The O. Henry Prize Stories 2008

SERIES EDITORS

2003–	Laura Furman
1997–2002	Larry Dark
1967–1996	William Abrahams
1961–1966	Richard Poirier
1960	Mary Stegner
1954–1959	Paul Engle
1941–1951	Herschel Bricknell
1933–1940	Harry Hansen
1919–1932	Blanche Colton Williams

PAST JURORS

2007	Charles D'Ambrosio, Ursula K. Le Guin, Lily Tuck
2006	Kevin Brockmeier, Francine Prose, Colm Tóibín
2005	Cristina García, Ann Patchett, Richard Russo
2003	David Guterson, Diane Johnson, Jennifer Egan
2002	Dave Eggers, Joyce Carol Oates, Colson Whitehead
2001	Michael Chabon, Mary Gordon, Mona Simpson
2000	Michael Cunningham, Pam Houston, George Saunders
1999	Sherman Alexie, Stephen King, Lorrie Moore
1998	Andrea Barrett, Mary Gaitskill, Rick Moody
1997	Louise Erdrich, Thom Jones, David Foster Wallace

The O. Henry Prize Stories 2008

Edited and with an Introduction by

Laura Furman

With Essays on the Stories They Admire Most by Jurors

Chimamanda Ngozi Adichie

David Leavitt

David Means

ANCHOR BOOKS

A Division of Random House, Inc.

New York

An Anchor Books Original, May 2008

Permissions appear at the end of the book.

Cataloging-in-Publication Data for *The O. Henry Prize Stories 2008* is available at the Library of Congress.

Anchor ISBN: 978-0-307-28034-3

Book design by Debbie Glasserman

www.anchorbooks.com

Printed in the United States of America
10 9 8 7 6 5 4 3 2 1

The editor thanks Amanda Frost and Domenica Ruta for their steady work, good reading, and honest words, and the staff of Anchor Books, whose energy, skill, and intelligence makes creating each new O. Henry collection a pleasure.

Publisher's Note

A Brief History of The O. Henry Prize Stories

Many readers have come to love the short story through the simple characters, easy narrative voice and humor, and compelling plotting in the work of William Sydney Porter (1862–1910), best known as O. Henry. His surprise endings entertain readers, even those back for a second, third, or fourth look. Even now one can say "'Gift of the Magi'" in a conversation about a love affair or marriage, and almost any literate person will know what is meant. It's hard to think of many other American writers whose work has been so incorporated into our national shorthand.

O. Henry was a newspaperman, skilled at hiding from his editors at deadline. A prolific writer, he wrote to make a living and to make sense of his life. He spent his childhood in Greensboro, North Carolina, his adolescence and young manhood in Texas, and his mature years in New York City. In between Texas and New York, he served out a prison sentence for bank fraud in Columbus, Ohio. Accounts of the origin of his pen name vary: one story dates from his days in Austin, where he was said to call the wandering family cat "Oh! Henry!"; another states that the name was inspired by the captain of the guard in the Ohio State Penitentiary, Orrin Henry.

Porter had devoted friends, and it's not hard to see why. He was charming and had an attractively gallant attitude. He drank too much and neglected his health, which caused his friends concern. He was often short of money; in a letter to a friend asking for a loan of $15 (his banker was out of town, he wrote), Porter added a postscript: "If it isn't convenient, I'll love you just the same." The banker was unavailable most of Porter's life. His sense of humor was always with him.

Reportedly, Porter's last words were from a popular song: "Turn up the light, for I don't want to go home in the dark."

Eight years after O. Henry's death, in April 1918, the Twilight Club (founded in 1883 and later known as the Society of Arts and Letters) held a dinner in his honor at the Hotel McAlpin in New York City. His friends remembered him so enthusiastically that a group of them met at the Biltmore Hotel in December of that year to establish some kind of memorial to him. They decided to award annual prizes in his name for short-story writers, and formed a Committee of Award to read the short stories published in a year and to pick the winners. In the words of Blanche Colton Williams (1879–1944), the first of the nine series editors, the memorial was intended to "strengthen the art of the short story and to stimulate younger authors."

Doubleday, Page & Company was chosen to publish the first volume, *O. Henry Memorial Award Prize Stories 1919*. In 1927, the society sold all rights to the annual collection to Doubleday, Doran & Company. Doubleday published *The O. Henry Prize Stories*, as it came to be known, in hardcover, and from 1984 to 1996 its subsidiary, Anchor Books, published it simultaneously in paperback. Since 1997 *The O. Henry Prize Stories* has been published as an original Anchor Books paperback.

How the Stories Are Chosen

All stories originally written in the English language and published in an American or Canadian periodical are eligible for consideration. Stories are not nominated; magazines submit the year's issues in their entirety by May 1.

The series editor chooses the twenty O. Henry Prize Stories, and each year three writers distinguished for their fiction are asked to evaluate the entire collection and to write an appreciation of the story they most admire. These three writers receive the twenty O. Henry Prize Stories in manuscript form with no identification of author or publication. They make their choices independent of one another and the series editor.

The goal of The O. Henry Prize Stories remains to strengthen the art of the short story.

To Grace Paley (1922–2007)

Last summer, Grace Paley died at the age of eighty-five at her home in Vermont. Her obituary in *The New York Times* showed a picture of her sitting among her books, her hair a frizzy aureole around her pretty face. She looked at the camera as if she might be friends with it someday if things went well.

It's easier to say what Grace Paley didn't do in her short stories than it is to pinpoint the source of their power.

She didn't often describe her characters or settings, though she was more than capable of pithy definition. In "Wants," the narrator describes her ex-husband: "He had had a habit throughout the twenty-seven years of making a narrow remark which, like a plumber's snake, could work its way through the ear down the throat, halfway to my heart. He would then disappear, leaving me choking with equipment." Why do we need description, when Paley has given us all we need to know about the man and the marriage?

Though they might use the past to make a point, Paley's characters grapple with what's in front of them, though not in conventional dramatic scenes. Her endings are often shy and lead the reader to begin the story again. The tools other writers might choose to work their stories were passed over by Paley. Her minimalism was of a friendly kind, dominated by the individuality of her voice and the determined hopefulness of her vision of human beings and their possibilities for good and evil.

Without declaring love, many of her characters are devoted to one another in an utterly convincing way. Her characters confront one another and wrestle a bit over the personal past or national politics, argue about the behavior of relatives or friends, and then they part. Even in a story as devastating as "Friends," in which a dying woman gives away photographs of her dead daughter, the movement of the story is toward serenity rather than a bitter howling at the moon. The reader might howl but the voice of the story continues, giving a tip of the hat to horror, combining pain with a salute to the complexity of feeling.

Only a really good writer could make her fiction seem truer than life.

Contents

Introduction

The O. Henry Prize Stories 2008 includes acknowledged masters, such as William H. Gass, Alice Munro, and William Trevor, along with talented beginners, such as Shannon Cain, Brittani Sonnenberg, Tony Tulathimutte, and Alexi Zentner. Though the twenty authors differ in age, nationality, gender, and style, it is a happy accident that their work consistently demonstrates the liveliness of the short story form.

Another happy accident—the invention of academic graduate programs in creative writing—contributes to the number of stories being written by young people. The benefit is accidental because the proliferation of short stories in writing workshops might be attributed to the practical demands of the average sixteen-week semester; the student can work on several drafts of a story in the course of a term with an intensity not possible for drafts of novels or even novellas. (There are exceptions to this, no doubt.)

The existence of graduate programs in creative writing is now an ordinary fact of literary life, though as recently as the 1940s it wasn't. The phenomenon often puzzles those who are neither teachers nor students, for what can be taught in any writing program? Talent can't be, nor can taste. Intelligence is there or not. Awareness of what is honest and what is false can be encouraged but must be innate also. Students can be educated as readers, as can anybody, and they can be introduced to the work of wonderful writers and be helped to understand what makes the work so good; educating readers is one of the higher callings of writing classes, if not the highest.

The most valuable contributions to a writer's education aren't insightful pronouncements or didactic urgings of method or subject matter from the teacher, or even the indispensable—the detailed consideration of the student's own efforts. The best learning, like the best writing, comes from instinct, never from logic. The most valuable and lasting gift is the unspoken example of the teacher's own integrity, devotion to literature, and passion for the work of writing. In the presence of the right teacher, the student is momentarily part of literature too.

A first reading of William Gass's "A Little History of Modern Music" is delightful for the situational humor of the classroom in which the teacher is free to say what he pleases and the students are under constraint. Subsequent readings show that there is more to the professor than a cranky fellow at the end of the term and perhaps his rope. The professor's history of modern music is also a guide to the role of the audience in the development of art. He teaches that new art creates its own new audience. "Home" to Mr. Gass's professor is the old music. A willingness to hear new music signals the courage to have new experiences and to leave home. "A Little History of Modern Music" is a portrait of the dissemination of knowledge, the encouragement of instinct, and the excitement of the intellectual adventure of connection and articulation.

Another teacher-student relationship, this one burdened by the giving and taking of grades and sex, is the spark for Sheila Kohler's "The Transitional Object," an age-old story of manipulation. Claire, a foreign student in Paris, learns what it is not to belong. The lessons she learns from her professor bring into question her own morality and acquaint her all too well with the power to be gained from being unscrupulous. As you read Kohler's story, consider, if you will, who is the transitional object, where Claire has been, and where she is going.

In Edward P. Jones's carefully calibrated story of social snobbery, "Bad Neighbors," the reader can decide just who the bad neighbors are. Are they the respectable and reprehensible residents of the 1400 block of Eighth Street NW, or the Bennington family, whose furniture is half broken and whose children can't quite be numbered by the street's established families? Jones's story delineates, as does Edith Wharton's work, the ways in which society's measurings fail the individual. Sharon Palmer, the Benningtons' beautiful across-the-street neighbor, almost crosses social barriers, for she and Neil Bennington share a love of literature. Sharon borrows from Neil a book of stories by the Irish writer Mary Lavin. In her preface to her *Selected Stories*, Lavin asked, "To whom does a story belong; to the writer or to the reader for whom it was written? To whom does the echo belong; to the horn or to the valley?" After reading Jones's story, we can ask: to whom does "Bad Neighbors" belong, the reader or Sharon? The story has undertones of *Romeo and Juliet*; we might also ask if that tragedy belongs to the audience or to the characters.

Ha Jin's "A Composer and His Parakeets" gives us a glimpse of the creation of a work of art and also of love. Bori, a parakeet, has been left in the care of the composer Fanlin. Slowly but surely, the bird wins Fanlin's attention and then his heart. The puzzle of Ha Jin's story is gradually revealed, and in the end concerns a fundamental question about how love—and art—comes into being. At the story's beginning, Fanlin believes that art cannot happen by accident, only by intention. As happens often in short stories, a conviction deeply held at first is turned on its head by the end.

Michel Faber's "Bye-bye Natalia" is another musical story, or rather the story of a difficult life held together by music. The overt problem facing Natalia is almost comical, whether or not she'll be able to persuade her tone-deaf cowboy to make her into a mail-order bride. Soon we realize how crucially Natalia needs rescuing, not only from poverty in a disintegrating society but from disease and petty criminality. Michel Faber has written a truly global story, including global culture, plague, and misunderstanding. "Bye-bye Natalia" reminds us that Babel was a global city. Nobly, Natalia remains faithful to Inward Path, a dark-metal band whose day has passed. Her final, plot-pivoting decision might seem whimsical, but it is an act of courage. Michel Faber's story is true not only in its tone but in its knowledge of what the human spirit will sacrifice in order to survive intact.

How children survive, how anyone survives the difficulties life dishes out, is the secret subject of Mary Gaitskill's unflinching story "The Little Boy." The failed mother at the plot's center ruminates on her many omissions in raising her own children and on the adult problems they blame on her. When she sees a child in need, it's her instinct to do the right thing, but can that alter her painful, unchangeable past or the child's present? The ending of Gaitskill's skillfully told story is almost a comfort.

Another child is at the center of "Taiping" by Brittani Sonnenberg. The fierce declaration at the beginning that his English father's blood in his veins "feels like insects crawling" puts the reader inside the narrator, and it isn't a comfortable place to be. He's divided against himself, contemptuous of other people, and in love with a street boy who hates him. Watching Taiping from a distance, the narrator stands as alone as he always will be, alienated even from his own blood. In her comment on her story, Sonnenberg asserts that grief is universal. Her story shows that love is too, however coercive and unwanted it might be.

In David Malouf's "Every Move You Make," Jo, a Hungarian immigrant to Australia, wishes for a love so deep that its loss would send her howling in the street. Her lover Mitch Maze's houses are as attractive and spontaneous-seeming as he is "remote, untouchable, self-enclosed." His mystery makes his attractions complete for Jo; romantic love is always about the unknown. "Every Move You Make" is an engrossing, lovely story with a steel underpinning; at its end Jo understands what howling for love really means.

Friendship as a variety of love is played out in Rose Tremain's "A Game of Cards," about the lifelong relationship between two Swiss men, Gustav, a hotel keeper, and Anton, a pianist. Through an English visitor to his hotel, Gustav learns the game of gin rummy, a simple game demanding little, requiring little skill, and supplying little excitement. Gustav tells us that gin rummy is "a game that, if you are both equally good and bad at it, strengthens a friendship." Leaving Switzerland, or making any significant changes, even for the good, threatens Gustav. The idea of stasis as security, friendship as imprisonment, haunts the story as Gustav's phobias and needs come to dominate his life and his friend's.

In Lore Segal's "Other People's Deaths," a circle of friends and colleagues seeks an etiquette for death, trying to formulate appropriate emotions and reactions while feeling contempt for the dead man and a perverse subgenre of Schadenfreude. Their fear of being contaminated by proximity to death causes them to shun the widow; surely their reaction will be recognizable to readers. The plurality of points of view in the story gives the reader access to the private thoughts and quibbles of all the characters. Perhaps the best joke in Segal's sharp, funny story is that the widow's unbearable but straightforward grief is a relief to the reader.

In "Folie à Deux" by William Trevor, the chance meeting of two men, friends when they were children and then at school, disrupts the carefully constructed subsistence of one and the smug equilibrium of the other. William Trevor's stories combine clarity and mystery. Those who love this great writer's work will recognize the subtle, pervasive anxiety that accompanies any contact between his characters. In the case of "Folie à Deux," the shadow of a shameful act committed long ago is the deciding factor in their moral lives, with profound consequences for one and, unfortunately, none for the other. Though Trevor doesn't judge his characters, his stories often turn on the characters' new vision of themselves in the harsh light of the story. They see themselves, judge themselves, and have to live with that.

An attempt at friendship between two middle-aged men drives Roger McDonald's "The Bullock Run." At the core of the story is a luscious piece of land, put together by Alan Corker's father for grazing young bulls. For Corker, the bullock run represents security and luxury in an often-harsh profession. The moment when Corker shows the bullock run to the artist and would-be rancher Ted Merrington, it's like one dog exposing his throat to another, an act of submission and an offer of friendship. The two are a fair match for rivalry, for the game of contesting who's the better man, but they're a poor match for friendship. McDonald's powerful story shows a man accepting his age, his place, and the measure of his possibilities.

By a lake with glacial water, a small hand-built cabin serves as a summer home for Oskar, Margret, and their small son, Jonas. In his story "On the Lake," Olaf Olafsson introduces into their peaceful existence a near-tragedy on the water and the subsequent wave of feeling that threatens devastation. The story is quiet, tense, and written with the deliberation of a mosaic maker; each sound in the silence that Olafsson creates has meaning.

Alexi Zentner's absorbing story "Touch," set in Canadian logging country, allows us into the life of another family living by the water, in this case a river that floats felled trees to market. There's a straight line in "Touch" from the father's mangled hand to the narrator's fate. Zentner writes movingly about the way his loggers and their families are uplifted, defined, and imprisoned by the place in which they live.

The form of "Scenes from the Life of the Only Girl in Water Shield, Alaska" by Tony Tulathimutte brings the story together for the reader. The story is broken into scenes, each titled, introducing us to Shelley, the only girl in Water Shield, Alaska, and her father, who's raised her very much alone. Shelley's world is circumscribed not only by place but by education and her father's single-minded devotion to survival at a basic level. In the course of the story, Shelley awakens to the limits of her surroundings and her father. The story has resonance and its own quiet madness, echoing the barks of the possibly rabid dog at its metaphorical core.

The power of parenthood to define and confine is the subject of Yiyun Li's "Prison." The profound, perverse, and all too understandable idea of Li's bereft couple is to replace their dead daughter with another child. The mother is too old to bear a child, so they decide to hire another woman to carry the child for them. The grieving parents seem rational, even scientific, but their coolness and practicality belies the madness of trying to compensate for an irreplaceable loss. Li's narration does everything to demonstrate subtly their avoidance of grief. Interesting issues are raised about nature versus nurture and seeing what money can buy, but the emotional center of the story is the imprisonment of the grieving mother by her love for her dead daughter, and the fatal quality of any mother's love for her child.

Shannon Cain's "The Necessity of Certain Behaviors" begins with the words "To escape," and for much of the story it seems that Lisa, an American tourist gone astray, has escaped from her city and country, from her friends and family, her job, her sexual identity, and her past. In the little society Cain creates for Lisa's idyll, men and women are equal, and homosexuality and heterosexuality are equally valid expressions of desire and love. From that premise, the story gives the reader a sojourn in a very different society and, along the way, examines Lisa's capacity for change. What she leaves behind of her past and what she will take into her future turn out to be as unpredictable as the new world she's discovered.

The relationship between the individual and society has always been an intrinsic subject of fiction, affording tension to be resolved and impossible dilemmas to solve. Alice Munro's "What Do You Want to Know For?" Anthony Doerr's "Village 113," and Steven Millhauser's "A Change in Fashion" all deal with that relationship.

In "A Change in Fashion" it isn't tension between characters driving the story, for there aren't any conventional characters here. Rather, the shifting of fashion from revelation to concealment (and inevitably back again) and the reactions to such changes by both the wearers and creators of fashion afford the story its action and movement. The fashion designer Hyperion is the closest thing the story has to an individual character, and the mystery of his true identity is never solved. The emotion and movement is controlled by Millhauser's tour-de-force sentences and his dry humor.

"*The river bottled, the nation fed.*" In "Village 113" by Anthony Doerr, the clash between the individual and society couldn't be more evident. Based on the creation of the Three Gorges Dam by the flooding of hundreds of villages, the displacement of 1.3 million people, the destruction of an ecosystem, and the loss of the archaeological past, Doerr's story focuses on the gradual emptying of one village and the reluctance of the village's seed keeper to abandon the life she cherishes. The contrast of her son's empty, bureaucratic city life with life in her doomed village, haunted as it is by layers of history, spiritual belief, and interaction with nature and community, is stunning. The seed keeper's sensible choice at the end is understandable. Sureness in a time of profound change is even enviable.

Alice Munro's earliest stories were about women who were caught by society, often represented by a man and a marriage, and who longed for another life and for self-knowledge. Her women recalled their childhoods or early womanhoods and came to an understanding of why they did certain things and chose not to do others. Gradually, Munro's stories have become less about a yearning for change and the unattainable than about how the past lives within the present, at least for those for whom the past is meaningful. The past is no longer only the personal one of the individual; now community life as it was lived and an examination of what that life has left behind are to be puzzled over by the living.

In "What Do You Want to Know For?" there are two kinds of excavation, one into a mysterious tomb discovered by chance during a country drive, and the other of the narrator's body as her breast cancer is discovered and diagnosed. Munro pulls the disparate threads through her story as her narrator explores the uses of knowledge and the usefulness of curiosity. The story's title questions not only why she would want to learn about a mostly forgotten piece of local history, but why she would want to know when exactly death is coming for her—and why she should fight it.

The image of the legendary lamp buried in the tomb echoes the familiar passage from Psalm 119, "Thy word is a lamp unto my feet, and a light unto my path." For Munro's readers, the word is literature, helping the reader to figure out what the path might be and what it's been for others.

—Laura Furman
Austin, Texas

The O. Henry Prize Stories 2008

Ha Jin

A Composer and His Parakeets

BEFORE DEPARTING for Thailand with her film crew, Supriya left in Fanlin's care the parakeet she had inherited from a friend. Fanlin had never asked his girlfriend from whom exactly, but was sure that Bori, the bird, used to belong to a man. Supriya must have had a number of boyfriends prior to himself. A pretty Indian actress, she always got admiring stares. Whenever she was away from New York, Fanlin couldn't help but fear she might hit it off with another man.

He had hinted to her several times that he might propose, but she would either dodge the subject or say her career would end before she was thirty-four, and she must seize the five years left to make more movies. In fact, she had never gotten a leading part, always taking a supporting role. If only she hadn't been able to get any part at all, then she might have accepted the role of a wife and prospective mother.

Fanlin wasn't very familiar with Bori, a small pinkish parakeet with a white tail, and he had never let the bird enter his music studio. Supriya used to leave Bori at Animal Haven when she was away; and if a trip lasted just two or three days, she'd simply lock him in the cage with enough food and water. But this time she'd stay abroad for three months, so she asked Fanlin to take care of the bird.

Unlike some other parakeets, Bori couldn't talk; he was so quiet Fanlin often wondered if he were dumb. At night the bird slept near the window, in a cage held by a stand like a colossal floor lamp. During the day he sat on the windowsill or on top of the cage, basking in the sunlight, which seemed to have blanched his feathers.

Fanlin knew Bori liked millet; having no idea where a pet store was in Flushing, he went to Hong Kong Supermarket down the street and bought a bag. At times he'd give the parakeet what he himself ate: boiled rice, bread, apples, watermelon, grapes. He found Bori enjoyed this food. Whenever he placed his own meal on the dining table, the bird would hover beside him, waiting for a bite. With his Supriya away, Fanlin could eat more Chinese food—the only advantage of her absence.

"You want Cheerios too?" Fanlin asked Bori one morning as he was eating breakfast.

The bird gazed at him with a white-ringed eye. Fanlin picked a saucer, put a fingerful of the cereal in it, and placed it before Bori. He added, "Your mother has dumped you, and you're stuck with me." Bori pecked at the Cheerios, his eyelids flapping. Somehow Fanlin felt for the bird that day, so he found a tiny wine cup and poured a bit of milk for Bori too.

After breakfast, he let Bori into his studio for the first time. Fanlin composed on a synthesizer, having no room for a piano. The bird sat still on the edge of his desk, watching him, as if able to understand the musical notes he was inscribing. Then, as Fanlin tested a tune on the keyboard, Bori began fluttering his wings and swaying his head. "You like my work?" Fanlin asked Bori.

The bird didn't respond.

As Fanlin revised some notes, Bori alighted on the keys and stomped out a few feeble notes, which encouraged him to play more. "Get lost!" Fanlin said. "Don't be in my way."

The bird flew back to the desk, again motionlessly watching the man making little black squiggles on paper.

Around eleven o'clock, as Fanlin stretched up his arms and leaned back in his chair, he noticed two whitish spots beside Bori, one bigger than the other. "Damn you, don't poop on my desk!" he screamed.

At those words the parakeet darted out of the room. His escape calmed Fanlin a little. He told himself he ought to be patient with Bori, who must be like an incontinent baby. He got up and wiped off the mess with a paper towel.

. . .

Three times a week he gave music lessons to a group of five students. The tuition they paid was his regular income. They would come to his apartment on Thirty-seventh Avenue in the evening and stay two hours. One of the students, Wona Kernan, an angular woman of twenty-two, became quite fond of Bori and often held out her index finger to him, saying, "Come here, come here." The parakeet never responded to her coaxing, instead sitting on Fanlin's lap as if also attending the class. Wona once scooped up the bird and put him on her head, but Bori returned to Fanlin immediately. She muttered, "Stupid budgie, only know how to suck up to your boss."

Fanlin was also collaborating with a local theater group on an opera based on the legendary Chinese folk musician Ah Bing. In his early years Ah Bing, like his father, was a monk; then he lost his eyesight and was forced to leave his temple. He began to compose music, which he played on the streets to eke out a living.

Fanlin didn't like the libretto, which emphasized the chance nature of artistic creation. The hero of the opera, Ah Bing, was to claim, "Greatness in art is merely an accident." To Fanlin, that kind of logic did not explain the great symphonies of Beethoven or Tchaikovsky, which could not have existed without artistic theory, vision, or purpose. No art should be accidental.

Nevertheless, Fanlin worked hard on the music for *The Blind Musician*. According to the contract he had signed, he'd get a six-thousand-dollar advance, to be paid in two installments, and twelve percent of the opera's earnings. These days he was so occupied with the composition that he seldom cooked. He'd compose from 7 A.M. to 2 P.M., then go out for lunch, often taking Bori along. The bird perched on his shoulder, and Fanlin would feel Bori's claws scratching his skin as he walked.

One afternoon at the Taipan Café on Roosevelt Avenue, after paying at the counter for lunch, Fanlin returned to his seat to finish his tea. He put a dollar tip on the table, which Bori picked up and dropped back in Fanlin's hand.

"Wow, he knows money!" a bulging-eyed waitress cried. "Don't steal my money, little thief!"

That night on the phone, Fanlin told Supriya about Bori's feat. She replied, "I never thought you'd like him. He wouldn't get money for me, that's for sure."

"I'm just his caretaker," Fanlin said. "He's yours." He had expected she'd be more enthusiastic, but her voice sounded as usual, mezzo-soprano and a little sleepy. He refrained from telling her that he missed her, often touching her clothes in the closet.

It was a rainy morning. Outside the drizzle swayed in the wind like endless tangled threads; traffic rumbled in the west. Lying in bed with a sheet crumpled over his belly, Fanlin was thinking of Supriya. She always dreamed of having children, and her parents in Calcutta had urged her to marry. Still, Fanlin felt he might be just her safety net—a fallback in case she couldn't find a more suitable man. He tried not to think too many negative thoughts and recalled those passionate nights that had thrilled and exhausted both of them. He missed her, a lot, but he knew that love was like another person's favor one might fall out of anytime.

Suddenly a high note broke from his studio—Bori on the synthesizer. "Stop it!" Fanlin shouted to the bird. But the note kept tinkling. He got out of bed and made for the studio.

Passing through the living room, its window somehow open and its floor scattered with sheets of paper fluttering in the draft, he heard another noise, then caught sight of a shadow slipping into the kitchen. He hurried in pursuit and saw a teenage boy crawling out the window. Fanlin, not fast enough to catch him, leaned over the sill and yelled at the burglar running down the fire escape, "If you come again, I'll have you arrested. Damn you!"

The boy jumped to the pavement below, his legs buckling, but he picked himself up. The seat of his jeans was dark-wet. In a flash he veered into the street and disappeared.

When Fanlin returned to the living room, Bori whizzed over and landed on his chest. The bird looked frightened, his wings quivering. With both hands Fanlin held the parakeet up and kissed him. "Thank you," he whispered. "Are you scared?"

Bori usually relieved himself in the cage, the door of which remained open day and night. Every two or three days Fanlin would change the newspaper on the bottom to keep the tiny aviary clean. In fact, the whole apartment had become an aviary of sorts, since Bori was allowed to go anywhere, including the studio. When he wasn't sleeping, the bird seldom stayed in the cage, inside which stretched a plastic perch. Even at night he avoided the perch, sleeping with his claws clutching the side of the cage, his body suspended in the air. *Isn't it tiring to sleep like that?* Fanlin thought. *No wonder Bori often looks torpid in the daytime.*

One afternoon as the parakeet nestled on his elbow, Fanlin noticed one of Bori's feet was thicker than the other. He turned the bird over. To his surprise, he saw a blister on Bori's left foot in the shape of half a soybean. He wondered if the plastic perch was too slippery for the parakeet to hold, and if the wire cage the bird gripped instead while sleeping had blistered his foot. Maybe he should get a new cage for Bori. He flipped through the yellow pages to locate a pet store.

That evening as he was strolling in Queens Botanical Garden, he ran into Elbert Chang, the director of the opera project for which Fanlin had been composing. Elbert had been jogging, and as he stopped to chat with Fanlin, Bori took off for an immense cypress tree, flitting in its straggly crown before landing on a branch.

"Come down," Fanlin called, but the bird wouldn't budge, just clasping the declining branch and looking at the men.

"That little parrot is so homely," observed Elbert. He blew his nose, brushed his sweatpants with his fingers, and jogged away, the flesh on his nape trembling a little. Beyond him a young couple walked a dachshund on a long leash.

Fanlin turned as if he were leaving, and Bori swooped down and alighted on his head. Fanlin settled the bird on his arm. "Afraid I'm going to leave you behind, eh?" he asked. "If you don't listen to me, I won't take you out again, understood?" He patted Bori's head.

The parakeet just blinked at him.

Fanlin realized that Bori must like the feel of the wooden perch. He looked around and found a branch under a tall oak and brought it home. He dismantled the plastic bar, whittled a new perch out of the branch, cut a groove on either end, and fixed it in the cage. From then on, Bori slept on the branch every night.

Proudly Fanlin told Supriya about the new perch, but she was too occupied to get excited. She sounded tired and merely said, "I'm glad I left him with you." She didn't even thank him. He had planned to ask her about the progress of the filming, but refrained.

. . .

The composition for the opera was going well. When Fanlin handed in the first half of the music score—132 pages altogether—Elbert Chang was elated, saying he had worried whether Fanlin had embarked on the project. Now Elbert could relax—everything was coming together. Several singers had signed up. It looked like they could stage the opera the next summer.

Puffing on a cigar in his office, Elbert gave a nervous grin and told Fanlin, "I'm afraid I cannot pay you the first half of the advance now."

"Why not? Our contract states that you must."

"I know, but we just don't have the cash on hand. I'll pay you early next month when we get the money."

Fanlin's face fell, his mothy eyebrows tilting upward. He was too deep into the project to back out, yet he feared he might have more difficulty getting paid in the future. He had never worked for Elbert Chang before.

"The bird looks uglier today," Elbert said, pointing his cigar at Bori, who was standing on the desk, between Fanlin's hands.

At those words the parakeet whooshed up and landed on Elbert's shoulder. "Hey, hey, he likes me!" cried the director. He brushed Bori off, and the bird fled back to Fanlin in a panic.

Fanlin noticed a greenish splotch on Elbert's jacket, on the shoulder. He stifled the laughter rising in his throat.

"Don't worry about the payment," Elbert assured him, his fingers drumming the desktop. "You have a contract and can sue me if I don't pay you. This time is just an exception. The money is already committed by the donors. I promise this won't happen again."

Feeling better, Fanlin shook hands with the director and stepped out of the office.

Upon signing the contract for *The Blind Musician* three months earlier, the librettist, an exiled poet living on Staten Island, had insisted that the composer mustn't change a single word of the libretto. The writer, Benyong, didn't understand that unlike poetry, opera is a public form of art and depends on collaborative efforts. Elbert Chang liked the libretto so much he conceded to the terms the author demanded. This, however, posed a problem for Fanlin, who had in mind a music structure that didn't always agree with the verbal text. Furthermore, some words were unsingable, such as *smoothest* and *feudalism.* He had to replace them, ideally with words ending in open vowels.

One morning Fanlin set out for Staten Island to see Benyong, intending to get permission to change some words. He didn't plan to take Bori along, but the second he stepped out of his apartment, he heard the bird bump against the door repeatedly, scratching the wood. He opened the door and said, "Want to come with me?" The parakeet leaped to his chest, clutching his T-shirt and uttering tinny chirps. Fanlin caressed Bori, and together they headed for the subway station.

It was a fine summer day, the sky washed clean by a shower the previous night. On the ferryboat Fanlin stayed on the deck all the way, watching seabirds wheel around. Some strutted or scurried on the bow, where two small girls were tossing bits of bread at them. Bori joined the other birds, picking up food but not eating any. Fanlin knew the parakeet was doing it just for fun, yet no matter how he called, the bird wouldn't come back to him. So he stood by, watching Bori walk excitedly among gulls, terns, petrels. He was amazed that Bori wasn't afraid of the bigger birds and wondered if the parakeet was lonely at home.

Benyong received Fanlin warmly, as if they were friends. In fact, they'd met only twice, both occasions for business. Fanlin liked this man, who, already forty-three, hadn't lost the child in him and often threw his head back and laughed aloud.

Sitting on a sofa in the living room, Fanlin sang some lines to demonstrate the cumbersomeness of the original words. He had an ordinary voice, a bit hoarse; yet whenever he sang his own compositions, he was confident and expressive, with a vivid face and vigorous gestures, as if he were oblivious of anyone else's presence.

While Fanlin was singing, Bori frolicked on the coffee table, flapping his wings and wagging his head, his hooked bill opening and closing and emitting happy but unintelligible cries. Then the bird paused to tap his feet as if beating time, which delighted the poet.

"Can he talk?" Benyong asked Fanlin.

"No, he can't, but he's smart and even knows money."

"You should teach him how to talk. Come here, little fellow." Benyong beckoned to the bird, who ignored his outstretched hand.

Without difficulty Fanlin got the librettist's agreement, on the condition that they talk before Fanlin made any wording changes. For lunch they went to a small restaurant nearby and each had a pan-fried pizza. Dabbing his mouth with a red napkin, Benyong said, "I love this place and have lunch here five days a week. Sometimes I work on my poems in here. Cheers." He lifted his beer and clinked it with Fanlin's water.

Fanlin was amazed by what the poet said. Benyong didn't hold a regular job and could hardly have made any money from his writing; few people in his situation would dine out five times a week. In addition, he enjoyed movies and popular music; two tall shelves in his apartment were loaded with CDs, more with DVDs. Evidently the writer was well kept by his wife, a nurse. Fanlin was touched by the woman's generosity.

After lunch they strolled along the beach of white sand, carrying their shoes and walking barefoot. The air smelled fishy, tinged with the stink of seaweed washed ashore. Bori liked the ocean and kept flying away, skipping along the brink of the surf, pecking at the sand.

"Ah, this sea breeze is so invigorating," Benyong said as he watched Bori. "Whenever I walk here, the view of the ocean makes me think a lot. Before this immense body of water, even life and death become unimportant, irrelevant."

"What's important to you, then?"

"Art, only art is immortal."

"That's why you've been writing full-time all along?"

"Yes, I want only to be a free artist."

Fanlin said no more, unable to suppress the image of Benyong's self-sacrificing wife. A photo in their study showed her to be quite pretty, with a wide but handsome face. The wind increased, and dark clouds were gathering on the sea in the distance.

As the ferryboat cast off, rain clouds were billowing over Brooklyn, soundless lightning zigzagging across the sky. On deck a man, skinny and gray bearded, was ranting about the evildoing of big corporations. Eyes shut, he cried, "Brothers and sisters, think about who gets all the money that's yours, think about who puts all the drugs on the streets to kill our kids. I know them, I see them sinning against our Lord every day. What this country needs is a revolution, so we can put every crook behind bars or ship them all to Cuba . . ." Fanlin was fascinated by the way words poured out of the man's mouth, as if the fellow were possessed by a demon, his eyes radiating a steely light. Few other passengers paid him any mind.

While Fanlin focused his attention on the man, Bori left Fanlin's shoulder and fluttered away toward the waves. "Come back, come back," Fanlin called, but the bird went on flying alongside the boat.

Suddenly a gust of wind caught Bori and swept him into the tumbling water. "Bori! Bori!" Fanlin cried, rushing toward the stern, his eyes fastened on the bird bobbing in the tumult.

He kicked off his sandals, plunged into the water, and swam toward Bori, still calling his name. A wave crashed into Fanlin's face and filled his mouth with seawater. He coughed and lost sight of the bird. "Bori, Bori, where are you?" he called, looking around frantically. Then he saw the parakeet lying supine on the slope of a swell about thirty yards away. With all his might Fanlin plunged toward the bird.

Behind him, the boat slowed and a crowd gathered on the deck. A man shouted through a bullhorn, "Don't panic! We're coming to help you!"

At last Fanlin grabbed hold of Bori, who was already motionless, his bill ajar. Tears gushed out of Fanlin's salt-stung eyes as he held the parakeet and looked into his face, turning him upside down to drain water out of his crop. Meanwhile, the boat circled back, chugging toward Fanlin.

A ladder dropped from the boat. Holding Bori between his teeth, Fanlin hauled himself out of the water. When he reached the deck, the gray-bearded man stepped over and handed Fanlin his sandals without a word. People massed around as Fanlin laid the bird on the steel deck and gently pressed Bori's chest with two fingers to pump water from his lifeless body.

Thunder rumbled in the distance and lightning cracked the city's skyline, but patches of sunlight still fell on the ocean. As the boat picked up speed heading north again, the bird's knotted feet opened, then clawed the air. "He's come to," a man exclaimed.

Sluggishly Bori opened his eyes. Cheerful cries broke out on the deck while Fanlin sobbed gratefully. A middle-aged woman took two photos of Fanlin and the parakeet, saying, "This is extraordinary."

Two days later a short article appeared in the Metro section of *The New York Times*, reporting on the rescue of the bird. It described how Fanlin had plunged into the ocean without a second thought and patiently resuscitated Bori. The piece was brief, under two hundred words, but it created some buzz in the local community. Within a week a small Chinese-language newspaper, the *North American Tribune*, printed a long article on Fanlin and his parakeet, with a photo of them together.

Elbert Chang came one afternoon to deliver the half of the advance he'd promised. He had read about the rescue and said to Fanlin, "This little parrot is really something. He doesn't look smart but is full of tricks." He held out his hand to Bori, his fingers wiggling. "Come here," he coaxed. "You forgot crapping on me?"

Fanlin laughed. Bori still didn't stir, his eyes half shut as if he were sleepy.

Elbert then asked about the progress of the composition, to which Fanlin hadn't attended since the bird's accident. The director reassured him that the opera would be performed as planned. Fanlin promised to return to his work with redoubled effort.

Despite the attention Bori proceeded to wither. He didn't eat much or move around. During the day he sat on the windowsill, hiccuping frequently. Fanlin wondered whether Bori had a cold or was simply getting old. He asked Supriya about the bird's age. She had no idea but said, "He must already be senile."

"What do you mean? Like in his seventies or eighties?"

"I'm not sure."

"Can you ask his former owner?"

"How can I do that in Thailand?"

He didn't press her further, unhappy about her lack of interest in Bori. Maybe she really wasn't in contact with the bird's former owner, yet Fanlin suspected that was unlikely.

One morning Fanlin looked into Bori's cage and, to his horror, found the parakeet lying still. He picked Bori up, the scrawny, lifeless body still warm. Fanlin couldn't hold back his tears while he stroked the bird's feathers; he had failed to save his friend.

He laid the tiny corpse on the dining table and observed it for a long time. The parakeet looked peaceful and must have passed in sleep. Fanlin consoled himself with the thought that Bori hadn't suffered a miserable old age.

He buried the bird under a ginkgo in the backyard. The whole day he couldn't do anything but sit absentmindedly in his studio. His students arrived that evening, but he didn't do much teaching. After they left, he phoned Supriya, who sounded harried. With a sob in his throat he told her, "Bori died early this morning."

"Gosh, you sound like you just lost a sibling."

"I feel terrible."

"I'm sorry, but don't be silly, and don't be too hard on yourself. If you really miss the budgie, you can buy another one at a pet shop."

"He was your bird."

"I know. I don't blame you. I can't talk anymore now, sweetie, I need to go."

Fanlin didn't sleep until the wee hours that night. He reviewed his conversation with Supriya, reproaching her as if she were responsible for Bori's death. What rankled him was her casual attitude. She must have put the bird out of her mind long ago. He wondered if he should volunteer to break up with her upon her return the following month, since it would be just a matter of time before they parted.

For days Fanlin canceled his class and worked intensely on the opera. The music flowed from his pen with ease, the melodies so fluent and fresh that he paused to wonder whether he had unconsciously copied them from master composers. No, every note he had put down was original.

His neglect of teaching worried his students. One afternoon they came with a small cage containing a bright yellow parakeet. "We got this for you," Wona told Fanlin.

While certain no bird could replace Bori, Fanlin appreciated the gesture and so allowed them to put the new parakeet in Bori's cage. He told them to return for class that evening.

The parakeet already had a name: Devin. Every day Fanlin left him alone, saying nothing to him, though the bird let out all kinds of words, including obscenities. At mealtimes Fanlin would put a bit of whatever he ate in Bori's saucer for Devin, yet he often kept the transom open in hopes that the bird would fly away.

The second half of the music for the opera was complete. When Elbert Chang read the score, he phoned Fanlin and asked to see him. Fanlin went to Elbert's office the next morning, unsure what the director wanted to discuss.

As soon as Fanlin sat down, Elbert shook his head and smiled. "I'm puzzled, this half is so different from the first."

"You mean better or worse?"

"That I can't say, but the second half seems to have more feeling. Sing a couple passages. Let's see what it sounds like."

Fanlin sang one passage after another with grief, as if the music were gushing from the depths of his belly. He felt the blind musician, the hero of the opera, lamenting through him the loss of his beloved, a local beauty forced by her parents to marry a general, to be his concubine. Fanlin's voice trembled, which had never happened before in his demonstrations.

"Ah, it's so sad," said Elbert's assistant. "It makes me want to cry."

Somehow the woman's words soothed Fanlin. Then he sang a few passages from the first half of the score, which sounded elegant and lighthearted, especially the beautiful refrain that would recur throughout the opera.

Elbert said, "I'm pretty sure the second half is emotionally right. It has more soul—sorrow without anger, affectionate but not soft. I'm impressed."

"That's true," the woman chimed in.

"What should I do?" sighed Fanlin.

"Make the whole piece more consistent," Elbert suggested.

"That will take a few weeks."

"We have time."

Fanlin set about revising the score, overhauling the first half. He worked so hard that after a week he collapsed and had to stay in bed. Even with his eyes closed, he could not suppress the music ringing in his head. The next day he resumed his writing. Despite his fatigue, he was happy, even rapturous in this composing frenzy. He ignored Devin entirely except to feed him. The parakeet came to his side from time to time, but Fanlin was too busy to pay him any mind.

One afternoon, after working for hours, he was lying in bed to rest. Devin landed beside him. The bird tossed his long blue-tipped tail, then jumped onto Fanlin's chest, fixing a beady eye on him. *"Ha wa ya?"* the parakeet squawked. At first Fanlin didn't understand the sharp-edged words, pronounced as if Devin were short of breath. *"Ha wa ya?"* the bird repeated.

"Fine, I'm all right." Fanlin smiled, his eyes filling.

Devin flew away and alighted on the half-open window. The white curtain swayed in the breeze, as if about to dance; outside sycamore leaves were rustling. "Come back," Fanlin called.

Lore Segal

Other People's Deaths

Everybody Leaving

The coroner's men put James in the back of the truck and drove away, and the Bernstines, once again, urged Ilka to come home with them, at least for the night, or to let them take the baby. Again, Ilka was earnest in begging to be left right here, wanted the baby to stay here with her. No thank you, really, she did not need—did not want—anybody sleeping over.

The friends and colleagues trooped down the path: Leslie Shakespeare, the director, and Joe Bernstine, the cofounder of the Concordance Institute—genus think tank, of which Ilka was, and poor Jimmy had been, junior members—and their colleagues the Ayes, the Zees, the Cohns, and the Stones. Outside the gate they stopped, they looked back, but Ilka had taken the baby inside and closed the door. They stood for a moment, they talked, not accounting to themselves for the intense charm of the summer hill rising behind Ilka's house, of standing, of breathing—of the glamour of being alive. Leslie asked everyone to come over for a drink.

The report of the accident had come at the very moment the committee was about to vote on Jimmy's retention.

Jimmy had told Ilka not to worry when he accepted the job as the institute's director of projects: what he didn't know about the *Who's Who* of scholarship he would pick up as he went along. Ilka had worried. She watched him not writing the book stipulated in his contract. She watched him worry when he screwed up the institute's directories on the new computer. Called on the carpet most recently for failing to file a duplicate of his letter to one conference participant, Jimmy had failed to confess that he couldn't find the fellow's address. Leslie Shakespeare had sent Jimmy out of town on institute business while his retention was under discussion.

The friends and colleagues began to move along the sidewalk in groups and pairs. Alfred Stone walked with his wife, Alpha. Alfred was a doctor, the only one of the group unconnected with the work of the institute. It was he who had attended at the scene of the accident. As he walked, he was arranging the sentence he ought to have spoken to the widow when he arrived at her house or at some moment in the hours since.

Everybody stopped at the corner. Ilka's door had opened and the two policemen came out. They had spent the day in the hallway trying to look inconspicuous. Now that the dead man, brought so inexplicably home from the scene of the accident, had been removed, they could finally leave. The small Puerto Rican policeman walked out the gate, but the big young policeman turned to wave. Ilka must be standing back in the darkness. The two policemen got into their car and drove away.

Inside her foyer Ilka closed the door and leaned her head against it, devastated at everybody's leaving.

WORDS TO SPEAK TO THE WIDOW

At the Shakespeares' there was the business of walking into the sitting room, of sitting down, of the drinks. "A lot of ice, Leslie. Thanks." "Martini, please, and hold the vegetables."

Little, agile Joe Bernstine smiled sadly. "I wonder if we retained Jimmy."

Leslie Shakespeare said, "Alpha will schedule us a new search committee."

Nobody said, We could hardly do worse than poor Jimmy.

Jenny Bernstine said, "Ilka is being very gallant and terrific."

Nobody said, She didn't cry.

Alicia Aye said, "Ilka isn't one to throw her hands up."

"Or the towel in, *or* the sponge," said Eliza Shakespeare. "Joke. Sorry!"

Alicia said, "Ilka is not one to drown in her sorrows."

"Well, I'm going to drown mine," Eliza said, holding her glass out to Leslie, who refilled it.

Alicia said, "We live on borrowed time."

Alpha asked her husband, "The policeman said there was fire?" and the friends' and colleagues' imaginations went into action to dim or scramble or in some way unthink the flames in which Jimmy—this person they knew—was burning. They wished to avoid an image of which they would never entirely be able to rid themselves.

Dr. Stone replied that Jimmy's body had been thrown clear of the burning car. The fall had broken his neck.

The flames went out. The friends envisaged an unnaturally angled head with Jimmy's face.

Dr. Alfred Stone took his drink and sat down. He was a very large man, with a large head that, Ilka had once told the Shakespeares, she thought would look good on Mt. Rushmore. Eliza said that jaw, that forelock were from the Sunday funnies—the muscle-bound superhero with the heart of tin. "Aw!" Ilka had said. "Poor Alfred! I like Alfred." Dr. Stone looked around the room and located his wife, Alpha, sitting beside Eliza Shakespeare. Were they talking about the death? Alfred had, earlier in the day, looked across another room and seen Alpha talking with Ilka. He had wondered what words Alpha might be saying to the widow: To refer to the death would be putting a finger in the wound, but how *not* to mention it? And wasn't it gross to be talking of anything else? Alfred mistakenly believed himself to be singularly lacking in what normal people—the people in this room—were born knowing. He thought that other people knew how to feel and what to say. He watched them walk out and return with drinks. They stood together, they talked. Dr. Stone remained sitting.

At eleven o'clock that first night a brutal loneliness knocked the wind out of Ilka. Then her phone rang. "We thought we'd see how you were doing," Leslie said. "Did the baby get to sleep?"

"The baby is OK. I'm OK. Is it OK to be OK? I could do with some retroactive lead time. I need to practice taking my stockings off with Jimmy dead. Relearn how to clean my teeth."

Leslie said, "Wait." Ilka heard him pass on to Eliza, who must be in the room, who might be lying in the bed beside him, that Ilka was OK but needed to relearn how to clean her teeth with Jimmy dead. His voice returned full strength. "Eliza says we're coming over in the morning to bring you breakfast."

SITTING SHIVAH

"I don't know how," said Ilka. Joe Bernstine remembered that when his father died his mother had turned the faces of the mirrors to the wall. Ilka was struck by the gesture but embarrassed by its drama. "I know I'm supposed to sit on a low stool, but I can't get any lower," she said. She was sitting on the floor tickling Maggie, the fat, solemn, comfortable baby. Baby Maggie's eyes were so large that they seemed to round the corner of the little face, with its hanging cheeks.

"A baroque baby," Eliza said.

"She's fun to hold because she collapses her weight in your arms." Ilka jumped Maggie up and down. "She must have heard me scream when the policemen told me."

Eliza unpacked the tiny tomatoes from her garden. She had baked two long loaves of white bread. Jenny was arranging the cold cuts that she had brought onto the platters she had brought. At some point in the morning Joe and Leslie rose to go to the institute. They would be back in an hour. Leslie bent his fine head over Ilka's hand and brought it to his lips.

Ilka said, "I called my mother and she's coming tomorrow."

IN THE INSTITUTE

Celie, the receptionist, sat at her desk across from the front entrance and fanned herself with an envelope, like someone trying to avoid fainting. She told Betty, one of the assistants, "I talked with him that actual morning! He comes running in, punches the elevator button, doesn't wait and runs right up those stairs, comes right down. He's stuffing papers in his briefcase. I told him, 'You have a good trip now,' and he says, 'Oh shit!' and he's going to run back up except the elevator door opens, and he gets in."

Betty was able to one-up Celie with her spatial proximity to the dead man, though at a greater temporal remove. The day *before* James drove to Washington he had tried to open the door into the conference room with papers under his arm, carrying a cup of coffee, saying, "Anybody got a spare hand?" Betty had held the door for him. He had said, "Oh! Thanks!"

Could a person for whom one held a door, who said "Oh shit!" and "Oh! Thanks!" be dead?

Words to Write to the Widow

Nancy Cohn and Maria Zee talked on the telephone and one-upped each other in respect to who was the more upset. "I got to my office," said Maria, "and just sat."

"I," Nancy said, "never made it to the office, because I kept waking up every hour *on* the hour."

"I never got to sleep! I kept waking poor Zack to check if he was alive. He was fit to be tied."

"Have you called her?"

"I thought I would write."

"That's what I will do. I'll write her," said Nancy.

Sitting Shivah, Day Two

"It's good of you to come," Ilka said to the visitors. The institute staff dropped over together, after office hours. Celie, Betty, Wendy, and Barbara sat around the table in Ilka's kitchen. The fellows sat in the living room. Ilka's mother held the baby on her lap. Ilka let out a sudden laugh and said, "What'll I do when the party is over!" She rose, picked up little Maggie, and carried her out of the room, up the stairs, past Dr. Stone hiding in the foyer.

Dr. Stone believed that by the time Ilka returned he would be ready with a sentence to say to her, but he was relieved, when she came down, that the baby's head intervened between his face and Ilka's face, and the front doorbell was ringing again. Martin Moses, a junior member, walked in, took Ilka and her baby into a big hug, and said, "Christ, Ilka!" Ilka said, "Don't I know it."

"Give her to me," Ilka's mother said and took the child out of Ilka's arms.

Alpha came out of the living room, saying, "Hello, Martin. Ilka, listen, take it easy. You take a couple of days—as long as you like, you know that! Alfred, we have to go." And the Ayes and the Zees had to go home. Celie and the rest left. Martin left. The Shakespeares said they would be back.

Ilka thought that everyone had gone when she heard a gentle clatter in the kitchen. Jenny Bernstine was washing dishes.

People trickled over in the evening—a smaller crowd, which left sooner. Jenny washed more dishes. When Joe came to pick her up, she looked anxiously at Ilka, who said, "I'm OK"

Writing to the Widow

Nancy Cohn went to look for Nat. He was on the living room couch, watching TV.

Nancy said, "I'm embarrassed not to know what to write to Ilka. It's embarrassing worrying about being embarrassed, for Chrissake!"

"Calamity is a foreign country. We don't know how to talk to the natives."

Nancy said, "*You* write her. You're the writer in the family."

"I'm not feeling well," said Nat.

"She's *your* colleague!" said Nancy.

And so neither of them wrote to Ilka.

Maria Zee called Alicia Aye and asked her, "I mean, we went *over* there. Do we still have to write?"

Alicia said, "Alvin says we'll have her over next time we have people in."

A Casserole

Celie cooked a casserole and told Art, her thirteen-year-old, to take it over to Mrs. Carl's house.

"The woman that her husband burned up in his car? No way!"

Linda, who was fifteen, said, "For your information, he did *not* even burn up. He broke his neck." She advised her brother to check his facts.

Art said, "Linda will go and take it over to her."

Well, Linda wasn't going over there, not by herself, so Celie made them both go.

Nobody answered the front bell.

Art said, "I never knew a dead person before."

Linda said, "You mean you never knew a person and afterward they died, and you didn't as a *fact* even know this person at all."

Art said, "But I know Mom, and Mom knew him. Ring it again."

They found a couple of bricks, piled one on top of the other, and took turns standing on them to look in the window. Those were the stairs the dead man must have walked up and down on. There was a little table with a telephone on it, and a chair. Had the dead man sat on that exact chair and lifted that phone to his ear?

Running Away

Yvette Gordot, the institute's economist, who had not called on Ilka, drove over, rang the bell, saw the casserole by the front door, thought, She's out, skipped down the steps, got in her car, and drove away.

"She was out," Dr. Stone reported to his wife.

"Who was?"

"Ilka was out, with the baby. I practically fell over the stroller, corner of Euclid."

"What did you say to her?" Alpha asked him.

"Say?" said Alfred. "Nothing. She was across the street on the other sidewalk."

Trying to imagine an impossibility hurts the head. Having failed to envisage Alfred falling over a stroller that was on the other sidewalk, Alpha chose to assume that she had missed or misunderstood some part of what he had told her.

Alfred came to remember not what had happened but what he said had happened. The unspoken words he owed the widow displaced themselves into his chest and gave him heartburn.

Night Conversation

"Celie left a casserole. Alfred fell into Maggie's stroller," Ilka reported to the Shakespeares when they phoned at eleven that night.

Leslie said, "Eliza says, 'What did Alfred say to you?' "

"He slapped his forehead the way you're supposed to slap your forehead when you remember something you've forgotten—and ran across the street to the other sidewalk. Poor Alfred! He's so beautiful."

Eliza took the phone from Leslie. "Why 'poor Alfred' when he's behaving like a heel?" she asked Ilka.

Ilka said, "Because Jimmy's death is making him shy of me. He thinks it's impolite of him to be standing upright."

Eliza said, "The good Lord intended Alfred to be your basic shit, and Alfred went into medicine in the hope of turning into a human being."

"Doesn't he get points for hoping?"

"Why can't you just be offended?"

"Don't know," said Ilka. "I mean, people can't help being heels and shits."

"You sound like Jimmy," said Eliza, and Ilka listened and heard the sound, over the telephone, of Eliza weeping for Ilka's husband.

Inviting the Widow

Nancy said, "We'll have her in when we have people over. The Stones are coming Sunday. Only, you think she wants to be around people?"

"Call her and ask her?" said Nat.

"You call her and ask her."

"*I'm* not going to call her. You call her."

"She's *your* colleague, *you* call her."

"I'm not well."

"I don't think she wants to be around people," Nancy said. "And her mother is staying with her."

Dr. Alfred Stone

Dr. Alfred Stone continued to mean to say to the widow what, as a doctor—as the doctor who had been on the scene of the accident—he ought and must surely be going to say to her. He always thought that by the next time he was face to face with her he would have found the appropriate words, and blushed crimson when he walked into the Shakespeares' kitchen and saw little Maggie sitting in a high chair and Ilka crawling underneath the table. She said, "Hi, Alfred. Look what Maggie did to poor Eliza's floor! And now Bethy is going to take Maggie to play in the yard so the grown-ups can sit down in peace and quiet. OK, Bethy. She's all yours!"

Bethy Bernstine had grown bigger and bulkier. The bend of Bethy's waist, as she buttoned the baby into her sweater, cried out to her parents, to her parents' friends, Watch me buttoning the baby's sweater! Bethy's foot on the back stair into the yard pleaded, This is me taking the baby into the yard. Notice me!

Murphy's Law seated Dr. Alfred Stone next to the widow. While the conversation was general, he tried for a sideways view of her face, which was turned to Eliza on her other side. Alfred was looking for the mark on Ilka, the sign that her husband had been thrown from a burning car and had broken his neck. Alfred studied his wife across the table. Would Alpha, if he, Alfred, broke *his* neck, look so regular and ordinary? Would she laugh at something Eliza said?

As they were leaving, Alpha asked Ilka to dinner and Ilka said, "If I can get a sitter. My mother has gone back to New York." Jenny Bernstine offered Bethy.

After that, and for the next few weeks, the friends and colleagues invited Ilka to their dinners. She always said yes. "I'm afraid," she told the Shakespeares, "that my first 'No, thank you' will facilitate the next no and start a future of noes." Then, one day, as she was driving herself to the Zees', Ilka drove past their house, made a U-turn, and drove home. She insisted on paying Bethy for the full evening.

"We missed you," Leslie said on the telephone.

"How come it gets harder instead of easier? You put on your right stocking and there's the left stocking to still be put on, and the right and the left shoe . . ." Ilka heard Leslie tell Eliza what Ilka said.

In the morning, Ilka called Maria Zee to apologize, and Maria said, "Don't be silly!"

"A rain check?"

"Absolutely," said Maria. "Or you call me!"

"Absolutely," said Ilka. But Ilka did not call her, and Maria did not call Ilka. One's house seemed more comfortable without Ilka from Calamity.

Bethy Bernstine

The Bernstines and the Shakespeares were the true friends. Ilka loved them and missed Jimmy because he was missing the pleasure of Eliza's risotto and of Leslie's wine that yielded taste upon taste on the tongue. Ilka held out her glass, watched Joe's hand tip the bottle, and thought, Joe will die, not now, not soon, maybe, but he will die. Ilka saw Jenny looking at her with her soft, anxious affection and thought, Jenny will die. "Will you forgive me," Ilka said to them, "if I take myself home?" Of course, of course! Leslie must drive Ilka. "Absolutely not! Honestly! You would do me the greatest possible favor if you would let me go by myself." "Joe will drive Ilka." "Let me drive you!" said Joe. "No, no, no!" cried Ilka. They could see that she was distraught. "Let Ilka alone," said Leslie. "Ilka will drive herself. Ilka will be fine."

Leslie and Joe came out to put Ilka into her car. She saw them, in the rearview mirror, as she drove away, two old friends standing together, talking on the sidewalk. There would be a time when both of them would have been dead for years.

Bethy was curled on the couch, warm and smelling of sleep, her skin sweet and dewy. Cruel for a sixteen-year-old to be plain—too much chin and jowl, the little, pursed, unhappy mouth. Ilka woke Bethy with a hand on her shoulder. She helped the girl collect herself, straighten her bones, pick her books off the floor. Ilka walked her out and stood on the sidewalk.

Maggie was sleeping on her back, arms above her head, palms curled. In her throat, and behind her eyes, Ilka felt the tears she could not begin to cry and she feared that beast in the jungle that might, someday, stop the tears from stopping.

When Leslie called to make sure she had got home, Ilka said, "I've been doing arithmetic. Subtract the age I am from the age at which I'm likely to die and it seems like a hell of a lot of years."

Though the words Dr. Alfred Stone had failed to say to Ilka had become inappropriate and could never be said, he tended, when they were in the same room, to move along the wall at the farthest remove from where Ilka might be moving or standing or sitting.

Anthony Doerr

Village 113

The Dam

The Village Director stands under an umbrella with the bare facade of the Government House dripping behind him. The sky is a threadbare curtain of silver. "It's true," he says. "We've been slated for submergence. Property will be compensated. Moving expenses will be provided. We have eleven months." Below him, on the bottom stair, his daughters hug their knees. Men shuffle in their slickers and murmur. A dozen gulls float past, calling to one another.

On project maps, amid tangles of contour lines, the village is circled with a red submergence halo scarcely bigger than a speck of dust. Its only label is a number.

One-one-three, one-thirteen, one plus one plus three is five. The fortune-teller crouches in her stall and shakes pollen across a field of numbers. "I see selfishness," she says. "I see recompense. The chalice of ecstasy. The end of the world."

Far-off cousins from other river towns, already relocated, send letters testifying to the good life. Real schools, real clinics, furnaces, refrigerators, karaoke machines. Resettlement districts have everything the villages do not. Electricity is available twenty-four hours a day. Red meat is everywhere. You will leapfrog half a century, they write.

The Village Director donates kegs; there's a festival. Generators rumble on the wharf and lights burn in the trees and occasionally a bulb bursts and villagers cheer as smoke ascends from the branches.

The dam commission tacks photos of resettlement districts to the walls of the Government House—two girls ride swings, pigtails flying; models in khaki lean on leather furniture and laugh. *The river bottled,* a caption says, *the nation fed. Why wait?* Farmers on their way back from market pause, rest their empty baskets across their shoulders, and stare.

QUESTIONS

Teacher Ke shakes his cane at passersby; his coat is a rag, his house a shed. He has lived through two wars and a cultural purge and the Winter of Eating Weeds. Even to the oldest villagers Teacher Ke is old: no family, no teeth. He reads three languages; he has been in the gorges, they say, longer than the rocks.

"They spread a truckload of soil in the desert and call it farmland?" he asks. He veers toward the seed keeper as she passes in front of the Government House. "They take our river and give us bus tickets?"

The seed keeper keeps her head down. She thinks of her garden, the broad heads of cabbages, the spreading squashes. She thinks of the seeds in her shop: pepper seeds, cream and white; kurrat seeds, black as obsidian. Seeds in jars, seeds in funnels, seeds smaller than snowflakes.

"Aren't you betrayed?" the schoolteacher calls after her. "Aren't you angry?"

OCTOBER

Blades of light slip between clouds; the air smells of flying leaves, rain, and gravel. Farmers drag out their wagons for harvest. Orchardists stare gray eyed down their rows of trees.

The dam has been whispered about for years: an end to flooding in the lower reaches, clean power for the city. Broken lines, solid lines, a spring at the center of every village—wasn't all this foretold in the oldest stories? The rivers will rise to cover the earth, the seas will bloom, mountains become islands; the word is the water and the earth is the well. Everything rotates back to itself. In the temple such phrases are carved above the windows.

The seed keeper ascends the staircases, past women yoked with firewood, past the porters in their newspaper hats, past the benches and ginkgo trees in the Park of Heroes, onto the trails above the village. Soon forest closes around her: the smell of pine needles, the roar of air.

Here, a thousand years ago, monks lashed themselves to boulders. Here a hunter stood motionless sixteen winters until his toes became roots and his fingers twigs.

Her legs are heavy with blood. Below, through branches, she can see a hundred huddled rooftops. Beyond them is the river: its big, sleek bend, its green and restless face.

Li Qing

After midnight the seed keeper's only son appears in her doorway. He wears huge eyeglasses; a gold-papered cigarette is pinched between his lips.

He lives two hundred miles downriver in the city and she has not seen him in four years. His forehead is shinier than she remembers and his eyes are damp and rimmed with pink. In one hand he extends a single white peony.

"Li Qing."

"Mother."

He's forty-four. Stray hairs float behind his ears. Above his collar his throat looks as if it is made of soft, pale dough.

She puts the peony in a jar and serves him noodles with ginger and leeks. He eats carefully and delicately. When he finishes he sips tea with his back completely straight.

"First-rate," he says.

Outside a dog barks and falls quiet and the air in the room is warm and still. The bottles and sachets and packets of seeds are crowded around the table and their odor—a smell like oiled wood—is suddenly very strong.

"You've come back," she says.

"For a week."

A pyramid of sugar cubes rises slowly in front of him. The lines in his forehead, the sheen on his ears—in his nervous, pale fingers she sees his boyhood fingers; where his big, round chin tucks in against his throat, she sees his chin as a newborn—blood whispering down through the years.

She says, "Those are new glasses."

He nods and pushes them higher on his nose. "Some of the other guards, they make fun. They say: 'Don't make spectacles of yourself, Li Qing,' and laugh and laugh."

She smiles. Out on the river a barge sounds its horn. "You can sleep here," she says, but her son is already shaking his head.

SURVEY

All the next day Li Qing walks the staircases talking to villagers and writing numbers in a pad. Surveying, he says. Assessing. Children trail him and collect the butts of his cigarettes and examine the gold paper.

Again he does not appear in her doorway until close to midnight; again he eats like an aging prince. She finds imperfections she didn't notice the day before: a fraying button thread, a missed patch of whiskers. His glasses are cloudy with smudges. A grain of rice clings to his lower lip and she has to restrain herself from brushing it free.

"I'm walking around," he says, "and I'm wondering: How many plants—how much of the structure of this village—came from your seeds? The rice stubble, the fields of potatoes. The beans and lettuce the farmers bring to market, their very muscles. All from your seeds."

"Some people still keep their own seeds. In the old days there was not even a need for a seed keeper. Every family stored and traded their own."

"I mean it as a compliment."

"Okay," she says.

He jogs a pencil up and down in his shirt pocket. The lantern is twinned in his glasses. When he was a boy he would fall asleep with a math book beneath his cheek. Even then his hair was the color of shadows and his pencils were cratered with teeth marks. She marvels at how having her son at her table can be a deep pleasure and at the same time a thorn in her heart.

The lantern sputters. He lights a cigarette.

"You are here to see how we feel about the dam," she says. "No one cares. They only want to know who will get the biggest resettlement check."

His index finger makes small circles on the table. "And you? Do you care?"

Out the window a rectangle of paper, a letter or a page of a book, spins past, blowing up the street and hurtling out over the roof toward the river. She thinks of her mother, cleaving melons with her knife—the wet, shining rind, the sound of yielding as the hemispheres came apart. She imagines water closing over the backs of the two stone lions in the Park of Heroes. She does not answer.

All That Week

Dam commission engineers pile ropes and tripods and blueprint tubes onto the docks. At night they throw noisy, well-lit banquets in the Government House; during the day they spray-paint red characters—water level markers—on houses.

The seed keeper disembowels pumpkins and spreads the pulp across ragged sheets of plastic. The seeds are shining and white. The insides of the pumpkins smell like the river.

When she looks up, Teacher Ke is standing in front of her, thin, impossibly old. "Your son," he says. "He is one of them."

It is drizzling and the garden is damp and quiet. "He's a grown man. He makes his own decisions."

"We're numbers to him. We're less than that. We're little stones in a game of *weiqi*. We're grains of sand in a dustpan."

"It's okay, Teacher," she says. "Here." She drags a wet hand across her forehead. "I'm almost done. You must be cold. I'll make some tea."

The schoolteacher backs away, palms up. The wind moves in his coat and she has the sudden impression his whole body is made of cloth and could blow away at any moment.

"He's here to arrest me," he hisses. "He's here to kill me."

Numbers

Memory is a house with ten thousand rooms; it is a village slated to be inundated. The seed keeper sees six-year-old Li Qing wading in mud at the edges of the docks. She sees him peering past the temple eaves at stars.

He was born with hair so thick and black it seemed to swallow light. His father drowned three months later and she brought up the boy alone. Math was the only schoolwork he cared for: algebra, geometry, graphs and equations; incorruptible rules and explicit conclusions. A world not of mud, trees, and barges, but of volumes, circumferences, and surface areas.

"Equations are complete," he told her once. "If they have a solution, the solution is the same for everybody. Not like"—he gestured at her seedlings, the house, the gorge beyond—"*this* place." At fourteen he started school in the city. By seventeen he had enrolled in civil engineering school and had no time for anything else. *I am so busy,* he would write. *The environment here is very competitive.*

He joined Public Security; he patrolled the aisles of train cars wearing a handgun, a short-brimmed cap, and trousers with stripes down the legs. Each time he returned, he looked slightly different, not merely older, but changed: a new accent, the cigarettes, three sharp knocks on the door. It was as if the city was entering his body and remaking it; he'd look at the low dark houses and wandering hens and farmers with their rope belts as if at film from another century.

There was no dramatic falling-out, no climactic fight. He'd send teapots for her birthdays. On New Year's he'd send a little glass dolphin, or an electric toothbrush, or seven clouds made from sequins. Whatever space that existed between them somehow extended itself, growing invisibly, the aerial roots of ivy burrowing into mortar. A year would revolve. Then another.

Now it is dusk again and Li Qing sits at her table in his jacket and tie and recites numbers. The dam will be made from eleven million tons of concrete; its parapet will be a mile long; its impoundment will swallow a dozen cities, a hundred towns, a thousand villages. The river will become a lake and the lake will be visible from the moon.

"The size of the thing," he says, and smoke rises past his glasses.

The Leaving

Heads of families are summoned to the Government House in groups of six. The choice is a government job or a year's wages in cash. Apartments in resettlement towns will be discounted. Everyone takes the money.

The ore factory closes. The owner of the noodle restaurant leaves. The barber leaves. Every day wedding armoires and baskets of cloth and boxes and crates trundle past the seed keeper's window on the backs of porters.

Hardly anyone buys seeds for winter wheat. The seed keeper stares at her containers and thinks: *It would be easier if I had traveled. I could have gone to see Li Qing in the city. I could have climbed onto a ferry and seen the world.*

By the end of the week the engineers are gone. The uppermost row of red markers bisects the rock face above town. The river will rise sixty-four meters. The tops of the oldest trees won't reach the surface; the gable of the Government House's roof won't come close. She tries to imagine what her garden will look like through all that water—china pear and persimmon, the muddy elbows of pumpkin vines, the underside of a barge passing fifty feet above her roof.

Outside her chicken wire, the neighbor boys whisper stories that revolve around Li Qing. He has killed men, they say; his job is to remove anyone who does not support the dam. A list is folded into his back pocket, and on the list are names; when he puts a body to a name, he takes you to the wharf and the two of you go upriver but only he comes back.

Stories, only stories. Not every story is seeded in truth. Still, she lies in bed and falls through the surfaces of nightmares: the river climbs the bedposts; water pours through the shutters. She wakes choking.

The Night Before Li Qing Leaves

They descend the old staircases to the docks and cross the Bridge of Beautiful Glances, and the buoys of fish traps welter and drag in the rapids and a half-dozen skiffs skim against their tethers.

The wind carries the smell of rain. Occasionally Li Qing loses his footing in front of her and little stones go trundling off into the water.

The river swallows all other sounds. There are only the faintly visible swoops of bats coming down from the high walls and the moonlight landing on rows of distant corn and the silver lines of riffles where the river wrinkles along its banks.

"Here we are," he says.

The cinder of his cigarette flares and his hand slips into his back pocket and a sudden coil of panic seizes around her throat and she thinks: *He knows. My name is on his list.* But he only produces a little square of cloth and wipes the lenses of his glasses.

With his eyes exposed Li Qing looks into the darkness as if he is standing on the edge of a cold and deep abyss, but then he replaces the glasses and he is merely Li Qing once more, forty-four, unmarried, deputy security liaison for Dam Commission Engineers' Division Three.

"I noticed you didn't collect your resettlement payment," he says. He speaks carefully; he is, she realizes, testing his words for balance. "You're getting older, Mother. All these staircases, all those hours you spend bent over your garden. Life is hard here. The cold, the wind. No one has electric heat. No one even has a telephone."

A drizzle starts to blow onto the river and she listens to it come, and within a few seconds it is on them and speckling his glasses. "A cash settlement or a government job. Plus your son living nearby. They aren't terrible options. Every day people leave the countryside for less."

Up and down the gorge the sound of the rain echoes and reechoes and the wind slips into caves and comes spiraling out again. The small orange point of his cigarette sails out over the river in an arc and disappears.

She says, "What about a third choice?"

Li Qing sighs. "There is no third choice."

The Schoolteacher

In the darkness, a half mile away, Teacher Ke stands in front of the Government House. Rain blows past the lanterns. He holds a candle inside a jar; its flame is buffeted back and forth. The wind flies and a plastic poncho draped over his shoulders flares behind him, rising in the rain like the wings of a wraith.

November

There is little work. She eats alone. Midnights feel emptier without Li Qing in them; she hangs his peony upside down over the doorway and the petals fall off one by one.

The dwarf oak behind her house drops its last acorns and she listens to high rustlings in the branches, the whistle and thud of the big seeds striking the roof. *Here*, the trees seem to say, and *here*.

A letter:

> *Mother—I wish we'd been able to talk. I wish a lot of things. We should start searching for your apartment. Something not too far away from me, something with an elevator. There are things here that will make your life easier. What I wanted to say is that you don't have to remain loyal to one place all your life.*
>
> *It would be a great help if you would please send in your relocation claim. July 31st isn't far away. The waiting lists get longer every day.*

Land transactions stop. Marriage proposals stop. Every afternoon another barge clanks into the docks and another family piles on their possessions—portraits and bed frames and naked dolls and slavering little dogs.

The Village Director's wife comes into the seed room and gazes into the mouths of a dozen envelopes. All summer her garden behind the Government House spilled over with asters: purple, magenta, white. Now she goes away with fifty seeds. "They say we'll have a balcony," she says, but her eyes are full of questions.

There is almost nothing, it seems, people cannot take with them: roofs, drawers, baseboards, window moldings. A neighbor spends all day on a ladder extracting shingle nails; another hacks flagstones out of the streets. A fisherman's wife exhumes the bones of three generations of house cats and rolls them up in an apron.

They leave things too: cracked makeup cases and spent strings of firecrackers and graded arithmetic homework and dustless circles on a mantel where statuettes once stood. All she can find inside the restaurant are the broken pieces of an aquarium; all she finds in the cobbler's shop are three blue stockings and the top half of a female mannequin.

That whole month the seed keeper does not see Teacher Ke once. She is starting, she realizes, to look for him. Her feet take her past the schoolteacher's tiny, slumping shed, but the door is closed and she cannot tell if anyone is inside.

Maybe he has already left. Li Qing's letter sits on her table, small and white. *July isn't far away. You don't have to remain loyal to one place all your life.*

Some evenings, sitting alone among the thousand dim shapes of the seed containers, she feels slightly nauseous, off balance, as though her son is pulling at her from one end of a huge and invisible cable, as though thousands and thousands of individual wires have been set into her body.

THE CHILDREN

Here is the Park of Heroes; here are the ginkgo trees, a procession in the dark. Here are the ancient lions, their backs polished from five centuries of child riders. On the full moon, her mother used to say, the lions come to life and pad around the village, peering in windows, sniffing at trees. Fog drags through the streets and moonlight pours into it like milk. Always, before first light, the lions would creep back to their pedestals and cross their paws and become stone once more. Don't disbelieve what you can't see.

She turns down the old alley with its collapsing walls. The schoolteacher's shed is barely a shape. The door is open.

"Hello?"

A cat hurries past. The seed keeper ascends one stair, then the other. The doorway is all darkness. The wood groans. "Teacher Ke?"

Inside are stacks of papers and a half-barrel stove, coal-stained and cold. Two pots hang from a nail; the cot is empty, the blanket folded.

The fog rolls. Down by the river a ferry blows its horn, a sound like a bull lowing, huge and prehistoric. She hurries away, shivering.

In the morning it is colder and outside her chicken wire the neighbor boys stack skim ice in piles and whisper.

You hear? You didn't hear? He took him upriver. The old teacher. He took him a hundred miles into the mountains. In a boat? In a boat. Then he dropped him off. No food? Gave him a gold cigarette. Made him swim for it. Miles from anyplace. That old man? He took him into nowhere and left him to die.

She leans back against the wire. She sits there a long time until the garden is bearded with shadow and dusk fills the sky with trenches and wounds.

Downriver

White cliffs flicker past in the mist. Within fifteen minutes the seed keeper is passing through country she has seen maybe five times in her life. The gorge opens and peels back: terraces of croplands scroll past, winter potatoes and mustard tubers and the yellow stubble of harvested rice.

All day the boat travels through gorges and all day the river gains strength, gathering tributaries—it is fifty meters across, then pinched between cliffs and surging. She can feel its power in her feet. The image of the schoolteacher's empty bed winks across the face of a passing village; it holds steady in the reflection of the overcast sun, flaking and shoaling and accusatory on the water.

She does not leave the deck. A family shares its rice. Daylight hurries into gloom and one by one the passengers retreat into the cabin to sleep. A dozen villages pass in the night, card parlors, tumbledown hotels, the skiffs of fishermen, lamps swinging above wharfs like wayward stars. She thinks: *The two of you go upriver but only he comes back.* She thinks: *In six months all of this will be underwater.*

The City

A soaring black facade, sheathed in glass, an exoskeleton of balconies. Li Qing's apartment is on the forty-eighth floor. The kitchen gradually fills with light. Li Qing heats dumplings in a microwave; he pours tea into mugs with engineering logos stamped onto them.

"Eat," he says. "Take my robe." Out the window, beyond a balcony, the sunrise is lost behind a convulsion of rooftops and antennas.

His mattress is small and firm. She breathes and listens to the muted roar of traffic and her son moving lightly about the room, putting on a suit, knotting his tie. Everything seems to take on the motion of the river, the bed rocking back and forth, a current drawing her forward.

"You rest," Li Qing says, and his face looms over her like a moon. "It's good you came."

When she wakes it's evening. A beetle traverses the ceiling, weltering in the whorls of plaster. Water travels the walls, the flushing of neighbors' toilets, the unstoppering of sinks.

She sits at the table and waits for her son. Sleep is slow to leave her. The drawn curtains are thick and heavy.

He is home before eight. He throws his jacket across the couch. "Did you sleep? I'll order some food." One of his socks has a hole in it and his heel shows through.

"Li Qing." She clears her throat. "Sit down."

He puts on the kettle and sits. His eyes are very steady. She tries to hold his gaze.

"Did you ever interview Teacher Ke? While you were in the village?"

"The retired teacher?"

"Yes. What did you say to him?"

The kettle groans as it heats. "I presented the case of the dam. He had some questions, I think. I tried to answer them."

"That's all?"

"That's all."

"You only talked to him?"

"I only talked to him. And gave him his resettlement check."

The balcony rails vibrate in the wind and the seed keeper swallows. Her son pulls a cigarette from his pocket, sticks it in his mouth, and strikes a match.

Days to Come

He lets her wear his sweaters; he buys her a towel. She watches the clothes in his dryer spin and spin. After meals he smokes on his balcony and the wind comes pouring over him and lifts his tie, flapping its loose end against the glass. The cigarette butts sail down in spirals until they disappear.

Maybe Teacher Ke left like everybody else. *Maybe,* she thinks, *I've got this all wrong. Maybe at some point a person should stop accumulating judgments and start letting them go.*

She rides with him to work in his black sedan. In the lobby of his office building a model of the dam sits on a massive table. Tourists crowd the Plexiglas and the flashes of cameras blink on and off.

The cool, uniform sweep of the dam's buttress is the size of Li Qing's car. It is studded here and there with elaborate cranes, swiveling back and forth and raising and lowering their booms. The riverbanks are crawling with model bulldozers and a convoy of tiny trucks slides along a mechanical track. Miniature shrubs and pines dot the hills; everywhere there are glowing lights and electric towers. Water flows through sluice gates, rattles down a spillway, sits placidly in the reservoir, all of it dyed a fabulous blue.

"Welcome," a voice from the ceiling says, over and over. "Welcome."

District 104

He drives her through a resettlement district. Vast new apartment structures, a block long, straddle central plazas. One after another they whisk past: white concrete, blue glass, neon, bird markets and meat stalls and growling, whirling street scrubbers and the cheery names of intersections—Radiance Way, Avenue of Paradise. Construction sheeting flaps in the wind; buckets swing from scaffolding. Coal dust streaks everything.

"This district here," Li Qing says, "is one of the nicest. Most of these people are from the First Twenty."

They stop at a traffic light. Motorbikes rattle on either side. Beyond them she can hear the boom of dull bass and the clinking of chisels and the whanging of a jackhammer. Li Qing is saying more, about how exciting it is for city engineers to construct neighborhoods from scratch, to plan proper sewers, wide roads, but she finds she can no longer pay attention. Women slip past on bicycles and a car alarm squeals to life and dies, and the idling tailpipes of the motorbikes exhale steadily. The traffic light turns green; televisions flare blue simultaneously in a thousand windows.

After dinner he wants to know what she thinks: Did she notice the high windows? Would she like to go back and look through a model apartment? Three-year-old Li Qing appears on the undersides of her eyelids, a mouth full of little teeth; he rolls a pinecone across the floor and practices telling lies: the wind spilled the seeds; a ghost stained his blanket.

Then he was twelve and tying centipedes to balloon strings and watching them rise up between the cliffs. How can he be forty-four years old?

"Some people do think the dam is a bad idea," he murmurs. "They call the radio stations; they organize. In one village they've threatened to chain themselves into their houses and drown against the rafters."

Words rise to her mouth but she finds she cannot assemble them into sentences. The whole city stretches beyond Li Qing's balcony, a riddle of rooftops and fire escapes, a haze of antennas. The wind wraps itself around the building; everything rocks back and forth.

"But really this is just a tiny percentage," Li Qing says. "Most everybody is in favor of the dam. The flooding downstream is awful, you know. It killed two thousand people last summer. And we can't keep burning all this coal. Talk is good. It is healthy. I encourage it."

One-thirteen. Selfishness, recompense, and the chalice of ecstasy. Her son wants to know about his father; what does she think his father would have thought about the dam? But everything reels; she is floating through rapids, trapped between the walls of a gorge. Limestone walls flash past, white and crumbling.

RETURN

In the village, two hundred miles away, another neighbor leaves: mother, father, son, daughter, a parade of furniture, a guinea pig, rabbit, and ferret, their cages suspended from the bamboo poles of porters, their black eyes peering into a snowfall, their breath showing in little spirals.

She has been in the city nine days when she rises and dresses and walks out into the other room where her son sleeps crammed onto his polyester couch. His glasses are folded on the floor beside him. His nostrils flare slightly with each breath; his eyelids are big and blue and traced with tiny capillaries.

She says his name. His eyes flutter.

"How does the water come, when it comes?"

"What do you mean?"

"Does it come fast? Does it surge?"

"It comes slowly." He blinks. "First the currents will go out of the river, and then the water will become very calm. The rapids will disappear. Then, after a day, the wharfs. To reach high water will take eight and a half days, we think."

She closes her eyes. The wind hisses through the rails on the balcony, a sound like electricity.

"You're going back," he says. "You're leaving."

THE VILLAGE

Nothing new has been built in months. Windows break and are left broken. Rocks as big as dogs fall into streets and no one bothers to remove them. She ascends the long staircase and creeps down the crumbling alley to the schoolteacher's house. His door is open; a kerosene lantern hangs from a beam. Teacher Ke sits over a sheet of paper in a shaft of light. A blanket hangs over his lap; he dips a brush in a bottle of ink. His beard wags over the paper.

He has not been arrested; he has not been killed. Maybe he was never gone at all—maybe he was in a nearby town drinking mao-tai.

"Good evening, Teacher," she calls, and continues up the street.

Her house sits unmolested. Her seeds are where she left them. She drags the coal bucket across the floor and opens the mouth of the stove.

There are maybe a hundred villagers left, some old fishermen and a few wives and a handful of rice farmers waiting until their seedlings are big enough to transplant. The children are gone; the Village Director is gone. The market is full of wet trash. But in the morning the seed keeper feels strangely unburdened, even euphoric: it feels right to be here, in the silver air, to stand in her garden amid the scraps of slush and listen to the wind stream through the gorge.

Light pours between clouds, glazing rooftops, splashing into streets. She lugs a pot of stew up the staircases and through the crumbling alley and leaves it steaming on the steps of the schoolteacher's house.

Spring

February brings rainstorms and the first scent of rapeseed. Threads of water spill from the canyon walls. Inside the temple six or seven women sing between blasts of thunder. The roof is leaking and rainwater leaches through great brown splotches and drips into pans scattered around the aisles.

There is no Spring Festival, no boat races down the river, no fireworks on the summits. She would be seeding rice now, a seed in each container of her plastic trays, then earth, then water. Instead she seeds her garden, and the neighbor's garden, and throws handfuls of seeds into the yards of abandoned houses too: kale, radish, turnip, chives. She is suddenly wealthy: she has the seeds for fifty gardens. In the evenings she cooks—spicy noodles, bean curd soup—and brings the pots to the steps of the schoolteacher and leaves them under lids and collects the pots she has left before, empty, clumsily washed.

Meanwhile the village disappears. The boards of the docks vanish. The wrappings are taken off trees. Clock hands disappear and the doors off the Government House and the guide wires from radio antennas and the antennas, too. Whole groves of bamboo are taken. Magnolia trees are dug up and carted in wheelbarrows onto barges. Hinges and knobs and screws and nuts evaporate. Every ounce of teak in every house is dismantled and packed away in blankets and lugged down the staircases.

In March the few farmers who are left thresh their wheat. When the wind is low she can hear them, the chop-chop of scythes. Every March of her life she has heard that sound.

She cannot remember a spring more colorful. Flowers seem to explode out of the mud. By April there is scarlet and lavender and jade everywhere. Behind the Government House zinnias are coming up with a deep, almost unnatural vigor—as if they are swarming up out of the earth. She kneels over them for a half hour, studying the tight fists of their buds.

Soon so many plants in her garden are coming up she has to start pulling them. It is as if someone is underneath the earth, pushing her vegetables up with his fingers. Has spring always been like this? Startling, overpowering? Maybe she is more sensitive to it this year. Bees drift through the alleys with their heavy baskets, seemingly drunk; to stand beneath the sycamores is to stand in a blizzard of seeds.

At night she walks the town and has the sense that the darkness is a great cool lake. Everything seems about to float away. Darkness, she thinks, is the permanent thing.

And silence. With the people gone, and the ore factory quiet, it is as if the village has become a trove of silence, as if the sounds of her shoes on the stairs, and the air passing in and out of her lungs, are the only sounds for miles.

Mail service stops. She does not hear from Li Qing. Any moment, perhaps, he will appear at her door and demand she leave with him immediately. But he never shows. At night there are only three or four lights against the huge background of the gorge and the dark sky and the darker river with its faint avenue of reflected stars.

FIREFLIES

Every night now thousands of fireflies float up the staircases and hang in the trees, flashing their sequenced trains of light, until the whole gorge looks as if it has been threaded with green bulbs. She bends to exchange a pot of soup for the empty one sitting on the schoolteacher's stairs when the door swings open.

"You're watching the beetles," he says. He clambers out the doorway and sits with the point of his cane balanced on the bottom step. She nods.

"I thought you had left," he says. "In the winter."

She shrugs. "Everyone is leaving."

"But you're still here."

"As are you."

He clears his throat. Out in his fruit trees the fireflies rise and flash, rise and flash.

"My son—" she says.

"Let's not talk about him."

"Okay."

"They're courting females," he says. "The beetles. In some of the big trees along the river, I've seen thousands of them all flashing in synchrony. On, off. On, off."

She stands to go.

"Stay," he says. "Talk awhile."

Memory

Every stone, every stair, is a key to a memory. Here the sons of her neighbors flew kites. Here the toothless knife sharpener used to set up his coughing, smoking wheel. Here, forty years ago, a legless girl roasted nuts in a copper wok and here her mother once let her drink a glass of beer on Old Festivals Day. Here the river took a clean shirt right out of her hands; here was once a field, furred with green shoots; here a fisherman put his hot, dry mouth on hers. The body odor of porters, the white faces of tombs, the sweet, bulging calves of Li Qing's father—the village drowns in memory.

Again and again her feet take her up the long staircases past the park to the crumbling alley, the tides of fireflies, and the sour perfume of the schoolteacher's yard. She brings a pot of hot water and a bag of sugar cubes, and the schoolteacher joins her on the steps and they drink and watch the beetles pulse and rise as if the whole gorge is smoldering and these are the sparks that have shaken free.

Before the Government House, before mail service, before the ore factory, this was a place of monks, and warriors, and fishermen. Always fishermen. The schoolteacher and the seed keeper talk of presidents and emperors, and the songs of trackers, and the temple, and the birds. Mostly she listens to the old man's voice in the darkness, his sentences parceling out one after another until his frail body beside her seems to disappear in the darkness and he is only a voice, a schoolteacher's fading elocution.

"Maybe," he says, "a place looks different when you know you're seeing it for the last time. Or maybe it's knowing no one will ever see it again. Maybe knowing no one will see it again changes it."

"Changes the place or how you see it?"

"Both."

She sips her sweet water.

He says: "Earth is four and a half billion years old. You know how much a billion is?"

One-thirteen, sixty-six, forty-four. A hundred billion suns per galaxy, a hundred billion galaxies in the universe. Teacher Ke writes three letters a day, a hundred words each. He shows them to her: the white paper, his wobbly calligraphy. He addresses them to newspapers, officials, engineers. He has a whole roster—hundreds of pages thick—of dam commission employees. She thinks: *My son's name is in there.*

"What do you say in the letters?"

"That the dam is a mistake. That they're drowning centuries of history, risking lives, working with faulty numbers."

"And do they make a difference?"

He looks at her; the moisture in his eyes reflects the fireflies, the soaring, glossy ruins of the cliffs. "What do you think?"

July

Everything accumulates a terrible beauty. Dawns are long and pink; dusks last an hour. Swallows swerve and dive and the stripe of sky between the walls of the gorge is purple and soft as flesh. The fireflies float higher up on the cliffs—a foam of green—as if they know, as if they can sense the water coming.

Is Li Qing trying to reach her? Is he right now racing up the river in a hydrofoil to take her away?

Teacher Ke asks her to carry his letters to the wharfs in the hope that passing boats will mail them. The fishermen almost always say no; they squint at the rickety script on the envelopes and sense they are dangerous. She has more luck with the hollow-eyed scavengers who come up on ramshackle motor launches to salvage scrap metal or paving stones; she bribes them with an old dress, or kerosene, or a paper bag filled with eggplant. Maybe they mail them; maybe they round the bend and pitch them into the rapids.

All the unbroken flagstones have been taken and sunflowers begin to rise from the center of the streets. Her improvised gardens in her neighbors' yards are unruly with bees and nettles.

"There are hours," the schoolteacher says, "when I think of the shoeshine boys making fun of me, and the piles of trash steaming in the rain, and the burns on my fingers from that old stove, and I cannot wait to see it all go underwater."

The long staircase, one landing after another, the front of each step edged with light. No chisels, no dogs, no engines. Just the sky, and light falling down between the buildings, like a fine rain, and her footfalls echoing through the empty alleys.

She stands in her house and stares into the mouths of containers, watching little polygons of light reflect off the smooth polish of seeds, their perfect geometries, their hibernal dreams.

She peers past the schoolteacher into his tiny shed, the scattered piles of papers and the books and his blackened lantern and the upturned husks of beetles in the corners.

She says, "You're going to drown with the village."

He is quiet a long time. "You're the one," he says, "we should be worried about."

Finally

There are two nights left in July when the schoolteacher appears in her doorway. He wears a suit, his shoes shined and his beard combed. His eyes gleam. Over his shoulder is a knapsack, in one fist his cane and in the other the neck of a large plastic bag.

"Look." Inside are hundreds, maybe thousands, of fireflies. "Honey and water. They can't get enough of it."

She smiles. He unloads his knapsack: a bottle of mao-tai and a stack of thirty or so letters.

"Two glasses," he says, and drags his stiff legs over to her chair and sits and wrestles the cork out of the bottle.

"To one last mailing."

"To one last mailing."

They toast. He explains what he needs and she empties every jar she has, pouring the seeds into buckets and trays. The schoolteacher strips corks with a penknife and rolls letters into the bottles and together they use a paper funnel to shake the fireflies in. The insects fly everywhere and clog the bottlenecks, but they manage to get thirty or so into each bottle.

They stack the corked bottles in a basket. Fireflies crawl the glass. The light from the lantern wavers and shadows lap the walls. She can feel the liquor burning in her stomach and down the lines of her arms.

"Good," Teacher Ke is saying, "good, good, good." When she extinguishes the lantern the bottles glow softly. She heaves the basket onto her shoulders and carries it down the staircases, and the schoolteacher limps beside her, leaning on his cane.

The air is warm and damp; the sky is a stripe of dark blue ink between the black shells of the cliffs. The basket on her shoulder buzzes softly. They reach what's left of the docks, fifteen or so piles driven into the riverbed, and she sets down the basket and studies it.

"They'll run out of air," she says, but she can feel the liquor working now, and Teacher Ke is breathing hard, already half drunk himself. Everything is silent except for the river.

"Okay," he says. "Let's put them in."

She wades out into the cold water. Pebbles stir beneath her shoes. The current parts lightly around her knees. The schoolteacher is a trembling weight at her elbow. She floats the basket out alongside them. The bottles flash and flash. Eventually the two of them—seed keeper and schoolteacher—are submerged to their waists.

Maybe the river is already beginning to slack, to back up and rise. Maybe ghosts pour out of the earth, out of the mouths of tombs up and down the gorges, out of the tips of twigs at the ends of branches. The fireflies tap against the glass. *More than anything*, she thinks, *I'll be sad to see the speed go out of the water*.

She hands the schoolteacher the first bottle and he sets it in and they watch the river slowly take it, a green-blue light winking out into the current, turning slightly as it picks up pace.

Twenty thousand days and nights in one place, each layered and trapped and folded on top of the last, the creases in her hands, the aches between her vertebrae. Embryo, seed coat, endosperm: What is a seed if not a link to every generation that has gone before it?

The bottle disappears. She hands him the next one. When he turns she can see he is crying.

Everything has trained her to expect this to work out badly. Li Qing with his cigarettes, the schoolteacher with his questions. *Our side, their side. But perhaps,* she thinks, *there is no good and bad to it at all.* Every memory will eventually be underwater. Progress is a storm and the wings of everything are swept up in it.

She leans forward and wipes the schoolteacher's eye with her thumb. The second bottle is gone.

Teacher Ke drags his forearm across his nose. "All this trouble," he says, "and still—doesn't it feel good? Doesn't it make you feel young?"

The river murmurs against their bodies and the bottles go out of the basket one after another. The old man takes his time. The bottles glow and flash in the current, round the bend, and are gone. She listens to the current, and the old man sends his letters downstream, and they stand in the water until they cannot tell where their legs end and where the river begins.

July 31

On the last day, five or six steady, level-faced servicemen with chainsaws come for the trees. They bring them down in four-foot sections and load the logs onto hand wagons, and bounce the hand wagons down what's left of the staircases, past the broken pavement and the sunflowers and the seed keeper's gardens in the neighbors' yards. They take the oaks, the ginkgoes, the three old sycamores from the garden behind the Government House. They leave the lions.

All day she does not see the schoolteacher and she hopes he is already gone, making his way upriver on some old trail, or squatting in the canoe of a passing fisherman, watching the gorges drift past. Maybe she is the last person in the village; maybe she is the last person on the river.

In the afternoon three policemen come to sweep the village, shining flashlights into rooms, lifting discarded plywood with the toes of their boots, but it is easy to hide from them and in an hour their hydrofoil is gone, roaring toward the next town.

She spreads a blanket across her table and upends containers of seeds onto it. Mustard tuber, pak choy, cabbage, eggplant, cauliflower. Millet, chestnut, radish. Her mother's voice: *Seeds are the dreams plants dream while they sleep*. Seeds big as coins, seeds light as breath. They all go onto the blanket. When all the containers are empty she folds the corners of the blanket over each other and ties the whole thing into a bundle.

In her arms it is maybe as heavy as a child. The sun rolls down behind the gorge. By now the diversion has been sealed off, and water is piling up behind the dam.

A wool cap. A jacket. She leaves her dishes stacked in the cupboards.

She walks down the staircases for the last time and out to the Bridge of Beautiful Glances and sits on the parapet. The day's heat rises from the stone into the backs of her thighs. Below her the river sucks and murmurs. Everything is radiant.

Birds land on the roof of the Government House. Coming up the river is the low growl of a motor launch, and when it rounds the corner she turns. Behind its windshield is a pilot and beside the pilot is Li Qing, waving at her and wearing his ridiculous eyeglasses.

YEARS LATER

She lives in a block-long building called New Immigrant 606. Her apartment has three rooms, each with a door and a single-paned window. The walls are white and blank. She never receives a bill.

Sundays Li Qing comes by and sits with her for a few hours, drinking beer. Lately he brings Penny Ou, a divorcée with a gentle voice and a trio of moles mushrooming off the side of her nose. Sometimes they bring her son, a round-faced nine-year-old named Jie. They eat stew, or noodles with bean sprouts, and talk of nothing.

Jie swings his feet back and forth beneath the table. A radio burbles on the sideboard. Afterward Penny takes the dishes to the sink and washes and dries them and stacks them in the cupboard.

The days seem made of twilight, immaterial as shadows. Memories, when they come, are often viscous and weak, trapped beneath distant surfaces, or caught in neurofibrillary tangles. She stands over the full bathtub but cannot remember filling it. She goes to fill the kettle but finds it steaming.

Her seeds sit moldering or cracking or expired altogether in a prefabricated pressboard dresser that came with the apartment. Occasionally she stares at it, its unfinished face, its eight shiny knobs, and a sensation nags at the back of her consciousness, a feeling like she has misplaced something but can no longer remember what it is.

Her mother used to say seeds were links in a chain, not beginnings or endings, but she was wrong: seeds are both beginnings and endings—they are a plant's womb and its coffin. For a school project Jie brings over six Styrofoam cups filled with peat. The seed keeper offers him six magnolia seeds, each bright as a drop of blood.

The boy pokes a hole into each cupful of dirt with a finger; he drops the seeds in like tiny bombs. They put the cups on her windowsill. Water. Soil. Light. "Now we wait," she says.

We go round the world only to come back again. A seed coat splits, a tiny rootlet emerges. On the news a government official denies reports of cracks in the dam's ship locks. Li Qing calls: He's going to be traveling this week. Things are very busy. Penny Ou will try to stop by.

The seed keeper goes to the window. In the plaza tides of people drift in a hundred directions: bicyclists, commuters, beggars, trash collectors, shoppers, policemen. Teacher Ke would have aged even more; it would hardly be possible for him to still be alive. And yet: What if he is one of those figures down there, inside one of those cars, one of the shapes on the sidewalk, a head and shoulders, the infinitesimal tops of his shoes?

Out past the square tens of thousands of lights tremble in the wind, airplanes and shopfronts and billboards, guide lights and lamps behind windows and warning lights on antennas. Above them a handful of stars show themselves for a moment, murky, scarcely visible between clouds, flashing blue and red and white. Then they're gone.

Steven Millhauser

A Change in Fashion

After the Age of Revelation came the Age of Concealment. Sleeves flowed along forearms and closed tight at the wrist, hems fell to the ankle, necklines rose above the collarbone. Young women at first resisted the new fashion, which reminded them of old photographs in boring albums on dreary Sunday afternoons, before succumbing to it with fervor. It became stylish to wear dresses that brushed the floor of high school hallways and allowed coy glimpses of polished boot toes; bands of girls strolling through malls wore kerchiefs over their hair and displayed lengthening gloves of lambskin and Italian leather that crept above the elbow toward the middle of the upper arm. Necks slowly disappeared behind rising collars as hat brims grew broader, casting the face in shadow. It was as if, after half a century of reckless exposure, a weariness had overcome women, a yearning for withdrawal, a disenchantment with the obligation to invite a bold male gaze. In every skirt fold and blouse button, one could sense the new longing for hiddenness.

As the fashion for more and more fabric spread from the pages of popular magazines, where the new models posed with turned-aside faces and downcast eyes, to the middle-class housewife and her daughters, a group of emerging designers on both coasts began to attract attention. They were young, imperious, and contemptuous of the recent past. Among the creators the most daring and secretive was one who signed his clothes with a small gold H in a blood-red circle. He refused to be photographed; in a spirit of irony or bravado, he called himself Hyperion.

At this time the long style still clung to the shape of the female body. It was Hyperion who took the decisive leap away from the body toward regions of high invention. In a celebrated autumn catwalk show, he shocked viewers by bringing back a version of the Victorian crinoline, with its hoops of flexible steel, and raising it to the level of the shoulders. Now a woman could walk hidden in a hemispheric ripple of wire-supported silk or velvet that fell from her shoulders to the floor. Although the hemi-dress was ridiculed by a number of fashion commentators for its awkwardness, its ugliness, its retro-kitsch jokiness, its air of mockery, others saw in it an expression of liberation from the tyranny of the body. Before the show, the history of women's fashion was a record of shifts of attention from one part of the body to another. With a single design, Hyperion had freed fashion from its long dependence on the female shape.

A brief and unsatisfactory geometric period—the pyramid dress, the octagon dress—was followed by the creation of the free style, which rejected symmetry altogether. Now women adorned themselves in free-floating designs that seemed intent on allowing fabric to explore its inner nature, to fulfill secret necessities. There were dresses with troubling structures that burst from the shoulders and waist and swooped up in arabesques of velvet and satin; aggressively long dresses with silk-lined trains that, raised and fastened about the neck, formed a kind of shimmering and ecstatic plumage; horizontal dresses; dresses like delirium dreams, dresses like feverish blossoms blazing in the heart of impenetrable jungles; dresses composed of synthetic fabrics specially developed to assume the appearance of thunderclouds, of swirling snow, of tongues of fire. It was as if dresses had become stricken with boredom, with impossible desires. Whereas fashion extravagances of the past—the Elizabethan farthingale, the horsehair bustle of the 1870s—had always emphasized and exaggerated some part of the female anatomy, the new shapes ignored the body entirely, while at the same time they seemed to express inner moods, forgotten dreams, buried realms of feeling. Teenage girls in particular embraced the Hyperion free style, with its double pleasure of secrecy and exposure—for they could plunge down, far down, into layers of costume that sheltered them from sight, while rivers of twisting cloth allowed them to bring forth forbidden longings.

. . .

Meanwhile the female face, which had hovered somewhat uncertainly above the early Hyperion dresses, began to be absorbed by the new designs. A petal collar, composed of lanceolate shafts of cloth, rose to the hairline; colorful wraps known as neckbands reached above the chin; elaborate head coverings swept down to the bodice. Even more remarkable was the development on the surface of dresses: new shapes sprang from folds of cloth, secondary growths that seemed to lead separate lives, like gargoyles sprouting in the corners of cathedrals.

Although the Hyperion free style was above all notable for its refusal to reveal the female body, commentators were quick to point out that the fashion of concealment was not without an erotics of its own. The direct and simple provocations of the old style—a bare stomach, a nipple pressing through a tight sweater—were replaced by indirection, disguise, and a vague suggestiveness. In the new style, the imagination was said to be stimulated to an unusual degree: beneath those lavish swirls of fabric, playful, and at times forbidding, lay a hidden body, inviting discovery. One fashion writer compared the free-style dress to the series of obstacles facing a medieval knight adventuring through a dark forest toward his mistress held captive in the tower of a distant castle guarded by an ogre. That sense of difficulty, of seductive impediment, was increased by elaborations of lingerie permitted by the new volume—beneath the vast skirts bloomed a garden of lace-trimmed petticoats in raspberry chiffon and black organdy, crimson silk half-slips with side slits, stretch-satin and dotted-mesh chemises with ruffle trim. Teenage girls, who a year earlier had reveled in their thongs and V-strings, led the way in adopting an excess of underclothes, holding contests in high school bathrooms to see who was wearing the greatest number of layers, in vivid and hidden colors: sunburst yellow, vermilion, ice blue. But quite apart from this development, which drew attention to new depths of concealment and thus to the veiled body itself, several commentators pointed out that it was not strictly accurate to speak of the complete covering of the female form. Beyond the neckbands and high collars, parts of the face continued to be visible, thereby reminding the observer of unseen portions of the body, which were helplessly summoned to the imagination. In addition, women concealed in Hyperion free-style dresses moved from place to place, so that the creations shook and swayed; now and then, a hidden arm or leg might press visibly against a portion of fabric. Stimulated by the unseen, lashed by the unknown, sexual fantasies became at once more violent and more devious. The new clothing was essentially paradoxical. Women, it was argued, were never more naked than when concealed from view.

Indeed one feature of the new style was its appeal to women who longed to inspire fiery passions but who judged their visible bodies to be inadequate or repellent. Beneath the Hyperion dress a woman could rest secure in the knowledge that her body, safely shut away, could become whatever she wished it to be, down there in the dark below distractions of fabric that seemed to tremble on the edge of dream.

Fashion is an expression of boredom, of restlessness. The successful designer understands the ferocity of that boredom and provides it with new places in which to calm its rage for a while. Even as Hyperion free-style dresses were displayed in photo spreads in international magazines and promoted in vigorous poster campaigns, the designer was preparing his next step. In his eagerly awaited spring/summer collection, he proclaimed the final liberation of costume from the female body. The new dress completed the urge toward concealment by developing the bodice upward into a complete covering for the face and head. Now the Hyperion dress entirely enclosed the wearer, who was provided with artful spaces for the mouth, nostrils, and eyes. The new top quickly developed a life of its own. It seemed determined to deny the existence of the head, to use the area between collarbone and scalp as a transitional element, by expanding the idea of a dress upward to include the space above the height of the wearer. Meanwhile the openings for eyes and nostrils, which had drawn attention to the concealed face and threatened to turn the dress into a species of mask, were replaced by an opaque fabric that permitted one-way vision. Women, who had gradually been disappearing into the hidden spaces of the new style, had at last become invisible.

Commentators welcomed the enclosure dress but were divided over its merits. Some argued that it represented the ultimate defense of the female body against visual invasion, while others saw in it the final liberation of costume from its demeaning dependence on the body. One fashion writer praised what she called the vanished woman and compared the enclosure dress to the development of the boudoir, or private sitting room in the eighteenth-century house—a secret domain in which a woman could be herself, safe from male control. A rival journalist, ignoring women and their desires, spoke only of the new aesthetic of costume, which at last was free to develop in the manner of landscape painting after it had become bold enough to exile the human figure.

And indeed there now began a period of excess, of overabundant fulfillment, as if the banishment of the face had removed some nuance of restraint still present in the earlier collections. Inspired by Hyperion, dresses became fevered with obscure cravings, with sudden illuminations and desolations, and threw themselves into hopeless adventures. Restless and dissatisfied, they grew in every direction; in some instances they exceeded the size of rooms and had to be worn in large outdoor spaces, like backyards or public parks. The vast lower depths of such dresses encouraged coarse speculation. It was said that beneath those coverings, naked women coupled madly with young lovers in the grass. One dress contained in its side a little red door, which was said to lead to a room with a bed, a mirror, and a shaded lamp. Another dress, designed for the wife of a software CEO, rose three stories high and was attached to the back of the house by a covered walkway. A celebrated fashion journalist with a fondness for historical parallels compared these developments to the fanatical elaborations of coiffure in the late eighteenth century, when three-foot castles of hair rose on wire supports. The new dresses were not so much worn as entered—it was as if they wished to carry the structural qualities of fashion to the point at which clothing began to merge with architecture.

Such excesses were not without a touch of desperation, as if the escape of costume from the female body had created in clothes an uncertainty, a sharp malaise. One summer afternoon during a party at an estate in northwestern Connecticut, an unusual immobility in the lavish dresses became apparent. Had the women taken a solemn vow not to move? The stationary costumes, arranged on a lawn that sloped down to a lake, resembled a form of sculpture. Four men, bored or excited by the motionless women, stood before one of them, talking and drinking hard. Suddenly two of the men bent over, grasped the heavy dress by the hem, and lifted it violently into the air. Voices shouted, cheered. Underneath they discovered only the lawn itself, stretching away.

The four men rushed over to the other dresses, yanking them up, knocking them over, tearing at them with their fingers, but the women had disappeared. Later that day they were discovered in the kitchen of a neighbor's house, dressed in old bathrobes and talking among themselves.

For a time the new fashion caught on. Women donned immense dresses and then quietly withdrew, wandering away to do whatever they liked. Dresses, freed at last from bodies, became what they had always aspired to be: works of art, destined for museums and private collections. Often they stood on display in large living rooms, beside pianos or couches.

But the complete separation of clothing from women's bodies created a new confusion. Women no longer knew how to dress, what to wear. Many dressed in a deliberately slatternly way, as if to express their sense of the unbearable distance between the perfection of high costume and the humiliating imperfection of the body it was meant to obliterate. It was as if a superior race of beings had been inserted into the world: the race of costume. A tension was building; there were rumors of an uprising of women, who would overthrow the dresses that had rendered them superfluous. Such talk, however absurd, revealed a longing for something new, for a redemptive leap. People spoke hungrily of new, impossible dresses—dresses worn on the inside of the body, dresses the size of entire towns. Others proposed an Edenic nakedness. As the new season approached, it was clear that something had to happen.

It was at this moment that Hyperion gave his only interview. In it he abjured the fashions that had made him famous; apologized to women for leading them astray; revealed that his name was Ben Hirschfeld, of Brooklyn; and announced his retirement after the coming show. The interview was analyzed relentlessly, attacked as a promotional stunt, dismissed as a hoax. On the nightly news a short, balding man stood under an umbrella as he blinked nervously behind small round lenses and said that yes, his name was Benjamin Hirschfeld, yes, he lived in Brooklyn, but no, he knew nothing about fashion, nothing about clothes, nothing. The public, skeptical and patient, waited.

And the moment came; it was not what anyone had expected. Along the catwalk strolled a tall model in a classic fitted dress, with a trim waist and a full, pleated skirt. Her face, entirely exposed, bore an indolent and haughty look that hadn't been seen for years. The new, impoverished dress represented a repudiation of everything Hyperion had stood for. At the same time, within the culture of the liberated dress it struck a radical note.

Women hesitated; here and there, in a spirit of daring, someone appeared at a party dressed in the new style. One day, as if by secret agreement, the fashion was everywhere. The monstrous old dresses drifted into attics, where young girls, climbing the stairs in search of an abandoned dollhouse or a pair of skates, came upon something looming against the rafters and stopped uneasily before continuing on their way. At dinner parties and family gatherings, people recalled the old style with amusement and affectionate embarrassment, as one might remember an episode of drunkenness. In memory the dresses became more vivid, more remote, until they seemed like brilliant birds rising in dark forests or like distant sunlit towns. Meanwhile the new dresses grew a little shorter, a little longer; slacks and blouses grew tighter, looser. One afternoon in late summer, on a sidewalk printed with the shade of maple leaves and flickers of sun, a woman walking with her young daughter had the sense that she was about to remember something, something about a dress, but no, it was gone, vanished among the overhead leaves already turning, the bits of blue sky, the smell of cut grass, the chimney shadows sharp and black on the sunlit roofs.

Sheila Kohler

The Transitional Object

On the Rue de la Faisanderie, about to ring the shiny brass bell that opens the heavy door, she hesitates. She looks up at the French windows, on the first floor, the curtains drawn, as they were on her first visit. That was in the evening. Now it is midafternoon, the dead time of day, not many people about.

What am I doing? What am I thinking? For a while now she has been talking to herself, her lips moving, certain words escaping aloud as she walks through the streets of Paris. *No! No! No!* she says. Since the university has closed its doors for the summer, since her first visit to her professor, she has wandered the lonely streets of Paris, increasingly distanced from herself. She hears a voice in her head constantly telling her what she is doing, as though she were writing the story of her life or had acquired a double, a secret sharer of her existence.

She leans against the blond stone wall, takes a pebble from her shoe, and notices a man across the street who walks under the chestnut trees. He is staring at her. She shouldn't have worn such a tight short skirt, she thinks. *Too noticeable.* She is exhausted, hot, and sweating, yet she shivers a little at the same time. She clutches her white handbag to her chest. *Crazy, out of the question. Not the place where I should be. Go home.*

But home is an odd word for where she has come from. She has slipped out her door and walked down all the stairs from the maid's room on the sixth floor, the air redolent with the rotting smell of drains. She has rushed out into the Rue du Cherche Midi, hoping to avoid the concierge, an elderly man with greasy locks who lurks in the dingy hall. She hasn't paid for her room for weeks.

She has telegrammed her mother but had no response. Now she has no money left with which to telegram anyone. Nor has she eaten or ventured out for two days, and the hot, humid air in the street makes her head spin, the voice in her ears louder and louder so that she no longer hears the sound of the cars, the wind in the leaves.

The big leaves of the chestnut trees hang down heavy as ripe fruit. Paris in late July, the streets half empty or filled with tired tourists. She had hoped to take the train and be at the beach by now with Richard. Instead, she has walked all the way from her hotel near the university, in the sixth, in the heat of the day, going along the quais in her uncomfortable high heels, toiling on up the hill to the professor's apartment on the other side of the Seine in the sixteenth. Even her Orange Card for the bus has expired. She has already pawned her two small, gold rings.

She reminds herself that tea was mentioned. She enters the door, steps into the cool shadows of the interior courtyard, green plants along the wall. There is a glass door covered with fine curtains on the left: the concierge's loge. She goes quickly past that, opens another door, and presses the button for the caged elevator, unable to walk another step, though the professor's apartment is only on the first floor, the piano nobile, as it is called. *Not much noble about him.*

On her first visit here, a month ago, summoned to talk about her paper, she had jogged up the carpeted stairs, two at a time. In her eagerness, she was early. She had taken the bus across Paris, contemplating various brilliant remarks with which she hoped to dazzle the professor. She had found his front door open that evening, as in a dream. She had not known whether to just walk in or ring the bell.

Today she is late, and the door is shut. She rings, breathless, afraid. *If he doesn't answer by the count of ten, I'm leaving. I'm out of here. One, two, three.*

He is completely bald and wears round, thick glasses and a shiny, gray expensive suit, which rustles as he moves to shake her hand. A pudgy man, with soft hands, small feet in shiny black shoes, he smells strongly of cologne—vetiver. He ushers her inside, without a word, looking appropriately solemn.

Never should have come back.

She has the impression of watching herself from a great distance: a slim young girl in a pink tank top, a tight white skirt, dark rings like ash beneath her slanting gray eyes. The girl follows a plump, bald man down a silent, shadowy corridor.

I'm going back into his office. I'm going back in there; the door is open.

She has lost the feeling of continuity.

Still, today she has made an effort. *You must make an effort.* She has washed her heavy, dark-blond hair in the sink in her room and tied it back from her face in a ponytail with a black velvet ribbon. She has found a clean skirt. She has put on pink lipstick, rubbed some on her pale cheeks. She has even remembered to wear short white gloves. *Wear gloves; make yourself look pretty.*

Dr. Soubrier seems to notice the effort, the short skirt, the prettiness. He glances at her appraisingly, his gaze lingering on her legs as he ushers her along the corridor and into his office.

"How nice you look today, my dear!" he says, and smiles, his round cheeks dimpling with optimism, she thinks.

She had asked Dr. Soubrier if he read English well enough to read her paper in English, but he had replied, "By next year I'm hoping it will be good enough," and smiled at her with his Buddha-like smile. An optimistic man, she thinks. He is the only psychoanalyst teaching them at the Institut Catholique. He has told them he is a Lacanian.

Now he asks her to sit down. She hesitates, looking around the muffled room, still contemplating escape into the street. Her hands, her knees, her whole body is trembling.

What am I doing?

She looks at all the learned, bound books in the bookcases behind his pompous Empire desk with the gold filigree: Freud's collected works in German, bound in black with gold lettering; several volumes by Durkheim. She sees the red bound volume with the title SUICIDE, written in big letters down the spine. She wonders how many of Dr. Soubrier's patients have committed suicide.

Perhaps Dr. Soubrier is more successful as a psychoanalyst than a professor, though she has her doubts about that, too, as she inspects his office, notices the box of Kleenex still on the table by the door.

He smiles at her and makes a gesture toward the brown velvet sofa, which she knows is soft and comfortable. The light is dim, the curtains drawn over the long French windows and the afternoon sunshine, a green lamp lit on his desk. His glasses catch the light, glint, when he looks at her.

"I'm so glad you came back. Somehow, I knew you would. I knew you would think things over and see them differently. An unfortunate misunderstanding," he says. He has a pleasant low voice. His patients must like his voice, she thinks. She supposes people usually do come back. Probably they come back again and again.

This is where she found him on that first visit, when she arrived, armed only with her thick paper in its blue folder, her thoughts on the transitional object. She walked into the room unannounced. The room with the large desk and the bookcases must be where he receives his patients, she presumes. One of them must have carelessly left the front door open as he went out that day.

Today, she notices a slim silver cigarette case with a crest on the lid, the sort of small cigarette case one could easily slip into a pocket. It shimmers invitingly. There doesn't seem to be any sign of a tea tray, however, let alone cake. At home in South Africa, at one of her teachers' houses, she thinks with longing, there would be something substantial provided: Marie biscuits, sandwiches on sliced lettuce, anchovy toast, or even cake. She imagines a thick slab of cake with white icing, granadilla icing, the kind her mother makes.

He tells her again, please, to sit down, to make herself comfortable, and indeed she cannot do otherwise now, her knees trembling so and overcome with giddiness. She sinks down into the dark velvet sofa, holding her handbag on her lap, closing her eyes for a moment. *I cannot do this. I cannot.* When she opens her eyes he stands over her, looking at her curiously, his eyes like two shiny currants pressed into the dough of his oily, smooth skin. For a moment it seems to her that there is something sardonic in his smile, that he is sneering at her, that he has guessed why she has come back. If she had the strength to rise she would run from him. But he only says, "The telephone has a way of distorting things," and smiles.

She lowers her gaze. She had called him on the phone after her visit and shouted at him in a rage. She had said something very rude, which he had not appreciated.

Today she says politely, "I really enjoyed talking to you about the transitional object, you know. I did. It meant a lot to me that you invited me here." She tells him that her mother told her that she, too, had carried a blue blanket around like this, herself, until it fell into pieces. She says that she found the idea quite fascinating: this object that enables the child to separate from the mother; something half real, half imbued with fantasy. She had read so many books in order to write her paper, sitting up at night in her small room, and she had been so pleased with the result. She had even secretly hoped that her professor might have some learned review in mind that would want to publish her paper, for he had sounded so enthusiastic.

He nods his head, smiles at her. "Thirsty? A drink? Gin and tonic?" he asks in his seductive voice.

Certainly, as a professor, his voice put them all to sleep. Dr. Soubrier mumbled in the classroom incomprehensibly, going on and on in a low, monotonous voice. He repeated certain half-understood phrases, like a mantra. Enough to drive you mad! Every now and then she would hear the word *foreclosure* and *the law of the father: la loi du père.*

She doesn't know much about that. Her father died before she knew him. Indeed, she doesn't know much about men.

She nods her head, though a drink on an empty stomach is not a good idea. Still, it may serve its purpose, she supposes. She would like to ask for something to eat, but he has already disappeared.

For a while now, her diet has been restricted to bread and cheese, and to an occasional piece of fruit slipped from a stall into her big white handbag. She doesn't want to get scurvy in France.

"Such civilized people. Such a civilized language," her mother had said after Claire matriculated from boarding school. "The country of the rights of man, unlike this place. I'm going to write to Mademoiselle Fanchon." Mademoiselle Fanchon, together with the Abbé Bertrand, directs the Institut Catholique. Mlle Fanchon was delighted to provide a scholarship for Claire at the small private university, providing her grades were all above 80 percent. Her mother had said, "No problem at all. Claire's never had anything below ninety," which has been the case up until now.

Dr. Soubrier comes back immediately with a silver tray he must have prepared earlier: two long drinks with lime and ice, and she sees to her delight a bowl of nuts. She takes a big handful, gobbles the salty almonds down, reaches for the drink nearer to him, and sips.

"Your hands are trembling, my dear," he says, glancing at her, looking concerned.

"I haven't been very well," she says.

"I'm so sorry to hear that," he says gravely.

She explains that her mother is unaware she is no longer in the au pair position with the French family, which she found for her daughter on her arrival in Paris, a year ago, though she still goes there to collect her mail. Unfortunately, the father in the family had understood her job was *au père*, not au pair.

Dr. Soubrier puts the tray down on the lacquered Chinese coffee table, sits down beside her, and swigs his drink. He mops his brow with a handkerchief, clucks his tongue, shakes his head. He looks at her with sympathy and then cocks his head, smiles.

He says, "Quite a temptation, you must admit!"

She gathers up her courage, thinks of Richard's words, his instructions, fumbles around in her handbag, checking. She watches him drink. She explains that she is not used to solitude. She has always been surrounded by people, mostly women, first at home with her devoted mother and sister and then the girls and teachers at the boarding school where she went for free, as her mother teaches French there.

"I understand," he says.

She says that was why she was so delighted when he invited her to his apartment to talk about her paper that day.

"And what about your colleagues, my dear, at the Institut?" he says in a fatherly way. "Surely you've made some friends?"

She explains that her colleagues are very different from her: all Catholics and many of them wealthy. There are even some aristocrats, like Sophie de Montesquieu. Besides, they are all away for the summer.

"Ah, yes, dear Sophie—a lovely girl," he says.

Claire explains that her mother is a widow, a schoolteacher, who teaches French. She doesn't have any money.

He nods his head with sympathy, explains that he, too, would have left Paris but is retained here by his patients. "They won't let me escape!" he says, and chuckles. He adds, "But surely, a pretty girl like you must have some *petit ami* in your life?" turning toward her, grinning.

She nods but says he has gone to the beach. Richard is in Saint-Jean-de-Luz. He has found a job there and might even find one for her, too, if she could find the money for the train fare. She says, breathless, her voice trembling, "I came to ask for your help."

"Of course," he says, as though he has expected these words. Perhaps he has heard them before from other scholarship students. "Of course, I'd be delighted to help. That's what I'm here for, my dear. What can I do for you?"

When she doesn't answer, the words stuck in her throat, he says, "You mustn't worry about that grade. That can easily be rectified," and he folds his hands together as in prayer. She thinks of Tartuffe in the play by Molière she saw at the Comédie Française. He really is a modern Tartuffe. She imagines him asking Laurent for his hair shirt.

"Really, a remarkable paper! Such an interesting concept, and I could see you had really understood it—'The Transitional Object.'"

"I worked so hard on it," she stammers.

"I can see that. Amazing bibliography. You read everything: Winnicott, of course, but Klein, too, all about the good and the bad breast, and even *Beyond the Pleasure Principle—eros* and *thanatos*."

Claire has done well in most of her subjects. To her surprise she particularly enjoyed psychophysiology and had no difficulty mastering the material. She liked learning about the nerves, the synapses, the way hormones—chemical messengers, she learned they are called—work.

He settles himself a little closer to her on the soft sofa, looks into her eyes.

She is so thirsty, so tired, so hungry. She would like, above all, to rest for a while, not to have to wander alone endlessly through the streets, with the voice in her head, not to lie sleepless and longing in her low-ceilinged room.

There's a wonderful long beach. I have a big room where I can see the sea. We could make love every night.

She finishes her drink and looks at Dr. Soubrier sitting next to her in his shiny suit. She is beginning to see him, too, doubled, blurred. What purpose does he fulfill in the world, she wonders. There are no photographs on his desk, no sign of a wife, a child, a friend. No maid or secretary present either now or on her first visit, of course.

"I've been having such a difficult time," she says. She wonders if it might be wise to weep.

"A difficult time? I am so sorry, my dear. You are so young and so lovely—I've seen many lovely young girls, you know, over the years, but you have something very special about you, something very natural. Such a lovely fresh smile. It must be having grown up in all that sunshine and freedom. Such lovely fresh skin," and he traces a line on the side of her cheek with one stubby finger. She notices he wears a gold signet ring on one finger with quite a substantial diamond in it.

She looks at him, blinks, feels the tears prick. Not difficult in this situation, after all. She has always been able to weep when she wishes. "Sarah Bernhardt!" she remembers her mother saying when she was having one of her wild tantrums as a child.

He puts his fingers into her hair and pulls off her velvet ribbon, lets her hair fall around her shoulders. "Such wonderful hair," he says. She shakes her head a little, making it sway. "Smile for me," he says, pursing his lips at her. "I like to see you smile. I like to see those lovely little teeth." She smiles for him.

"Another gin and tonic, perhaps?" he says, and puts his hand, his little fat paw, on her bare knee.

"I don't think I should," she simpers, "my head is already spinning," and looks at him.

"It will do you good. You look so hot and so worried. I feel your pain, my dear, and I don't want you to be worried. We'll see what we can do for you. You were worrying about the grade, of course? Your scholarship? I understand. We'll arrange all of that; shall we say ninety percent?"

He had given her 54 percent on her paper, not a failing grade but certainly a poor one, one of the lowest in the class, she had noticed, her name down the bottom of the list. Only Natalie de la Tour, the girl who had scored so low on the intelligence test they had all given one another, was below her. Claire had stood there staring at the grades, her eyes burning with shame and anger, unable to believe the figures she saw. How could he!

Sophie de Montesquieu, in her pink cashmere cardigan and her Gucci shoes with the tassels, stood beside her and asked, "What did you get?" when she went to find the grades pasted up on the bulletin board at the Institut Catholique. And when she didn't respond, Sophie looked down the list and said, "You poor thing, and you worked so hard for it."

"It's like committing incest!" she had shouted at Dr. Soubrier over the phone after the visit, perhaps exaggerating a little, though it was not entirely false, in her estimation. Claire is still only seventeen and she is his student, after all. She has no idea how old Dr. Soubrier is, nor does she care. To her he is just old, evil, and useless, though he has a smooth, ageless face, cherubic cheeks. He is surely old enough to be her father.

He looks at her, and she stares back at him coolly without responding. Sophie de Montesquieu, she noticed, had a 92.

"Ninety-four, perhaps? You want to be the best in the class, don't you!" He laughs at her. "*Voilà!* Ninety-four for you. Will that do?" He smiles triumphantly and claps his hands gleefully, like a child. She gives a slight nod. "Such a good paper, after all. Well-earned. An error, that grade, brought on by—" He pauses, looking for the right word, waving his hands in the air: "A moment of aggravation, overwork on my part. Such a difficult profession. The Abbé Bertrand will understand. Such an understanding man."

There is a moment of silence while he contemplates her with obvious pleasure. She does not smile. *You must be firm, polite, but arrogant.*

"I'm sure he must be, but would you mind terribly putting that in writing for me on your own stationery, and signing it, please?" she says, blinking back her tears. He stares at her, his little cupid mouth slightly open. "You don't trust me?" he asks.

"Just to avoid any sort of misunderstanding. It would mean so much to me. I could get my scholarship back. I would so like to complete my degree, next year."

"Of course, my dear, of course, I quite understand," and he rises fast. He is a surprisingly agile man for someone of his size. He goes to his desk, plucks one of his fat Montblanc pens from the pretty blue glass where he keeps a bouquet of them. She rises, too, follows him, tilting her head and looking across the desk as she watches him write.

"Perhaps you would date it back a bit? Say the last week in June?" she asks. He looks a little puzzled by this request but gamely tears up the note, throws it into the wastepaper basket. She watches the pieces flutter in the air, makes a mental note of them. He says, "Whatever you wish, my dear. Your word is my command. I'm sure they'll give you the money whatever the date," and he laughs at what he must consider her caprice and writes another note on his doctor's prescription pad. He gives it to her. "Will this do?" he says, and smiles at her, the teeth even but rather yellow like the skin.

She takes the note, reads the date, his words, the signature, folds it and puts it into her handbag. "Thank you," she says as she sits down, "thank you so much." He comes to sit close beside her, his leg against hers. "And we'll go out for some dinner, shall we, a little later? I know a nice place near here. We'll have a good bottle of wine to celebrate our—reunion, our renewed friendship, and you'll tell me all about your little troubles. I want to hear them all, you know, my dear."

She nods, leans back against the sofa, and shuts her eyes again. She allows him to rub her leg, to slip his fat fingers between her legs, stroke her sex.

"Perhaps another drink?" she says.

"Ah, my dear, what you do to me, what you do to me," he murmurs, but he gets up obediently and goes for more drinks.

He manages to make a considerable amount of cash with his phony platitudes, she thinks, as he goes out of the door.

When he comes back with the drinks, she lets him take a few sips and looks down at his trousers. *I cannot.* But she puts her white-gloved hand where she knows he would like it to be. He turns his head and smiles at her. His face shines as it did on her first visit.

As they were standing there and she was awkwardly saying good-bye, thanking him for his kindness, the interesting conversation about the transitional object, he had suddenly held her against him with one arm, fumbling with his fly, his little member, and her skirt. Such swift dexterous hands. For a moment she was unable to react, stunned, silenced, trapped, her back against the wall, his thin lips on hers. *This respectable, intelligent man, my professor, a psychoanalyst, cannot be doing this to me.* She saw another girl, her white panties lowered and another man pushing his little pink penis inside her.

"Standing up like stallions," he breathed in her ear, and then, "A Kleenex?" It hadn't taken him but a moment to do what he wanted to do. She glances at the box of Kleenex still conveniently on the table by the door.

"You *are* growing up, Claire. I'm proud of you. You are learning the ways of the world, how things work. There's always a quid pro quo, isn't there?" he says now.

She nods and says, "Yes, I suppose there is. There definitely is."

"Things are never as simple as they seem," he says. "People are more complex than we believe: things are never black or white; there are always the transitional objects, things that are not quite what they seem, as Winnicott says."

She nods and smiles. She says, "I'm afraid I'm in need of another kind of transitional object today: a sum of money to tide me over until my mother's check arrives." She explains that her mother has been ill. She had mentioned a bad back in her letters, problems with her position at the private girls' school where she teaches French. Unfortunately, no one seems to have remembered to send her check this month.

He looks at her and blinks. "Well, of course, my dear, of course. Will this do?" He takes out his smooth, shiny, black wallet from his inner breast pocket, pulls out a few bills. *The cheapskate!*

She shakes her head. "I have something *bigger* in mind. I have rather substantial debts," she says, and she mentions a not inconsiderable sum and puts her hand back on his little penis with a smile. He pushes the bills back in his wallet and frowns at her. She says, "Is that too much for someone so special, someone with such hair, such teeth, such skin? Someone who is just seventeen, a minor, after all? Would you?" She shakes her hair at him, smiles.

For a moment he hesitates, looks at her, and then he laughs. "Well, well, you do surprise me, Claire. Growing up in a hurry, I see," he says. "Do you have a bank account? A check?"

"Cash," she says. "Cool cash in order to really feel the transaction. You understand?" And she makes the gesture for money, with her fingers rubbing the tips of her little white gloves together.

He smiles and her gaze goes beyond him to the books behind which lies, she knows, the safe.

On her first visit she had pushed open the front door, put her head inside the hall, and said a discreet "Hallo," which he must not have heard. She listened, heard a clicking sound, and walked down the corridor and into his shadowy study, where he stood with his back to her, to the door. He had not heard her enter the room, busy as he was in his safe, hidden behind the books, putting away the pile of cash his patient must have given him. She had cleared her throat and said, "Dr. Soubrier? May I come in?"

He startled, turned toward her in alarm, and said, "Oh, my dear, you gave me such a fright!" and put his hand to his heart.

He must have seen how she was staring at the big stacks of bills in the open safe, behind his back, before he had time to turn from her and close it up, because he had thought to explain that in his business he asked for cash so that his patients were more aware of the money they were paying. "It is a necessary part of the process, you see, so that they really feel the transaction," he explained to her and rubbed the tips of his little fat fingers together.

"It makes sense," she replied, nodding, but even then she had thought that it must also make sense when he was paying his taxes.

Richard was right. This can actually be fun. She is actually enjoying herself now. She sees Dr. Soubrier more clearly, the sweat on his brow. She is particularly enjoying the glimmer of something like fear in his eyes. He is no longer smiling. She feels better, not so giddy, not so hungry. She feels a sense of her own power.

"Could this wait until after . . . dinner, perhaps?" he asks. She almost feels sorry for him, but really she is performing a useful service for society, she thinks. She has always wanted to be useful, to do something about the evil in the world. Her mother has always been afraid she might run off and marry a missionary.

She shakes her head and fumbles to open his fly. She strokes his little squid of a sex with the tips of her gloved fingers. "It's rather urgent, rather urgent, I'm afraid," she says, and shows him her small white teeth again. Then she takes her hand from his penis, crosses her arms, her legs, and says, "Of course, I could come back some other time."

He looks at her, presses his lips together. Then he shrugs, sighs, and gets up. He says curtly, "I'm trusting you to repay me within the week. If not, you understand, there will be consequences."

"Of course, there are always consequences."

He has his back to her as he pulls out the books, Durkheim's *Suicide* with the blood-red cover. He twists the knob on the safe to find the right combination. She rises quietly behind him but waits until she hears him swing open the door.

The man still has his back to her and his hands in the piles of bills. She sees herself again from a distance: someone else, a girl staring at the big stacks of bills, opening up the white handbag she holds in her white-gloved hands.

Olaf Olafsson

On the Lake

THEY SAT in the living room drinking coffee, looking out at the lake. Margret got up every now and then to check on their son. He had fallen asleep in her arms in the living room, and she had taken him into his bedroom and laid him down. He was sleeping peacefully, but she kept looking in on him every few minutes to listen to his breathing. When she couldn't hear it, she put her ear to his nose and mouth. Only then could she relax.

They had started using the summer cabin just over a year before. Margret's parents had a cabin farther up the hillside and had given them a piece of their land for a wedding present. Oskar had built the cabin himself. It had taken a long time, since he was busy with so many other things. The cabin wasn't large, but it was well situated, with an uninterrupted view of the lake. A hollow cut by a stream and some tall trees, mostly fir and birch, separated them from Margret's parents. Although Oskar got on well with his in-laws, he liked having the stream and the hollow between them.

They had come down after work on Friday. The weather forecast had been uncertain, but Margret paid it no attention, knowing from experience that it could seldom be relied on. She had spent her childhood summers by the lake with her mother and her siblings, her father coming out as often as he could. She had hoped it would be the same for her and Oskar. Until this evening, she had been confident that it would.

They were drinking their coffee. Oskar had his back to the window; the men who had rescued him and their son, Jonas, sat facing him across the coffee table. Margret was sitting beside Oskar. When she got up yet again to check on the boy, Oskar said: "Leave it. He's all right."

She gave him a sharp glance but said nothing. Once she had left the room, Oskar said: "How about some scotch? A man can't live on coffee alone."

He was filling their glasses when she returned.

"Scotch?" he asked.

She shook her head.

He added a little water and an ice cube to each of their glasses. The water came from the spring below the hollow. It was delicious and cold, even on hot days, he told the rescuers while mixing their drinks. He also told them that he had built the cabin with his own hands, as well as installed the electricity and piped the water from the spring.

"The water at Margret's parents' place always had a muddy taste," he said. "But now they get their water from our spring."

Easter was behind them; it was the end of April. The earth was gray and the air raw, but one could sense that spring wasn't far away. It was light past nine and then dusky for a while before it got dark. The snow was gone.

"Not a breath of wind now," said Oskar. "Cheers!"

Margret studied the men. One of them had bought the cabin next door to her parents' place earlier that year. She had seen him in the distance but had not spoken to him until now. Her parents often complained of his noisy boat, which roared around the lake while they were trying to appreciate the silence and sound of the Great Northern Divers.

"A banker," said her father. "Nouveau riche."

From time to time the new neighbor held parties—with the barbecues pouring out smoke and people swilling beer and wine on the veranda, according to Margret's father, who spied on them with the binoculars that Oskar and Margret had given him for his sixtieth birthday. Margret had the same kind of binoculars. Her father reported that his neighbor had two barbecues: one coal, one gas. "He'll end up setting the whole place on fire," he predicted.

The rescuers introduced themselves after the boy had fallen asleep. There hadn't been time before. The banker's name was Vilhelm, his friend's, Bjorn. Still frantic, Margret flung her arms round them. Oskar stood to one side, watching.

"All right, all right," he had said. "No need to make such a big deal out of it."

The look she gave him did not escape Vilhelm or Bjorn, who exchanged glances. Vilhelm said: "Glad we could help."

It had been after dinner when Oskar suggested to the boy that they go out on the lake. He and Margret had eaten salad and lamb, drinking white wine with the salad and red with the meat. They were content.

Jonas was their only child, just turned six. He was named after Margret's father and was thought to have his features. His grandparents had given him a fishing rod for Christmas, and a couple of times Oskar had taken him out on the water to fish from their boat. Jonas had caught his first fish the prior weekend, a small trout that Margret fried for lunch. He had been very proud of it.

"Wouldn't it be better to go tomorrow morning?" she asked. "It's already eight thirty."

"We won't be long," answered Oskar. "I promised him."

She did the dishes, and Oskar finished his wine as he cleared the table. It had been a rule when Margret was growing up that people shouldn't go out on the lake when they had been drinking, but she decided not to bring that up now. She had mentioned it before, and Oskar hadn't hidden his opinion that her father's rules had no place in their home. He was far from drunk, anyway, and Margret made sure that Jonas's life jacket was securely fastened before father and son went down to the shore. She had been waiting for a moment to herself; as soon as they were gone, she took a seat by the window with a crime novel and a bowl of raisins. By the time they reached the lake, she was already immersed.

There was a breeze, and the boat rocked a little as they fished. They had no luck in the first spot and motored farther out. They got nothing there either. When the wind picked up, Oskar told Jonas they should be getting home. Jonas begged to stay just a little longer. Oskar agreed, but the trout still weren't biting. "The fish have gone to bed," he said, "and so should we."

Jonas hung his head, disappointed.

"I never catch any fish with you." he said, "and you never do anything fun like the man in the white boat. You never spin around or anything."

The man in the white boat was Vilhelm. He sometimes amused himself by making tight turns on the lake, and Jonas would watch him, enthralled. "Bloody fool," said Margret's father, but this had no effect on Jonas, who saw the white boat sending big waves up the beach.

"Shall we do a few turns?" Oskar asked.

"You never do," said Jonas. "You never do turns like the man in the white boat."

"Right," said Oskar. "Hold tight."

They weren't far from land when Oskar turned round, headed out into the lake, and increased his speed. Keeping within what he thought a safe limit, he swerved to the left and right before slowing down again.

"Wasn't that fun?" he asked.

"No," said Jonas, "not like the man in the white boat. It was boring."

Oskar sped up again, heading for land this time. He was feeling irritable and wanted to go home. He opened the throttle as far as he could, then thrust the tiller hard right. The boat capsized.

They went under. Oskar surfaced and then gasped. He couldn't see Jonas anywhere. Oskar splashed round the boat and found Jonas, coughing up water. Oskar gripped the gunwale with one hand and pulled Jonas to him with the other. The water was too cold for them to swim to land. The boy was crying and kept choking on water every time a wave washed over them.

Margret didn't see the boat capsize. The murderer had struck again, this time with good reason. She felt more sympathy for him than for the victim. Eventually she stretched, put down the book, and looked out.

She screamed, snatched up the binoculars, and dashed out to the veranda. First Oskar appeared, then Jonas. There was nothing she could do, but she set off down to the lakeside anyway. Trying to run despite the steepness of the slope, she quickly lost her footing. When she got up again, she noticed the white boat. She reached for the binoculars.

After nearly ten minutes in the water Oskar was losing strength. He had tried to hoist Jonas up on the side of the boat but couldn't manage it, his grip on the boy loosening. Jonas was no longer whimpering, and Oskar was afraid he was losing consciousness. The water was glacial. One wouldn't last long in it.

. . .

Vilhelm cut the boat's engines a short distance from Oskar and Jonas, careful not to bump against them. He and Bjorn leaned over the side, holding out their hands. Oskar set off with Jonas; but, unable to hold on to his son, he used the last of his strength to get to the rescuers himself. They quickly hauled him aboard, then peered around for Jonas, who vanished briefly beneath a wave before reappearing. Vilhelm jumped into the water, grabbed the boy, and swam back. Then they returned to land, towing the capsized boat.

Without waiting for the boat to dock, Margret waded into the water and took Jonas in her arms. Speechless, she briefly collapsed on the shore. As the men disembarked, she rose and set off up the slope with the boy. Bjorn and Vilhelm followed her, with Oskar between them. He was still weak and couldn't walk without help. When Margret reached the steepest pitch, she stopped to gather her strength. Vilhelm let go of Oskar and helped her up the last stretch.

There was a hot tub by the cabin, and Margret stripped off Jonas's wet clothes and held him in the hot water. Vilhelm and Bjorn borrowed some old swimming trunks from Oskar, and they all got into the tub with Jonas. They didn't say much. Oskar just stared out at the lake. From a distance the waves looked insignificant, and when the setting sun broke through the clouds they were struck with gold.

Oskar loaned Vilhelm some dry clothes. The jeans were too big, so Oskar fetched some rope from the toolshed. In an attempt to put a good face on things, he joked: "We'll make a country boy of you yet."

Oskar drained his glass. Bjorn and Vilhelm were taking their time, and Oskar decided not to have another until they had finished. He started talking about the fishing in the lake, keeping an eye on their glasses as he talked. As soon as Bjorn took his last mouthful, Oskar leaped to his feet and fetched the bottle and some ice.

"Another drop?" he asked.

Bjorn nodded, but Vilhelm declined.

"We haven't eaten," he said. "The steak was on the barbecue when you capsized."

Margret, who had been silent until now, looked up.

"You didn't see it happen?" Vilhelm asked her.

"No," she said. "I didn't see."

Oskar interrupted: "I bought this whiskey in London last spring. We were there on a weekend trip. Glenlivet. Sixteen years old."

"It's good," said Bjorn.

"We had the steak on the grill," said Vilhelm. "I can't remember if we turned it off."

"Neither can I," said Bjorn.

"Filet mignon," continued Vilhelm. "A beautiful cut."

"We've got some leftovers from dinner," said Oskar. "Why don't we heat them up for you?"

"We ran out the moment you capsized," said Vilhelm. "The steak's probably burnt to a cinder."

"I'll heat up the lamb," said Oskar.

"What happened?" asked Margret.

The men looked at each other.

"I didn't see," said Bjorn. "I was inside."

Margret stared at Oskar, waiting for an answer. She had not spoken to him since they had come in. He twisted the glass in his hands.

"I don't really know," he said. "I turned and must have been hit broadside by a wave. That sort of thing shouldn't happen. The boat's supposed to be stable."

He glanced at Vilhelm, who was silent. Margret got up.

"I'll fetch the lamb," she said.

She checked on Jonas before putting the meat in the pan. She heated the gravy too and divided the rest of the salad onto the plates along with the lamb.

"Here you go," she said.

Oskar refilled his and Bjorn's glasses. Vilhelm was still nursing his first.

"People have died of hypothermia in a shorter time than you were in the water," Vilhelm said.

"I tried to hold Jonas out of the water," said Oskar. "That's probably what saved him. I was pretty cold myself by then."

He looked at Margret. She looked away.

"We must have been in the water for at least twenty minutes," he continued.

"It was less than ten," said Vilhelm. "I'd been watching you."

"Really," said Oskar.

"I was watching you while the barbecue heated up."

"We watch you too sometimes when you're out in your boat," said Oskar. "My father-in-law thinks you set a bad example."

Vilhelm smiled.

"He's got a good set of binoculars, your father-in-law. He doesn't seem to have much else to do but look through them. Do you know what make they are?"

Oskar glanced around. "Where are the binoculars?" he asked.

"Down by the lake," said Margret.

"Down by the lake? What are they doing there?"

She said nothing.

"It turned out all right," said Vilhelm. "Everybody's safe. Perhaps I will have another whiskey."

Oskar filled his glass.

"How about a game of cards?" he asked.

"Yes, why not?" said Bjorn.

"I'm not playing," said Margret.

"Oh, come on," said Oskar.

"You can play," she said.

"Perhaps we should be going anyway," said Vilhelm, handing Margret his empty plate. "Thank you. I was starving."

Their hands touched briefly and she said quietly: "All right, perhaps for a little while."

"Good," said Oskar. "Whist?"

"Sure," said Bjorn.

"Of course we could play bridge, but that wouldn't be fair," said Oskar.

"Why not?" said Bjorn.

"I'm two-time Icelandic champion."

He began to shuffle.

"Then this should be a walk in the park for you," said Vilhelm.

Margret sat down diagonally opposite Vilhelm, making them partners in the game. Oskar shuffled showily, unaware of his wife's look of contempt. Vilhelm stood up and splashed some water in his glass.

"Are you sure you won't have any?" he asked Margret.

Oskar looked up.

"Well," she said, "why not?"

"How about that," said Oskar.

"Ice?" asked Vilhelm.

She nodded.

Vilhelm handed her the glass and sat down. Oskar dealt, then suddenly looked up.

"What were you doing while we were on the lake?" he asked.

Margret didn't answer.

"It was just luck that I happened to be watching you," said Vilhelm.

"She must have been reading," said Oskar. "Give her a book and she won't notice if the house is burning down."

He laughed. Margret looked away.

Bjorn and Oskar won the first couple of games. Vilhelm noticed that Margret forgot herself every now and then, her eyes straying to the window. Dusk had fallen, but the lake was still visible.

"You've got better hands than we do," said Oskar, "yet you still manage to lose."

Getting up, he fetched the whiskey bottle and filled Bjorn's and Vilhelm's glasses. There wasn't much left, but he took care to save a few drops for Margret. When he went to top off her glass she snatched it from the table and said quietly: "No."

"Right," he said, "in that case I'll finish it myself."

He and Bjorn kept winning. Oskar couldn't contain himself and pointed out Vilhelm's mistakes as he made them. Oskar didn't usually behave like this. Vilhelm listened with a half smile on his lips.

"Are you sure the engine didn't cut out?" he asked suddenly.

Oskar waited without answering.

"Just a thought," said Vilhelm.

"There's nothing wrong with the engine," said Oskar.

"What made you think that?" asked Margret.

"The boat slewed round so oddly," said Vilhelm. "I thought perhaps something had come loose. A screw, maybe."

Margret looked at them both in turn. Oskar stared at his cards. Vilhelm smiled.

"Let's finish this," said Oskar. "Who's out?"

"I'm out," said Bjorn. "Don't you have any more scotch?"

"No," said Oskar. "It's finished."

He saw that he was losing control of the evening. "It's nearly midnight anyway," he added, hoping to get rid of them.

"There's whiskey at my parents' place," said Margret. "You could go and get it."

"I don't want any more whiskey," said Oskar.

"I do," said Margret.

"I'll go with you," Bjorn told Oskar. "I could do with some fresh air."

Oskar thought for a moment. He didn't see a way out.

"All right," he said. "Let's go."

Margret and Vilhelm stayed in their seats.

"We'll practice while you're gone," said Vilhelm. "We need it."

They walked quickly. Bjorn had trouble keeping up with Oskar. The temperature had dropped, and the wind was blowing off the lake, swaying the trees in the hollow.

"Where's the spring?" asked Bjorn.

"What?" said Oskar.

"The water supply you set up," said Bjorn.

"Over there," said Oskar, gesturing down the hollow without slowing his pace. From time to time he looked back to their cabin, though he could see nothing from this distance but a faint light in the living room window.

His in-laws were in the Canaries, so Oskar fetched a key from their toolshed and opened the door to the cabin, which held the usual smell of damp. He headed straight for the cupboard where the liquor was kept and found half a bottle of Johnnie Walker. After locking up in a hurry, he returned the key to the shed.

"That should do," said Bjorn.

They walked back the same way. When they came to the stream, Bjorn remembered the binoculars.

"Shouldn't we go down to the lake and get them?" he asked. "It won't take us a minute."

They stepped over the stream, and Oskar quickened his stride even more. After a short search of the shore they found the binoculars lying among the rushes where Margret had sat down with Jonas. They had just started for the cabin when Oskar stopped abruptly. Bjorn stopped too and waited.

Oskar hesitated, then raised the binoculars to his eyes. There was no one in the living room. He searched outside the cabin but found no one there either.

"Is everything all right?" asked Bjorn.

"Let's go," said Oskar, setting off at a run.

Reaching the cabin before Bjorn, he opened the door. He stopped short in the doorway, sweating and out of breath. Vilhelm and Margret were in the living room, still in their seats. But Oskar was sure they had only just sat down; he thought he could see the change in them. Margret looked at him, then away.

"You didn't take long," said Vilhelm.

"We ran," said Bjorn. "Oskar was in a hurry to get back."

"It's late," said Vilhelm, looking at his watch. "We really should be going. The whiskey can wait till another time."

He stood up. The door was still open.

"Thanks for the lamb," said Vilhelm. "I'll return your clothes tomorrow."

As they left, Margret remained in her seat, staring out at the lake. Oskar still hadn't moved. When he opened his mouth he had difficulty talking.

"What happened?" he said. "Tell me what happened."

She was trembling and didn't answer immediately. Then she buried her face in her hands.

"You let go of him," she said in a low voice. "That's what happened. You let go of him."

Brittani Sonnenberg

Taiping

My father was a white man from England, a rubber salesman. When I think about him, his blood in my veins, it feels like insects crawling and I start scratching as hard as I can. He chose my unwilling mother from the town. When my grandfather finally found his daughter, bruised, huddled, bleeding, my father had already fled. But he is still here in me; I am half as British as all of the furniture they left in this house and the cigar breaths they exhaled and the stiff white undergarments they took back to England, bras and briefs too hot for the Malay sun.

Every day the house crumbles in new places: split furniture, ripped screens, fading paint on the portraits. Only the ants are thriving. Their hard bodies glint under the fluorescent kitchen light, slash diagonals of black each night across my peeling bedroom walls.

Under the British, Bukit Larut was called Maxwell Hill, and they built vacation homes here to escape the heat down in Taiping. After independence our government seized their properties and converted them into guesthouses. Now they pay me to run the place, renting bug-ridden rooms for ten dollars to foreigners, three dollars to locals.

There's a boy here who helps me out. No one knows where he came from; he simply showed up in the middle of the monsoon five years ago and never left. It's not our house, but we keep each other company, and he distracts me. Whenever I feel something painful surfacing from before, I call for the boy and tell him stories about Taiping. If I can't find him I walk outside, over to the lookout, and watch the town itself. From Bukit Larut you can see all of Taiping, and the roads leading to it.

Sometimes the boy catches me staring at the town. He sneaks up from behind and makes a noise to frighten me, laughs loudly when I jump. He says I jump like a girl. But then he sticks around; he stares too. He watches the town with a fierce look. I know I am looking at where I used to live, wondering if the motorbikes leaving Taiping still carry people I know. But what is he watching? I laugh at him for staring at the town for no reason. Then I go inside and leave him there, looking.

Today I awake late, heavy and sweated with nightmares. Damp sheets lie tangled at the foot of the bed and the sun makes hot, burning squares on the carpet. Stinking and ravenous, I haul myself out of bed and call for the boy, fumbling with the doorknob, tripping on backpackers' sandals in the hallway.

I step into the kitchen, blinking in the natural light that floods the room midday. I call again for the boy. No answer. I glance out the window to a hot empty yard, fuchsia bougainvillea dangling limp in the heat. I boil water for tea. As the kettle starts to shrill I hear the distant creak of the front door opening.

I hurry there to scold him, my sarong catching on a pine dresser in the front hallway. Cursing in Malay, I collide in the dark with a backpacker, a woman, who has just come in. Not the boy. Disappointed, I slink to one side. After the blinding kitchen, the hallway is like night, and I strain my eyes to find her face.

Her shadowy figure stops next to me. As my eyes adjust I see it is the middle-aged American woman who arrived last night with her husband. Her dyed-blond hair is swept back in a sweaty ponytail. She lays her backpack down by the front door and walks past me to the kitchen. "These are some wonderful pieces you have," she says, her hands drifting along the top of a rattan lounge crammed in the hallway last week.

"They are not really my pieces," I reply, my voice dying as she leaves the hallway. I steal a quick glance out the front door she left open. The boy is not in the yard. Fighting a growing panic, I decide to leave the house to look for him. In the doorway, however, her muffled voice from the kitchen draws me back.

"Excuse me?" I call.

Her reply is unintelligible. Reluctantly, I shut the door and return to the kitchen, where I find her fingering oven dials, lifting up lids and sniffing pots. She smiles expansively as I enter. "I was just wondering who taught you how to cook," she says.

"My mother," I reply stiffly, turning to go.

She continues, not taking the hint. "I think it's wonderful when men, like you, know how to cook. You should teach my husband a few things while we're here. I don't think John even knows how to turn on the oven in our kitchen back home. Those noodles you made last night were delicious." As her stream of chatter continues, she walks to the cabinet above the sink, casually removing the jade teapot I brought with me from Taiping. "Extraordinary color," she murmurs. I force a smile. She replaces the teapot and moves to the spice rack, unscrewing each jar, making "mmm," "hmmm," and "delicious" noises after sniffing each one. I ignore the performance and sneak a look at the clock. It is one P.M. Where could he be? Finished with the spices, the American woman strides to the refrigerator and removes a bottle of water.

"How long have you lived here?" she asks.

I ignore the question and point to the sweating bottle. "The water is eight R.M."

"Eight?" An edge creeps into her tone, the panic of a foreigner who suspects they are being cheated. I shrug, smile consolingly, tell her what I tell the rest of them: "Yes, eight. It costs me more money to order it up from the town."

She returns to the refrigerator in a huff, jostling soft drink cans around angrily before removing a Sprite. I look out the window. Perhaps the boy has gotten lost on the jungle path, I think. Perhaps he thought an old riverbed was the path back and followed that instead. Shadows from gathering black clouds spot the yard. It will rain hard this afternoon.

An approaching storm always reminds me of the day the boy arrived. For two weeks before he came the rain fell in curtains. Guests stayed away. After so many days alone in the house, I started leaving it to stand naked in the storm. From the yard, Taiping was nothing but white clouds. I pictured the town's streets and houses cloaked in water. I was standing in the rain when the boy walked into the yard, though the storm around us was so loud I couldn't hear his approach. When I finally noticed him all I saw was a dark shape beside me, as though through a waterfall. I assumed the shadow was my imagination until it spoke.

"How old is your son?" At the sound of the American woman's voice I swivel around guiltily. I had forgotten she was here.

"My son?"

"He helped us with our bags last night. He was very polite. How old is he?"

"Not my son," I say. In the awkward silence that follows, I put the water bottle she left on the counter back in the refrigerator. I point at her Sprite. "Five R.M., please."

She removes a wad of bills from her pocket, thumbs through them. "I don't even know what all these are. Here, can you help?"

I pick out a five note and hand back the rest.

"So the boy just works for you?"

I nod, taking a rag from the sink to wipe the counter, my back to her.

"He has a beautiful face," she says. "Such wonderful skin."

I am silent, concentrating on a fried noodle stuck to the surface of the counter. When the rag fails, I try using my long fingernail, careful not to break the nail.

"I would give anything for skin like that. His girlfriends at school must be jealous."

I laugh out loud at the idea of the boy at school, the idea of the boy having a girlfriend.

She looks at me shrewdly. "Do his parents live nearby?"

"Yes," I lie, and go to the sink to rinse my hands.

As she begins to ask another question, I interrupt. "What time you want to eat dinner?"

"Dinner?" She is confused by the sudden change in topic. "Dinner. Well, I don't know. Let me speak to John. We'll let you know later this afternoon. Does that sound all right?"

"Of course," I say. To my horror, the words come out in my high voice. My face burning, I walk quickly out of the kitchen, nodding brusquely as I pass her. I cross the living room in three quick strides, open the sliding door to the front yard. I head to the Japanese guests eating sunflower seeds and laughing on the old iron swing, then make a swift right turn instead. I take the path into the jungle, a shortcut to the main road leading to Taiping, and start running.

. . .

I shout for the boy from the safety of the trail. I know its roots, broad leaves, and vines better than I know the furniture of the house. "Boy!" I echo into the woods, but only hear late-afternoon responses: birds, the electric hum of crickets. The smell of jungle, rotten and metallic. The sky is covered by the tops of the trees, and my body streams with sweat.

Even now, mid-frenzy, I take a little comfort in the way the sun falls once I have left the clearing. Bright beams hit spots on the jungle floor and illuminate whole leaves; ants pass through the lit circles and then dip back into shade again. A faint breeze rustles through the green. I slow a little, cowed by the heat, branches slapping my face.

In one ragged inhalation, I long for the boy. I think of how he looks when he sleeps and am embarrassed by the thought of my own body at night: aged, flabby, sweating. I understand all too well why he left. His lithe feet gratefully slapping old jungle paths to escape my stench.

Another breeze fumbles with the trees. Then a fiercer one. Here it comes, I think. Just as the thought falls, the shower starts. A few calm, wet plops that barely make it through the knit cover of treetops. I hear the rain before I feel it, crashing onto wide waxy leaves. The downpour makes the search feel even more hopeless. I head back for the house, muttering to myself, muttering to the boy: "Leave all day, think you can still come home, have dinner just like that? What about your work? What about all the rooms you're supposed to clean? Monkeying around all the time. So I go search for you like your mother."

Slick mud shines on the path. I slip several times, my heel sticking and my sandal stubborn in one sucking patch. A mosquito tugs on the back of my neck. My sarong is soaked. Though I know the house is near, I scold myself for leaving it to look for the boy. To look for nothing.

I emerge from the path onto the sick grass of the front yard. There he is, naked, standing with his arms out, head back, in the center. Too beautiful to scold. He sees me and runs back inside, grabbing his clothes. It is only when he is fully dressed, washed, sullen, sitting on a dank armchair in the night of the living room, that I sit beside him and try to hug him, as the backpackers chat loudly to each other on the porch. Bony, all sharp angles, he breaks away, but only to the front porch, to join the guests.

. . .

For supper that night, I make his favorite: kway teow. He appears in the kitchen once the smell of garlic explodes from the frying oil. While I cook I speak anxiously with him. Or, I am anxious, but I try to cover it up with quick, easy questions. "Where did you go today? Did you find a new path?" I do not ask "Why did you leave? Did you plan to run away?" because I am afraid of the answer.

He responds to my questions reluctantly at first, but when I do not scold he grows more animated, describing how far he went, what the plants looked like. A hiss of oil cuts him off as I fry the noodles with bean sprouts, kai lan, beef. We sigh happily in the smell. My smile dies when I look at him through the steam. It is like looking at another man's face through fog. I divide the noodles onto six plates and ask him to deliver four of them to the front porch. We will eat alone inside together tonight. As he leaves the kitchen I squeeze his shoulders. He shivers. I am right, I think. He meant today to leave for good.

Waiting for the boy to return, my stomach growls at the glistening noodles below me. The clock ticks emptily in the kitchen and soon the kway teow grows cold. I hear the boy's high laughter in the distance, the American woman's low chuckle. I serve myself and begin eating alone, barely tasting the noodles. Twenty minutes later, the boy returns to the kitchen and scarfs down the noodles like a dog. I glare at him, awaiting an apology. In the silence that follows, broken only by the boy's slurping sounds and the crash of his silverware against the plate, I remember what the boy was like before—the boy when he first arrived.

The first thing he ever said to me, in the rain on the day he came here, was a question shouted over the storm: "Where are your clothes?"

"What are you doing here?" I asked him, instead of answering his question.

"I don't know." The storm nearly swallowed it.

"Do your parents know you are here?"

He didn't answer. I squinted at his shadowy form. He looked thin and small and dirty, even in the rain.

I put out a hand experimentally, to touch him on the shoulder. He jerked. I had not touched anyone in years, except for a handshake, except for an accidental brush against a guest's arm in the hallway.

"Can I work here?" the boy asked, when my hand had gone away.

"Work here?" I laughed and my open mouth filled with water. "How old are you?"

"Fifteen."

He was ten, or maybe eight.

"Yes, you can work here," I said. "Come inside."

He came in and stood in the worst part of the house, the empty entranceway with moldy paintings and tapestries, flying ants covering the floor. The ants had arrived just before the rain and moved quickly over the carpet now, like trucks leaving Taiping.

I picked an ant off the wall and squished it in between two long nails. The boy watched me. The sound of our dripping echoed in the passage.

"Are you afraid of them?" I asked.

"No." His voice rose in scorn at the idea.

"Are you afraid of snakes?"

"No."

"Are you afraid of foreigners?"

"No."

"Are you afraid of ghosts?"

"Are there ghosts here?"

He looked around. He was so small. I ignored his question and said, "You should get warm," even though the rain had been warm, and now, inside the house, I was already sweating.

I gave him an old shirt and started to run the water in the old clawfoot tub. He ran out after I had closed the door to the bathroom, and into the bedroom where I was putting on a sarong.

"What's wrong?" I asked.

I went to the bathroom to see what had frightened him and he followed timidly behind, pointing to centipedes crawling across the floor.

"I thought you weren't scared," I said. "Come here."

I lifted him over the centipedes and placed him gently in the tub, in my T-shirt.

I left and he took a bath. He shouted when he was finished and I lifted him out again, shirt dripping.

That night I made him kway teow and he ate twice as many noodles as I did.

"That's all right," I told him. "I have lots of food. I keep guests here most of the time. Tomorrow you can start to work."

"Have you always lived here?" he asked me.

"No," I told him. "I am from Taiping. That's the town at the bottom of the hill."

That first night was four years ago. Now he helps me with the guests and in return I show him the love that he can't get from parents, from friends. Most nights before I sleep, I pause outside of his door, ask if he is awake. If he is silent I walk in.

His little cot is in the corner of the room. He sleeps curled like a snake. I move to his bed and watch him breathe, softer than the insects and the geckoes. A more human rhythm. I kneel by the bed and stroke his hair. He moans lightly but does not wake. I move my fingers along his arms, lightly down the nearly hairless limbs. He lies sheetless and naked. I trace the shadows the windowpane makes on his stomach. I massage his legs, his thighs; I kiss his toes, the soles of his feet.

Last night his breathing quickened, caught. I looked up to his face and saw two eyes in little slits, barely open, still pretending to sleep. Full of hate. I acted as if I had not noticed and continued rubbing his feet. Then I stood up, left the boy to himself, as I have since the night he came here. But last night I lingered a little at the door, watching. I was waiting, I think, for him to come to me. Embrace me, cry out, whisper one thing. Instead he rolled over in bed, his back to the door.

I love the boy like a mother, father, girlfriend, boyfriend. I feel sorry for him. He must be lonely without anyone his own age around. I was thirteen in Taiping when I first fell in love, fourteen when I had my first kiss, eighteen when Masjid was killed in a motorcycle accident. Nobody in Taiping understood why I didn't leave my room after his funeral. When I finally left my room, two weeks later, I caught a ride in a soldier's jeep to Bukit Larut.

I have never told the boy that story. I tell him funny stories about the Muslim coffee shop owners in Taiping, and the old Chinese shopkeeper's monkey. The boy laughs at the right parts and never complains if I tell the same story twice. Recently, though, his gaze has begun to wander. Tonight as I gather our plates from the table I see he is staring out to the porch, at the American woman sitting alone.

"You are exhausted," I say. "Go to bed."

His eyes dart back to me. "I'll clean up now, take care of things," I say. "See you in the morning."

I bring the dishes into the dark kitchen, flipping on the fluorescent light. In the day, the kitchen is my favorite part of the house. Light swells inside of it and I cook for hours. The heavy ghosts of the furniture do not sit in here as they do throughout the rest of the place. I keep bougainvillea near the window to look at as I chop, fry, stir the dishes my mother taught me to make.

But now, at night, the world outside is black and the windows only reflect the kitchen. Large bugs flying around the fluorescent lights make the room look conquered. The smells are no longer fresh; leftover odors mingle to create a heady overripe scent, like afternoon jungle, but without a path through it. I hurry now through the dishes, cringing at the dead bugs that crunch underfoot.

I go into each room turning off the lights, bumping into furniture on my way out. Geckoes click on the walls and dead portraits stare at me through the new dark. I am terrified of which Western eyes might resemble my father's, which portraits' faces resemble my own.

I open the sliding door to the front porch and step outside where things are gentler. Crickets creak on either side, in concert. A soft breeze blows across my bare chest.

I watch Taiping. The cars travel in and out of town with bright headlights. It feels good to see the town flashing down there. Sometimes there is too much to stare at during the day, old friends from my childhood growing older. I get a feeling when watching Taiping in the morning and early afternoon, like watching an ant carry an insect five times its size. I am stagnating in this moldy British house, keeping my eyes down so I won't look into the eyes of the backpackers, eyes of the portraits. Or unconsciously close my eyes and find Masjid's face.

I never liked the gravel that crept into my words when I turned thirteen. I tried hard to keep my high voice with me, speaking in high tones to myself at night. I never used the high voice at school, since the other boys' voices were changing too, and they growled around me like new animals. I spoke like them to speak with them. Sometimes my other voice would slip out by accident and it was terrible, as though my face had fallen off and there were only bulging eye sockets, blood vessels gleaming like in our science book.

Even before puberty, I never fit in well with the other kids. They made fun of my ang mo looks and called my mother a pelacur. Masjid moved to Taiping from Kuala Lumpur when I was ten, but I didn't fall in love with him until I was thirteen. He had a funny limp and I teased him with the other kids. The day we became friends we had both been beaten up at recess. He had fallen down trying to chase a ball and they kicked him; when they heard me laughing, they turned on me. "What are you laughing at, you son of a whore?" They didn't stop kicking until I begged them to stop, in my high-low voice, and by then I was bleeding all over. They left us both lying there when the bell rang for class. When he came over to see if I was all right I tackled him. Despite his limp, his upper body was strong and he pinned me to the ground easily. I was too tired to keep struggling and lay there hating him. Then he lifted one of my arms and blew on the cuts, just as my mother did later that day when I got home.

When Masjid died, he was sixteen and I was eighteen. I stayed in the room we had shared in secret some afternoons and did not leave it. In the days that followed, I spoke in the high voice more and more. The walls closed in and I could not differentiate between the voices, I spoke half a sentence high and the rest of the sentence low, or maybe the other way around, it felt like singing and crying to have those two pitches. I roamed around my tiny room humming and weeping, my mother leaving uneaten plates of chicken rice by the door, refusing to speak to me.

I remember visiting the smoking temple after Masjid died. I could not breathe; I ran out choking, my eyes streaming. Sometimes I think of going down to Taiping, returning to the streets we walked together. The afternoon after he died, when I did not come down for lunch, my mother came in my room with a bowl of steaming laksa. She set it down on my bed and sat down on a chair in the corner of the room. The shutters were drawn and the light was gray. I poured the curry onto my white sheets, watching the stain grow. "You always hated him," I said, as she slammed the door. I wouldn't be welcome back there now. I don't like to think of it.

. . .

I dream of tying the boy to his bed. I awake just before sunrise, soaked in sweat, ashamed. Sleep has fled, and I leave the dim room with a mind to make roti pratha for breakfast. The boy's second favorite, after kway teow.

Walking outside with the dawn reassures me. Chilly air and fresh dew on my bare feet make my skin rise pleasantly. The mist over Taiping is melting away and the town resurfaces slowly, surrounded by pale green jungle. My guilty dreams fade as I enter the kitchen. The sun is just starting to gleam off the metal pots.

Before the boy came I did not cook on the days without guests but now I enjoy making food for just the two of us. As I remove the rotis and pour oil into the pan, I think, it is the smell of my food that keeps him here. The kitchen is one of the only places that we talk; I am in a good mood and he sits on the counter, watching me, asking me questions about Taiping.

When the boy eats he chews thoughtfully and distantly. I watch him closely then, and it is different than watching him at night, when everything is silver and black. He is not a half-caste like me, he is Malay, with smooth brown skin, hair that curls black and wiry. He is not old like me, or heavy, or tired, but he is lonely like me. I know by the way he used to look around when he was younger, playing alone in the yard, as if he was looking for someone else to run down the jungle path to him. I still look for Masjid that way. I look for him every day from the kitchen window.

The boy does not play alone in the yard anymore; he is too old for that. His body is changing, though I only notice that in the moonlight, in the silver blackness of the bedroom. New brittle hairs poking up. And his voice. His voice is deepening. The boy has never shown surprise at my voice that comes out high-low. I wonder what he thinks now that he has the high-low voice, too. If he thinks it is the way men talk. Though I doubt I seem to him like a man.

When the rotis are ready I go to find the boy, surprised that the smells of cooking have not brought him to the kitchen already. I find him again with the American backpacker woman on the patio, laughing. He is pointing to the town below and telling her about it in broken English. Bastard, I think. Show-off. I leave the two of them to their jokes and go back to the kitchen. I stuff a roti into my mouth and throw the rest away.

I begin chores. Hanging laundry outside, raking the yard. Once I found a cobra under the rose bush, dead. It terrified me to nudge its limp body with my rake. Now I leave that bush alone. I put the rake back in the house and retrieve a bucket of wet clothes.

Sometimes I wonder what the guests think about the boy and me. He always distances himself from me when foreigners are around. Like with this American woman. When I walked by just now and saw them talking he didn't even turn his head. I know he knew I was there.

I finish hanging the first bucket of clothes and walk back to retrieve the second. I think of how clumsy the boy was with chores when he first came here. Too small to reach the highest kitchen cabinets, too frail to wield heavy gardening tools. Mostly he just sat in the dirt. I remember once he stuck a stick down a red ant hole and came up howling, covered in bites. I took care of him like he was my baby. He was easier with my touch at night after that.

The bucket is not in the hallway where I remember leaving it. Sweat pours down my back. It is too hot here, I think, even in the morning, even on top of this bloody hill. I walk through the living room to look for the bucket on the patio. As I open the sliding door I see the American woman stroking the boy's face. I forget the bucket and stalk over to them. The woman looks startled, but does not remove her hand. "I was trying to tell him what wonderful skin he has, but I don't think he understands my English. Can you translate for me?" The boy hasn't looked at me since I came over. He is staring at the woman's low-cut blouse, at her breasts, at the expanse of white thigh revealed by her tiny hiking shorts.

"Boy," I say.

He does not turn around.

"Hey, boy."

"Hey, kayu." When he does not respond to the insult, I jerk him to his feet. He curses at me in Malay and heads toward the house.

"Boy," I call after him. He keeps walking. I follow him and grab the back of his shirt. I hear the woman cry out as I take the boy's right wrist and spin him around. I slap the boy's face. When he looks up again his face is so full of hate that my arm, ready to strike again, stays frozen. The boy shakes his right hand free of my grasp. We stand there staring at each other, breathing shallowly. Dimly, I hear the woman running over. Her approach unfreezes the boy and he spits in my left eye with such force that

I cry out in pain. The woman wants to take him in her arms, comfort him, but he is already running.

I do not make dinner for the guests that night. I ignore their knocks at my door. I watch the long line of ants that stretches from the ceiling above my bed to the floor. The next morning all of the guests check out. The American woman glares at me as I settle their bill. "In America people like you get sent to jail," she hisses, before following her husband out the door.

When the house is silent again, I go to the boy's room and watch an enormous black ant crawl across the carpet before I step on it. I rearrange a few things on the table. Rocks, trash, pens and paper the boy got from foreigners. I arrange them neatly and patiently. I should go look for him, I think, and a wave of grief courses through me. Then the pain passes and I am numb. It is hotter than yesterday, I realize, as I walk to the kitchen. I look out the window at a cloudless sky. No rain today.

Later that day, I walk to the front of the garden, to look at Taiping. The shadows grow. For some reason, the cars look smaller than usual today. Still no clouds.

The afternoon the boy came I said to myself I will be like his father. But my own father is a foreign ghost and I never knew how to be the boy's father. From the first night I desired the boy and despised him. Some days I would approach him in the house, jerk him roughly to his feet, send him to a task. On the worst days, days I slept in past noon, unwilling to face the furniture outside my bedroom, exhausted with guilty dreams' pleasures, I would shake the boy for looking cheeky, chide him for being lazy.

The nights that followed those bad days overflowed with my apologies. I always waited until the moonlight leaked in before entering his bedroom, stroking him in his sleep, kissing his feet.

"Why are you crying?" I asked the boy once, in the garden. It was shortly after he had arrived.

"I'm not crying," he had said, wiping his face.

A week or so ago, I remember him entering the kitchen, surprising me. "Why are you crying?" he had asked.

"Because I love you," I said, and tried to kiss him.

He ran away from me. I watched him from the kitchen window as he stumbled onto the jungle path. I was still standing there when he returned, a half an hour later.

The next day, when I saw him crying, I scolded him.

"Stop crying," I had said, and shook him.

It is a painful thing to remember now.

The garden is black. Taiping blinks uselessly below. I am suddenly starving and return to the kitchen to cook myself dinner. The curry I make is delicious and the smells are my own. The sight of the orange gravy pooling over rice on my plate reminds me of Masjid, whose mouth always tasted like curry.

I eat in heaping spoonfuls, until my stomach aches and my throat burns. I make my way to the bedroom and fall asleep in my clothes. I awaken early the next morning to heavy rain and cannot fall back asleep. I slept dreamless and sweatless but as I shift under the sheets now I feel the memories of the past days resurfacing. I get out of bed overburdened.

When I open the front door, I hear rain pounding, crashing, drowning out the usual morning noises. I remove my sarong and step into the storm. It pelts my brown-white, white-brown skin. I wonder, as I walk to the lookout, if my father ever turned around to look as he left my mother, if it was raining the night that he fled from Taiping. I wonder if the boy has reached the town yet. I know he did not look back yesterday after he began running.

Alice Munro

What Do You Want to Know For?

I SAW the crypt before my husband did. It was on the left-hand side, his side of the car, but he was busy driving. We were on a narrow, bumpy road.

"What was that?" I said. "Something strange."

A large, unnatural mound blanketed with grass.

We turned around as soon as we could find a place, though we hadn't much time. We were on our way to have lunch with friends who live on Georgian Bay. But we are possessive about this country and try not to let anything get by us.

There it was, set in the middle of a little country cemetery. Like a big woolly animal—like some giant wombat, lolling around in a prehistoric landscape.

We climbed a bank and unhooked a gate and went around to look at the front end of this thing. A stone wall there, between an upper and a lower arch, and a brick wall within the lower arch. No names or dates, nothing but a skinny cross carved roughly into the keystone of the upper arch, as with a stick or a finger. At the other, lower end of the mound, nothing but earth and grass and some big protruding stones, probably set there to hold the earth in place. No markings on them, either—no clues as to who or what might be hidden inside.

We returned to the car.

. . .

About a year after this, I had a phone call from the nurse in my doctor's office. The doctor wanted to see me. An appointment had been made. I knew without asking what this would be about. Three weeks or so before, I had gone to a city clinic for a mammogram. There was no special reason for me to do this, no problem. It is just that I have reached the age when a yearly mammogram is recommended. I had missed last year's, however, because of too many other things to do.

The results of the mammogram had been sent to my doctor.

There was a lump deep in my left breast, which neither my doctor nor I had been able to feel. We still could not feel it. My doctor said that the mammogram showed it to be about the size of a pea. He had made an appointment for me to see a city doctor who would do a biopsy. As I was leaving he laid his hand on my shoulder. A gesture of concern or reassurance. He is a friend, and I knew that his first wife's death had begun in just this way.

There were ten days to be put in before I could see the city doctor. I filled the time by answering letters and cleaning up my house and going through my files and having people to dinner. It was a surprise to me that I was busying myself in this way instead of thinking about what you might call deeper matters. I didn't do any serious reading or listening to music, and I didn't go into a muddled trance as I so often do, looking out the big window in the early morning as the sunlight creeps into the cedars. I didn't even want to go for walks by myself, though my husband and I went for our usual walks together or for drives.

I got it into my head that I would like to see the crypt again and to find out something about it. So we set out, sure—or reasonably sure—that we remembered which road it was on. But we did not find it. We took the next road over and did not find it on that one either. Surely it was in Bruce County, we said, and it was on the north side of an east-west unpaved road, and there were a lot of evergreen trees close by. We spent three or four afternoons looking for it and were puzzled and disconcerted. But it was a pleasure, as always, to be together in this part of the world looking at the countryside that we think we know so well and that is always springing some sort of surprise on us.

The landscape here is a record of ancient events. It was formed by the advancing, stationary, and retreating ice. The ice has staged its conquests and retreats here several times, withdrawing for the last time about fifteen thousand years ago.

Quite recently, you might say. Quite recently now that I have got used to a certain way of reckoning history.

A glacial landscape such as this is vulnerable. Many of its various contours are made up of gravel, and gravel is easy to get at, easy to scoop out, and always in demand. That's the material that makes these back roads passable—gravel from the chewed-up hills, the plundered terraces, that have been turned into holes in the land. And it's a way for farmers to get hold of some cash. One of my earliest memories is of the summer my father sold off the gravel on our river flats, and we had the excitement of the trucks going past all day, as well as the importance of the sign at our gate. *Children playing.* That was us. Then when the trucks were gone, the gravel removed, there was the novelty of pits and hollows that held, almost into the summer, the remains of the spring floods. Such hollows will eventually grow clumps of tough flowering weeds, then grass and bushes.

In the big gravel pits you see hills turned into hollows—as if a part of the landscape had managed, in a haphazard way, to turn itself inside out—and hollows where before there were only terraces or river flats. The steep sides of the hollows grow lush, in time, bumpy with greenery. But the tracks of the glacier are gone for good.

So you have to keep checking, taking in the changes, seeing things while they last.

We have special maps that we travel with. They are maps sold to accompany a book called *The Physiography of Southern Ontario*, by Lyman Chapman and Donald Putnam—whom we refer to, familiarly but somewhat reverentially, as Put and Chap. These maps show the usual roads and towns and rivers, but they show other things as well—things that were a complete surprise to me when I first saw them.

Look at just one map—a section of southern Ontario south of Georgian Bay. Roads and towns and rivers appear, as well as township boundaries. But look what else—patches of bright yellow, fresh green, battleship gray, and a darker mud gray, and a very pale gray, blue and tan and orange and rosy pink and purple and burgundy brown. Clusters of freckles. Ribbons of green like grass snakes. Narrow fluttery strokes from a red pen.

What is all this?

The yellow color shows sand, not along the lakeshore but collected inland, often bordering a swamp or a long-gone lake. The freckles are not round but lozenge shaped, and they appear in the landscape like partly buried eggs, with the blunt end against the flow of the ice. These are drumlins—thickly packed in some places, sparse in others. Some qualifying as big smooth hills, some barely breaking through the ground. They give their name to the soil in which they appear (drumlinized till—tan) and to the somewhat rougher soil that has none of them in it (undrumlinized till—battleship gray). The glacier in fact did lay them down like eggs, neatly and economically getting rid of material that it had picked up in its bulldozing advance. And where it didn't manage this, the ground is naturally rougher.

The purple tails are end moraines. They show where the ice halted on its long retreat, putting down a ridge of rubble at its edge. The vivid green strokes are eskers, and they are the easiest of all features to recognize when you're looking through the car window. Miniature mountain ranges, dragons' backs—they show the route of the rivers that tunneled the ice, at right angles to its front. Torrents loaded with gravel, which they discharged as they went. Usually there will be a little mild-mannered creek running along beside an esker—a direct descendant of that ancient battering river.

The orange color is for spillways, the huge channels that carried off the meltwater. And the dark gray shows the swamps that have developed in the spillways and are still there. Blue shows the clay soil, where the ice water was trapped in lakes. These places are flat but not smooth, and there is something sour and lumpy about clay fields. Heavy soil, coarse grass, poor drainage.

Green is for the beveled till, the wonderfully smooth surface that the old Lake Warren planed in the deposits along the shore of today's Lake Huron.

Red strokes and red interrupted lines that appear on the beveled till, or on the sand nearby, are remnants of bluffs and the abandoned beaches of those ancestors of the Great Lakes, whose outlines are discernible now only by a gentle lift of the land. Such prosaic, modern, authoritative-sounding names they have been given—Lake Warren, Lake Whittlesey.

Up on the Bruce Peninsula there is limestone under a thin soil (pale gray), and around Owen Sound and on Cape Rich there is shale at the bottom of the Niagara Escarpment, exposed where the limestone is worn off. Crumbly rock that can be made into brick of the same color it shows on the map—rosy pink.

My favorite of all the kinds of country is the one I've left till last. This is kame, or kame moraine, which is a chocolate burgundy color on the map and is generally in blobs, not ribbons. A big blob here, a little one there. Kame moraines show where a heap of dead ice sat, cut off from the rest of the moving glacier, earth-stuff pouring through all its holes and crevices. Or sometimes it shows where two lobes of ice pulled apart and the crevice filled in. End moraines are hilly in what seems a reasonable way, not as smooth as drumlins, but still harmonious, rhythmical, while kame moraines are all wild and bumpy, unpredictable, with a look of chance and secrets.

I didn't learn any of this at school. I think there was some nervousness then about being at loggerheads with the Bible in the matter of the creation of the Earth. I learned it when I came to live here with my second husband, a geographer. When I came back to where I never expected to be, in the countryside where I had grown up. So my knowledge is untainted, fresh. I get a naïve and particular pleasure from matching what I see on the map with what I can see through the car window. Also from trying to figure out what bit of landscape we're in before I look at the map—and being right a good deal of the time. And it is exciting to me to spot the boundaries, when it's a question of the different till plains, or where the kame moraine takes over from the end moraine.

But there is always more than just the keen pleasure of identification. There's the fact of these separate domains, each with its own history and reason, its favorite crops and trees and weeds, its special expression, its pull on the imagination. The fact of these little countries lying snug and unsuspected, like and unlike as siblings can be, in a landscape that's usually disregarded, or dismissed as drab agricultural counterpane. It's the fact you cherish.

I thought that the appointment I had was for a biopsy, but it turned out not to be. It was an appointment to let the city doctor decide whether he would do a biopsy, and after examining my breast and the results of the mammogram, he decided that he would. He had seen only the results of my most recent mammogram—those from 1990 and 1991 had not arrived yet from the country hospital where they had been done. The biopsy was set for a date two weeks ahead, and I was given a sheet with instructions about how to prepare for it.

I said that two weeks seemed like quite a while to wait.

At this stage of the game, the doctor said, two weeks was immaterial.

That was not what I had been led to believe. But I did not complain—not after a look at some of the people in the waiting room. I am over sixty. My death would not be a disaster. Not in comparison with the death of a young mother, a family wage earner, a child. It would not be *apparent* as a disaster.

It bothered us that we could not find the crypt. We extended our search. Perhaps it was not in Bruce County but in next-door Grey County? Sometimes we were sure that we were on the right road, but always we were disappointed. I went to the town library to look at the nineteenth-century county atlases, to see if perhaps the country cemeteries were marked on the township maps. They appeared to be marked on the maps of Huron County, but not in Bruce or Grey. (This wasn't true, I found out later—they were marked, or some of them were, but I managed to miss the small faint *C*s.)

In the library I met a friend who had dropped in to see us last summer shortly after our discovery. We had told him about the crypt and given him some rough directions for finding it, because he is interested in old cemeteries. He said now that he had written down the directions as soon as he got home. I had forgotten ever giving them. He went straight home and found the piece of paper—found it miraculously, he said, in a welter of other papers. He came back to the library where I was still looking through the atlases.

Peabody, Scone, McCullough Lake. That was what he had written down.

Farther north than we had thought—just beyond the boundary of the territory we had been doggedly covering.

So we found the right cemetery, and the grass-grown crypt looked just as surprising, as primitive, as we remembered. Now we had enough time to look around. We saw that most of the old slabs had been collected together and placed in the form of a cross. Nearly all of these were the tombstones of children. In any of these old cemeteries, the earliest dates were apt to be those for children, or young mothers lost in childbirth, or young men who had died accidentally—drowned, or hit by a falling tree, killed by a wild horse, or involved in an accident during the raising of a barn. There were hardly any old people around to die in those days.

The names were nearly all German, and many of the inscriptions were entirely in German. *Hier ruhet in Gott.* And *Geboren*, followed by the name of some German town or province, then *Gestorben*, with a date in the sixties or seventies of the nineteenth century.

Gestorben, here in Sullivan Township in Grey County in a colony of England in the middle of the bush.

Das arme Herz hieniedan
Von manches Sturm bewegt
Erlangt den renen Frieden
Nur wenn es nicht mehr schlagt.

I always have the notion that I can read German, even though I can't. I thought that this said something about the heart, the soul, the person buried here being out of harm's way now, and altogether better off. *Herz* and *Sturm* and *nicht mehr* could hardly be mistaken. But when I got home and checked the words in a German-English dictionary—finding all of them except *renen*, which could easily be a misspelling of *reinen*—I found that the verse was not so comforting. It seemed to say something about the poor heart buried here getting no peace until it stopped beating.

Better off dead.

Maybe that came out of a book of tombstone verses, and there wasn't much choice.

Not a word on the crypt, though we searched far more thoroughly than we had done before. Nothing but that single, amateurishly drawn cross. But we did find a surprise in the northeastern corner of the cemetery. A second crypt was there, much smaller than the first one, with a smooth concrete top. No earth or grass, but a good-sized cedar tree growing out of a crack in the concrete, its roots nourished by whatever was inside.

It's something like mound burial, we said. Something that had survived in Central Europe from pre-Christian times?

In the same city where I was to have my biopsy, and where I had the mammogram, there is a college where my husband and I were once students. I am not allowed to take out books, because I did not graduate, but I can use my husband's card, and I can poke around in the stacks and the reference rooms to my heart's content. During our next visit there, I went into the Regional Reference Room to read some books about Grey County and to find out whatever I could about Sullivan Township.

I read of a plague of passenger pigeons that destroyed every bit of the crops one year in the late-nineteenth century. And of a terrible winter in the 1840s, which lasted so long and with such annihilating cold that those first settlers were living on cow cabbages dug out of the ground. (I did not know what cow cabbages were—were they ordinary cabbages kept to be fed to animals or something wild and coarser, like skunk cabbage? And how could they be dug up in such weather, with the ground like rock? There are always puzzles.) A man named Barnes had starved himself to death, letting his family have his share, so that they might survive.

A few years after that a young woman was writing to her friend in Toronto that there was a marvelous crop of berries, more than anybody could pick to eat or dry, and that when she was out picking them she had seen a bear, so close that she could make out the drops of berry juice sparkling on its whiskers. She was not afraid, she said—she would walk through the bush to post this letter, bears or no bears.

I asked for church histories, thinking there might be something about Lutheran or German Catholic churches that would help me. It is difficult to make such requests in reference libraries because you will often be asked what it is, exactly, that you want to know, and what do you want to know it for? Sometimes it is even necessary to write your reason down. If you are doing a paper, a study, you will of course have good reason, but what if you are *just interested*? The best thing, probably, is to say you are doing a family history. Librarians are used to people doing that—particularly people who have gray hair—and it is generally thought to be a reasonable way of spending one's time. *Just interested* sounds apologetic, if not shifty, and makes you run the risk of being seen as an idler lounging around in the library, a person at loose ends, with no proper direction in life, *nothing better to do*. I thought of writing on my form: *research for paper concerning survival of mound burial in pioneer Ontario.* But I didn't have the nerve. I thought they might ask me to prove it.

I did locate a church that I thought might be connected with our cemetery, being a couple of country blocks west and a block north. St. Peter's Evangelical Lutheran, it was called, if it was still there.

In Sullivan Township you are reminded of what the crop fields everywhere used to look like before the advent of the big farm machinery. These fields have kept the size that can be served by the horse-drawn plough, the binder, the mower. Rail fences are still in place—here and there is a rough stone wall—and along these boundaries grow hawthorn trees, chokecherries, goldenrod, old-man's beard.

Such fields are unchanged because there is no profit to be gained in opening them up. The crops that can be grown on them are not worth the trouble. Two big rough moraines curve across the southern part of the township—the purple ribbons turning here into snakes swollen as if each of them had swallowed a frog—and there is a swampy spillway in between them. To the north, the land is clay. Crops raised here were probably never up to much, though people used to be more resigned to working unprofitable land, more grateful for whatever they could get, than is the case today. Where such land is put to any use at all now, it's pasture. The wooded areas—which everybody in our part of the country calls the bush—are making a strong comeback. In country like this the trend is no longer toward a taming of the landscape and a thickening of population, but rather the opposite. The bush will never again take over completely, but it is making a good grab. The deer, the wolves, which had at one time almost completely disappeared, have reclaimed some of their territory. Perhaps there will be bears soon, feasting again on the blackberries and thimbleberries and in the wild orchards. Perhaps they are here already.

As the notion of farming fades, unexpected enterprises spring up to replace it. It's hard to think that they will last. SPORTS CARDS GALORE, says a sign that is already weathering. TWO-DOOR DOGHOUSES FOR SALE. A place where chairs can be re-caned. TIRE SUPERYARD. Antiques and beauty treatments are offered. Brown eggs, maple syrup, bagpipe lessons, unisex haircuts.

We arrive at St. Peter's Lutheran Church on a Sunday morning just as the bell is ringing for services and the hands on the church tower point to eleven o'clock. (We learn later that those hands do not tell the time, they always point to eleven o'clock. Church time.)

St. Peter's is large and handsome, built of limestone blocks. A high steeple on the tower and a modern glass porch to block the wind and snow. Also a long drive shed built of stone and wood—a reminder of the days when people drove to church in buggies and cutters. A pretty stone house, the rectory, surrounded by summer flowers.

We drive on to Williamsford on Highway 6, to have lunch and to give the minister a decent interval to recover from the morning service before we knock at the rectory door to seek out information. A mile or so down the road we make a discouraging discovery. Another cemetery—St. Peter's own cemetery, with its own early dates and German names—making our cemetery, so close by, seem even more of a puzzle, an orphan.

We come back anyway, at around two o'clock. We knock on the front door of the rectory, and after a while a little girl appears and tries to unbolt the door. She can't manage it and makes signs for us to go around to the back. She comes running out to meet us on our way.

The minister isn't home, she says. She has gone to take afternoon services in Williamsford. Just our informant and her sister are here, looking after the minister's dog and cats. But if we want to know anything about churches or cemeteries or history, we should go and ask her mother, who lives up the hill in the big new log house.

She tells us her name. Rachel.

Rachel's mother does not seem at all surprised by our curiosity or put out by our visit. She invites us into her house, where there is a noisy interested dog and a self-possessed husband just finishing a late lunch. The main floor of the house is all one big room with a wide view of fields and trees.

She brings out a book that I did not see in the Regional Reference Room. An old soft-covered history of the township. She thinks it has a chapter about cemeteries.

And in fact it does. In a short time she and I are reading together a section on the Mannerow Cemetery, "famous for its two vaults." There is a grainy photograph of the larger crypt. It is said to have been built in 1895 to receive the body of a three-year-old boy, a son of the Mannerow family. Other members of the family were placed there in the years that followed. One Mannerow husband and wife were put into the smaller crypt in the corner of the cemetery. What was originally a family graveyard later became public, and the name of it was changed from Mannerow to Cedardale.

The vaults were roofed with concrete on the inside.

Rachel's mother says that there is only one descendant of the family living in the township today. He lives in Scone.

"Next door to the house my brother's in," she says. "You know how there's just the three houses in Scone? That's all there is. There's the yellow-brick house and that's my brother's, then the one in the middle, that's Mannerows'. So maybe they might tell you something more, if you went there and asked them."

While I was talking to Rachel's mother and looking at the history book, my husband sat at the table and talked to her husband. That is the proper way for conversations to go in our part of the country. The husband asked where we came from, and on hearing that we came from Huron County, he said that he knew it very well. He went there straight off the boat, he said, when he came out from Holland not long after the war. In 1948, yes. (He is a man considerably older than his wife.) He lived for a while near Blyth, and he worked on a turkey farm.

I overhear him saying this, and when my own conversation has drawn to a close, I ask him if it was the Wallace Turkey Farm that he worked on.

Yes, he says, that was the one. And his sister married Alvin Wallace.

"Corrie Wallace," I say.

"That's right. That's her."

I ask him if he knew any Laidlaws from around that area, and he says no.

I say that if he worked at Wallaces' (another rule in our part of the country is that you never say *the* so-and-sos, just the name), then he must have known Bob Laidlaw.

"He raised turkeys too," I tell him. "And he knew Wallaces from when they'd gone to school together. Sometimes he worked with them."

"Bob Laidlaw?" he says, on a rising note. "Oh, sure, I knew him. But I thought you meant around Blyth. He had a place up by Wingham. West of Wingham. Bob Laidlaw."

I say that Bob Laidlaw grew up near Blyth, on the Eighth Line of Morris Township, and that was how he knew the Wallace brothers, Alvin's father and uncle. They had all gone to school at S.S. No. 1, Morris, right beside the Wallace farm.

He takes a closer look at me and laughs.

"You're not telling me he was your dad, are you? You're not Sheila?"

"Sheila's my sister. I'm the older one."

"I didn't know there was an older one," he says. "I didn't know that. But Bill and Sheila. I knew them. They used to be down working at the turkeys with us, before Christmas. You never were there?"

"I was away from home by then."

"Bob Laidlaw. Bob Laidlaw was your dad. Well. I should have thought of that right away. But when you said from around Blyth, I didn't catch on. I was thinking Bob Laidlaw was from up at Wingham. I never knew he was from Blyth in the first place."

He laughs and reaches across the table to shake my hand.

"Well now. I can see it in you. Round the eyes. That's a long time ago. It sure is. A long time ago."

I am not sure whether he means it's a long time ago that my father and the Wallace boys went to school in Morris Township, or a long time since he himself was a young man fresh from Holland and worked with my father and my brother and sister preparing the Christmas turkeys. But I agree with him, and then we both say that it is a small world. We say this, as people usually do, with a sense of wonder and refreshment. (People who are not going to be comforted by this discovery usually avoid making it.) We explore the connection as far as it will go and soon find that there is not much more to be got out of it. But we are both happy. He is happy to be reminded of himself as a young man, fresh in the country and able to turn himself to any work that was offered, with confidence in what lay ahead of him. And by the looks of this well-built house with its wide view, and his lively wife, his pretty Rachel, his own still alert and useful body, it does look as if things have turned out pretty well for him.

And I am happy to find somebody who can see me still as part of my family, who can remember my father and the place where my parents worked and lived for all of their married lives, first in hope and then in honorable persistence. A place that I seldom drive past and can hardly relate to the life I live now, though it is not much more than twenty miles away.

It has changed, of course, it has changed utterly, becoming a car-wrecking operation. The front yard and the side yard and the vegetable garden and the flower borders, the hayfield, the mock-orange bush, the lilac trees, the chestnut stump, the pasture, and the ground once covered by the fox pens are all swept under a tide of car parts, gutted car bodies, smashed headlights, grilles, and fenders, overturned car seats with rotten, bloated stuffing—heaps of painted, rusted, blackened, glittering, whole or twisted, defiant, and surviving metal.

But that is not the only thing that deprives it of meaning for me. No. It is the fact that it *is* only twenty miles away, that I could see it every day if I wanted to. The past needs to be approached from a distance.

Rachel's mother asks us if we would like to look at the inside of the church before we head off to Scone, and we say that we would. We walk down the hill, and she takes us hospitably into the red-carpeted interior. It smells a little damp or musty as stone buildings often do, even when they are kept quite clean.

She talks to us about how things have been going with this building and its congregation.

The whole church was raised up some years ago to add on the Sunday School and the kitchen underneath.

The bell still rings out to announce the death of every church member. One ring for every year of life. Everybody within hearing distance can listen and count the times it rings and try to figure out who it must be for. Sometimes it's easy—a person who was expected to die. Sometimes it's a surprise.

She mentions that the front porch of the church is modern, as we must have noticed. There was a big argument when it was put on, between those who thought it was necessary and even liked it and those who disagreed. Finally there was a split. The ones who didn't like it went off to Williamsford and formed their own church there, though with the same minister.

The minister is a woman. The last time a minister had to be hired, five out of the seven candidates were women. This one is married to a veterinarian and used to be a veterinarian herself. Everybody likes her fine. Though there was a man from Faith Lutheran in Desboro who got up and walked out of a funeral when he found she was preaching at it. He could not stand the idea of a woman preaching.

Faith Lutheran is part of the Missouri Synod, and that is the way they are.

There was a great fire in the church some time ago. It gutted much of the inside but left the shell intact. When the surviving inside walls were scrubbed down afterward, layers of paint came off with the smoke, and there was a surprise underneath—a faint text in German, in the Gothic German lettering, which did not entirely wash off. It had been hidden under the paint.

And there it is. They touched up the paint, and there it is.

Ich hebe meine Augen auf zu den Bergen, von welchen mir Hilfe Kommt. That is on one side wall. And on the opposite wall: *Dein Wort ist meines Fusses Leuchte und ein Licht auf meinem Wege.*

I will lift up my eyes unto the hills, from whence cometh my help.

Thy word is a lamp unto my feet and a light unto my path.

Nobody had known, nobody had remembered that the German words were there, until the fire and the cleaning revealed them. They must have been painted over at some time, and afterward nobody spoke of them, and so the memory that they were there had entirely died out.

At what time? Very likely it happened at the beginning of the First World War, the 1914–18 war. Not a time to show German lettering, even spelling out holy texts. And not a thing to be mentioned for many years afterward.

Being in the church with this woman as guide gives me a slightly lost feeling, or a feeling of bewilderment, of having got things the wrong way round. The words on the wall strike me to the heart, but I am not a believer, and they do not make me a believer. She seems to think of her church, including those words, as if she were its vigilant housekeeper. In fact she mentions critically that a bit of the paint—in the ornate *L* of *Licht*—has faded or flaked off and should be replaced. But she is the believer. It seems as if you must always take care of what's on the surface, and what is behind, so immense and disturbing, will take care of itself.

In separate panes of the stained-glass windows are displayed these symbols:

The Dove (over the altar).

The letters Alpha and Omega (in the rear wall).

The Holy Grail.

The Sheaf of Wheat.

The Cross in the Crown.

The Ship at Anchor.

The Lamb of God bearing the Cross.

The Mythical Pelican, with golden feathers, believed to feed its young on the blood of its own torn breast, as Christ the Church. (The Mythical Pelican as represented here resembles the real pelican only by way of being a bird.)

Just a few days before I am to have my biopsy I get a call from the city hospital to say that the operation has been canceled.

I am to keep the appointment anyway, to have a talk with the radiologist, but I do not need to fast in preparation for surgery.

Canceled.

Why? Information on the other two mammograms?

I once knew a man who went into the hospital to have a little lump cut out of his neck. He put my hand on it, on that silly little lump, and we laughed about how we could exaggerate its seriousness and get him a couple of weeks off work so that we could go on a holiday together. The lump was examined, but further surgery was canceled because there were so many, many other lumps that were discovered. The verdict was that any operation would be useless. All of a sudden, he was a marked man. No more laughing. When I went to see him he stared at me in nearly witless anger. He could not hide it. It was *all through him*, they said.

I used to hear that same thing said when I was a child, always said in a hushed voice that seemed to throw the door open, half-willingly, to calamity. Half-willingly, even with an obscene hint of invitation.

We do stop at the middle house in Scone, not after visiting the church but on the day after the hospital phoned. We are looking for some diversion. Already something has changed—we notice how familiar the landscape of Sullivan Township and the church and the cemeteries and the villages of Desboro and Scone and the town of Chesley are beginning to seem to us, how the distances between places have shortened. Perhaps we had found out all we are going to find out. There might be a bit more explanation—the idea of the vault might have come from somebody's reluctance to put a three-year-old child under the ground—but what has been so compelling is drawn now into a pattern of things we know about.

Nobody answers the outside door. The house and yard are tidily kept. I look around at the bright beds of annuals and a rose of Sharon bush and a little black boy sitting on a stump with a Canadian flag in his hand. There are not so many little black boys in people's yards as there used to be.

Grown children, city dwellers, may have cautioned against them—though I don't believe that a racial insult was ever a conscious intention. It was more as if people felt that a little black boy added a touch of sportiness and charm.

The outside door opens into a narrow porch. I step inside and sound the house doorbell. There is just room to move past an armchair with an afghan on it and a couple of wicker tables with potted plants.

Still nobody comes. But I can hear loud religious singing inside the house. A choir singing "Onward, Christian Soldiers." Through the window in the door I see the singers on television in an inner room. Blue robes, many bobbing faces against a sunset sky. The Mormon Tabernacle Choir?

I listen to the words, all of which I used to know. As far as I can tell these singers are about at the end of the first verse.

I let the bell alone till they finish.

I try again, and Mrs. Mannerow comes. A short, competent-looking woman with tight grayish-brown curls, wearing a flowered blue top to match her blue slacks.

She says that her husband is very hard of hearing, so it wouldn't do much good to talk to him. And he has just come home from the hospital a few days ago, so he isn't really feeling like talking. She doesn't have much time to talk herself, because she is getting ready to go out. Her daughter is coming from Chesley to pick her up. They are going to a family picnic to celebrate her daughter's husband's parents' fiftieth wedding anniversary.

But she wouldn't mind telling me as much as she knows.

Though being only married into the family, she never knew too much.

And even they didn't know too much.

I notice something new in the readiness of both this older woman and the energetic younger woman in the log house. They do not seem to find it strange that anybody should wish to know about things that are of no particular benefit or practical importance. They do not suggest that they have better things to think about. Real things, that is. Real work. When I was growing up, an appetite for impractical knowledge of any kind did not get encouragement. It was all right to know which field would suit certain crops, but not all right to know anything about the glacial geography that I have mentioned. It was necessary to learn to read, but not in the least desirable to end up with your nose in a book. If you had to learn history and foreign languages to pass out of school, it was only natural to forget that sort of thing as quickly as you could. Otherwise you would *stand out.* And that was not a good idea. And wondering about *olden days*—what used to be here, what happened there, why, why?—was as sure a way to make yourself stand out as any.

Of course some of this kind of thing would be expected in outsiders, city people, who have time on their hands. Maybe this woman thinks that's what I am. But the younger woman found out differently and still seemed to think my curiosity understandable.

Mrs. Mannerow says that she used to wonder. When she was first married, she used to wonder. Why did they put their people in there like that, where did they get the idea? Her husband didn't know why. The Mannerows all took it for granted. They didn't know why. They took it for granted because that was the way they had always done it. That was their way and they never thought to ask why or where their family got the idea.

Did I know the vault was all concrete on the inside?

The smaller one on the outside too. Yes. She hadn't been in the cemetery for a while, and she had forgotten about that one.

She did remember the last funeral they had when they put the last person in the big vault. The last time they had opened it up. It was for Mrs. Lempke, who had been born a Mannerow. There was just room for one more, and she was the one. Then there was no room for anybody more.

They dug down at the end and opened up the bricks, and then you could see some of the inside, before they got her coffin in. You could see there were coffins in there before her, along either side. Put in nobody knows how long a time ago.

"It gave me a strange feeling," she says. "It did so. Because you get used to seeing the coffins when they're new, but not so much when they're old."

And the one little table sitting straight ahead of the entranceway, a little table at the far end. A table with a Bible opened up on it.

And beside the Bible, a lamp.

It was just an ordinary old-fashioned lamp, the kind they used to burn coal oil in.

Sitting there the same today, all sealed up and nobody going to see it ever again.

"Nobody knows why they did it. They just did."

She smiles at me with a sociable sort of perplexity, her almost colorless eyes enlarged, made owlish by her glasses. She gives a couple of tremulous nods. As if to say, it's beyond us, isn't it? A multitude of things, beyond us. Yes.

The radiologist says that when she looked at the mammograms that had come in from the country hospital, she could see that the lump had been there in 1990 and in 1991. It had not changed. Still in the same place, still the same size. She says that you can never be absolutely 100 percent certain that such a lump is safe, unless you do a biopsy. But you can be sure enough. A biopsy in itself is an intrusive procedure, and if she were in my place, she would not have it. She would have a mammogram in another six months instead. If it were her breast, she would keep an eye on it, but for the time being she would let it alone.

I ask why nobody had told me about the lump when it first appeared.

Oh, she says, they must not have seen it.

So this is the first time.

Such frights will come and go.

Then there'll be one that won't. One that won't go.

But for now, the corn in tassel, the height of summer passing, time opening out with room again for tiffs and trivialities. No more hard edges on the days, no sense of fate buzzing around in your veins like a swarm of tiny and relentless insects. Back to where no great change seems to be promised beyond the change of seasons. Some raggedness, carelessness, even a casual possibility of boredom again in the reaches of earth and sky.

On our way home from the city hospital, I say to my husband, "Do you think they put any oil in that lamp?"

He knows at once what I am talking about. He says that he has wondered the same thing.

Shannon Cain

The Necessity of Certain Behaviors

TO ESCAPE from the hot city and the people in it, Lisa goes on an ecotourism trek in the mountains of a foreign country. To get there she endures a long airplane ride. There is the usual business of camping equipment and protein bars and local guides in odd headgear carrying packs containing tea and dried meat. One day she becomes separated from her group of Americans, and after trudging half a day on a narrow path that doesn't look all that well traveled, she comes to a village.

Lisa is thirsty, and relieved to have stumbled across civilization. She spent the last hour considering the possibility that when night fell the mountain goats could become aggressive. She'd read a novel set in Wyoming in which a wild sheep attacks a tourist on a motorcycle. She is teary and grateful when a woman comes out of a hut and gives her a bowl with water in it. With a great deal of kindness the woman watches her drink, and then takes her by the hand. She brings Lisa into the hut and feeds her a stew of meat and a starchy root vegetable, flavored with sweetish spices and featuring a pleasant pungency caused, Lisa guesses, by someone having aged, or possibly smoked, a key ingredient. She thinks of a wedge of stinky cheese dredged in honey and almonds that someone brought to an office party.

Their stools sit six inches off the dirt floor. Lisa smiles and points at the food. She flashes a thumbs-up to the woman, who clearly doesn't understand. The woman is young, about Lisa's age, with muscular arms. She has a straight long nose and black eyes and moves with economy around her little hut. The woman points to a mat on the floor and Lisa removes her two-hundred-dollar hiking boots and falls asleep.

When she wakes up it is still dark, and the woman is at the other side of the hut. She is washing herself, sitting cross-legged on an animal skin rug with a bowl of water in front of her. A single candle burns, illuminating her brown body. It occurs to Lisa that the woman might know she's being watched.

In the city where she's from, Lisa knew a man named Bennett with full Greek eyelids, a cynical urban grin, and unappeasable curiosity about Lisa's feelings. Some mornings while she showered they'd pretend she wasn't aware he was watching her through the vinyl curtain, which was clear but tinted a flattering pink. Her selection of the curtain was deliberate. In the city where she is from, people in love understand the necessity of certain behaviors.

The woman's name is unpronounceable, but Lisa tries: "Hee-nara," she says. They laugh at her. Now, in the morning, there is another woman in the hut, someone who appears to have stopped by for the purpose of staring. Her hair is braided and piled on top of her head in a complicated arrangement. She wears a red cowboy shirt and a skirt made of a soft animal skin. She and Heenara sit with thighs touching, talking in low voices and looking at Lisa. They seem to be very close, like sisters. The woman leans over and deposits a long kiss on Heenara's lips. Lisa realizes she was wrong about the sister thing. They look at Lisa, apparently for a reaction. To put them at ease, she smiles.

Heenara and her girlfriend take Lisa for a walk in the village. People emerge from their huts and look at her. Each hut seems to contain only one person. Everyone is young and robust looking. All in all, this is a very attractive tribe, or clan, or whatever.

In the parlance of the city she is from, Lisa does not "identify" as bisexual. She is a straight girl who on occasion will take a woman home. After having spent some time in her early twenties thinking about the issue, she settled on the strategy of refusing to adopt a label with regard to her sexuality. This train of thought has not rumbled unprovoked into Lisa's head.

Heenara has received another visitor, this time a man, who, like the other men of the village, walks around bare chested and has a shiny mane of black hair. With this guy Heenara repeats the show of kissing. They take a break and regard Lisa, who offers what she believes to be an encouraging expression. Heenara throws back her head and laughs. Her neck is both soft and muscular. The man's name sounds something like "Luck." He smiles brilliantly when she tries to pronounce it. Lisa wonders how he keeps his teeth so white.

The villagers are exceptionally good cooks. Lisa sees no children and no old people. Their language sounds like a stream over stones.

Lisa becomes the village guest. She spends a night or two in the huts of a dozen different people, each cheerful and attentive. One afternoon, she is helping her latest host prepare a batch of root stew and it occurs to her to wonder whether anyone has been feeding her dog. His name is Digit, and he's a fairly good-natured animal, considering the fact he lives in a six-hundred-square-foot box five stories above the ground. The man named Bennett was particularly fond of him. If he could speak, Digit would be the kind of dog who wouldn't mind being pressed to reveal information, at any given moment, on his current state of mind.

If the villagers experienced curiosity about Lisa, it now appears to be satisfied. Although the language barrier is undoubtedly a factor in their failure to inquire where she's from, Lisa suspects even if she could talk with them freely they would not be particularly interested in her place of origin or whether she plans to return. Their unconditional acceptance feels both welcoming and indifferent, like a warm hug from an uncle who keeps forgetting your name. But what would be the point of going home? Only twenty or so people will have even noticed she's gone, if you count her coworkers, her doorman, and the super. During her years in the city Lisa has failed to work toward establishing a circle of friends, a practice that seems important to other city dwellers. Here in the village, a community has made itself available to her, with practically no effort on her part. Sticking around feels logical, plus the people are sexy.

She makes Heenara understand, through a comic series of gestures, that she's evolved past the guest phase and wants a hut of her own. Twenty villagers show up to build it for her. There is no mention of how or whether Lisa will pay for building materials, which mostly consist of mud and fronds and such. During construction they sing slow, melodic songs in a companionable harmony. Lisa experiences a frothy happiness. An unusually tall woman with a high forehead teaches Lisa how to weave her roof from strands of ropy grass. In two days the hut is finished, and people come by with gifts for her: a rug, some wool for her mattress, a candle. The emergency supplies in her backpack now seem foreign and useless: waterproof matches, freeze-dried chicken noodle soup, a flare gun.

One night Heenara and Luck drop by for a visit. Heenara has been crying. Drawing stick figures in the dirt floor, Heenara explains that she and the woman with complicated hair are no longer together. Luck makes a sympathetic face and puts his arm around Heenara's shoulder. Lisa is impressed with his ability to conceal his pleasure at this development. She serves them bowls of a fermented plum beverage brought as a housewarming present. They pass the time attempting to teach Lisa more of their impossible language and after they're all fairly drunk, Lisa draws two stick figures in her dirt floor meant to represent Heenara and Luck. She puts a circle around the two figures and smiles at Luck. She reaches for their hands and clasps them together, pantomiming something like, Now you have Heenara all to yourself.

Heenara looks at Luck. They frown at one another and exchange a series of rapid sentences. She shakes her head and glances sideways at Lisa.

Luck picks up the stick. He draws, outside the circle Lisa has made but standing next to his own image, a figure of a man. He points at that figure and pronounces a name that sounds as if he's trying to say "Frederick" with a mouthful of stones. He draws another circle, now around this new man and himself. Luck stands in the overlap of the two circles. Lisa smiles politely at the dirt diagram and raises her eyebrows. Heenara makes an exasperated sound. She draws a figure of the woman with complicated hair, next to her own image, and then a circle that encompasses the two of them, but not Luck. She pauses to see if Lisa understands. Then she erases the figure of her ex-girlfriend, leaving a blank space. She holds her two hands out to Lisa. She smiles at her left hand, which is cupped, as if holding something, and nods toward Luck. She shrugs sadly at the other, whose fingers are splayed open, empty.

Lisa takes a swallow of the plum wine. In the blank space left by the woman with complicated hair, she draws a woman with a backpack. Luck ducks his head, grinning into his wine. He kisses them both on the cheek and leaves the hut.

Heenara keeps her awake until sunrise. She performs a ritual involving a paste made of wine mixed into a palmful of dirt gathered from under Lisa's sleeping mat. She hums a soulful tune and nakedly dances a series of steps around Lisa's front door. She removes Lisa's clothes and washes her with maternal tenderness from head to toe, using a latherless soap that smells like oregano and fruit nectar. It leaves an oily film. Finally she hoists Lisa over her shoulder like a sack, drops her ungently onto the sleeping mat, and pours the remaining wine over her torso, her legs, her shoulders, and her arms. They slide together with the wine as lubricant until it becomes sticky, whereupon Lisa demonstrates with her mouth one or two cleansing rituals commonly practiced among a certain tribe of humans she used to know.

When Heenara is asleep Lisa stands in the open doorway. In the flat tones of their urban language, the man Bennett had told her he was building a three-bedroom house in Westchester for himself and a woman named Julie. He said he admired Julie's devotion to transparency. Lisa's relationship with Bennett had long since ended; there was no particular reason for him to tell her all this. Still, months after he moved away from the city Lisa carried on interior dialogues with the memory of him. It was to be expected that he'd have identified someone new, but nevertheless the matter of Julie had startled her. Since her arrival in the village she hasn't had a single imaginary conversation with him. The stars above the village crowd the sky. How could there possibly be room for them all? How is it that they didn't smash into each other in chaotic collisions of light and heat?

Lisa wakes up at dawn with Heenara pushing her gently off the mat. She accepts a bowl of hot tea. As soon as she's standing, Heenara pulls the mat from the floor and lays it outside, in the dirt. The plum wine has left a stain in the outline of Lisa's body. Heenara sips tea in the yard. Villagers appear. They approach, smiling, slapping Heenara on the back and raising their eyebrows in the direction of Lisa's door. Through a crack in the wall, Lisa watches.

A caravan of donkeys led by a couple of men in odd headgear arrives in the village. The men pull packs off the animals and open their contents, spreading a blanket on the ground and displaying aluminum cookware, athletic socks, sewing needles. Lisa would like to have a necklace made of carved bone beads, but has nothing with which to trade. There was a time when she would purchase beautiful things. A set of vintage turquoise martini glasses. A distressed calfskin briefcase with copper buckles. Jade earrings set in Balinese silver. She waits for a feeling of longing to occur but the memory of these items is akin to a foreign object in her eye. How silly she used to be! Yet how comfortable.

One of the traders stares at her. Heenara says something sharp to him and he turns away.

The opening weeks of her relationship with Heenara are spent in a sexual frenzy broken up only by Heenara's perfunctory visits to Luck's hut. Upon her return Lisa smells him on Heenara's skin, which she finds not unpleasant. Beating her mat clean on the rocks at the stream, Lisa runs into him. He's polite but has a pained look that suggests his patience is wearing thin. She learns from Heenara that Luck's lover Frederick is away from the village with a group of hunters, tracking a herd of mountain goats across the plateau.

One evening Luck appears at her door. He's had a fair amount of plum wine. Her remedial knowledge of their language results in a distressing conversation in which she understands that Luck wants her to break up with Heenara. When he sees Lisa's tears he leaves and returns with Heenara, who rolls her eyes in the direction of the sheepish Luck and informs Lisa via their semi-efficient system of communication that it's time for Lisa to find a boyfriend.

Among the village inhabitants there is a specialist in such matters. She visits Lisa's hut and cheerfully submits her to a series of questions Lisa only halfway understands, having mostly to do with matters such as eyes, hair, and body type. She strikes Lisa as being awfully young for the job. Lisa defers to her judgment about borrowing a dress that displays her cleavage, and together they spend the following morning visiting a handful of potential boyfriends. Each of them is beautiful beyond belief. Their upper bodies trigger a hazy memory of men lifting weights in a gym located in the gay section of the city where she used to live. The men look at her as if she were some exquisite yet puzzling object they uncovered while digging a hole.

She finds herself judging them by the way they move around their huts.

She finally settles on one whose name she mispronounces less comically than those of the others and who betrays his nervousness by splashing a bit of boiling water on his foot in the process of making her a cup of bitter tea. He's called Toruk, more or less, and she finds herself flirting uncontrollably with him, as if overcome by some Darwinian instinct to snag a hunter-gatherer of her own.

In the days following Bennett's revelations about Julie and Westchester, Lisa experienced an accelerated interest in her psyche by certain people in her life. Her mother; a previously indifferent coworker; her gay boyfriend. They grilled her regarding what had occurred between her and Bennett and what had not; what was said and what was left unsaid. They berated her for her failure to expose herself, as is apparently standard practice in the pursuit of modern urban love. Such a fuss, Lisa thinks now. How did she endure it? Why didn't she leave the city so much earlier?

In preparation for her date with Toruk, Heenara coaches Lisa on the first-night ritual, the initiation of which turns out to be the responsibility of the aggressor, in this case Lisa. Teaching her the steps to the front-door dance and the nonsensical lyrics of the song that accompanies it, Heenara becomes teary and in need of assurance. It's possible Lisa is witnessing a moment of emotional fallout brought on by culturally coerced non-monogamy. Or maybe Heenara is preoccupied with something she can't translate—crop failure, perhaps a sick parent. Which would constitute a mystery in itself, Lisa realizes: she still hasn't encountered any old people. Heenara and Lisa get very drunk and make bittersweet, dramatic love until Lisa gets out of bed to vomit in the bushes behind her hut.

In the morning she awakes to Heenara's voice in the front yard. She goes outside. Heenara is talking to the trader who came to the village and stared at Lisa. She uses words Lisa more or less understands to explain that the man has said that people in the town at the base of the mountain are asking about a woman with yellow hair. "A woman who is lost," she says.

Lisa shakes her head and says something like, "Not lost, me." Heenara smiles.

The man has brown teeth. He lets loose a current of words. He gestures in Lisa's direction. Heenara raises her voice and flaps her hand, shooing him from the yard. Lisa goes inside and pulls the hiking boots from her backpack. She runs after the man and gives them to him. She looks him carefully in the face. "Not lost, me," she says.

He takes the boots and nods. He doesn't meet her eye. Surely he understands, though, about payment in exchange for complicity. Lisa walks back to her hut. The trader will sell her boots for a nice amount of money. He'll feed his family for a month.

In the city at the bottom of the mountain there are people looking for her, probably, people paid by her mother. It's not too late to chase the trader. To erase any ambiguity regarding her desire for his silence. She should appeal to his love of homeland, his indigenous understanding that this is the place, not her city, where humans are meant to live.

Heenara has seen the exchange. She frowns and goes inside. Slung by their laces over the trader's shoulder, Lisa's boots retreat down the mountain. She tries to make Heenara understand, but she lacks the words to explain that she no longer knows the difference between *lost* and *found*.

For the occasion of their first night together, Toruk has shaved his beard. As part of this procedure he has applied to the skin of his face a berry-scented oil that reminds Lisa of a sweet drink she often consumed as a child. He remains still, waiting for her to move toward him, and when she arrives at his bare chest he raises his arms as if to offer his underbelly. She reaches up to pull on his biceps, to place his arms around her waist, but he refuses to move them. She pulls harder, and he smiles at her and shakes his head. If necessary she could hang the entire weight of her body on these arms.

She performs the ritual to the best of her ability. Toruk smiles understandingly when she screws up the dance and also skips an entire verse of the song. In the washing of his skin she finds herself in a trance of sorts, focused and consumed by the task, unbothered by a soap that won't yield suds. She becomes giggly when the time comes for her to toss him into bed, unsure how to approach the feat of physically moving a mountain of muscle, but he solves the problem by throwing himself onto the mat with what appears to be a painful thud.

She pours the wine on him. Finally, he abandons his ritual passivity and pulls her sharply to the floor to land hard on his body, very nearly knocking her breath away. She is thrilled by the jolt of it, and by her own desire: she found it so rarely in the city.

In the morning she sleeps late. When she wakes up Toruk is glaring at her. She's forgotten to display the stained mat in his front yard. She's forgotten to receive congratulatory visitors. She doesn't know how to say *I'm sorry* in his language. She pouts in a shamefaced way and sucks his dick by way of apology.

Sometimes the man named Bennett would step inside the shower. In the pink light he'd wash her hair. He'd ask if she was okay. When he performed these tender acts she was careful to maintain a neutral expression. Since her face was already wet she could cry without provoking questions as long as she kept her lip from trembling. She didn't want to explain her happiness to him. The joy she harbored was easily scared away; a timid, furry creature.

Heenara retreats to Luck's sleeping mat to wait out Lisa's infatuation with Toruk. After only two days, however, Frederick returns from the hunt, triumphant with goat meat and horny for Luck. Lisa is at the village well when the hunters return. Luck dashes across the dusty compound to slam into Frederick's body, their mouths joining in a display of sweaty lust. Everyone stops to watch.

Lisa runs into Heenara outside the shower hut. She cups her neck affectionately, but Heenara is stiff. Lisa pulls her by the hair into a shower stall and closes the woven straw curtain. She turns the warm water on their bodies and methodically works half her hand into Heenara's vagina. This, it turns out, was the right thing to do. Heenara is smug and satisfied.

Lisa finds herself unable to apply to her new life the wisdoms she knew in the old. For example: Don't meet the eyes of strangers. Don't be tempted to take the local train; sit tight for the express. Walk at night to the Laundromat with your pepper spray ready; however, do feel free to yell at men pissing against your building: no one with a limp penis in his hand is a threat. Expect that all lovers, eventually, will leave.

Lisa comes to the realization that on any given night, one third of the huts in the village are empty. She speculates on the efficiency, resource-wise, of this arrangement. She wonders if this condition is related to the eerie absence in the village of anyone under the age of eighteen. One night she draws in the dirt floor of Toruk's hut a stick figure of a small person holding the hand of a larger person. She circles the child figure and says, "Where?"

Given Toruk's tender laughter, Lisa's expression must reveal her fear of his answer. He points to the hills. He talks, he smiles fondly, he says a lot of words. She doesn't need to understand their meaning to know the children have not, after all, been sold into slavery or sacrificed to some grumpy god.

Slowly, Lisa's comprehension of the stream-over-stones language gets better. She knows now, for example, that when Toruk looks pensively at the ceiling and utters a masculine yet lilting series of words, he's not making an observation on the vast and mysterious wonders of the universe. As a public works laborer of sorts—preparing communal garden plots, digging sewage canals—he turns out to be mostly preoccupied with moving piles of dirt from one end of the village to another. As for Lisa's own preoccupations, either Toruk doesn't know how to ask or he isn't especially interested.

As time passes, the domino effect created by the prolonged absence of Frederick the goat hunter gets sorted out. Lisa settles into a routine with Heenara and Toruk. They don't have anything so formal as a schedule of visits, but there emerges between them an understanding that things always even out, more or less.

On a calm morning with huge white clouds in the sky, Bennett arrives in the village, unshaven, dirty, and limping. Behind him is the trader. Filling her water gourd at the well, Lisa spots him before he realizes it's her. When she approaches, he holds her and he cries. "I've been looking for you," he says. He is oblivious to the people staring.

"I'm fine," she says into his shirt. Underneath the old sweat he smells like Bennett.

Heenara appears, unsmiling, at Lisa's side. Lisa introduces him.

"You speak their language?" Bennett says.

"Not really." She shrugs. She shouldn't be proud of this.

He turns to see why Lisa is looking over his shoulder. Toruk stands at the entrance to his hut, observing them. His arms are folded across his chest. She is surprised to notice he's not any taller than Bennett. Heenara removes the water gourd from Lisa's hand and gives it to Bennett for a drink. She takes his arm and walks them to Lisa's hut. She gives Lisa a look and comes inside with them.

"I'm sorry," Lisa says to Bennett.

"What were you thinking?" he says. "Did you lose your passport? Or something? Were you hurt? Are you sick?" He lowers his voice. He watches Heenara. "Are these people keeping you here?"

Heenara is banging around in Lisa's cooking area. Her cheeks are flushed. Lisa is overcome with loyalty toward her. "It's good here," she says.

"You've been living here? In this woman's hovel?" he says.

"Did your wife come too?" she asks.

He looks at Heenara, who is blowing earnestly on the fire. "What's going on, Lisa?"

"Go back," Lisa says. "Call my mother."

"And tell her what?"

"I don't know. Tell her not to worry."

"Tell me this is a joke," he says. "Is this some kind of joke?"

Bennett pitches an orange pup tent and for two days skulks around the edges of the village. He stakes out her movements, watching from behind his tent flap. Lisa brings him food, which he accepts wordlessly. The villagers stay clear of him. Apparently they don't know much about stalkers. Lisa's never had one before and is disappointed hers is so benign and morose.

It becomes colder at night. Toruk presents her with a finely woven goat wool blanket. During an afternoon of cleaning she discovers the backpack in the corner of her hut, behind a large pile of wool. She caresses the items inside the pack and thinks about the relative usefulness or frivolity of each. She boils water and prepares the freeze-dried chicken noodle soup. She gives a taste to Heenara, who finds it disgusting.

"I wish you wouldn't spit food on my floor," Lisa says in the stream-over-stones language.

"You call that food?" Heenara says.

Lisa recalls a brunch of salmon benedict and roasted rosemary potatoes at a sidewalk café on the Upper West Side.

"I love you," she says. It's possible she's now speaking English.

"I don't understand," Heenara says.

"Me neither," Lisa replies.

Heenara wipes her thumb across Lisa's forehead, as if to rub out the worry.

Late one afternoon, it snows. The villagers quicken the pace of their work. Many are smiling in a distracted, anticipatory way, lifting their faces to the falling flakes. When it becomes dark, the temperature drops. Lisa approaches Bennett's campsite at the edge of the village and calls his name. He unzips the tent flap, sits back on his heels, and gazes up at her.

"Why don't you come inside," she tells him.

"I've been squatting here for three days," Bennett says. "Not much to do."

"It's cold," Lisa says. "I'll heat some stew." She tightens Toruk's blanket around her shoulders.

Bennett stands, stretches his limbs. "I do have some things to ask you about," he says.

The moon rises with characteristic drama over the eastern mountains. "It's pretty enough," Bennett says after a while. "I can see the appeal."

On the moonlit hillside to the north of the village, a line of people appears, making its way down the path. Lisa and Bennett wait for the group to approach. Snow falls thickly, coating rocks, everything.

The travelers are led by a woman with long gray hair and a thin neck. She leans hard on her walking stick, though her pace is steady. The children behind her seem as if they would break into a run if not for a duty to support teetering grandparents. A small group of women follows, carrying babies and toddlers in cloth slings. An ancient man lying in a litter is transported via the muscled shoulders of four very young men. At the rear of the line, attractive teenagers lead pack animals by their halters. Theatrically illuminated by an accommodating moon, the faces in the procession reveal fatigue and communion and anticipation of home.

"Wow," Bennett says. The spectacle passes them by. To the south, Lisa sees villagers wrapped in blankets and waiting in their doorways, each cupping with ritualistic tenderness a steaming bowl of tea. Light from cooking fires behind them creates a series of soft yellow squares on the ground.

From the little hill selected by Bennett for its convenient view of village activity, Lisa witnesses the homecomings. Bennett remains heavily quiet.

The boys carrying the old man stop at Toruk's hut and bring him inside. At Heenara's door, one of the women with an infant sling removes the baby from its pouch and hands it, squalling, to her. Their heads are thrown back in laughter. Together they drink from her bowl of tea. At each hut, women and men and children reassemble themselves into clusters. One at a time the doors close, until every yellow square is extinguished.

Bennett sets his arm across Lisa's shoulders and guides her down the path to her hut. In the warm interior he ladles her stew into bowls. She answers a question, and then he asks another. Through the walls of grass and mud comes the muted gurgle of families in conversation.

Rose Tremain

A Game of Cards

LET ME tell you the story of my friend Anton Zwiebel.

You will soon realize that any story about Anton Zwiebel is also a story about me, Gustav Perle. In fact, I can't imagine how I could set down any account of Anton Zwiebel's life that didn't include me. I am at the heart of Anton Zwiebel's life and he is at the heart of mine.

We were both born in 1942, during the Second World War, but we were born in Switzerland, where the war didn't trespass. A little later, in 1947, when we attended kindergarten in Zorin, the village where we lived, we began learning about the war and how, beyond our country, there was this other, destroyed world, which the teachers found it difficult to talk about. We were shown pictures of ruined cities. I recall that in one of these pictures a white dog was sitting all alone among the rubble, and the sight of this abandoned dog made me feel lonely, as though I, and not the dog, were the creature sitting there.

Did you know that the word *Zwiebl* means *onion*? *Herr Zwiebel* translates as "Mr. Onion." In the kindergarten days, the other kids used to laugh at Anton because he had this name, Zwiebel, but I didn't laugh; I felt sympathetic toward him. I think my mother had already taught me to show compassion toward others, because she was such a kind and understanding woman. When I first invited Anton Zwiebel home for coffee and Mutti's cinnamon cake, my mother took his hand in hers and led him out into the yard, where our flowering cherry tree was so weighed down with white blossoms that its lower branches almost touched the stones beneath. Anton Zwiebel began stamping up and down, up and down, up and down in a little, crazy dance of wonderment. Later, after we'd had the coffee and the cinnamon cake, my mother said: "I like this boy, Gustav. I hope he will be your friend."

I have to move forward now. I know it can be annoying, in stories, to be suddenly told that twenty years have passed. You can't stop yourself from wondering what happened in all that time the author has chosen not to talk about. But let me reassure you that nothing out of the ordinary happened to Anton Zwiebel and me. We went through school. We played table tennis. We learned to skate. No tragedy came our way. I entered catering school and then acquired a job as the assistant manager of a *Gasthaus* in the spa town of Matzlingen. Anton became a piano teacher at a small school, also in Matzlingen. We continued to see each other almost every day.

At the age of twenty-seven, after I'd been promoted to manager of the Gasthaus, my modest aspirations were roughly as follows: first of all, I wanted to stay put in Switzerland, not too far from my mother's village. I had a peculiar fear of traveling outside my country, as though what I might find beyond its borders were places only partially rebuilt, where I would become lost. I enjoyed my work. The role of host, who makes everything clean and warm and convivial for those who are forced to spend their lives traveling about, appealed to my conservative nature. I expected that one day I would own my own hotel.

As to Anton, I think I can describe with reasonable confidence what he felt when we were young men. He, too, was very fond of his country. His nature was more passionate than mine, but this intense, susceptible side of his personality found all the outlet it needed in his piano playing. He was extremely diligent about his practice and would get up every morning at six to play Bach for one hour. He was also working rigorously through the one hundred studies in Clementi's *Gradus ad Parnassum*, but he told me that he had no ambition to be a concert pianist. He knew he was gifted, but not exceptional. And he often joked that a concert pianist called "Anton Onion" was an impossibility.

It was around this time, in our late twenties, that a retired English colonel, Colonel Ashley-Norton, came to stay at the Gasthaus. He was in Matzlingen to take the spa waters and he was doing this on what he called "the cheap," as he found that his army pension didn't go as far as he'd hoped. He spoke good German, which he said he had learned in the war. "However, Herr Perle," he said to me, "let's not talk about the war. Do you by any chance know the English card game of gin rummy?"

It transpired that this game, which is ideal for two players and in which scores are slowly built up and laid down on the table for all to see, was the consolation of Colonel Ashley-Norton's old age. He was addicted to it. He and his late wife used to play it for hours at a time, but now his wife was no longer there, and this was the thing about her death that caused him the greatest pain: he no longer had a gin rummy partner.

Despite my managerial duties, I was able to find enough time during the stay of Colonel Ashley-Norton to learn this card game. After Ashley-Norton left, I taught it to Anton and we both agreed that we found it a very agreeable pastime. There is a little skill attached to it—deciding when to hoard cards in your hand, for instance, or when to risk throwing something away in order to gain fruitful access to the discard pile at a later moment—but it's not an exacting game like bridge, where you're benighted by the need for perpetual vigilance. It's a game that, if you are both equally good and bad at it, strengthens a friendship. And I think Anton and I knew that, in addition to table tennis and skating, we'd discovered a leisure activity that could last a lifetime.

You will be wondering by now what was happening to us in what my mother called "the department of love."

Although we had reached the 1960s and sometimes listened to the songs of Serge Gainsbourg, the wilder notions of that decade concerning "free love" and "flower power" did not seem to have quite reached Switzerland. We still behaved with a certain reserve toward girls. And I know that I speak for Anton, too, when I say that we found them confusing creatures. They seemed to be full of longing. But we felt that it was impossible to fathom what these longings were, or how they might be satisfied. The notion that we should marry two girls and then become responsible for making them happy filled us with dread. We liked to go skating with them sometimes. I certainly enjoyed watching them dancing and swooping round the Matzlingen ice rink, wearing tiny little skirts and fur hats, and afterward drinking a glass of mulled wine with them by the side of the rink. Once or twice, inspired by their grace on the ice, I tried kissing one of the girls, but I have to say that this always disgusted me. Their tongues were wet, frenzied, and searching. It was as though some newly hatched blind eel had slithered its way inside my mouth. I can vividly remember lying in my bed at the Gasthaus and thinking about the way marriage would entail repeated encounters with this newborn eel and feeling cold and sick. I knew, also, that if I married, I would no longer be able to live at the Gasthaus in my comfortable room with its Biedermeier furniture and its red-and-white check curtains. And this upset me too. In short, I began to feel that marriage, for me, was a wretched idea.

I discussed my anxieties with Anton during the gin rummy games. He admitted to me that he quite liked the feeling of the eel in his mouth and that he'd even gone to bed with a girl named Gisela, which he'd also enjoyed. "But," he said, "marriage is out of the question for me too. I need to live alone to play my music. The idea of someone listening to me while I'm practicing is intolerable."

I now have to move the story forward again, to the time when the event of greatest significance occurred in our lives.

For most people, I've noticed, the momentous crises tend to happen before the age of about forty-five. And if this had been the case for us, then everything might have turned out differently. But the years of our thirties, forties, and fifties went slowly by without disturbance. I was able to purchase a modest two-star hotel in Matzlingen, which I redecorated and renamed the Hotel Perle, and in which I lived very comfortably in an apartment on the top floor, with a distant view of open countryside. Anton remained in his job at the school. His name was mentioned once in our local newspaper, the *Matzlinger Zeitung*, when a former pupil of his, Mathias Zimmerli, won an international piano competition and in his acceptance speech personally thanked "Herr Anton Zwiebel, for being the most inspirational teacher any piano student could wish for."

It is true that, after the "Zimmerli incident," as I refer to it in my mind, Anton went through a period of what I would have to term wistfulness. During our games of gin rummy, for instance, I would suddenly catch him staring out of the window, instead of down at his cards. He developed the habit of sighing for no reason. He returned to the vexed question of his name, saying that it was lucky for Zimmerli he wasn't called "Onion." He said that the trouble with being sixty was that now one was able to predict how everything would end.

What neither of us anticipated was the arrival in Matzlingen of Hans Hirsch.

Hans Hirsch was the uncle of one of Anton's students and he came in the winter of 2003 to the annual Christmas Eve concert at the school, at which performances by the pupils were traditionally followed by the playing of two or three short pieces—usually by Chopin—by Anton himself.

You will have worked out that by 2003, Anton and I were sixty-one years old.

I can remember that it was a particularly cold and icy Christmas and I was unable to attend the concert because of problems with the central heating boiler at the Hotel Perle. I spent the evening making sure that the emergency plumber I'd had to call out stayed until the heating system was fixed and reassuring those few residents who had booked in for Christmas that the rooms would be warm again in a few hours.

It was not until after Christmas that I learned what had happened to Anton.

He came round to my apartment with a bottle of champagne and told me that Hans Hirsch owned a small record company called CavalliSound. Hirsch had approached Anton after the concert and told him that he had never heard Chopin waltzes played "with such sweet, underlying melancholy." On the spot, he invited Anton to go to Zurich and record a selection of waltzes for release on the CavalliSound label.

We drank the champagne. I noted that Anton's face was flushed and that he couldn't stay still, but paced about my living room with agitated steps. "Imagine, Gustav," he burst out, "imagine if, after all this time, I can have some proper recognition!"

I tried as hard as I could to feel happy for my friend. I knew that he deserved more than just being mentioned in passing in the *Matzlinger Zeitung*. But I now have to admit to you that what I felt about this turn of events was terror. The prospect of Anton's departure, the appalling idea that he would become famous, made me feel so utterly cast down that I found it impossible to move from my armchair. In this godforsaken hour, my own life as a hotelier—from which it was far too late to escape—

suddenly appeared to me as irredeemably mundane, shallow, and pointless. The champagne felt bitter in my stomach. I was impatient for Anton to leave so that I could give way to my feelings in the privacy of my rooms.

Anton went away to Zurich to make his Chopin recordings in the late spring, when the cherry trees were in flower.

During his absence, my mother fell ill. I dragged myself from the hotel to the hospital and back again, sunk in a misery so deep I wished it had been I and not my beloved Mutti who was dying. It was as though the world around me, so quietly agreeable to me for so long, had turned to rubble.

I saw, too, that the Hotel Perle, where the clientele had fallen off in recent times, was in desperate need of refurbishment. The bathrooms were dingy and outmoded. Some rooms *had* no bathrooms. The dining-room carpet was stained and worn, and the noxious smell of gravy had seeped into the walls. I stared at all this and knew that taking it in hand, finding the money and the will to hire builders and decorators, was beyond me.

When Anton returned, full of tales about the recording studios of CavalliSound, full of hope that he might soon be invited to play recitals in Geneva or even Paris, he was disappointed by my melancholy mood.

"I'm sorry, Anton," I said, "but worry about Mutti seems to have made me wretched. Please forgive me."

CavalliSound released Anton's recording of the Chopin waltzes the same week in which my mother died. I tried to think only about giving Mutti a good funeral and nothing else. The dazzling recital tours that might soon take Anton away from me forever I tried to banish from my mind.

Then, a few weeks later, I picked up the *Matzlinger Zeitung* one morning and read a headline that ran: "Disappointment Looms for Zimmerli Mentor." The article reported that national criticism of Anton Zwiebel's Chopin recordings had been universally unfavorable. "Across the board," said the *Zeitung*'s arts reporter, "music critics have attacked Zwiebel's 'muddy sound' and questioned the policy of the CavalliSound supremo, Hans Hirsch, of 'discovering' unknowns such as local man Zwiebel. Although it was anticipated that recital venues would be interested in Zwiebel, once the tutor of the celebrated Mathias Zimmerli, it now looks as though this is unlikely to happen."

I was eating my breakfast. I laid everything aside and telephoned Anton and invited him to supper. I didn't mention the article I'd just seen. I said: "We haven't played gin rummy for a while, but we can take up where we left off. What do you say, Anton? I'm pretty sure it was you who won the last round."

In the years that have followed, we've never really talked about what happened at that time, so it's difficult for me to judge what Anton feels about it, deep down. He did say once: "Perhaps if I'd had your name—Perle—it might have happened for me, but who knows?" But he also told me that no matter what, he would carry on playing Bach for an hour every morning.

He's retired from the school now. And I'm contemplating selling the hotel. It's really become too much for me. When we last talked about our future, Anton and I decided that we would rather like to return to Zorin and live quietly together in the old house I've inherited from Mutti, with, perhaps, a white dog for company.

Alexi Zentner

Touch

THE MEN floated the logs early, in September, a chain of headless trees jamming the river as far as I and the other children could see. My father, the foreman, stood at the top of the chute, hollering at the men and shaking his mangled hand, urging them on. "That's money in the water, boys," he yelled, "push on, push on." I was ten that summer, and I remember him as a giant, though my mother tells me that he was not so tall that he had to duck his head to cross the threshold of our house, the small foreman's cottage with the covered porch that stood behind the mill.

He had run the water when he was younger, poling logs out of eddies and currents and breaking jams for the thirty miles from Sawgamet to Havershand. Once there, the logs went by train without him: either south for railway ties or two thousand miles east to Toronto, and then on freighters to Boston or New York, where the giant trees became beams and braces in strangers' cities. The float took days to reach Havershand, he said. There was little sleep and constant wariness. Watch your feet, boys. The spinning logs can crush you The cold-water deeps beneath the logs always beckoned. Men pitched tents at the center of the jam, where logs were pushed so tightly together that they made solid ground, terra firma, a place to sleep for a few hours, eat hard biscuits, and drink a cup of tea.

Despite his bad hand, my father could still man one end of a long saw. He kept his end humming through the wood as quickly as most men with two hands. But a logger with a useless hand could not pole on the river; when the men floated the trees my father watched from the middle of the jam, where the trees were smashed safely together, staying away from the bobbing, breaking destruction of wood and weight at the edges.

I never knew how my father felt about his mangled hand, and I was afraid to ask. He did not talk about the dangers; the river was swift and final, but it was out in the cuts, among the trees, when each day unfolded like the last—the smooth, worn handles of the saw singing back and forth in an almost domestic motion, like a mother kneading dough—that men's minds wandered. Men I knew had been killed by falling trees, had bled to death when a dull ax bounced off a log and into their leg, been crushed when logs rolled off carts, had drowned in the river during a float. Every year a man came back dead or maimed.

Two years before that float, on my sister Marie's fifth birthday, I had asked my mother about my father's hand.

"I was thankful," she said. We sat on the slope by the log chute, looking out over the river, waving uselessly at the black flies. My father had taken Marie into the woods, the preserve of the men, a present for her birthday.

"You were thankful?"

"It was only his hand," my mother said, and she was right.

That summer morning, Marie had carried her own lunch into the cuts, all bundled together and tied in a handkerchief: two slices of blueberry bread; a few boiled potatoes, early and stunted; a small hunk of roast meat. My father let her carry his ax, still sharp and gleaming though he had not swung it since his accident, and as they walked away from the house, I argued that my father should take me as well, that other boys helped their fathers on Saturdays and during the summers. I was old enough to strip branches, to help work the horses, to earn my keep.

"You've been enough," my mother said, though she knew I had been only twice, on my birthdays. "It's too dangerous out there." She was no doubt thinking of the way the log had rolled onto my father's hand, crushing it so tightly it did not begin to bleed until the men had cut him free. I must have made a face, because she softened. "You'll go again next month, on your birthday."

They returned late that night, the summer sun barely drowned, Marie still bearing the ax and crying quietly, walking with a stiff limp, spots of blood showing on her socks where her blisters had rubbed raw, my father keeping a slow pace beside her. My mother stepped off the porch toward Marie, but my sister moved past her, climbing up the three steps and through the door. My father shook his head.

"She wouldn't let me carry her."

"Or the ax?"

"I tried."

"And?"

He kissed my mother and then shook his head again. "It's a hard day for a child. She'll go again next year, if she wants." My mother nodded and headed inside to see to Marie's blisters, to give her dinner, to offer her a slice of pie.

The next week, Charles Rondeau, bucking a tree, did not hear the yells from the men, and Mr. Rondeau had to carry his son Charles bloodied and dead from the bush. Charles was only a few years older than I was then, and a month later, when I turned eight, my mother gave me a new Sunday suit, hot and itchy, and my father went to the cuts without me.

Despite Charles Rondeau's death, the season I turned eight was a good one, the cold holding back longer than usual. My father kept the men cutting late into October. There had not even been a frost yet when they started sending logs down the chute from the mill into the river.

When the last log was in the water, my father waved to us from the middle of the jam, and Marie and I ran along the banks with the other children for a mile or two, shouting at the men. Three weeks later, my father, like every other man that year, came back from Havershand laughing. They all had their coats off, their long, sharp peaveys resting on their shoulders, and small gifts for their wives and children tucked under their arms. Even the winter that year was easy, and when the river did finally freeze up in December, the latest the ice had ever been, Marie and I had our first new skates. There was still tissue paper in the box. Christmas had come early.

Even though we wanted to be with my father in the cuts during the summers, the winters were better, because at least then we had him to ourselves. School days, he took to the mill, filing blades, checking the books, helping the assistant foreman, Pearl, tend to the horses, but he was home when we were, sitting at the stove at night, listening with us as my mother, a former schoolteacher at the Sawgamet schoolhouse, read from her books. He carved small wooden toys for Marie—a rough horse, a whistle—using his destroyed hand to pin the block of wood to the table. Mostly, though, he told us stories.

I know that out in the cuts he was a different man. He had to be. He kept the men's respect and, in turn, they kept the saw blades humming through green wood. While their axes cut smiles into pines and stripped branches from fallen trees, while they wrapped chains around the logs, my father moved through the woods, yelling, talking, making them laugh, taking the end of a saw when it was needed. He pushed them hard, and when they pushed back, he came home with bruises, an eye swollen shut, scabs on his knuckles. He made them listen.

At home, he was gentle. He told us his stories. They were true stories. He told us how the sawdust grew wings and flew down men's shirts like mosquitoes, how one tree picked itself up and walked away from the sharp teeth of the saw. He told us about splitting open a log to find a fairy kingdom, about clearing an entire forest with one swing of his ax, about the family of trees he had found twisted together, pushing toward the sky, braided in love.

Our favorite story, however, the story that we always asked him to retell, was about the year he finally convinced our mother to marry him. The last time I remember him telling the story was the spring before I turned ten.

"Every man had been thrown but me and Pearl Gasseur," he said.

"Old Pearl?" Marie giggled, thinking of Pearl as I thought of him, riding the middle of the float with his close, gray hair bristling crazily from his scalp, yellowed long underwear peeking from the cuffs of his shirt.

My father had told the story so many times that Marie probably could have recounted it word for word by then, but like me, like our mother, she still laughed and clapped.

"Old Pearl? Old Pearl?" my father roared, his teeth flashing. "Old Pearl wasn't always old," he yelled happily. "Old Pearl could sink any man and would laugh at you while he spun the log out from under your feet."

"And Mrs. Gasseur was happy to tell you about it," my mother said. "She was happy as winter berries watching him dunk the boys." My mother smiled at this. She always smiled.

Logrolling in Sawgamet was a tradition. Every year the entire town came down to the river the day before the float. They carried blankets and baskets full with chicken, roasted onions and potatoes, bread, blueberry pies, strawberry wine. My father—and before him Foreman Martin—would roll out a few barrels of beer, and the men took to the water. They spun logs, a man on either end, turning the wood with their feet, faster and faster, stopping and spinning the other way, until one, or sometimes both, pitched into the cold water to raucous cheers from the banks.

"Pearl won ever since I could remember," my father said. "He'd never been unseated, but I had to win." He slapped the worn pine table with his mangled hand and winked at my mother. "Oh, your mother was a clever one." He stood up from the table and hooked his arm around her waist, pulling her close to him and looking over her shoulder at Marie and me. "She still is."

He kissed her then, and it surprised me to see my mother's cheeks redden. Before she pushed him away, she whispered something into his ear and he reddened as well, pausing a moment to watch her take the plates from the table.

"Papa," Marie said, demanding more.

"Oh, but you know all this already. She married me," he said, turning back to us and waving his hand, "and here you are."

"Papa," Marie said again, shaking her finger at him like our schoolmarm.

"Tell it right," I said.

He smiled and leaned over the top of his chair. "She wouldn't marry me."

"But Mama," Marie asked, "why didn't you love Papa?"

My father stopped and looked at my mother. This was not part of the story. "Why didn't you love me?" he said.

"You asked every girl in Sawgamet to marry you," my mother answered.

"But I only asked them once," he said, turning back to Marie. "Your mother, I asked every day. All of the men had asked her to marry them, even some of the ones who were already married, but I kept asking. Every day for three years I called on her at the boardinghouse, and every day I asked her to marry me."

"And she always said no." Marie reached out and cupped the withered fingers of my father's bad hand in her two hands. He sat down next to her. "Mama," she asked again, "why didn't you love Papa?"

"I always loved him, sweetheart," she said, pouring hot water from the stove into the dish tub. She leaned in toward the steam, letting it wash across her face. "I just didn't know it yet."

"So I kept asking her to marry me, until one day, she didn't say no."

"What did she say?" Marie could not stop herself.

"She said the day she'd marry me was the day I got Pearl into the water."

"I thought it was a safe bet," my mother said. "Your father never could seem to stay dry."

My father was leaning back in his chair now, staring at the moon through the window. He had taken his hand back from Marie, and he rubbed the fingers of his good hand across the back of the bad, as if it ached.

I wanted to hear about his triumph, how that was the year the log spun so fast he could not see his feet, and how it was not until he heard a splash, and a roar from the banks of the river, that he knew he had finally dunked Pearl Gasseur. I wanted to hear him describe the feel of the cold water when he dove from the log and swam to the bank, the river dripping from his clothes as he walked to my mother. I wanted to see the wink he gave us when he said that our priest, Father Hugo, was asleep with drink at the barrels of beer. I wanted to hear how Father Earl, who had arrived from Ottawa only the day before and who was Anglican and younger than my father, performed the wedding right then and there on the bank of the Sawgamet. But before he could tell us that, before he could tell us how he had to leave the next morning for the float, and how he ran home all the way from Havershand, running to his wife, instead I asked him, "Do you miss it? Do you miss the float?"

He looked at me for a moment, as if he had not heard my question, and then my mother spoke. "You and Marie wash up now, get ready for bed."

As I rose from the table, he stopped me. He raised his ruined hand, the fingers curled like a claw. "I miss it," he said.

He did not tell many stories for the next few weeks, and then when the snow finally melted enough for the men to take out their saws and axes and get into the woods, my father pushed them terribly, as if he knew how bad the coming winter would be. He kept them working from dawn to dusk with not a day's break until the first of September, when the trees were stacked and lined beside the mill.

The logs had to run the river of course for the money to come in, and the winter that Foreman Martin had misjudged the weather and waited too long, the river froze with the logs still in it. That had been a hard winter, with money tight and credit long. When cutting started again in the spring, snow still on the ground, my father crushed his hand the first week, and then later that month Foreman Martin died when the errant swing of an ax caught him across the back of the head. The company gave my father the foreman's job.

The year I was ten, ice clung to the banks of the river on the morning of the float, and the men glanced appreciatively at my father, knowing that the freeze-up would not be far behind. The winter was coming early and fierce, troubling even for the few men who remembered the original rush and the year Sawgamet had turned hard and lean; the boomtown had gone bust and rumors of desperate men eating their mules to stay alive through the snowed-in winter had been overshadowed by whispers of their eating more pernicious meat than what came from the mules.

My father pushed the men to send the logs down the chute, screaming at them, adding his weight to the poles when needed, and by supper Father Hugo and Father Earl had both blessed the float; the men were gone, the logs gone with them.

The men came back from Havershand in the snow, cold but laughing, flush and ready for a winter of trapping and hunting, a chance to file saw blades and sell a few furs. But by the end of October, the cold ate at us, wind pulling tears from our eyes, solid on our cheeks in moments. Men stacked firewood three rows deep outside their houses, the thump of axes a constant sound. Mothers kept their stoves burning all day, the dishwater they threw out the door freezing as it hit the ground.

The river froze inward, flat and even near the banks at first, but by November even the fast-moving water at the center of the river, the dangerous meeting of the Sawgamet and Bear rivers, had iced over. Daylight fading, we skated on the river after school while shoreline bonfires raged, giving us a place to warm our hands. Girls played Crack the Whip while the men and boys played hockey on the broad run of ice swept clear of snow.

Sundays, before dinner, we usually went down to the river. That Sunday, however, my mother stayed in the house to finish her baking, so only my father came down with us, carrying his and Marie's skates slung over the hockey stick he rested on his shoulder. With the cold, which had shattered the schoolhouse's thermometer the week before, even my father wore a scarf over his face. My mother had swaddled Marie and me with so many layers that we had trouble with the steps. Still, the cold seeped through our clothes like water, and we were eager to skate and warm ourselves a little.

Down at the river, we sat on the packed snow at the banks, and my father helped Marie with her skates. He tied her laces and sent her off on the river. As he tied his own laces, she skated slowly toward the tip of the channel, pushing away from us with timid steps, like a newborn moose with shivering legs. The sun was already setting, and I could feel the temperature falling away and getting colder, if such a thing was even possible.

I had my head bent down over my skates and was pulling the laces tight, eager to take my stick and join the other boys playing shinny, when my father suddenly jumped from the snow along the bank, one skate still unlaced. He screamed Marie's name, skates chewing the frozen water, flying toward the thin ice at the confluence of the two rivers. There was just a dark hole where Marie had broken through the ice and disappeared.

Other men raced behind my father, but he was the first to the open water, screaming her name. For a moment, he stopped at the edge of the fissure. Suddenly, we saw her—we all saw her—gasping, bobbing, taking a last breath at the surface of the table-sized breach in the ice, too cold or too scared to even scream, and as I reached the water, I saw my sister's eyes lock on to my father.

He dove into the water.

And then they were gone.

I hesitated at the edge, staring at the water, surprised at how smooth it was. Pearl grabbed my shoulder roughly. "No," he said, holding me back, and I realized that I had not even thought of following my father in.

The black water in the hole that Marie's fall had opened up started icing even as Pearl held my arm. The men yelled for rope, but then, not willing to wait, they linked arms, Pearl the first one into the breach. I could see the shock on his face at the first touch of the water. It was a minute at most before the men hauled him back from the water, the skin on his hands gone white from the cold. He could not stand when they pulled him out, his legs shaking uselessly beneath him.

The sun seemed to have fallen from the sky, pulling the temperature down with it. In the dark, I could barely see the hole in the ice freezing back over, like a mouth that had briefly yawned open and was now closing again. Even though it was too late, another man, and then another, went into the river, reaching beneath the water to feel for my father and Marie. As the last man was dragged from the water, the ice almost sealed shut around his legs, as if the river wanted one more.

Father Earl was the one who brought my mother down to the river, and she found me sitting around the bonfire on the bank, near the men with the blue chattering lips. Boiling sap in a burning pin log popped, sending up a shower of sparks; a few embers floated out over the river before dying in the night.

Later, there were the other wives and mothers, quiet murmurs, Pearl sitting beside me, changed into dry clothes but crying, and then, finally, my mother and I turning home.

What little warmth there had been in October and November dropped completely away from us, and even with a constant fire in the stove, my mother and I took to wearing our overcoats in the house, hats and mittens to bed. Though there were no bodies, there was a funeral, and afterward my mother spoke little to the women who brought plates of food, little to Mrs. Gasseur, to Pearl, little to Father Hugo or to Father Earl, who visited us even though we were not in his flock. She did not speak to me, even when I lifted my father's ax from the wooden pegs over the stone lintel of the doorway and took it out behind the house. I split wood every morning, and the sound of the ax on the wood seemed to linger, floating through our house long after I had returned from school. Every evening I sharpened the blade, the rasp of the stone on metal making my mother shiver.

The winter punished us into December. Snow fell hard, our roof creaking until angry winds beat the white dust onto the ground. The same winds cleared a great swath of snow from the Sawgamet, until finally, between Christmas and New Year's, the sun came out and the men and children, bundled against the cold, took their skates down to the river again. Except for the whip of the wind and the crackling of wood in the stove, our house was quiet.

The knock on the door sounded like a shot.

Pearl led us to the river, helping my mother down the snow-crusted steps cut into the hill next to the log chute, holding her arm as we walked across the ice to the small circle of men. The ice was smooth and clean after a month of scouring from the wind.

The hands were not touching. Even through the plate of frozen water covering them, we saw clearly that little more than the width of an ax blade separated my father's two hands from my sister's one. His mangled fingers on one hand, the smooth, alabaster fingers on the other hand, all stretched toward Marie's small hand. The ice, like glass above their hands, thickened as we tried to look farther out, to see the rest of their bodies and their faces. The lines blurred, only shadows, dark shapes.

There was talk of axes, of chopping at the ice, but my mother forbade it, as if they had suggested pulling my father and Marie from their graves, and then the men left, gliding away from us on their skates. Pearl touched me on the back and headed toward the bank, leaving my mother and me over the ghosts of our family. As the sun dropped below the peak of the hill, we turned from the ice and trudged back up the stairs, holding the side of the log chute for balance.

The next morning, when I woke, my mother sat in her chair by the stove, rocking slowly, staring at the fingers of flame that showed through the gaps in the metal. I dressed slowly for church, waiting for her to pin back her hair, to put on her gray Sunday dress. But she stayed in the chair.

After a little while she looked up at me. "Go on, then."

I thought about taking communion, the wafer melting in my mouth like a chip of ice, the wine, diluted by Father Hugo, more water than blood. Then, instead of going to the church, I walked down to the river, the ice and snow screeching under my boots. In the sun, the winter felt like it had flown away, and I sweated during the short walk.

I kneeled down above them, waiting to see them move. I put my hand on the ice above my father's fingers. I wondered if Marie had known how close my father's hands had been to hers. I waited for something to happen, for my father to reach out and bridge the gap separating him from Marie, but neither of them moved. Finally, as I heard the first yells of the other children rushing down to the river after church, I rose and returned to the house.

My mother had not moved from her chair by the stove. She kept shivering, even with the blankets wrapped around her, even with the surprising heat of the day, so I fed more logs into the fire. And then, as the screams and laughter drifted up from the river, the slaps of sticks on ice, my mother startled with every sound. My skates hung from their laces on a rusty nail half-driven into the corner post of the mill, and I thought of taking them down to the river, of skating over my father and Marie, of carving the ice above them, but I did not want my mother to ask me where I was going.

I woke in the middle of the night, thinking I heard Marie calling me. Out the window, something looked wrong, as if the entire world were underwater with my father and Marie, and I realized that thin sheets of rain were falling from the sky, icing the trees, turning all of Sawgamet into a frozen river. I went to check the fire in the stove, remembering my mother's shivering, and I saw that the ax no longer hung above the door.

The steps beside the log chute were slick, and the mist was star-bright, neither water nor ice—diamonds falling from the sky. When I reached the river, my mother was swinging the ax. The ice shone below her, as if the river had swallowed the moon, and the sound of the ax striking the ice was ringing and clear, like metal on metal.

I walked closer to my mother and almost expected the river to shatter under the sharp, oiled blade, the ice to cleave beneath our feet. The river would take us and freeze us alongside my father and Marie. Or my father would step from the open ice himself, pulling Marie behind him, holding her hand, the four of us walking to the house, where we could sit in front of the fire and he could tell us stories about fish made of ice.

My mother kept swinging the ax, and between the pings of the blade skittering off the surface of the ice, I heard her crying. She stopped when she saw me and fell to her knees, shaking. I knelt beside her. The ice was still smooth and clean, as if she had never been here with the ax, and when I put my hand flat on the ice it was warm against my palm, like bread cooling from the oven. Then the light beneath the river disappeared, leaving us on the ice, the film of rain covering us.

In the house, my mother covered me with my blanket and kissed me on my forehead. "I'm sorry," she said, so quietly that I was unsure whether she had really spoken or I had only imagined it.

I lay in bed and fell asleep listening to her sharpen the ax, the rhythmic grind of metal on stone.

The next morning, when Mrs. Gasseur, who was, as usual, the first to morning prayers, found Father Hugo frozen on the bench outside the church, she did not realize right away that he was dead.

"I asked him if he had been well during his morning walk," she said, "since I had such a terrible time with the frozen rain, and when he didn't answer, I touched his hand."

I did not see Father Hugo, but Pearl told me later that the old man looked alive under the clear coating of ice, still holding the communion cup full of the blood of Christ. The men had to build a small fire in front of the church, waiting until the ice melted to pull him from the bench. Pearl said he thought Father Hugo might have passed before he was frozen, but with the wine he could not tell.

They tried to dig a grave, but even with pickaxes the ground was too hard. Father Earl said prayers over the body, and then Father Hugo spent the rest of the winter in the woodshed behind the church, wrapped in layers of oilcloth.

At nights, when the cold left the sky so clear that the stars were within easy reach, sap froze in the trees, breaking them open like the sound of river ice cracking. Many of the days, the men could not trap or even chop wood, the wind burning their skin, hands too cold to hold ax handles. During that winter, Father Earl visited my mother and me frequently and stayed for dinner many nights. He was a small man. He looked like I did when I wore one of my father's coats, and I could not picture him taking down a tree. My mother said he had not seemed so small before his wife and unborn child died, during the winter before I was born.

One night, when I should have been sleeping, I heard him ask my mother what she would do in the spring, when the company took the house back, when they gave the foreman's cottage to Pearl and Mrs. Gasseur.

"I can go back to teaching," my mother said, though we all knew that Sawgamet did not need another teacher.

"I have a house," Father Earl said, but then his voice trailed off. He tried again: "I know it's only been a few months, but if you're willing."

I could not hear my mother's response, but a few minutes later I felt the cold draft of the door and heard the latch drawing shut. And when he visited us later that week, they talked of the weather, of books and plays, of gossip about Father Hugo's replacement, as if Father Earl had never offered marriage.

Sometimes I saw him walking on the river, his hands in his pockets, and once, I saw him walk to the clear circle of ice above my father and Marie, stopping to kneel, putting one hand flat on the ice the same way I had the night of the freezing rain.

The cold finally left in May, the trickle of water underneath the snow becoming a constant stream, the sound of running water a relentless reminder in our house of the coming breakup. The river groaned, and the sound of shifting ice replaced the clattering of skates and sticks.

The morning the river opened, I pulled the ax down from above the doorway.

My mother looked up from her sewing, pulling the needle and thread through the cloth of my father's pants, mending the rips that she had not had time to attend to while he was alive, setting each pair aside for me as if I would wear them when I was older. "Where do you think you're going?"

"To the cuts." I waited for her to speak, but she stayed quiet. "We need the money."

She kept sewing, not looking at me. I wanted to go. I had to go. Pearl and Mrs. Gasseur had not said anything, but this was the company house. This was their house now.

"You're not going," she said finally.

I ran my thumb across the blade of the ax and then turned my hand over and scraped a white shaving from my thumbnail. "You can't stop me."

She stood up and walked to me, and without a word, she slapped me. Then, carefully, she took the ax and placed it above the door again.

I turned and walked out the door.

At the cuts, Pearl looked at me for a moment and then handed me his ax. I bucked trees and stripped branches, the ache in my arms familiar from a winter of chopping firewood. At lunch, Pearl gave me a few biscuits and shared some water.

The next morning, my mother told me to wash and put on my Sunday suit, and after the wedding, instead of going into the cuts, I helped my mother and Father Earl—my new stepfather—carry our belongings to his tidy house.

The furniture belonged to the company, so there was only our clothing and my mother's books, pots and pans, drawings, the toys my father had carved, my skates and stick. My mother left my father's mended clothes. For Pearl, she said, though I knew that Mrs. Gasseur would not keep the clothes of a dead man. After three trips, when all that was left were some jars of summer berries in syrup and a few bundles of clothes, Father Earl reached over the door to take down my father's ax.

"No." He stopped at the sound of my voice, his hand almost touching the handle. He moved aside as I stepped past him. The ax felt heavier than it had the day before. When I pulled it down, the blade struck against the lintel stone, the sound ringing and clear, like the sound of my mother chopping at the ice.

But the last sound I heard in the house was my mother's voice. "No more to the cuts," she said.

A few summers later—after Pearl and Mrs. Gasseur died in the fire that burnt down the mill and the company house—the railway linked into Sawgamet, and I knew that I would never get a chance to join a float like my father had. I spent many of the days that summer by myself, down by the river, fishing and picking wild blueberries.

Near the end of the summer I walked down the banks for an hour or two, toward Havershand, to no end in particular, just getting distance from Sawgamet. The rocks had stopped holding their heat past the setting of the sun, and I knew it was almost time to return to school. It was my last year before I would go to the seminary in Edmonton, the same seminary where my stepfather had studied.

At lunch that day, I stopped and ate my sandwich while sitting on a small rock, my feet splayed in the cold shallows of the river. I finished, and then leaned down and pulled a flat oval stone from the water, and threw it out into the whitewater. The stone disappeared without a trace, and when I reached down again for another rock to throw I saw the skate.

Even with the blade rusted through, the black leather eaten in places, it was clearly a child's skate. I turned it over in my hands, water dripping onto my legs. There were no markings on the skate, and I held it awhile, looking out into the water.

I wondered if their hands had met, if the breaking ice, the tumultuous destruction of winter, had pushed Marie and my father together, or if it had torn them apart. I wanted to believe that my father had taken hold of Marie's hand, that as the water roared down the Sawgamet, his hands, both of them made whole again, held her hand tightly against the current.

I put the skate back into the water and started home, thinking of my father as a young man, walking back from Havershand after the float, walking to Sawgamet.

Edward P. Jones

Bad Neighbors

EVEN BEFORE the fracas with Terence Stagg, people along both sides of the 1400 block of Eighth Street NW could see the Benningtons for what they really were. First, the family moved in not on a Saturday or on a weekday but on a Sunday, which was still the Lord's Day, even though church for many was now a place to visit only for a wedding or a funeral. Perhaps Easter or Christmas. And those watching that Sunday, from behind discreetly parted brocade curtains and from porches rarely used except to enter and leave homes, had to wonder why the Bennington family had even bothered to bring most of their furniture. They had a collection of junk that included a stained queen-size mattress, a dining-room table with three legs, a mirror with a large piece missing from one corner, and a refrigerator dented on two sides. One neighbor joked to his wife that the Bennington refrigerator probably wouldn't work without a big block of ice in it. During the move, the half-dressed little Benningtons occupied themselves by running to and from the two small moving trucks, carrying in clothes that had busted out of cardboard boxes during the trip from whatever countrified shack they had left behind. Over the next two weeks, it became clear that the house at 1406 Eighth, with its three bedrooms, would be home to at least twelve people, though that number was fluid. The neighbors could never get a proper accounting, and they would never know who was related to whom.

They came in the middle of October, the Benningtons, bringing children—a bunch of perhaps five, from a two-year-old to a girl on the verge of being a teenager. Children who sometimes played outside on Friday and Saturday nights until nearly nine thirty. And they were loud children, loud in a neighborhood where most of the kids were now in their teens and did no more harm than turn their portable radios up too high as they washed their parents' cars. Then, there was Neil, a tenth grader, and Amanda, a girl of no more than eighteen, who seemed to live night and day in tight blue jeans. She would be wearing them in her yard one early afternoon months later when Bill Forsythe, next door at 1408, stood at his bedroom window looking down at her with his second drink in his hand.

And the Benningtons came with a few young men, who sat on the porch on a legless couch covered with a cheap bedspread, drinking from containers in paper bags. But over the first two months that the Benningtons lived on Eighth Street most of those men, none more than forty years old, simply disappeared, until, by mid-December, the only one the neighbors still saw was Derek. He was a well-built and often shirtless loudmouth in his early twenties, who seemed to go off, maybe to some job, whenever he could get his nineteen-year-old Ford to run; it was the kind of car most of the established men on Eighth Street had owned on their way up to where they were now.

Grace Bennington appeared to be the matriarch; she might have been fifty, but, with her broad weight and her gray hair, it was difficult for anyone to be certain. On a good day, her Eighth Street neighbors might have said forty or forty-five, but on a bad day seventy-five would not have seemed unfair. Only one thing was certain—she had known hard work, and it showed in face and body. She moved about on stubby legs, favoring the outer sides of her feet as she walked, so that all her shoes were run down on those edges. There was also a man who looked far older than Grace, tallish, whom the neighbors sometimes saw. He always came walking up—never down—Eighth Street with bags of groceries, and he was always in the uniform of a train's sleeping-car porter. Finally, there was a woman who was rarely seen, and, when she was, the older children would be holding her hands as they took her for a walk. She wore coats and sweaters even on the warmest days, and that fall and winter saw many good days. She might have been beautiful, but no one could tell, because she was also always wearing sunglasses and a scarf pulled around to cover most of her face.

In early November, after the Benningtons had been in the neighborhood a tad more than two weeks, Sharon Palmer noticed Neil Bennington, the tenth grader, peering into his locker, in the second-floor hall at Cardozo High School. She knew very little about the family beyond what her parents and the rest of the Eighth Street neighbors were saying, and nothing they said was at all positive. Sharon lived at 1409, across from the Benningtons. A senior, she had, in the eleventh grade, become aware of her effect on boys—almost all of them. (Terence Stagg, next door at 1407, for whom she had long had eyes and heart, was a month or so from paying her any attention.) And Sharon, coming rather late to this awareness of her womanhood, had begun to take some delight in seeing boys wither as they stood close enough to her to smell the mystery that had nothing to do with perfume and look into the twinkling brown eyes she had inherited from a grandmother who had seen only the morning, afternoon, and evening of a cotton field.

When Sharon said hello Neil rose slowly, as though he knew all too well the accidents that came with quick movements. He seemed more befuddled by than taken with her femaleness after she told him who she was, and his innocence made her wish that just this once she could turn down the mystery that transformed boys into fools. He squinted and blinked, and with each blink he appeared to get closer to knowing who she was. As the brief conversation went on, it occurred to her that he was very much like one of her younger brothers—Neil and the brother forever had the look of true believers who had to start every sad morning by learning all over again that the Easter Bunny and Santa Claus did not exist.

That day, she saw Neil walking alone down Eleventh Street after school and she separated from her friends to go with him the rest of the way home. She thought Neil, like her brother, was adorable, a word she had just started using. Her father, Hamilton Palmer, saw them turn the corner from P and thought nothing of it. As the morning and afternoon supervisor at the main post office, on North Capitol Street, he was home most days by three thirty. He was watering plants on his porch, and as Neil said good-bye to his daughter Hamilton opened the little gate on the porch that had been installed ages ago, when his children were too small to know all the ways the world beyond the gate could hurt them.

It was three weeks later that Hamilton Palmer began to think something might be amiss. Thanksgiving had come and gone, and people all over Washington were complaining that it just didn't feel like Christmas weather. Who could think of Christmas with people still in their fall sweaters and the trees threatening to bud? Neil and Sharon turned the corner again, this time accompanied by three other students, who lived farther down Eighth. Before the four left Sharon in front of her house, Hamilton's daughter touched Neil's shoulder and the boy smiled. It was not the touch so much as the smile that bothered Hamilton. He noticed for the first time that Derek Bennington was watching everything from across the street. He could not tell for certain, but he thought he saw Derek smirking.

Two days later, the Prevosts, at 1404, were robbed, with a television the most expensive thing taken. No one said anything, but the neighbors knew it had to be Derek. The next week, the Thorntons, at 1414, had their car stolen. The car was only a Chevy, five years old, but that was not the point, said Bill Forsythe, at 1408. His wife, Prudence, had complained about what a noisy heap the Thornton car was and that the neighborhood was well rid of it. A man's property is a man's property, Bill said, even if it's one skate with three wheels. After the car was taken, someone called the police and they came and spoke to the Benningtons in their house for some fifteen minutes. No one knew what went down, because the police left without talking to any of the neighbors. Derek walked out onto the porch soon afterward and stood, smoking a cigarette. He was alone for a good while, and then his mother, Grace, came and said something that made him put the cigarette out in the ashtray. She continued talking, and for every second she was speaking he was nodding his head slightly.

In December, more than a month before the fracas between Derek and Terence Stagg, Sharon Palmer returned a book she had borrowed from Neil. It was a Saturday afternoon, and when she went up the steps to the Bennington home, she saw that the screen door was shut but the main door was open. She couldn't see anyone from the threshold and she called "Hello" and "Neil," and then she knocked on the wood frame of the screen door. The radio and the television were playing. She did not want to think it, but she felt that this said something about them, maybe not about Neil but about all the rest of them. She waited about two minutes, and after she again called for Neil she opened the screen and stepped into the house, saying "hello, hello, hello" all the way. The woman in the sunglasses was sitting on the couch, and when Sharon asked for Neil the woman said nothing. There was a small child on either side of her, and they were watching a black-and-white television. Sharon immediately thought about the Prevosts' television, but she did not know if it had been color or black-and-white.

"I knocked, but I got no answer," Sharon said. "Is Neil here? I brought his book back." The woman tilted her head to the side as though to consider what she had heard. "Is he here?" The children were silent and their eyes were big, as though Sharon were a creature they had not seen before. Sharon told the woman again that she was looking for Neil. It would be better, Sharon thought, if I could see her eyes. Finally, the woman turned her face toward the next room. "Thank you," Sharon said.

The dining room was crowded with boxes, the state it must have been in since the day the Benningtons moved in. The dining table's missing leg had been replaced with one that had yet to be painted the color of the rest of the table.

"Hello, Neil? Neil?" She stepped into the kitchen, and she was not prepared for what she saw. It was immaculate, the kind of room her mother would be happy with. The floor was clean, the counters were clean, the stove was clean, the tiny table and its three chairs were clean. "Hello?" She turned and looked about the room with great curiosity. When she turned back, Derek was standing at the open screen door to the back yard, watching her.

"You lost?"

"No, I'm sorry. I knocked but no one answered."

"The May maid swayed away to pray in the day's hay," Derek said, not smiling. "Thas why you got no answer."

"I just came to return Neil's book. Is he here?"

Derek shouted twice for Neil. "Well, you can just leave it on the table, lady from across the street."

"He said that I could borrow another one. A book of Irish stories the library doesn't seem to have."

He shouted for Neil again, and, as she listened to his voice thunder through the house, she noticed a small bookcase beside the refrigerator. Four shelves, each a little more than two feet across. He saw her looking at it. "Just leave the book on the table. That readin fool'll get it."

"I can come back for the next one another time." She set the book on the table.

"Which one was it?" He was wearing an undershirt, and it hung on him in a way that did not threaten as those shirts often did on other men. The bare muscular arms were simply bare muscular arms, not possible weapons. It was a small moment in the kitchen, but Sharon was to think of those arms years later as she stood naked and looked down at the bare arms of her husband while the red light of an expensive German clock shone down on him.

"A book of stories—Mary Lavin's *Tales from Bective Bridge*. My teacher shared two with me and I'm hooked."

"Hooked is good cept with junk, ask any junkie," Derek said, and he looked across at the bookcase. "The almighty reader might have it upstairs or in some box somewhere. His shit is all over the fuckin place." Shit, fuckin, she thought. Shit, fuckin. In a few quiet, swift steps he was at the table. He took up the book and looked at the spine and wrinkled his face. "Hooked, hooked," he said. The same kind of steps took him to the bookcase. He knelt, peered a moment, and put the book between two green books on the second shelf up from the bottom. " 'L' is for Lavin," Derek said, and found the collection. " 'M' is for Mary." He looked at it front and back. "I know one thing for sure: he loves this woman's work, so you bet not lose it. I think the almighty reader is part Irish and don't know it yet." In two more steps he was before her and she took the book and promised to return it just as it was. There was nothing untoward in his face—the lust, the hunger, that was in all the boys except Neil, boys with pimples and boys without. There was no smile from him and he did not look into her eyes, the twinkling and brown. He turned and went to the refrigerator and opened it. "You know," he said, his back to her and the light of the refrigerator pouring out over him, "you shouldn't be afraid of wearin blue." He took out a beer and closed the icebox with great care. "Forget the red. You wear too much red." He did not turn around but found an opener for the beer on the counter beside the icebox.

"What?"

Neil came in, with the same befuddled look he'd had the day Sharon introduced herself to him, and Derek pointed to him. "Where you been, boy?" Derek said. "Your girlfriend been waitin. You the worse fuckin boyfriend in the world."

"She ain't my girlfriend," Neil said, and raised his hand hello to Sharon.

"I gave your girlfriend one of Lavin's books, man."

"I told you she's not my girlfriend, Dee."

"Whatever, man." He drank from the beer as he walked to the back door. "You should tell your girlfriend that red really doesn't suit her. She ain't believin me, so maybe if it comes from her boyfriend." He went out the door, and Neil walked her to the front of the house.

Three neighbors saw Sharon Palmer leave the Bennington house that day—her father, Hamilton, from his upstairs bedroom, Terence Stagg next door to the Palmers, and Prudence Forsythe next to the Benningtons. Terence was standing at his living-room window and watched Sharon walk down the Bennington steps with a book in her hand. Neil Bennington was a wisp of a boy, not worth the notice of a young man like Terence. But Terence had seen Derek about, and like most of the men on Eighth Street he didn't think much of him; men like Derek had never seen the inside of Howard University, where Terence was in his second year, and they never would. As Sharon waited to cross Eighth, she lowered her head in a most engaging way, lowered it only for a second, as if to consider something, and Terence could see how she had filled out. Filled out in her red sweater, and her blue jeans not trampy tight but tight enough to let a man know if he should bother or not. She had filled out since the last time he had really taken a look at her, and that was a time he could not remember.

Terence was at her door that evening, asking a beaming Hamilton Palmer, who had also gone to Howard, how he was doing these warm days and then asking the father if he might talk a bit with his daughter this evening. Terence and Sharon stepped out onto the porch, and he invited her to a movie and a meal on Friday night. She had had two dates before—and one of those had been with a young man who was brother to her cousin's husband. Sharon was not one to keep a diary, but, if she had been, that meeting of a few minutes with Terence would have taken up at least two pages.

Terence called good-bye to Hamilton Palmer, who came out of the kitchen with Sharon's mother. They asked him how his studies were going, and Terence told them they were going very well and that he was hitting his stride. He was, in fact, going with a fellow Howard student, but Howard students who were not D.C. natives were taught from Day One never to venture into Washington neighborhoods except those where they could find a better class of people, meaning white people, for the most part, and so that girl from Newark would never know about Eighth Street. That Newark girl was so clingy, with her "Terence this" and her "Terence that." And, as he had watched Sharon come across Eighth, he had remembered something that his father, Lane, had recently told him: You are young and the world is your oyster. You shuck it, don't let it shuck you. What oyster would Derek ever shuck? Terence thought, as he listened to Hamilton. Well, fine, Hamilton said about Terence hitting his stride, and he came across the living room with his hand extended.

Sharon, ecstatic, did not get to Mary Lavin's *Tales from Bective Bridge* that night as she had planned. She could think of nothing but the evening with Terence. She tried sleeping, but found it was no use and so got up from bed and sat in the dark at her window, which, like the one in her parents' bedroom, faced Eighth Street. She was at the window again two weeks later, near about midnight three days before Christmas, when she saw Neil Bennington, carrying a small package that was bright even in the dark, dash across the street to her house, take the steps two at a time, and then dash back across the street to his place, his hands now apparently empty. By then, she had had a second date with Terence, and he had kissed her three times, once surprising her as he thrust his tongue into her mouth. She mistook what she felt at that moment for blossoming love. It was a rare cold night for that December, and she was tempted not to go downstairs. But she did. She opened the front door to find a small gift-wrapped package on the threshold between that door and the storm door. It had her name on it. With anxious fingers, just inside the living room, she tore open the shiny wrapping and found in a velvet-covered box a figure of brown wood, nearly perfectly carved. It was of a little girl no more than an inch and a half tall, in a dress that came down to her feet. She had on a bonnet. When Sharon held the figure to the light of a lamp, she could tell by the shape of the nose that it was a black girl. One of the girl's arms was extended somewhat, and there was a bracelet on it. That the bracelet was shining told her that it might be gold; that it was from a boy of no means from across the street told her that it might not be.

She was disappointed, because she did not want Neil to think that there could ever be anything between them, and such a thing, with such intricacy, with such compellingly quiet beauty, told her that was what he was thinking. But she did not want to hurt his feelings by returning the gift. Adorable people should not be hurt. She thought for a day and decided to give him a book, and she chose a small paperback edition of Ann Petry's *The Street.* She came up to him as he stood at his locker at school, his head cocked to the side as if he were trying to decide what was needed for the final period of the day. Terence was picking her up after school. Neil seemed genuinely surprised by the gift. "I didn't get you anything," he said, blushing and blinking. "This is straight up embarrassin."

"That doesn't matter," Sharon said. "It's the season for giving. What are neighbors for?"

"I'll get you somethin, I promise," he said, biting his lip.

"You've already done a great deal. Believe me."

"All right," Neil said, moving his hand slowly down the table of contents. "All right, but I won't forget this. Ever."

More than five years later, on her way to becoming a nurse, she would attend a party at the home of one of her Georgetown professors. Her husband would not be able to be with her that night, but that was the way it had become. She would spend a good part of the evening in a corner with a glass of ginger ale. Just as she was about to excuse herself and leave, a white woman of some seventy years came up to her.

"I have been admiring that wondrous thing you're wearing," the white woman said. "Even from across the room, you can see how unique it is." She looked closer. "The carver must have used up all his eyesight making it. You have exquisite taste." The woman smiled, not at Sharon but at the Christmas gift that she had unearthed only recently from a trunk in her parents' basement.

"Someone gave it to me. It isn't much."

"It is much in that other way," the woman said. "I know a place down on F Street that would give you two hundred dollars for it. Please. May I?" And the woman raised a tentative hand, and Sharon nodded, and the woman took up the little girl in the bonnet and rested it between her fingers and then looked fully into Sharon's eyes. "It's not very old, perhaps less than ten years since it was created, but the artistry makes up for that. If the carver lost his sight, he may have thought it was worth it." That evening, for the first time, Sharon would notice the initials carved into one of the folds of the girl's dress. The initials were far from evident, but they were there if the time was taken to look for them. No, she said to herself, alone in the apartment she shared with her husband, I would not sell it. I don't even know if the carver is living anymore.

It was Amanda Bennington who first got into it with Terence Stagg. Late on a Saturday morning in mid-January, she and Derek had come home from the Safeway. They parked in front of the Staggs' house, across the street, while Derek took bags of groceries into their house and Amanda tidied up the car's trunk.

Sharon Palmer was watching from her bedroom window. Nothing had really been said, but it was known by then that she and Terence were a couple and might well have a nice future together. They had driven up in his father's Cadillac one evening the week before, and she saw Neil watching from his porch. She waved and he waved back. She and Neil were not walking home together as much as they had been, but they still shared books. Derek came out as Terence walked Sharon into her house.

Terence, that Saturday morning, was heading out his door when he saw Amanda fussing around in the trunk of Derek's Ford, which was parked in the spot where his father, Lane Stagg, had been parking his Cadillacs since before Terence knew what good things life had in store for him. It might as well be said that Lane Stagg owned that dot of public real estate. Before his family had awakened, Lane had gone out on an errand, purring quietly away in his new tan Cadillac, which had less than three thousand miles on it.

"Hey, you," Terence said to Amanda, and came down the steps to the sidewalk, too upset to take full notice of her behind as she bent over and puttered in the trunk. He was to excel in anatomy and dermatology when he got to Howard's medical school, but genetics and neurology would nearly cost him his future. Amanda straightened up, holding jumper cables, and looked Terence up and down. "Hey! You know you parked in my father's space?" Then, watching Amanda toss the cables back in the trunk and try to clean the dirt from her hands with a Kleenex that she had pulled from her back pocket, he pointed to Derek's car and said again, "Hey, do you know that you are parked in my father's space?" Since his first month at Howard, he had stopped referring to Lane as "my daddy."

"Hay for horses, not for people. Go down Hecht's and get em cheaper," Amanda said. They were the words of a small child, and they upset Terence even more. "It's a free country, man," Amanda said. "We all got a right to park where we wanna park." She pulled another bunched-up Kleenex from the back pocket of her jeans. She was dark and pretty, and in another universe Terence would have been able to appreciate that. "And besides"—she turned and pointed across the street—"somebody's got my brother's regular spot." That Saturday, the Forsythes, at 1408, had company from out of town, and the visitors' Trans Am was where Derek's Ford would have gone, in a spot covered with the oil that was forever leaking from his car. "We had stuff to take and it whatn't no use parkin way down at the corner. Maybe that Trans Am'll move before your daddy gets back."

"I don't care about that," Terence said. "You're just going to have to move that thing somewhere else."

Grace had been trying to teach Amanda to control her temper, but there were days and then there were days. "First off," Amanda said, "I ain't movin shit. Second off, it ain't no thing. It's a classic. Third off, you better get out my damn face. This a free country, man. You ain't no fuckin parkin police." She closed the trunk with both hands to make the loudest sound she could manage.

"I would expect something like this from trash like you," Terence said.

She flicked the Kleenex at him and he dodged it. "Since it's that way, you the biggest trash around here," she said. In another universe, before that moment, Amanda would have liked him to come across the street and knock at her door and invite her to the Broadway on Seventh Street for a movie and a hamburger and soda afterward. She had seen Terence's well-dressed mother, Helen Stagg, quite often, had studied the woman as she came out of her house and looked up and down Eighth Street as if waiting for the world to tell her that it was once again worthy of having her. Amanda loved her own mother, in all her dowdiness, more than any human being, but she knew Grace would never be Helen Stagg. "If I'm trash, you trash."

"Typical," Terence said. "Real damn typical."

"Whas up here?" Derek came across the street, his keys in his hand.

"Derek, this guy say we gotta move the car cause his father got the spot."

"Ain't nobody own no parkin spot, neighbor. This a free country, neighbor," Derek said, the keys jingling at his side.

"I'm not your neighbor."

"Oh, oh, it's like that, huh?" Derek said, turning around twice and raising his arms in faux surrender. "You one a those, huh? All right." Amanda had stayed in the street behind the car, but Derek had continued on up to the sidewalk. "All right, big shot. Les just clear away, cause I don't want no trouble. Nobody want any trouble." He stepped back into the gutter. "All I can say is we got a right to be there, as much right as your daddy and that Cadillac of his with that punk-ass color." He looked at Amanda. "You done?"

"Yeah, I'm cool."

"Well, les go," and they waited to cross as two cars passed going up Eighth Street.

"I told you to move that damn thing," Terence said. His knuckles tapped the top of the trunk. "You people should learn to wash your ears out." He spat on the car.

Derek turned. "Just leave that somebitch alone, Derek," Amanda said. "He ain't worth it."

Grace Bennington came out of her house and yelled at Derek to come on in. Neil stood beside her, holding the hand of a girl of seven or eight. "Wipe that shit off," Derek said of the spit, a slow-moving blob on the black paint heading down toward the fender. The car didn't always run, but he kept it clean.

Derek counted all the way to ten, and Terence said, "Tell your funky mother to wipe it off."

"Even you, even poor you," Derek said calmly, "should know the law against sayin somethin like that. Man oh man oh man . . ."

It took but one hit to the lower part of the jaw to send Terence to the ground. He had seen the fist coming, but, because he had not been in very many fights in his life, it took him far too long to realize the fist was coming for him. Grace and Amanda screamed. The Bryants, at 1401, and the Prevosts, at 1404, came out, as did the Forsythes and their company who had the Trans Am, all of them still digesting their breakfasts. Sharon Palmer had watched with growing concern from her bedroom window. She had not been able to hear all that was said by the three, but, already on the path to love, she had admired the way Terence seemed to be standing up to Derek. By the time she got downstairs and out to the sidewalk, Amanda and Grace were tending to Terence. Seconds later, he awoke and saw the women, and told them to get the fuck away from him. Derek was already back across the street, sitting on the legless couch, watching the group around Terence and smoking a cigarette and waiting for the police to show up.

Lane Stagg was more disturbed about what had happened to his son than he would have been if this had been a fight between young men of equal age and status and Terence had simply lost after doing his best. No doubt, Lane Stagg thought, men like Derek Bennington had never learned to fight fair. Terence, after a quick trip to the hospital, was out of it for a day and a half, but he suffered no permanent damage and would recover to become the first person anyone in the neighborhood knew to become a doctor. "Let them crackers," Lane Stagg said after his second drink at the dinner to celebrate his son's medical-school graduation, "write that up in the immigration brochures about how descendants of slaves aren't any good and so all you hardworking immigrants just come on over."

The police came out that Saturday, but, because they didn't like doing paperwork and because no white person had been hurt, Derek was not arrested. He would not fare as well after the complaint weeks later by the white man from Arlington who owned the Bennington home. The white man and his family had been the last whites to live in the neighborhood. "Come on over to Arlington," his former neighbors kept telling him after they themselves had moved. "Over here, the blacks are all off in their own neighborhood, so you hardly ever see them." The white man and his wife had a son, deep into puberty, and the son was growing ever more partial to blondes, which Eighth Street didn't grow anymore.

After Terence came home from the hospital, Lane, working on his first drink, broached the idea of buying the house that the Benningtons were renting from the white man. He sat in his living room with his wife perched on the arm of his easy chair, and across from him, on the couch, were Hamilton Palmer, Arthur Atwell, and Bill and Prudence Forsythe. Lane Stagg started in on how the neighborhood was changing for the worse. And Hamilton, already seeing the Staggs as future in-laws, agreed. He was not drinking. And neither was Bill Forsythe. Prudence had quietly come upon Bill two weeks earlier looking out their bedroom window at Amanda Bennington collecting toys in her front yard. Prudence had watched him for more than five minutes before going to see what had captured him. Bill had a drink in his hand, and Amanda was wearing those tight blue jeans and it was not even one thirty. "Nice day," Bill said to his wife, already drifting toward happy land and so unable to compose something better. "I'm fucking tired of you getting ideas," Prudence said. "I'm fucking tired of you and your ideas." "Honey," Bill said, "keep your voice down. The neighbors, honey. The neighbors." Meaning not the Benningtons, on one side, but Arthur and Beatrice Atwell, on the other. Prudence took the drink from Bill, and she did it in such a way that the ice cubes did not clink against the sides of the glass.

Lane Stagg, pained about his son, was as eloquent that evening as he would be at the last meeting of the neighbors, years later, as he argued that the building had really not housed the proper sort of folks in years. "What," he asked, "does that white man across the river in Arlington care about our neighborhood?" Lane Stagg had been the captain of his debating team in high school, when the schools had such things. He would have made a good lawyer, everyone said, but the son of a coal-and-ice man rose only so far. His wife, whose father and mother were lawyers, had married him anyway.

It was not a long meeting, but before it ended the good neighbors of Eighth Street decided that they would raise the money and buy the house and rent it to more agreeable people. "Let's drink to that," Lane said, and stood up. About then, Sharon Palmer came down from upstairs, where she had been comforting Terence. The medicine had finally overcome him and he had fallen asleep. "Thank you, sweet Sharon, thank you, thank you," Lane said, and he set his drink on the table beside his chair and put his arms around her. "It was the least I could do," she said.

After everyone had left, and his wife had gone to bed, Lane sat beside his son's bed. He had enjoyed his house for a long time, and it saddened him, beyond the effects of the liquor, to think that he would not see his grandchildren enjoy it. He loved Washington, and as he sat and watched Terence sleep he feared he would have to leave. He was hearing good things about Prince George's County, but that place, abutting the more redneck areas of the Maryland suburbs, was not home to him like D.C. He had heard, too, that the police there were brutes, straight out of the worst Southern towns, but he had come a long way since the boyhood days of helping his father deliver coal and ice throughout Washington. "Dirty nigger coal man and his dirty nigger coal son," children had called them. And that was in the colored neighborhoods of maids and shoeshiners and janitors and cooks and elevator operators. But he was a thousand lives from that now, even though he wasn't anybody's lawyer. With his reputation as a GS-15 at the Commerce Department and a wife high up in the D.C. school system and a big Maryland house and a son on his way to being a doctor, he could let the police in Prince George's know just what sort he was.

The good neighbors were helped by one major thing: the white man and his wife across the Potomac who owned the Bennington house had been thinking for some time about moving to Florida. Lane Stagg, Hamilton Palmer, Arthur Atwell, and Prudence Forsythe met with the white man on the highway in Arlington named for Robert E. Lee, in a restaurant that was named for Stonewall Jackson. They offered him thirty-one thousand dollars for the Bennington house. The white man whistled at the figure. Arthur Atwell was silent, as usual. He was semiretired and liked to think he had more money than he really did have. The white man, Nicholas Riccocelli, whistled again, this time even louder, because the thirty-one thousand sounded good—he really had no idea how much the house was worth. For several moments, he studied a cheap print of a Dutch windmill on the wall beside the table and thought about how many days on a Florida beach thirty-one thousand dollars would provide.

Riccocelli said to give him a week to think it over, but he called Lane Stagg in four days and said they had a deal. The white man had never had any trouble with the Benningtons and so he felt he owed it to Grace and her family to tell them himself formally that they would have to move. He came late one Saturday afternoon in early February. When Derek told him that his mother wasn't home, Riccocelli wanted to know if she would be gone long.

"If there's something important," Derek said, "you can tell me." And when the white man told him that they would have to be gone in two months, Derek turned from his spot in the middle of the living room to look at Amanda and Neil standing in the doorway to the dining room. "Can you believe this shit?" he said. Then, to Riccocelli, he asked, "Why? Ain't we always paid rent on time? Ain't we?"

"Yes, but the new owners would like to start anew."

"Who are they?" Derek said. "You tell em we good tenants and everything'll be all right."

"I'm afraid," the white man said, "that will not work. The new owners wish to go in another direction altogether."

"Who the fuck are these people? What kinda direction you talkin about?" Derek said, and came two steps toward the man.

"Why . . . why . . . " Riccocelli was unable to complete the sentence, because he had thought their neighbors would have somehow let the Benningtons know. "Why, your neighbors around you." The man sensed something bad was about to happen and backed toward the front door. Where, he wondered, was the mother? She had always seemed so sensible.

"Get the fuck out!" Derek said, and grabbed the man by his coat collar. Riccocelli opened the door and Derek pushed him out. "You sorry motherfucker!" The woman who always wore sunglasses, seated between two children on the couch, began to cry, and the children, following her, began crying as well.

"Derek, leave him alone," Amanda said. "Leave him be."

Out on the porch, Derek still had Riccocelli by the collar. He pulled him down the stairs. "Derek!" Amanda shouted. "Please!"

"Don't hurt me, Mr. Bennington." The ride over from Arlington had been pleasant enough. Riccocelli was a small man, and his eyes barely came above the dashboard, but he enjoyed driving. There had been gentle and light snow most of the way from Arlington, and a few times he had seen lightning across the sky. Snow and lightning. How could a day like that go wrong? He would miss the snow in Florida, he had thought as he drove across Key Bridge. Now, as the two men stumbled and fell down the steps to the sidewalk, there was rain, also gentle, but the sky was quiet. "You mustn't molest me, Mr. Bennington." Riccocelli had parked behind Derek's Ford, and Derek half pushed and half carried him to the car and slammed him against it. "You come back and you dead meat."

After Riccocelli had gone, Derek went up and down both sides of the street shouting to the neighbors to come out and confront him. "Don't be punks!" he shouted. As he neared the Palmers' house, Grace came around the corner, and she and Amanda and Neil, who had been standing in the yard, went to him. "We got babies in that house, man! It's winter, for God's sakes!" Derek shouted. Sharon opened her door and came out onto the porch, but she was the only neighbor to do so. "We got sweet innocent babies in that house, man! What can y'all be thinkin?" His family was able to calm him, but before they could get him across the street the police arrived.

Arthur Atwell died of a heart attack at the end of February, not long after the Benningtons moved, and two days before Derek got out of D.C. jail. Arthur's widow, Beatrice, found that despite all Arthur had said there was not much money, and so she had to back out of the Bennington-house deal. She moved to Claridge Towers, on M Street, into an apartment with a bathroom where she could hide when thunder and lightning came. Everyone was sad to see her leave, because she had been a better neighbor than most. Those still in on the Bennington-house deal did manage to buy the house, but the good neighbors rarely found their sort of people to rent the place.

Sharon Palmer Stagg's car had been in the shop two days when she finished her shift at Georgetown University Hospital one Saturday night in March. It was too late for a bus and she thought she would have a better chance for a cab at Wisconsin Avenue, so she made her way out of the hospital grounds to P Street. She was not yet a nurse, but she did have a part-time job as a nurse's assistant at the hospital, where she often volunteered on her days off. Near Thirty-sixth Street, she saw a small group of young men coming toward her, loud, singing a song too garbled for her to understand. She was used to such crowds—Georgetown students, many with bogus identification cards that they used to buy drinks at the bars along Wisconsin Avenue and M Street.

She had been married for nine months. She was a little more than three weeks from meeting the white woman at the party. Terence Stagg was in medical school at Howard. His maternal grandparents, the attorneys, had been killed in a car accident by a drunken driver who was himself an attorney, and they had left their only grandchild more money than was good for him. Terence and his wife lived quite well in a part of upper Northwest Washington where the likes of the Benningtons could only serve.

Just before Sharon reached Thirty-fifth Street, the group of young men walked under a street light and she could see that two of them were white and the third was black. The black student, six or so feet from her, said to the white students, "I spy with my little eye something good to eat," and the three spread out and blocked her from passing. "I always have these fantasies about nurses and sponge baths," the black one said. She was wearing her uniform and that had told them all they needed to know. They came to within three feet of her and one of the white students held his arms out to Sharon, while the other two men surrounded her. She did not hear the car door behind her open and close.

The black student touched her cheek and then her breasts with both hands, and one of the white students did the same, and both young men breathed sour beer into her face. Sharon pulled away, and the two looked at each other and giggled. As the black student inhaled deeply for another blast into her face, something punched him in the side of the face and he fell hard against a car and passed out. "Hey! Hey!" the white student who had had his hands on Sharon said to the puncher. "Whatcha do to our Rufus?" The puncher pulled Sharon back behind him and she saw a face from a long time ago and her knees buckled to see it. He might well have been a ghost, because she had not seen him in many years. "They spoil the best nights we have," Derek said to her.

The white student who had not touched her pulled out a knife, the blade more than three inches long. Derek reached into his own pocket, but before his hand came out the white student had stabbed him in his left side, through his leather jacket, through his shirt, into the vicinity of his heart, and Sharon screamed as Derek first faltered and then pulled himself up. In a second his switchblade was out and the blade tore through the student's jacket and into his arm, and the student ran out into P Street and down toward his university. "I wanted to keep this clean," Derek said. "But white trash won't let me."

"We didn't mean anything," the second white student said as he sobered up. He raised his arms high. "See—"

"Oh, you fucks always mean somethin," Derek said, holding his knife to the man's cheek and flicking it once to open a wound in the cheek, less than an inch from his nostrils. The man crumpled, both hands to his face. His black friend was still unconscious, and the man with the arm wound was shouting as he ran that they were all being killed by niggers. Derek sheathed the knife and returned it to his pocket and then pulled Sharon down the street to his car.

Within moments he had driven them down P, slowly, across Wisconsin, and to a spot just before the P Street Bridge. He turned on the light and inspected his side. "Shit!" he said. "Bad but maybe not fatal. Damn!"

"Let me help you," Sharon said.

After looking in the sideview mirror, he continued down P Street again, slowly. Two patrol cars sped past them, and she watched him watching them go in the rearview mirror. "Dead or alive, the black dude won't matter," he said to the mirror, joining the traffic moving around Dupont Circle. "But them white dudes are princes and the world gon pay for that." He became part of the flow going up Connecticut Avenue. "And it happened in Georgetown. They'll make sure somebody pays for that. But they were drunk and so describin might be a problem. Real drunk." He seemed unaware that she was there. "Thas why you never went to college, Derek. Black people gotta leave all their common sense at the front door. College is the business of miseducatin. Like them people would ever open the door anyway." She feared he might pass out, and she was comforted by the fact that in the near darkness of the car she could not see blood creeping around to the right side from the left. Two more police cars passed them, screaming. "They gonna pull that one patrol car they have in Southeast and the only one they got in Northeast and bring em over here to join the dozens they keep in Georgetown. You watch, Derek," he said to a carved wooden figure dangling from the rearview mirror. "You just watch."

"Derek," she said. "Stop and let me help you."

They had crossed Calvert, they had crossed Woodley, and he looked at her for the first time since they had entered the car. "I lied," he said. "I lied. Red wasn't a bad color. It was way good enough for you. Any color you put on is a good color, didn't you know that? You make the world. It ain't never been the other way around. You first, then the world follows." They were nearing Porter. Two blocks from the University of the District of Columbia he stopped, not far from her condominium building, which had one of the few doormen in Washington. "You can walk the rest of the way home," he said. "All the bad thas gonna happen to you done already happened."

She moved his jacket aside and saw where the blood had darkened his blue shirt, and when she touched him the blood covered her hand and began to drip. "Come with me and let me help you." And as she said this her mind ticked off the actual number of years since she had last seen him. Three days later she would have it down to months as well. She took a handkerchief and Kleenex from her pocketbook and pressed them gently to his side. "It's bad, but manageable, I think. We need to get you help, though."

He took her hand and placed it in her lap. "Let me be," he said. "You best get home. You best go home to the man you married to."

"Come in. You helped me, so let me help you."

"You should tell that glorious husband of yours that a wife should be protected, that he shouldn't be sleepin while you have to come home through the jungle of some white neighborhood. Tell him thas not what bein married should be about."

She took the bloody handkerchief and Kleenex and returned them to her pocketbook. She did not now want to go home. She wanted to stay and go wherever he was going to go to recover. She snapped the pocketbook shut. Her father had walked her down the aisle, beaming all the way at the coming together of his two favorite families. The church had been packed and Terence had stood at the altar, waiting, standing as straight as he could after a night of drinking and pals and two strippers who had taken turns licking his dick.

"You best go home."

"Please," she said. "Let me stay."

He reached across her and opened the door. "And one last thing," he said. "Neil been at me for the longest time to have me tell you it was never him. He was always afraid that you went about thinkin he was stuck on you, and he wanted me to set the record straight. He was always doin my biddin and now I'll do his and set the record straight." How long can the heart carry it around? How long? The answer came to her in a whisper.

She got out and shut the door, and he continued on up Connecticut Avenue, his back red lights, brightly vital, soon merging with all the rest of the lights of the Washington night. The man in the shop had promised that her BMW would be ready by the end of the week. Terence's Mercedes had never seen a bad day.

As soon as she locked the door to their condominium, she heard the hum of the new refrigerator, and then the icemaker clicked on and ice tumbled into the bucket, as if to welcome her home. The fan over the stove was going, and she turned it off, along with the light over the stove, the two switches side by side. In the living room, she noticed the blood on her uniform; if the doorman had seen the blood, he made no comment. In the half-darkness, the spots seemed fresh, almost alive in some eerie way, as if the blood had just that second come from Derek's wound. Bleeding. Bleedin. She had emerged unscathed. The overhead fan of grand golden wood was going, slowly, and she considered for the longest time whether to switch it off. In the end, she chose to stop the spinning. Her family had moved away from Eighth Street when she was in college, more than two years after the Benningtons left. And they had been followed by the Forsythes and the Prevosts and all the people she had known as she grew into womanhood. We are the future, Lane Stagg had proclaimed at a final dinner party at the Sheraton Hotel for the good neighbors. Who was left there now? Bad neighbors, her father had called those who came after them. Bad neighbors. The dinner party was held not long before the first contingent of whites had come back and planted their flags. The motor on the fish tank hummed right along; the light over the tank was on, and she turned that off. The stereo, which had cost the equivalent of seven of her paychecks, was not playing, but the power light was on, and she pushed the button to put the whole console to rest. She placed one finger against the fish tank, and all the fish in their colorful finery ignored it. Her father had risen at that hotel dinner and given the first toast, his hand trembling and his voice breaking at every fifth word.

Terence was sleeping peacefully, his arms and shoulders bare, and one foot sticking out of the covers, the fine German clock's dull red numbers shining down on him from the bedside table with the reassurance of a child's night-light. Her father hated such clocks, the digital ones that told the time right out; he believed, as he had tried to teach Sharon and her brothers, that children should learn to tell time the way he had learned, with the big hand and the little hand moving around a circle of numbers. She stood in the doorway and watched Terence and the clock, and for all the time she was there he did not stir. A burglar could come in, she thought, and he would never know it. She could stab him to death and end his world and he would never know it. She could smother him. The whole world could end and he would not know that, either. The insurance they paid on all that they owned—not including the cars and their own lives, which had separate policies—came to $273.57 a month. It is worth it, the white insurance man had said as he dotted the final "i," "because you will sleep better at night knowing you are protected." Knowing. Knowin.

She got out of her clothes in the bathroom, took off everything she had on, even her underwear, and found that the blood had seeped through all the way to her skin. She held her uniform up before her. She stared at her name tag and found it hard to connect herself with the name and the uniform and the naked person they belonged to. Am I really who they say I am? Bleeding. Bleedin. None of Derek's people had ever used the "g" on their -ing words; one of the first things she herself had been taught early in life was never to drop the "g." The "g" is there for a reason, they had told her. It separates you from all the rest of them, those who do not know any better. Sharon did not shower. Another Sharon in another time might have been unsettled by his appearing from nowhere, by the thought that he had been following her. But the idea that he had been there, out there in weather of whatever sort, out there in the dark offering no sign and no sound, out there for months and perhaps years, seemed to give her something to measure her life by. She did not yet know how to do that. After she turned out the bathroom light, she stood in the dark for a long time. In their bedroom, she decided against putting on underwear and so got into bed the way she came into the world. Terence stirred, pulled his foot back under the covers, but beyond that he did nothing. Almost imperceptibly, the rightmost red number on the expensive German clock went from two to three.

David Malouf

Every Move You Make

When Jo first came to Sydney, the name she heard in every house she went into was Mitchell Maze. "This is a Mitchell Maze house," someone would announce, "can't you just tell?" and everyone would laugh. After a while she knew what the joke was and did not have to be told. "Don't tell me," she'd say, taking in the raw uprights and bare window frames, "Mitchell Maze," and her hostess would reply, "Oh, do you know Mitch? Isn't he the limit?"

They were beach houses, even when they were tucked away in a cul-de-sac behind the Paddington Post Office or into a gully below an escarpment at Castlecrag. The group they appealed to, looking back affectionately to the hidey-holes and tree houses of their childhood, made up a kind of clan. Of artists mostly, painters, session musicians, filmmakers, writers for the *National Times* and the *Fin Review*, who paid provisional tax and had kids at the International Grammar School, or they were lawyers at Freehills or Allen, Allen & Hemsley, or investment bankers with smooth manners and bold ties who still played touch rugby at the weekends or belonged to a surf club. Their partners—they were sometimes married, mostly not—worked as arts administrators or were in local government. A Mitchell Maze house was a sign that you had arrived but were not quite settled.

Airy improvisations, or—according to how you saw it—calculated and beautiful wrecks, a lot of their timber was driftwood blanched and polished by the tide, or had been scrounged from building sites or picked up cheap at demolitions. It had knotholes, the size sometimes of a twenty-cent piece, and was so carelessly stripped that layers of old paint were visible in the grain that you could pick out with a fingernail, in half-forgotten colors from another era: apple green, oxblood, baby blue. A Mitchell Maze house was a reference back to a more relaxed and open-ended decade, an assurance (a reassurance in some cases) that your involvement with the Boom, and all that went with it, was opportunistic, uncommitted, tongue-in-cheek. You had maintained the rage, still had a Che or Hendrix poster tacked to a wall of the garage and kept a fridge full of tinnies, though you *had* moved on from the flagon red. As for Mitch himself, he came with the house. "Only not often enough," as one of his clients quipped.

He might turn up one morning just at breakfast time with a claw hammer and rule at the back of his shorts and a load of timber on his shoulder. One of the kids would already have sighted his ute.

"Oh, great," the woman at the kitchen bench would say, keeping her voice low-key but not entirely free of irony. "Does this mean we're going to get that wall? Hey, kids, here's Mitch. Here's our wall."

"Hi," the kids yelled, crowding round him. "Hi, Mitch. Is it true? Is that why you're here? Are you goin' t'give us a *wall*?"

They liked Mitch, they loved him. So did their mother. But she also liked the idea of a wall.

He would accept a mug of coffee, but when invited to sit and have breakfast with them would demur. "No, no thanks," he'd tell them. "Gotta get started. I'll just drink this while I work."

He would be around then for a day or two, hammering away till it was dusk and the rosellas were tearing at the trees beyond the deck and dinner was ready; staying on for a plate of pasta and some good late-night talk, then bedding down after midnight in a bunk in the kids' room, "to get an early start," or, if they were easy about such things, crawling in with a few murmured apologies beside his hosts. Then in the morning he would be gone again, and no amount of calling, no number of messages left at this place or that, would get him back.

Visitors observing an open wall would say humorously, "Ah, Mitch went off to get a packet of nails, I see."

Sensitive fellows, quick to catch the sharpening of their partners' voice as it approached the subject of a stack of timber on the living room floor, or a bathroom window that after eleven months was still without glass, would spring to the alert.

As often as not, the first indication that some provisional but to this point enduring arrangement was about to be renegotiated would be a flanking attack on the house. "Right, *mate*," was the message, "let's get serious here. What about that wall?"

Those who were present to hear it, living as they did in structures no less flimsy than the one that was beginning to break up all around them, would feel a chill wind at their ear.

All this Jo had observed, with amusement and a growing curiosity, for several months before she found herself face to face with the master builder himself.

Jo was thirty-four and from the country, though no one would have called her a country girl. Before that she was from Hungary. Very animated and passionately involved in everything she did, very intolerant of those who did not, as she saw it, demand enough of life, she was a publisher's editor, ambitious or pushy according to how you took these things, and successful enough to have detractors. She herself wanted it all—everything. And more.

"You want too much," her friends told her. "You can't have it, you just can't. Nobody can."

"You just watch me," Jo told them in reply.

She had had two serious affairs since coming to Sydney, both briefer than she would have wished. She was too intense, that's what her friends told her. The average bloke, the average *Australian* bloke—oh, here it comes, *that* again, she thought—was uncomfortable with dramatics. Intimidated. Put off.

"I don't want someone who's average," she insisted. "Even an average Australian."

She wanted a love that would be overwhelming, that would make a windblown leaf of her, a runaway wheel. She was quite prepared to suffer, if that was to be part of it. She would walk barefoot through the streets and howl if that's what love brought her to.

Her friends wrinkled their brows at these stagy extravagances. "Honestly! Jo!" Behind her back they patronized and pitied her.

In fact they too, some of them, had felt like this at one time or another. At the beginning. But had learned to hide their disappointment behind a show of hard-boiled mateyness. They knew the rules. Jo had not been around long enough for that. She had no sense of proportion. Did she even *know* that there were rules?

They met at last. At a party at Palm Beach, the usual informal Sunday-afternoon affair. She knew as soon as he walked in who it must be. He was wearing khaki shorts, work boots, nothing fancy. An open-necked unironed shirt.

Drifting easily from group to group, noisily greeted with cries and little affectionate pecks on the cheek by the women, and with equally affectionate gestures from the men—a clasp of the shoulder, a hand laid for a moment on his arm—he unsettled the room, that's what she thought, refocused its energies, though she accepted later that the unsettlement may only have been in herself. Through it all he struck her as being remote, untouchable, self-enclosed, though not at all self-regarding. Was it simply that he was shy? When he found her at last she had the advantage of knowing more about him, from the tales she had been regaled with, the houses she had been in, than he could have guessed.

What she was not prepared for was his extraordinary charm. Not his talk—there was hardly any of that. His charm was physical. It had to do with the sun-bleached, salt-bleached mess of his hair and the way he kept ploughing a rough hand through it; the grin that left deep lines in his cheeks; the intense presence, of which he himself seemed dismissive or unaware. He smelled of physical work, but also, she thought, of wood shavings—blond transparent curlings off the edge of a plane. Except that the special feature of his appeal was the rough rather than the smooth.

They went home together. To his place, to what he called "The Shack," a house on stilts, floating high above a jungle of tree ferns, morning glory and red-clawed coral trees in a cove at Balmoral. Stepping into it, she felt she had been there already. Here at last was the original of all those open-ended, unfinished structures she had been in and out of for the past eight months. When she opened the door to the loo, she laughed. There was no glass in the window. Only a warmish square of night filled with ecstatic insect cries.

. . . .

She was prepared for the raw, splintery side of him. The sun-cracked lips, the blonded hair that covered his forearms and the darker hair that came almost to his Adam's apple, the sandpapery hands with their scabs and festering nicks. What she could not have guessed at was the whiteness and almost feminine silkiness of his hidden parts. Or the old-fashioned delicacy with which he turned away every attempt on her part to pay tribute to them. It was so at odds with the libertarian mode she had got used to down here.

He took what he needed in a frank, uncomplicated way; was forceful but considerate—all this in appreciation of her own attractions. She was flattered, moved, and in the end felt a small glow of triumph at having so much pleased him. For a moment he entirely yielded, and she felt, in his sudden cry, and in the completeness afterward with which he sank into her arms, that she had been allowed into a place that in every other circumstance he kept guarded, closed off.

She herself was dazzled. By a quality in him—*beauty* is what she said to herself—that took her breath away, a radiance that burned her lips, her fingertips, every point where their bodies made contact. But when she tried to express this—to touch him as he had touched her and reveal to him this vision she had of him—he resisted. What she felt in his almost angry shyness was a kind of distaste. She retreated, hurt, but was resentful too. It was unfair of him to exert so powerful an appeal and then turn maidenly when he got a response.

She should have seen then what cross-purposes they would be at, and not only in this matter of intimacy. But he recognized her hurt, and in a way, she would discover, that was typical of him, tried out of embarrassment to make amends.

He was sitting up with his back against the bedhead enjoying a smoke. Their eyes met, he grinned; a kind of ease was reestablished between them. She was moved by how knocked about he was, the hard use to which he had put his body, the scraps and scrapes he had been through. Her fingertips went to a scar, a deep nick in his cheekbone under the left eye. She did not ask. Her touch was itself a question.

"Fight with an arc lamp," he told her. His voice had a humorous edge. "I lost. Souvenir of my brief career as a movie star."

She looked at him. The grin he wore was light, self-deprecatory. He was offering her one of the few facts about himself—from his childhood, his youth—that she would ever hear. She would learn only later how useless it was to question him on such matters. You got nowhere by asking. If he did let something drop it was to distract you, while some larger situation that he did not want to develop slipped quietly away. But that was not the case on this occasion. They barely knew one another. He wanted, in all innocence, to offer her something of himself.

When he was thirteen—this is what he told her—he had been taken by his mother to an audition. More than a thousand kids had turned up. He didn't want the part, he thought it was silly, but he had got it anyway and for a minute back there, because of that one appearance, had been a household name, a star.

She had removed her hand and was staring.

"What?" he said, the grin fading. He gave her an uncomfortable look and leaned across to the night table to stub out his cigarette.

"I can't believe it," she was saying. "I can't believe this. I know who you are. You're Skip Daley!"

"No, I'm not," he said, and laughed. "Don't be silly."

He was alarmed at the way she had taken it. He had offered it as a kind of joke. One of the *least* important things he could have told her.

"But I saw that film! I saw it five times!"

"Don't," he said. "It was nothing. I shouldn't have let on."

But he could have no idea what it had meant to her. What *he* had meant to her.

Newly arrived in the country, a gangly ten-year-old, and hating everything about this place she had never wanted to come to—the parched backyards, the gravel playground under the pepper trees at her bare public school, the singsong voices that mocked her accent and deliberately, comically got her name wrong—she had gone one Saturday afternoon to the local pictures and found herself tearfully defeated. In love. Not just with the hard-heeled freckle-faced boy up on the screen, with his roundheaded, blond pudding-bowl haircut and cheeky smile, his fierce sense of honor, the odd mixture in him of roughness and shy, broad-voweled charm, but with the whole barefoot world he moved in, his dog Blue, his hard-bitten parents who were in danger of losing their land, the one-story sunstruck weatherboard they lived in, which was, in fact, just like her own.

More than a place, it was a world of feeling she had broken through to, and it could be hers now because *he* lived in it. She had given up her resistance.

On that hot Saturday afternoon, in that darkened picture theatre in Albury, her heart had melted. Australia had claimed and conquered her. She was shocked and the shock was physical. She had had no idea till then what beauty could do to you, the deep tears it could draw up; how it could take hold of you in the middle of the path and turn you round, fatefully, and set you in a new direction. That was what he could know nothing of.

All that time ago, he had changed her life. And here he was more than twenty years later, in the flesh, looking sideways at her in this unmade lump of a bed.

"Hey," he was saying, and he put his hand out to lift aside a strand of her hair.

"I just can't get over it," she said.

"Hey," he said again. "Don't be silly! It was nothing. Something my mother got me into. It was all made up. That stupid kid wasn't me. I was a randy little bugger if you want to know. All I could think about was my dick—" And he laughed. "They didn't show any of that. Truth is, I didn't like myself much in those days. I was too unhappy."

But he was only getting himself in deeper. Unhappy? He caught the look in her eyes, and to save the situation leaned forward and covered her mouth with his own.

From the start he famished her. It was not in her nature to pause at thresholds but there were bounds she could not cross and he was gently, firmly insistent. He did give himself, but when she too aggressively took the initiative, or crossed the line of what he thought of as a proper modesty, he would quietly turn away. What he was abashed by, she saw, was just what most consumed her, his beauty. He had done everything he could to abolish it. All those nicks and scars. The broken tooth he took no trouble to have fixed. The exposure to whatever would burn or coarsen.

A series of "spills" had left him, at one time or another, with a fractured collarbone, three bouts of concussion, a broken leg. These punishing assaults on himself were attempts to wipe out an affliction. But all they had done was refine it: bring out the metallic blue of his eyes, show up under the skin, with its network of cracks, the poignancy—that is how she saw it—of his bones.

Leaving him sprawled, that first morning, she had stepped out into the open living room.

Very aware that she was as yet only a casual visitor to his world, and careful of intruding, she picked her way between plates piled with old food and set on tabletops or pushed halfway under chairs, coffee mugs, beer cans, gym socks, ashtrays piled with butts, magazines, newspapers, unopened letters, shirts dropped just anywhere or tossed carelessly over the backs of chairs. A dead lightbulb on a glass coffee table rolled in the breeze.

She sat a moment on the edge of a lounger and thought she could hear the tinkling that came from the closed globe, a distant sound, magical and small, but magnified, like everything this morning. The room was itself all glass and light. It hung in midair. Neither inside nor out, it opened straight into the branches of a coral tree, all scarlet claws.

She went to the kitchen bench at the window. The sink was piled with coffee mugs and more dishes. She felt free to deal with those, and was still at the sink, watching a pair of rainbow lorikeets on the deck beyond, all his dinner plates gleaming in the rack, when he stepped up behind her in a pair of sagging jockey shorts, still half asleep, rubbing his skull. He kissed her in a light, familiar way. Barely noticing the cleared sink—that was a *good* sign—he ran a glass of water and drank it off, his Adam's apple bobbing. Then kissed her again, grinned and went out onto the deck.

The lorikeets flew off, but belonged here, and soon ventured back.

Over the weeks, as she came to spend more time there, she began to impose her own sort of order on the place. He did not object. He sat about reading the papers while she worked around him.

The drawers of the desk where he sometimes sat in the evening, wearing reading glasses while he did the accounts, were stuffed with papers—letters, cuttings, prospectuses. There were more papers pushed into cardboard boxes, in cupboards, stacked in corners, piled under beds.

"Do you want to keep any of this?" she would inquire from time to time, holding up a fistful of mail.

He barely looked. "No. Whatever it is. Just chuck it."

"You sure?"

"Why? What is it?"

"Letters."

"Sure. Chuck 'em out."

"What about these?"

"What are they?"

"Invoices. 1984."

"No. Just pile 'em up, I'll make a bonfire. Tomorrow maybe."

She had a strong need for fantasy, she liked to make things interesting. In their early days together, she took to leaving little love notes for him. Once under the tea caddy, where he would come across it when he went out in the morning, just after six, to make their tea. On other occasions, beside his shaving gear in the bathroom, in one of the pockets of his windcheater, in his work shorts. If he read them he did not mention the fact. It was ages before he told her, in a quarrel, how much these love notes embarrassed him. She flushed scarlet, did not make that mistake again.

He had no sense of fantasy himself. He wasn't insensitive—she was often touched by his thoughtfulness and by the small things he noticed—but he was very straight-up-and-down, no frills. Once, when his film was showing, she asked if they could go and see it. "What for?" he asked, genuinely surprised. "It's crap. Anyway, I'd rather forget all that. It wasn't a good time, that. Not for me it wasn't."

"Because you were unhappy?" she said. "You told me that, remember?"

But he shut off then, and the matter dropped.

He told her nothing about his past. Nothing significant. And if she asked, he shied away.

"I don't want to talk about it," was all he'd say. "I try to forget about what's gone and done with. That's where we're different. You go on and on about it."

No, I don't, she wanted to argue. You're the one who's hung up on the past. That's why you won't talk about it. What I'm interested in is the present. But all of it. All the little incidental happenings that got you here, that got *us* here, made us the way we are. Seeing that she was still not satisfied, he drew her to him, almost violently—offering her that, his hard presence—and sighed, she did not know for what.

He had no decent clothes that she could discover. Shirts, shorts, jeans—work clothes, not much else. A single tie that he struggled into when he had an engagement that was "official." She tried to rectify this. But when he saw the pile of new things on the bed he looked uncomfortable. He took up a blue poplin shirt, fingered it, frowned, put it down.

"I wish you wouldn't," he said. "Buy me things. Shirts and that." He was trying not to seem ungracious, she saw, but was not happy. "I don't need shirts."

"But you do," she protested. "Look at the one you've got on."

He glanced down. "What's wrong with it?"

"It's in rags."

"Does me," he said, looking put out.

"So. Will you wear these things or what?"

"I'll wear them," he said. "They're bought now. But I don't want you to do it, that's all. I don't *need* things."

He refused to meet her eye. Something more was being said, she thought. I don't deserve them—was that what he meant? In a sudden rush of feeling for something in him that touched her but which she could not quite catch, she clasped him to her. He relaxed, responded.

"No more shirts, then," she promised.

"I just don't want you to waste your money," he said childishly. "I've got loads of stuff already."

"I know," she said. "You should send the lot of it to the Salvos. Then you'd have nothing at all. You'd be naked, and wouldn't be able to go out, and I'd have you all to myself." She had, by now, moved in.

"Is that what you want?" he asked, picking up on her lightness, allowing her, without resistance for once, to undo the buttons on the offending shirt.

"You know I do," she told him.

"Well then," he said.

"Well then what?"

"Well, you've *got* me," he said, "haven't you?"

He had a ukulele. Occasionally he took it down from the top shelf of the wardrobe and, sitting with a bare foot laid over his thigh, played—not happily, she thought—the same plain little tune.

She got to recognize the mood in which he would need to seek out this instrument that seemed so absurdly small in his hands and for which he had no talent, and kept her distance. The darkness in him frightened her. It seemed so far from anything she knew of his other nature.

. . .

Some things she discovered only by accident. "Who's Bobby Kohler?" she asked once, having several times now come across the name on letters.

"Oh, that's me," he said. "*Was* me."

"What do you mean?"

"It's my name. My real name. Mitchell Maze is just the name I work under."

"You mean you changed it?"

"Not really. Some people still call me Bobby."

"Who does?"

"My mother. A few others."

"Is it German?"

"Was once, I suppose. Away back. Grandparents."

She was astonished, wanted to ask more, but could see that the subject was now done with. She might ask but he would not answer.

There were times when he did tell her things. Casually, almost dismissively, off the top of his head. He told her how badly, at sixteen, he had wanted to be a long-distance runner, and shine. How for a whole year he had got up in the dark, before his paper run, and gone out in the growing light to train on the oval at their local showground at Castle Hill. He laughed, inviting her to smile at some picture he could see of his younger self, lean, intense, driven, straining painfully day after day toward a goal he would never reach. She was touched by this. But he was not looking for pity. It was the folly of the thing he was intent on. It appealed to a spirit of savage irony in him that she could not share.

There were no evocative details. Just the bare, bitter facts. He could see the rest too clearly in his mind's eye to reproduce it for hers. She had to do that out of her own experience: Albury. The early-morning frost on the grass. Magpies caroling around a couple of milk cans in the long grass by the road. But she needed more, to fix in a clarifying image the tenderness she felt for him, the sixteen-year-old Bobby Kohler, barefooted, in sweater and shorts, already five inches taller than the Skip Daley she had known, driving himself hard through those solitary circuits of the oval as the sunlight came and the world turned golden around him.

One day she drove out on her lunch hour to see the place. Sat in her car in the heat and dazzle. Walked to the oval fence and took in the smell of dryness. There was less, in fact, than she imagined.

But a week later she went back. His mother lived there. She found the address, and after driving round the suburb for a bit, sat in her car under a paperbark on the other side of the street. Seeing no one in the little front yard, she got out, crossed, climbed the two front steps to the veranda, and knocked.

There was no reply.

She walked to the end of the veranda, which was unpainted, its timber rotting, and peered round the side. No sign of anyone.

Round the back, there was a water tank, painted the usual red, and some cages that might once have held rabbits. She peeped in through the window on a clean little kitchen with a religious calendar—was he a Catholic? He'd never told her that—and into two bedrooms on either side of a hall, one of which, at one time, must have been his.

He lived here, she told herself. For nearly twenty years. Something must be left of him.

She went down into the yard and turned the bronze key of the tap, lifting to her mouth a cupped handful of the cooling water. She felt like a ghost returning to a world that was not her own, nostalgic for what she had never known; for what might strike her senses strongly enough—the taste of tank water, the peppery smell of geraniums—to bring back some immediate physical memory of the flesh. But that was crazy. What was she doing? She had *him*, didn't she?

That night, touching the slight furriness, in the dark, of his earlobe, smelling the raw presence of him, she gave a sob and he paused in his slow lovemaking.

"What is it?" he said. "What's the matter?"

She shook her head, felt a kind of shame—what could she tell him? That she'd been nosing round a backyard in Castle Hill looking for some ghost of him? He'd think she was mad.

"Tell me," he said.

His face was in her hair. There was a kind of desperation in him. But this time she was the one who would not tell.

He was easy to get on with and he was not. They did most things together; people thought of them as a couple, they were happy. He came and went without explanation, and she learned quickly enough that she either accepted him on these terms or she could not have him at all. Without quite trying to, he attracted people, and when "situations" developed was too lazy, or too easygoing, to extract himself. She learned not to ask where he had been or what he was up to. That wasn't what made things difficult between them.

She liked to have things out. He wouldn't allow it. When she raged he looked embarrassed. He told her she was over-dramatic, though the truth was that he liked her best when she was in a passion, it was the very quality in her that had first attracted him. What he didn't like were scenes. If she tried to make a scene, as he called it, he walked out.

"It's no use shouting at one another," he'd tell her, though in fact he never shouted. "We'll talk about it later." Which meant they wouldn't talk at all.

"But I *need* to shout," she shouted after him.

Later, coming back, he would give a quick sideways glance to see if she had "calmed down."

She hadn't usually. She'd have made up her mind, after a bout of tears, to end things.

"What about a cuppa?" he'd suggest.

"What you won't accept—" she'd begin.

"Don't," he'd tell her. "I've forgotten all about it." As if the hurt had been his. Then, "I'm sorry. I don't want you to be unhappy."

"I'm not," she'd say. "Just—exasperated."

"Oh, well," he'd say. "That's all right then."

What tormented her was the certainty she felt of his nursing some secret—a lost love perhaps, an old grief—that he could not share. Which was there in the distance he moved into; there in the room, in the bed beside her; and might, she thought, have the shape on occasion of that ukulele tune, and which she came to feel as a second presence between them.

It was this distance in him that others were drawn to. She saw that clearly now. A horizon in him that you believed you alone could reach. You couldn't. Maybe no one could. After a time it put most people off; they cut their losses and let him go. But that was not her way. If she let him go, it would destroy her. She knew that because she knew herself.

There was a gleam in him that on occasion shone right through his skin, the white skin of his breast below the burn line his singlet left. She could not bear it. She battered at him.

"Hey, *hey*," he'd say, holding her off.

He had no idea what people were after. What she was after. What she saw in him.

For all the dire predictions among the clan, the doubts and amused speculations, they lasted; two people who, to the puzzlement of others, remained passionately absorbed in one another. Then one day she got a call at work. He had had a fall and was concussed again. Then in a coma, on a life-support system, and for four days and nights she was constantly at his side.

For part of that time she sat in a low chair and tuned her ear to a distant tinkling, as a breeze reached her, from far off over the edge of the world, and rolled a spent lightbulb this way and that on a glass tabletop. She watched, fascinated. Hour after hour, in shaded sunlight and then in the blue of a hospital night lamp, the fragile sphere rolled, and she heard, in the depths of his skull, a clink of icebergs, and found herself sitting, half frozen, in a numbed landscape with not even a memory now of smell or taste or of any sense at all; only what she caught of that small sound, of something broken in a hermetic globe. To reach it, she told herself, I will have to smash the glass. And what then? Will the sound swell and fill me or will it stop altogether?

Meanwhile she listened. It demanded all her attention. It was a matter of life and death. When she could no longer hear it—

At other times she walked. Taking deep breaths of the hot air that swirled around her, she walked, howling, through the streets. Barefoot. And the breaths she took were to feed her howling. Each outpouring of sound emptied her lungs so completely that she feared she might simply rise up and float. But the weight of her bones, of the flesh that covered them, of the waste in her bowels, and her tears, kept her anchored—as did the invisible threads that tied her body to his, immobile under the crisp white sheet, its head swathed in bandages, and the wires connecting him to his other watcher, the dial-faced machine. It was his name she was howling. Mitch, she called. Sometimes Skip. At other times, since he did not respond to either of these, that other, earlier name he had gone by. Bobby, Bobby Kohler. She saw him, from where she was standing under the drooping leaves of a eucalypt at the edge of a track, running round the far side of an oval, but he was too deeply intent on his body, on his breathing, on the swing of his arms, the pumping of his thighs, to hear her.

Bobby, she called. Skip, she called. Mitch. He did not respond. And she wondered if there was another name he might respond to that she had never heard. She tried to guess what it might be, certain now that if she found it, and called, he would wake. She found herself once leaning over him with her hands on his shoulders, prepared—was she mad?—to *shake* it out of him.

And once, in a moment of full wakefulness, she began to sing, very softly, in a high far voice, the tune he played on the ukulele. She had no words for it. Watching him, she thought he stirred. The slightest movement of his fingers. A creasing of the brow. Had she imagined it?

On another occasion, on the third or fourth day, she woke to find she had finally emerged from herself, and wondered—in the other order of time she now moved in—how many years had passed. She was older, heavier, her hair was gray, and this older, grayer self was seated across from her wearing the same intent, puzzled look that she too must be wearing. Then the figure smiled.

No, she thought, if that is me, I've become another woman altogether. Is that what time does to us?

It was the night they came and turned off the machine. His next of kin, his mother, had given permission.

Two days later, red-eyed from sleeplessness and bouts of uncontrollable weeping, she drove to Castle Hill for the funeral.

His mother had rung. She reminded Jo in a kindly voice that they had spoken before. Yes, Jo thought, like this. On the phone, briefly. When she had called once or twice at an odd hour and asked him to come urgently, she needed him, and at holiday times when he went dutifully and visited, and on his birthday. "Yes," Jo said. "In June." No, his mother told her, at the hospital. Jo was surprised. She had no memory of this. But when they met she recognized the woman. They *had* spoken. Across his hospital bed, though she still had no memory of what had passed between them. She felt ashamed. Grief, she felt, had made her wild; she still looked wild. Fearful now of appearing to lay claim to the occasion, she drew back and tried to stay calm.

The woman, Mitch's mother, was very calm, as if she had behind her a lifetime's practice of preserving herself against an excess of grief. But she was not ungiving.

"I know how fond Bobby was of you," she told Jo softly. "You must come and see me. Not today. Ring me later in the week. I can't have anyone at the house today. You'll understand why."

Jo thought she understood but must have looked puzzled.

"Josh," she said. "I've got Josh home." And Jo realized that the man standing so oddly close, but turned slightly away from them, was actually with the woman.

"I can't have him for more than a day or so at a time," the woman was saying. "He doesn't mean to be a trouble, and he'd never do me any harm, but he's so strong—I can't handle him. He's like a five-year-old. But a forty-year-old man has a lot of strength in his lungs." She said this almost with humor. She reached out and squeezed the man's hand. He turned, and then Jo saw.

Large-framed and heavy-looking—"hulking" was the word that came to her—everything that in Mitch had been well knit and easy was, in him, merely loose. His hands hung without occupation at the ends of his arms, the features in the long large face seemed unfocused, unintegrated. Only with Mitch in mind could you catch, in the full mouth, the heavy jaw and brow, a possibility that had somehow failed to emerge, or been maimed or blunted. The sense she had of sliding likeness and unlikeness was alarming. She gave a cry.

"Oh," the woman said. "I thought you knew. I thought he'd told you."

Jo recovered, shook her head, and just at that moment the clergyman came forward, nodded to Mitch's mother, and they moved away to the open grave.

They were a small crowd. Most of them she knew. They were the members of the clan. The others, she guessed from their more formal clothes, must be relatives or family friends.

The service was grim. She steeled herself to stay calm. She had no wish to attract notice, to be singled out because she and Mitch had been—had been what? What had they been? She wanted to stand and be shrouded in her grief. To remain hidden. To have her grief, and him, all to herself as she had had him all to herself at least sometimes, many times, when he was alive.

But she was haunted now by the large presence of this other, this brother who stood at the edge of the grave beside his mother, quiet enough, she saw, but oddly unaware of what was going on about him.

He had moments of attention, a kind of vacant attention, then fell into longer periods of giant arrest. Then his eye would be engaged.

By the black fringe on the shawl of the small woman to his left, which he reached out for and fingered, frowning, then lifted to his face and sniffed.

By a wattlebird that was animating the branches of a low-growing grevillea so that it seemed suddenly to have developed a life of its own and began twitching and shaking out its blooms. Then by the cuff of his shirt, which he regarded quizzically, his mouth pouting, then drawn to one side, as if by something there that disappointed or displeased him.

All these small diversions that took his attention took hers as well. At such a moment! She was shocked.

Then, quite suddenly, he raised his head. Some new thing had struck him. What? Nothing surely that had been said or was being done here. Some thought of his own. A snatch of music it might be, a tune that opened a view in him that was like sunlight flooding a familiar landscape. His face was irradiated by a foolish but utterly beatific smile, and she saw how easy it might be—she thought of his mother, even more poignantly of Mitch—to love this large unlovely child.

The little ukulele tune came into her head, and with it a vision of Mitch, lost to her in his own world of impenetrable grief. Sitting in his underpants on the floor, one big foot propped on his thigh. Hunched over the strings and plucking from them, over and over, the same spare notes, the same bare little tune. And she understood with a pang how the existence of this spoiled other must have seemed like a living reproach to his own too easy attractiveness. It was that—the injustice of it, so cruel, so close—that all those nicks and scars and broken bones and concussions, and all that reckless exposure to a world of accident, had been meant to annul. She felt the ground shifting under her feet. How little she had grasped or known. What a different story she would have to tease out now and tell herself of their time together.

The service was approaching its end. The coffin, suspended on ropes, tilted over the hole with its raw edges and siftings of loose soil. It began, lopsidedly, to descend. Her eyes flooded. She closed them tight. Felt herself choke.

At that moment there was a cry, an incommensurate roar that made all heads turn and stopped the clergyman in full spate.

Some animal understanding—caught from the general emotion around him and become brute fact—had brought home to Josh what it was they were doing here. He began to howl, and the sound was so terrible, so piteous, that all Jo could think of was an animal at the most uncomprehending extreme of physical agony. People looked naked, stricken. There was a scrambling over broken lumps of earth round the edge of the grave. The big man, even in the arms of his mother, was uncontrollable. He struck out, face congested, the mouth and nose streaming, like an ox, Jo thought, like an ox under the hammer. And this, she thought, is the real face of grief, the one we do not show. Her heart was thick in her breast. This is what sorrow is that knows no explanation or answer. That looks down into the abyss and sees only the unanswering depths.

She recalled nothing of the drive back, through raw unfinished suburbs, past traffic lights where she must dutifully have swung into the proper lane and stopped, her mind in abeyance, the motor idling. When she got home, to the house afloat on its stilts among the sparse leaves of the coral trees, above the cove with its littered beach, she was drained of resistance. She sat in the high open space the house made, feeling it breathe like a living thing, surrendering herself to the regular long expansions of its breath.

Against the grain of her own need for what was enclosed and safe, she had learned to live with it. What now? Could she bear, alone, now that something final had occurred, to live day after day with what was provisional, which she had put up with till now because, with a little effort of adjustment, she too, she found, could live in the open present—so long as it *was* open.

Abruptly she rose, stood looking down for a moment at some bits of snipped wire, where he had been tinkering with something electrical, that for a whole week had lain scattered on the coffee table, then went out to the sink, and as on that first morning washed up what was there to be washed. The solitary cup and saucer from her early-morning tea.

For a moment afterward she stood contemplating the perfection of clean plates drying in the rack, cups turned downward to drain, their saucers laid obliquely atop. She was at the beginning again. Or so she felt. Now what?

There was a sock on the floor. Out of habit she retrieved it, then stood, surveying the room, the house, as you could because it was so open and exposed.

Light and air came pouring in from all directions. She felt again, as on that first occasion, the urge to move in and begin setting things to rights, and again for the moment held back, restrained herself.

She looked down, observed the sock in her hand, and had a vision, suddenly, of the place as it might be a month from now when her sense of making things right would already, day after day, imperceptibly, have been at work on getting rid of the magazines and newspapers, shifting this or that piece of furniture into a more desirable arrangement, making the small adjustments that would erase all sign of him, of Mitch, from what had been so much of his making—from her life. Abruptly she threw the sock from her and stood there, shivering, hugging herself, in the middle of the room. Then, abruptly, sat where she had been sitting before. In the midst of it.

So what did she mean to do? Change nothing? Leave everything just as it was? The out-of-date magazines, that dead match beside the leg of the coffee table, the bits of wire, the sock? To gather fluff over the weeks and months, a dusty tribute that she would sit in the midst of for the next twenty years?

She sat a little longer, the room darkening around her, filling slowly with the darkness out there that lay over the waters of the cove, rose up from the floaty leaves of the coral trees and the shadowy places at their roots, from around the hairy stems of tree ferns and out of the unopened buds of morning glory. Then, with a deliberate effort, she got down on her knees and reached in to pick up the match from beside the leg of the coffee table. Shocked that it weighed so little. So little that she might not recall, later, the effort it had cost her, this first move toward taking up again, bit by bit, the weight of her life.

Then, with the flat of her hand, she brushed the strands of wire into a heap, gathered them up, and went, forcing herself, to retrieve the sock, then found the other. Rolled them into a ball and raised it to her lips. Squeezing her eyes shut, filling her nostrils with their smell.

Then there were his shirts, his shorts, his jeans—they would go to the Salvos—and the new things she had bought, which lay untouched in the drawers of his lowboy, the shirts in their plastic wrappers, the underpants, the socks still sewn or clipped together. Maybe Josh. She had a vision of herself arriving with these things on his mother's doorstep. An opening. The big man's pleasure as he stroked the front of his new poplin shirt, the sheen of its pure celestial blue.

She sat again, the small hoard of the rolled socks in her lap, the spent match and the strands of wire in a tidy heap. A beginning. And let the warm summer dark flow in around her.

Tony Tulathimutte

Scenes from the Life of the Only Girl in Water Shield, Alaska

The Dalmatian

Among the tall clusters of evergreen that obscured the horizon in all directions, Shelley looked up and saw that the sun was disappearing behind the thick, darkening cloud cover. By now, her left hand was too cold to grip the metal strings, and every so often she stuck her fingers in her mouth to warm them. She felt a wet tap on her neck, and as the wind propelled from the west, she felt another on her cheek. The autumn showers had started three days earlier, which perennially grayed the skies, making it impossible to see the pale aurora at night and even more impossible to get out as often as she wanted. Shelley felt a jab of dread at staying holed up with her father for the next three months; the longer she was stuck with the Moose, the more she thought about jobs she could take, or correspondence classes, or just getting up and leaving.

Dark rain spots soaked the dirt around Shelley. She wiped the body of her guitar clear with the elbow of her plaid hunting jacket. She placed her instrument in the case, snapped it shut, and brushed the trails of her rat-dark hair behind her ear. There were boot steps and the swish of jeans coming from the west: the Moose returned with his rifle gripped in one hand, nothing in the other. He was whistling. His shades were settled on top of his faded blue baseball cap, and his suspenders dangled out from under the sides of his tan jacket.

"Damn bitch got away," he called out to Shelley, still distant. "Heard me coming."

Shelley waited until he was near, picked up her guitar case and started walking with him as he passed. He was small, almost shorter than Shelley, so they kept an equal stride. They walked side-by-side, making a straight path through the berry-green muskeg and out of the thicket of dully glinting evergreens. Shelley wanted to linger, but she was driven onward toward the shore by blasts of wind that filtered through the collar of her jacket. Her fingers ached with chill as she gripped the handle of her guitar case. Sheets of rain drenched the surrounding pines, which shed fat drops from their lowest needles, and under the drizzle, Shelley heard a creak of metal.

"What's that?" Shelley said, slowing her stride to a halt.

Again, the sound: it wasn't a creak, but a living, fluttering sound—a whimper.

"Hold up, Shel." The Moose pushed his shades onto the bridge of his sunburned nose, gripped his rifle close to his chest, slid his finger into the cradle of the trigger. Whatever it was, it was hurting. Shelley stopped, searched her pocket with her free hand for the smooth bone handle of her hunting knife, and rested her fingertips on it as the sound grew clearer through the rain and the Moose approached.

The feeble sound was only a few yards away from where they were walking, closer than she'd expected. It was a dog, a real dog, a Dalmatian. Its coat stood out against the green-gray terrain, and as soon as its black eyes found the Moose, it bolted at him, barking furiously. Shelley's shoulders bucked in surprise, and the Moose took a step backward, but then Shelley saw that the dog was hitched to a moss-covered log by a yellow nylon rope, farther back. The rope was cinched tense around the dog's neck. The Dalmatian braced with its throat rumbling, and Shelley and the Moose stared at it. The Moose walked a safe distance to it and leaned in.

"No tags, no collar," said the Moose to himself, holding the animal's gaze.

In a rough circumference around the mossy log, the dirt was pitted and grooved where the dog had taken to restless pacing. Shelley saw the outline of the dog's rib cage, spine, hips; it was starving. It was missing an ear. Snarling and oblivious to its wretched condition, the dog hauled against the rope again. There was no house around here and no boot tracks around; it could have been waiting there forever.

HOME

Water Shield, Alaska: population, two.

Home was a row of two squat structures, each no larger than a two-car garage: the house and the sauna. Both structures bore the same rough-cut paneling and hand-split cedar shingles, dull yellow from half a decade of weathering. The house was a single room, packed with all the clutter of the simple life: television, stove, space heater, two mattresses in the corner, lamps, tools and guns, a pantry, a VHF radio, hunting equipment and fishing tackle, old *Time* magazines, garbage, a dozen cats. A gas generator and a solar energy kit. No windows.

Out front was the twelve-foot satellite dish, an American flag on a raw cedar shaft, and a trailer, hand-painted flame yellow and red, filled with dog food for the cats, and barrels of fuel.

A small chicken coop was under the base of the house, visible only by a door that barricaded them in during the day. When Shelley was seven, the Moose had warned her not to let the chickens out, because the weasels would come quick, bite and steal them away.

"Even if you let 'em out, where would they go?" he'd asked her.

"They would fly away," Shelley said, convinced.

"Aw, that's dumb. You know chickens can't fly," said the Moose, poking Shelley on the forehead with a calloused thumb.

"They would learn! Birds can fly."

"Some ain't meant to," said the Moose.

One night after that, Shelley kneeled by the door in the ground that led to the coop. She undid the latch, lifted open the splintery door.

"Chickens, come out, he's asleep!" Shelley yelled in. She stepped into the dark coop, and the thick brown smell crammed her lungs. She poked at nests, kicked hay. "Come out!"

A scramble of feathers burst out in the room, scratching and cackling and fighting. Shelley was struck in the face by the chest of a flapping chicken that she'd knocked off its top shelf; she grabbed hold of it, held it as the dirty thing thrashed and twisted in her arms. She carried it up the few steps to the exit and dumped it on the ground outside, expecting it to spread its wings over the ground and take flight into the black night sky. She breathed the cold air, waited—the small, buckshot-black hen quivered its head, scrabbled at the ground. Then, flapping its wings unsteadily, it started to run a drunken path, pitching to the left and then back toward Shelley, past her, and with a crack, it ran into the house. Shelley froze, watched it squawk loudly, heard the Moose throw open the door of the house.

"Goddamnit, Shelley, what did you do?" said the Moose, the frigid air gusting his boxer shorts.

"I wanted to help," Shelley said, warbling.

"The chickens are blind, you brat! We raised them in the dark! They're all blind!"

The Moose took a few steps toward the hen, but it had regained its feet and was running off, away.

Shelley's First Song

Always the same, nothing's different,
No escape, no place I want to go, I want to be alone
The skies, they are always this gray
The world is a whirling top and
Oh, the pain, the loneliness,
I need you close to me, please, I'm dying here.

The first and only time the Moose heard Shelley playing this song and singing to herself in unsteady tones, he'd interrupted with a whiny falsetto: *Whyyyyyyy don't the boys like meeeeeeee!* And then he slapped her on the back, grinning wide.

That's why Shelley only played when the Moose wasn't around.

Blood

The blood had started coming while Shelley was watching MTV and the Moose was out back, splitting wood for the sauna. She felt a little twinge in her body, like the snapping of a thread, and it flowed numbly out. A mother would have told her what was happening and whether she was going to die or not, but all Shelley had was the Moose and the television.

Her momma died during childbirth, and she went out with a hoot and both fists clenched and that's the right way to go and that's all that mattered: the Moose told Shelley this story once when she was eight, and then never again. Whenever Shelley asked, he would shake his head, say, "She went out with a hoot." Shelley was left to wonder.

She couldn't tell him about this. When she was eleven, she had sliced into the tip of her thumb while cleaning a halibut; she had screamed at the jagged flap of white skin and showed the Moose. He'd dropped his fish and held her thumb, scrutinized it.

"Think that hurts?" he'd said.

Shelley nodded, and her father let go of her hand, his lips smiling crookedly through his dense beard. He picked up his cleaning knife, hitched up his plaid sleeve around his bicep, touched the point of the knife along the back of his hand, and flicked. A vertical red line appeared along his thumb, and it began to ooze almost immediately. Holding his trickling hand close to Shelley's face, the Moose grimaced, then laughed, saying, "You're right, that does hurt. Now I'll show you how to bandage it up."

Since then, she didn't tell the Moose about pain, or anything else that hurt. She didn't ask about Momma. And now, as she hunched close to herself, pressing her pale thighs together to stanch the bleeding, Shelley waited for the Moose to turn in before stealing off to the sauna to examine herself. As she drew a cold bucket bath to clean herself up, she caught a glimpse of long, thin streaks of red on her knee. She placed a hand on her thigh, and then wobbled and passed out, briefly.

FRIENDS

"We need diesel," said the Moose, standing at the gas stove and stirring a breakfast paste of beans and Tabasco. "So I'm going into town today."

"Your dick's out," Shelley said.

The Moose looked down, placidly tucked himself in. "I'm pickin' up ammo, too. Gonna come, so you can see your friend?"

Shelley shook her head, and the Moose grunted in reply. No way was she going. The girl the Moose always called "her friend" was Rena Langford, who was three years older than Shelley and smelled like trash and was such a total slut and was definitely not her friend. She was the daughter of

Garry from Garry's Hunting Supplies down at Randall Cove, who was a longtime friend of the Moose's since back when they both lived in Alberta. Every time Shelley went with the Moose for supplies, the Moose made her hang out with Rena while he and Garry talked about trap hunting, politics, women. The Langfords were from Valdez up in the north, and with Rena, it was always the same talk about how things were in Valdez, how the men are hotter and how they do stuff, how guys from around these parts just jerk off and die. Shelley mostly felt the same way, felt the monotony of days that ran together and were separated only by rare events; but she hated Rena's stupid tight shirts and chalky makeup so much that she fell into tacit disagreement.

"Up in Valdez, me and the guys, you know, we would go down and take shots at the pipeline sometimes," Rena once said, peering down the sight of a used Winchester. Its yellow price tag dangled from the hammer. "Even with as close a shot as you can get, it never cracks. But it makes a real loud noise when you blast it. *Blam*. Now that was some fun. Can you imagine all that oil?"

Shelley didn't respond. The thought of a place even more boring than home made Shelley tired.

Home, Part Two

"Dad, I want my own room."

The Moose was baiting a longline with chicken liver. He wiped his greasy hands on his camouflage pants and squinted at Shelley. He had a wide, smooth face with a big forehead, and his thin hair tassled down to the thick plastic rims of his glasses. His was an easygoing face, but when it spoke about how Bill Clinton was going to send the world to damnation, or when it was shouting down Forest Service agents about a goddamn unfair overfishing fine, it could reveal a frightening hardness, like wrung iron. As Shelley sat beside him, she could see him gathering stern authority, and she already regretted her words.

"No," he said, and he went back to his work.

"It would only take a half a season, and I can do all the construction," Shelley said, her jaw set. "All you have to do is help me with the wood."

The Moose looked back up again, his face screwed up in annoyance. "I said no, Shelley. What do you need your own room for?"

Shelley felt a flame of anger; she thought about the blood. "I just want one."

"I ain't got time," he said.

"But I said I could—"

The Moose squinted, his eyes dark slits. He stuck his tongue out, moistened his lips, and Shelley's shoulders braced as his teeth came together and his thumb and forefinger went to his gums and he blew a shrieking whistle, a high ascending note that broke to shrill screeching. Shelley cringed; she knew he was done talking. The Moose's whistle was his hello and good-bye, and moreover, his way of saying "shut up." He'd learned it and honed it back in the days when he lived in Alberta with Shelley's mother and hunted small game with dogs. He would make his whistle with its two trilled notes, loud enough to call the dogs back from brush or pond two hundred yards away; he bragged that whenever his whistle caught one of the dogs in the middle of a crap, it would come scuttling back proud as a soldier with all that shit still coming out as it ran. And Shelley agreed, yes, that it was an effective whistle, and she knew because he'd used it to call her ever since she was a kid, whenever something needed doing.

By the next afternoon, she was out in the woods on the other side of the island with her mind made up, holding an idling chainsaw against the side of a tall spruce. Her goggles were loose around her head, and they slid as she prepared to fell her third tree that afternoon. She was feeling good; she'd never even used a chainsaw before, but she was sure that she could handle it, just as sure as she was going to build her room twice as high as the Moose's house, spit on its roof from the second story. The two trees she'd finished were limbed and bound behind her, and their great fallen lengths made her feel tough. She was tough.

With arms tensed, Shelley squeezed the trigger of the chainsaw and pushed the blurred edge of the blade into the side of the tree. It chewed uneven inches through the tree, scattering chips that pricked Shelley's skin through her sleeves. When she was almost a quarter of the way through, she struck something hard inside the tree—a knot or growth—and she couldn't push the saw farther. Before she could release the trigger, the saw kicked back at her, ripping itself out of the tree and out of one of Shelley's hands. She steered it out and it came back toward her chest too fast, and the base of the blade caught the side of her unzipped jacket. Shelley dropped the saw just as the blade wound itself around the jacket, sucked it in and tied it into a twisted hitch. As it came to a stop, it had eaten the jacket up to Shelley's armpit. It dangled loose, and its friction-seared chain was pressed up against her stomach. She stood rigid in fear, reached to switch the chainsaw off. When it was off, she pulled off her jacket, stood back. The chain was convoluted impossibly in the fleece of her jacket. Shelley would have to tell the Moose that it was broken, that she broke it. He would have to fix it; he would say that it was all right, just don't do it without him. Don't do anything without him. Shelley cried.

Shelley came home at night to the sound of the television, the CNN broadcast, the Moose propped on the couch, inert. The only light came from the glare of the screen; it reflected off the plastic that covered the bright yellow insulation in the walls, which gave the room a pale glow; he stuffed popcorn into his face even though he was allergic to it. The more Shelley watched the Moose, the more she was sure he'd always be there, always lying limp on some recliner, watching some TV, eating something out of a bag. Her stomach tightened.

Blood, Part Two

Shelley had made a rag for herself out of a tatter of lining that she'd retrieved from her torn jacket, and the Moose must have found it sometime while she was drying it on the clothesline, because one day he said:

"So, you're gettin' your monthlies now, huh?"

Shelley stared at him, with no honest idea of what he was talking about. It was a cool evening, and they were on the dock, snag fishing with unbaited treble hooks.

"Your monthly . . . womanlies," the Moose said, clearing his throat. "Bleeding?"

"Yeah, I bleed." Shelley reeled, not expecting the hook to snag.

The Moose looked out at the water. He scratched at his bare chest, around a thick red circular scar.

"Well do you need a how-to, you think?"

Shelley's brow arched. "I don't know what you're gonna say, but say it anyway."

"Listen, I know that I can't tell you much, 'cause this is a woman thing, a womanly burden, shall we say, and I guess I wish your mother was around, 'cause this womanly kind of thing just ain't my thing, Shel." The Moose began reeling in his line, waving the pole right and left to zigzag the hook. He cleared his throat. "Is not my thing."

She heard it. The Moose had mentioned her mother. Shelley's eyes widened, and her tongue tensed to find a phrase or word that would keep him talking. She felt too much time pass before she spoke.

"Why, what would Mom have to say?"

"Huh?" the Moose said, as if he'd thought the talk had ended.

"I mean, what do you think Mom would tell me? Like, you know, what was she like?"

The Moose was silent. He shifted on one butt cheek and then the other. Shelley was about to repeat herself when her rod tipped and pitched forward in her hand.

"You got something," said the Moose.

"I asked you what she was like," Shelley said, putting the rod down.

"Hey, damn it now, Shelley, you do not let the rod go when you got a catch!" The Moose tucked his pole between two planks of the dock and reached across Shelley to take hers. He faced the water with his whiskered lower jaw jutting, reeling in the taut line.

"Why won't you tell me about my mother?"

"Because," the Moose said, watching the line travel a rippling path through the water, "she ain't for you to know."

"Just tell me why. Tell me her name."

"Alice," he said, raising his voice. The catch coming closer.

"Her maiden name?"

Shelley saw tendons make a long ridge in the Moose's arm as he jerked the catch violently out of the water. He stood, and the catch swung like a pendulum past his face. It was a small-fry salmon; the Moose had snagged it so fast that the treble hook had torn down its whole body from its gill nearly to its tail. A crooked red streak stood out against the slick pewter of the fish skin.

The Moose threw down the rod, and the salmon fell, lay between two slats on the dock, its tail flapping and dispersing a spray of bloody water. Its eye was lidless, wide, mouth shocked open. The Moose gave Shelley his iron stare, then turned and walked back home.

Friends, Part Two/Blood, Part Three/Home, Part Three

At Garry's, Rena Langford said something gross.

"Pads, huh? Yeah, I use those too, I gotta. Every month I flow like the goddamn Nile, Jesus Christ, I swear."

They were out in front of Garry's, sitting on an unpainted picnic table; Shelley was waiting for the Moose to come back with the supplies. Rena was smoking cloves, pushing wisps of thin smoke through her wired teeth as she spoke. She was proud because she was the only one with braces, one of the few with a straight and complete set of teeth at Randall Cove. She also wore gel in her hair, rings on each finger.

"Yeah, every month," said Shelley. A frosty wind blew Rena's smoke into Shelley's face.

"But they feel like diapers."

"Yeah," said Shelley, staring at her shoelaces.

"Up in Valdez, there was a guy who didn't mind I wore them. He said he liked to feel them through my panties," Rena said.

"Gross."

"Nah, it wasn't. That's how it is in the city," Rena said. She laughed.

Shelley looked up. "What do you mean, the city?" Valdez was four thousand people large.

"Well, it's more city than this shithole is," said Rena, flicking her spent stub on the dirt.

"Have you ever been to any real cities?" said Shelley.

"No."

"Are you ever gonna move to one?"

"Aw, nah, I couldn't do that. Couldn't leave." Rena pulled out another clove.

"Why?"

"Because, you know, I grew up here." She flicked a blue lighter at her lips behind cupped hands.

"So?"

Rena looked at Shelley and said, "What, are you planning to leave?"

"If I can."

"To where?"

"The lower forty-eight. Maybe California," Shelley said.

"The hell? You think you're too good for Alaska now?"

Shelley saw that Rena's face was becoming severe. "Aren't you always saying how much it sucks here?"

"Yeah, but I'm not gonna leave my home," said Rena. "All my friends are here."

"Why can't you make new friends?"

Rena blew smoke in Shelley's face. "Fuck you. Not like you have any friends."

"At least I don't smell like a litterbox."

Rena held her cigarette up to her mouth, and for a moment, Shelley thought she was going to burn her with it. Rena opened her mouth, and a small smile formed at its sides.

"You wanna know something?" Rena said. "About your mom?"

Shelley stared cold. Her heart awoke, strummed in rhythm. "What?"

"My dad." Rena smiled wider. "He says your mom is your dad's sister. You're a freak."

Shelley's eyes were wide.

"You've got freak blood. That's why you're so ugly, why you got all those fucking red spots on your skin," Rena said calmly, taking a drag.

"Shut up!"

Shelley wound up, slapped Rena. The cigarette flew from Rena's lips, and her stiff dark hair fell across her face. Shelley got off the picnic table, preparing to fight the taller girl. Rena regained herself and looked Shelley in the eyes. Her pale face was blotching on one side. She smiled, stood up.

"Your dad's a pervert," Rena said. "Careful he doesn't fuck you next." She jumped off the picnic table, ran into the hunt shop, and Shelley didn't follow her.

Shelley was staggered, shaken. She sat on the dirt and took her face in her hands, did not cry. She had a thought, and it slipped away like an eel; more came and went.

Fifteen minutes later, she heard a car's tires crunching on the gravel road. It was the Moose, driving Garry's pickup truck. In the back of the truck, Shelley saw dozens of corded-down bulk packages of maxi pads, pastel blue and pink boxes piled high over the cab. The Moose parked and got out, holding a slip of paper in his hands, a receipt.

"They're, let's see here, uh, Always Ultra with . . . uh, Flexi-wings," he said, rubbing his furrowed brow. He looked up. "Where's your friend?"

Shelley's Second Song

My mother is my mother
Dad's the brother of my mother
They must have loved each other
Falling one after another.
My mother is my mother
Dad's the brother of my mother
They must have loved each other
And then they had me.

Shelley never played this song, only kept it in her head, secret.

Why They Call Him the Moose

The scar on the Moose's chest was heart sized, red and rubbery, and it was surrounded by dark clusters of chest hair. At home, slouched on the sofa, Shelley watched it as it rose and sank with his breathing while he fixed his eyes on the television. The room stank with the week's stale garbage, sweltered with the space heater turned to high.

"I talked to Rena yesterday," she said.

"Yeah," said the Moose.

"She told me something."

"What's that."

"She told me that my mother was your sister."

The Moose didn't move or blink, he just sat there. He grimaced. "Well. She's lying," he said, flat.

Shelley said it almost at a whisper: "Are you sure?"

"Yes. Rena is a goddamn liar."

"Why did she say it, then?"

"Because people are goddamn liars! Now shut your mouth and watch the TV."

"Why are you getting so mad?"

"You said Rena told you? That fuckin' whore." He stood up, wobbled a little, paced.

"I'm not angry, Dad. I don't care."

"That fucking whore."

Shelley raised her voice, high, to an unaccustomed wail. "Dad, I don't care!"

The Moose ran his hands down his cheeks, then dropped his arms to his sides. He sat back down, into the couch.

"Sorry, Shel," said the Moose. His small body, his short hair, his broad face, none of them faced Shelley. "She ain't dead. Nope."

"Where is she?"

"Dunno. I dunno." The Moose shook his head. "I ain't seen her."

"Why not?"

"Because I did it to her."

"Did what?"

"Um," said the Moose, his voice breaking into a tremor. He swallowed and turned to face Shelley with his eyes red rimmed and wet. "I did a bad thing, and she ran away." The Moose turned back away and wiped his nose. "And she gave me you because she didn't want you. But I did. Okay? And I brought you here so I could keep you here and you could grow up in a good way. All right? No more to say than that."

Shelley nodded. Her mother was gone now, lost to her, and Shelley let it be lost.

"I just want to know something," said Shelley. "Then I won't ask you anything after that."

"Shelley, I'm sorry, that's all there is."

"Why do they call you the Moose?"

The Moose looked at Shelley, wavered an awkward smile. "Because of this," he said, gesturing with an open hand to the pendant of scar on his chest. "Moose got patches of hair on their chest. I got a hairless patch, and since people already call him Eagle 'cause of the bald spot on his head, I guess Garry thought it'd be funny to call me that. The Moose."

"Oh," said Shelley. "I thought it was because . . . I mean, didn't you say before that you were hunting moose when you got that? When your father shot you?"

"No," said the Moose, "I wasn't."

The Dalmatian, Part Two

"It'll freeze to death if we leave it here," said Shelley. The rain had become a downpour, and the Dalmatian was still strained against its rope, blinking against the drops that fell in his eyes.

"It ain't our problem," said the Moose.

"We could take it home."

"No."

"It's going to die," said Shelley.

"We're not taking it home, and we're not stealing someone's dog," the Moose said, raising his voice.

The dog barked, and the Moose bared his own gapped teeth, whistled lightly and pointed away. Instead of obeying, the dog curled his lip, showing a crest of red gums and yellow teeth.

"It's not fair to keep it here," said Shelley. "We have to let it go."

"I ain't gonna argue."

"Well, I'm not going to leave it here."

The Moose scratched his scalp under his cap with his thumbnail. "Shelley. Come on."

"Why don't you ever care about anything?" Shelley set her jaw. "What if I was that dog?"

"Shelley, quit."

"If I was that dog, I know I wouldn't like it. I'm going to take care of this dog."

"No you ain't."

"And I'm going to feed it. And give it a name. You know what, in fact? He'll live in my room, with me—"

The Moose took his rifle in his left hand, crammed two dirty fingers of his right hand in his cheek and blew a loud, ragged whistle that jabbed Shelley's ears. She scowled as he finished, and behind the Moose just then Shelley saw a spatter of mud and pine needles as the Dalmatian pitched forward, and with a soggy sound, its nylon rope went slack and it charged. The leash had broken through the rot of the damp log, and it trailed behind the Dalmatian as it lunged at the Moose, crashing the small man down. All its teeth went to the Moose's rifle arm, and its hind legs stood quaking on the Moose's chest. Shelley's hand went to her knife; she wiped the rain from her eyes, and she grabbed the bony back of the Dalmatian and stabbed it once, four times in its side, inhaling between thrusts. The knife tip slid in as if on oiled tracks. The dog lurched back with a gasp, a suffering cry. The Moose pushed it off, and it landed tense on the ground, curled. The Moose stood—Shelley saw a broken red oval on his arm—and he cocked and fired his rifle into the dog's flank. It was pushed back a few inches by the discharge, and after a long half-minute of struggle, its breaths receded into the silent contraction of its chest and it died. The Moose touched his left hand to his right forearm, came up with a bloody palm.

"Are you all right?" said Shelley, glancing back at the dead dog. "Did it get you?"

"Doesn't hurt," said the Moose.

Shelley sheathed her knife, blade slick with gore—either the Moose's or the Dalmatian's. Her own blood ran scorching within her. The sound of the rain became apparent again—the rain itself was again cold. Shelley took the Moose's arm and examined the fresh bite; it was mangled, multiple.

"We need to get back," said Shelley. "Let's go to the boat. We can call a doctor on the VHF."

"This is no problem. Quit babying me," said the Moose, taking his arm back.

"But what if it was rabid?"

The Moose turned and started walking toward the boat, and Shelley took her guitar and caught up to walk beside him. As they walked, Shelley watched the Moose's forward-facing eyes, certainly out of concern and helplessness, and while she watched she tried to look through him, into him, searching for lies, symptoms, silences, some emerging sign of madness.

Roger McDonald

The Bullock Run

ALAN CORKER spent the whole wet afternoon with Ted Merrington walking cows and calves down narrow gullies to a set of yards and drafting them out. It was miserable weather but satisfying work for men.

The two had opposite styles. Corker was a quiet prodder, whereas Merrington swore and whacked the animals' rumps with a length of plastic pipe to get them moving. If a beast proved stubborn, red eyed and craning its neck across a bony shoulder, Merrington took it personally while Corker whistled and waited.

Rain slanted from the south and ran over their hat brims and down their noses to their chins. Corker was a tall, lean, light-complexioned man with a narrow, intelligent face and a flattened nose from boxing. In his youth he had won the regional light-heavyweight belt, and few ever forgot.

Merrington was short, gloweringly handsome and gave his opinions freely. He was a relative newcomer to the district, and Corker was getting to know him. When a cow lurched heavily through the wrong gate, banging it sideways and splintering a panel, Merrington squatted in a puddle and belted mud with his polypipe, swearing in a rhythm of frustration and sending splats of wet manure all over himself.

Alan Corker had never quite seen that kind of thing before.

When they got the cows away, Merrington switched in the middle of a rant and turned to Corker, raising a wild eyebrow. "Shall we take horses next time? Do you ride?"

No answer needed to that. Alan Corker had been raised in dealing stock, scouring the gullies of the Great Dividing Range from early youth with a hardheaded father on an irascible fat-bellied pony kept for the muster. There didn't seem much point in taking horses when a walk along a ridgetop with a cattle dog was effective. But if Merrington wanted some galloping fun, he'd oblige.

Why Merrington had this effect on him Corker couldn't say. The man was past fifty but like a spoiled child. It was the charm of the cheeky kid making demands, Corker supposed. You might want to kick them, but they made you grin, made you feel you could get them what nobody else could.

Merrington looked for trouble on the simplest pretext.

"You don't always have to please me, Alan."

"I like to try."

"I don't have to please you, though." Merrington threw a piratical grin. "Use your agent as a floor mop as the old saying goes."

Corker enjoyed the banter, the game of words. Merrington brought matters chin-to-chin and then swerved away with opposite meanings. So many of Corker's clients were hard-dealing men with no imagination to be otherwise. Colonel Robertson-Duff, who'd sold Merrington his land, was a good example. Yet Merrington's fancy, it appeared, was to be in the Robertson-Duff class. Tussock barons, Corker's father used to call them.

Six months before, on auction day, Corker wielded the hammer, and Merrington had won the homestead block excised from the larger spread. It barely offered a basic living, but Merrington bragged an impressive costs-to-income potential through his adroitness in beating the arse off Robertson-Duff.

Except Merrington was a mere trier, really—Corker's rare experience of an owner who wasn't an authentic hard case but wanted to be seen as one. The money Merrington had paid for plant and equipment after the auction was above what anyone else in the district wanted to give. It reversed the usual trend of gentlemanly conduct when he wrote a check without much haggling. Obviously the money came from off-farm, and it was Corker's precaution, Dun-and-Bradstreet-wise, to bite the silver back to the source.

Merrington looked the part, though, wearing a pair of stiff leather leggings found in a shed. Draped around his shoulders was an oilskin cape left hanging on a peg since the 1940s. He brought to mind a squatter from the Jolliffe cartoons in *Pix*: a comical geezer with galahs in his corn and a Bugatti in the woolshed. Corker calculated bringing Merrington up to date from the work-wear side of the agency. He felt warm about his ironical client in the cold rain, catching a glint in Merrington's eye that seemed to suggest Merrington reading Corker's thoughts and finding them agreeable. They might even become friends. Corker had reached a stage in life of wanting more zest from his usual cronies: denizens of the Apex Club and the Five Alls Hotel Galloping Wombats Polocrosse Squad. Merrington was a stiff breeze battering up from somewhere.

"That's the way, Ted," said Corker, with the calves jammed black and glistening in the race, smelling of panic. "You've got them sitting pretty."

Merrington accepted the tribute with a twisted smile.

"You're limping," said Corker.

"It's from a rodeo fall forty years ago."

"No kidding?"

Merrington gave a toss of the head. "I went jackarooing up Wanaaring way, in the school hols. Entered the bullock ride as a dare. I was a stupid young booger, and now the sciatica stabs like a knife. Our generation needed a war but didn't get it. Cracked ribs and a fractured pelvis—they're my battle scars, while the old Colonel got his medals at Tobruk and Balikpapan."

"We had Vietnam," countered Corker.

"You believe so?" Merrington's neck elongated, and his head wove like a snake's, in exaggerated surprise. "You were in that?" He steadied and stared hard.

"I was in the lottery, but my number never came up."

"Would you have gone if it had?"

Corker nodded. Of course he would have gone. That was the deal offered, just as it was when his father, Careful Bob, went to North Africa to fight the Eyeties and then to New Guinea against the Nips. Only later might he have seen things differently.

"I was too old for that game of marbles," said Merrington, giving his polypipe a flick on the rails to clean it of muck. "So I wasn't given the privilege to serve."

What seemed like a sneer accompanied these last words, leaving Corker wondering what Merrington meant. That Corker should have enlisted anyway? Or that he was wrong to have even taken his chances?

A phone call came. From under an umbrella Merrington's wife, Patricia, relayed information at the side garden gate. The semitrailer Corker had promised was delayed past dark.

Merrington said, "Well!" and shot an intense blaming glare at the agent. Corker said, "Easy does it," and reminded him that nine calves were not a full semi load, and the driver was doing the rounds of the district, so might he just be patient like everyone else? Thus reprimanded, Merrington became almost craven and asked Corker down to the house.

Double whiskies were replenished twice while they awaited the semi. It arrived past seven in the sodden winter dark. Half sloshed by then, they loaded the stock by headlights, the driver using an electric prod and scampering terrified calves up the race in the rain. Merrington took the prod and tried it, liking the feeling. "This is more humane than people make out," he said, jolting a poor animal more than was warranted. Then, with a reckless leer, he reached around behind his back and gave himself a wallop of volts in the left rear buttock.

"Whoa baby! Order me one in the morning!" he yelled.

"Done."

They took more drinks afterward to rewarm their saturated bones. Patricia attentively plied them with pumpkin soup and slices of homebaked bread, telling Corker he must bring his wife next time. Corker then rang Liz to explain his lateness and heard the arch humor in her voice, the note of interested surprise over who was getting him plastered. "He came to the school one day," she said, "and talked to the Year Twelve art class. They thought he was funny."

"As in?" asked Corker guardedly.

"Ha-ha."

"You've met my Lizzie then," said Corker when he came off the phone.

Merrington shot Corker an empty look, grinding his bottom jaw sideways as if about to spit. "Have I?"

"She's a teacher."

"Oh, delightful. The little English one in plaits?"

"Yes, she's a Pom," acknowledged Corker.

The two men moved into the living room with dogs on the rugs and a fire of red gum in the grate. Corker talked about his kids: his own twin daughters by his first marriage and Lizzie's two boys by hers. The twins lived with their mother in Sydney and visited their hometown irregularly. It broke his heart to miss them through their growing years, and now when they visited, it was only for a few days at a time because there was too much else going on for them in the big smoke.

"How old are the girls?"

"Sixteen."

"I understand that age," said Merrington in a tone that implied, mysteriously, that Corker didn't. "They should come and sit for me sometime."

"Sit?"

"Model."

Merrington gestured above the fireplace, where a painting of female figures gave an impression of half-circles overlapping. Small floating leaves like tentative bikinis covered the obvious bits.

"I never know what to make of modern art," Corker said. "But I like that one."

"Twins pay double," barked Merrington.

Corker whistled. "For doing nothing!"

"There would be no funny stuff," growled Merrington, "I can assure you of that."

Corker felt as if he'd had an unworthy thought, when really he was just giving the man his due, while reflecting warmly, through a haze of red wine, how there were more ways of skinning a cat than were dreamed of in his little corner.

Corker stood, yawned, stretched, patted the dogs, and said he'd better be going. The thought of Lizzie and the life they had was a magnet in the night: her warm toes pulling him over to her side of the bed when he came in, and the way they slept hooked in each other's arms until the early rooster crowed and they woke holding hands as trustingly as children.

"It's still early," taunted Merrington. "She's got you by the short and curlies."

"Maybe so." Corker grinned.

"Dear me, Ted," chided Patricia, joining the farewells at the door, "I imagine Alan doesn't have the luxury of sleeping in like you do."

Feeling blindly toward his car, Corker heard Merrington's voice answering her back. It seemed the wife was being paid out for verbal slips.

But why shouldn't a man sleep late if he was able? Give Corker the chance, he told himself, he'd sleep past noon every break he got. Merrington, thought Corker, was lucky in not having to show up at daylight at yet another set of frosty yards, running through the same whiskery old palaver every day of his life for the sake of the national debt.

Although not every day really. There were times mid-month or early in the week previous to cattle sales' Fridays when Alan Corker's phone fell silent for up to an hour and the winter sunshine poured across the oiled boards of the agency. Then Corker went around wiping dust from old photographs and chasing blowflies with a ruler. Then he gave the indispensable Jenny Garlick the morning off to visit her mother in the elderlies' wing of the district hospital and sent Henry Tuck delivering hardware around town from the back of the old Bedford.

Then Corker was ready for visitors to his alcove under the stairs, the green-stained electric kettle ready on the boil, instant coffee spooned from a jar, and a packet of Chocolate Wheatens ripped open and available to anyone who wanted to grab. And intermittently, in they came and grabbed: old cow cockies on their stick-assisted rounds, former loyal clients of Corker & Corker, bygone strong men of the Trout district, now diminished in their bones and down from their outlying acres and wind-rattled pioneer homesteads for good. For the betterment of their old age, and the pleasure of their wives, they'd bought brick-veneer bungalows in town with workable plumbing and cement driveways painted green.

Corker always knew what was coming as they nudged him in the ribs and told him another one about his old man, Careful Bob, and the one time Careful had got the better of them, the cunning old rat of Tobruk. Except Corker knew it wasn't just the one time because Careful Bob had taken the long view always.

The best example of this was the Bullock Run. Along the rim of the Dividing Range were parcels of land Bob had bought for barely the cost of a packet of fags in the 1950s and 1960s at mortgagees' auctions, estate clearances, and the like. Once intersected by logging tracks, the paddocks passed to Corker amalgamated whole.

The Bullock Run, four thousand acres of mountain fastness, responded to years of aerial supering and low stocking rates, whereas on Corker's home block, a rocky three hundred acres just out of town (the house within sightline of the St. Aidan's belltower), Corker ran fine wool merinos until they nibbled the ground almost bare, a choice little flock biding time and building up numbers among the wild turnip and Scotch thistle. Corker guarded their increase from marauding town dogs with a policy of once warned, never reminded. They would remain a mere sideline until wool improved and Hollywood Boy III paid his way, handsomely serving ewes. Meantime on the Bullock Run, Corker's herd of red cattle covered the twins' maintenance and school fees and left change for a red MGB—or some such whim of nature—that Corker planned wheeling in for Liz's fortieth-birthday surprise.

Then there was the time, the old men cackled, competing for Corker's attention, when Alan was too young to remember, so they said, when Careful had driven warily around the corner near the Catholic church—this was back postwar, when the roads in town were rough dirt—and the passenger door flipped open and infant Alan rolled out on the gravel.

"You wouldn't remember. You sat there like a little king, directing the traffic, covered in dust."

"Did I just," said Corker with a smile.

"Yeah, till Bob in the Saloon Bar of the Five Alls bought you a raspberry syrup, then looked around, wonderin' where you was."

So he had the old men. But since that evening with Ted Merrington, Corker came back to a thought—opening the door to the street and advancing his indefinable understanding with that peppery man. It was what he wanted, and why this should be so Corker could only wonder. There had been no sight of him since the night of the big headache, when Corker had driven home seeing double all the way. At the end of that week, the monthly statements had gone out as usual, a few necessary adjustments made to Merrington's.

One day it snowed down to the thousand-meter contour line. In a distant gap of steely-gray clouds, Corker saw the Bullock Run dappled through the state forest. He imagined the Herefords with snow striping their spines and lacing their sturdy haunches.

Suddenly there was Merrington, haggard and huddled in a houndstooth sports coat with the collar turned up, crossing windswept, deserted, inhumanly bitter-cold Currockbilly Street and meeting Corker face-to-face. "Hello, bud," he wheezed through his teeth.

"Ted, good to see you."

Merrington's tongue, white as limewash, rattled as he shaped his words. Corker had the feeling Merrington had forgotten his name, though not his function, as he grabbed him by the jumper and drew him close.

"Where's my cattle prod?"

"Wasn't that a joke?" answered Corker, grinning because Merrington had that effect on him, and he was glad.

"That says a lot."

"Ted, I'll get you one."

Merrington bit again. "The statement you sent me was a fine piece of work. My wonderful price for calves wasn't so great after you cut it to ribbons with your costs and deductions and whatever else you chose to whittle it down with."

"Just trying to help you, Ted."

There'd been a load of hardwood planks, Corker reminded his client, six twenty-kilo bags of Lucky Dog, and a galvanized steel wheelbarrow with a pneumatic tire, top of the range, for which Merrington had overlooked paying since auction day and which Corker, after the three-month allowance for terms had run out, had taken care of for him, as Careful Bob would say.

"Sharp!" snapped Merrington, without the trace of a grin.

"I don't like being touched, Ted." Best to make that clear.

Merrington rocked back on his heels and gave a small, uncertain laugh. There came again that almost apologetic appeal in the collapsed body language—the retreat into meekness Corker remembered from reprimanding him in the yards.

It needed to be said, but made the friendly side of Alan Corker feel sick and sorry. "Come over to the shop for a cuppa?"

"The legendary old-men's club."

"Is that what they call it?"

"Oh, crafty. As if there's nothing you don't know."

A car went past, separating them. When Corker stepped back onto the road, he saw Merrington making his way uphill toward the post office, waving farewell as if nothing uneasy had passed between them, as if soon enough—though not today—he would drop in for that hot drink and friendly yarn.

Yet a fact Corker knew about the path up the hill was that just over the rise, Kinloch United Sandison & Ball pitched for business, no matter how small it was. Could be that Merrington was already taking trade to Kinloch the Farmer's Friend, as the franchiser, new to town, called himself, fitting out the staff in Akubra hats and issuing monogrammed cotton shirts and moleskin trousers to both sexes.

Liz said there must be only one farmer using that lot because of where Kinloch put the apostrophe. Corker liked her loyalty but noticed his cash flow wobble a bit through the year.

He walked down through the backroom storage shelves and went to the dim windows facing out into the lane. There he coiled cobwebs with his finger and gazed up into the western hills at the far end of town. He knew every twist of track and crooked boundary line disputed and argued over since Careful Bob first piggybacked him through the kangaroo grass and showed him the Bullock Run. A shaft of sunlight passed along the Dividing Range, and snow showers seemed to melt from the far-distant slopes as Corker watched. In these years when snow fell, the smell of spring was constantly in the air—rich and clean, half humid—and close behind was the excitement of a good flush of feed translating itself into people's well-being.

There were no cattle prods in stock, so Corker ordered one by express post. As soon as it arrived, he threw it on the passenger seat of the Fairlane and drove the fifty minutes to Merrington's home, "Burnside." Nobody was there. Even the dogs were gone. A small flush of green in the driveway wheel tracks showed there'd been nobody home for possibly a week.

When Corker drove around the back of the house to check the sheds, a bunch of cows galloped along the fenceline toward him, just that little bit hungry and wanting a bale of hay. There was hay in the shed, and Corker wondered where Merrington had bought it. Seventeen cows meant that Merrington had bought five more from somewhere, and paid good money, too, because they weren't cheap anywhere.

With the parcel tucked under his arm, Corker walked down the side of the house and looked for a place to leave it. He tried the back door and entered the kitchen. This was not how he did business, not unless the favor owed was considerable, and in this case the favor was hardly more than a niggle raised to vague importance. Nor was it like Alan Corker to go walking through an empty house uninvited. But on he went, nose weaving like a ferret's.

Entering the next room on from the kitchen, he was drawn by the thickly lingering aromas of turps and oils. It was Merrington's studio, which, Corker had been given to understand, when they had their drinks, was the inner sanctum, the room that Patricia Merrington entered at her peril if Merrington was working.

It gave Corker a stab of satisfaction to break a rule. "He owes me for the drive," the calculating part of him rationalized—always a ledger in the back of his mind. Another thought was that Liz wouldn't stand for being excluded from anything he did, and he wouldn't want her excluded either, and so in his head a small argument with Merrington began. Who was the better man?

That question was certainly in the air with Merrington—had been since they first met, when Merrington bid up to prove his worth and overpriced himself against the district norms. Tracing it back, Corker identified the question as what separated Merrington out from his other clients—the source of attraction. Possessing an artistic temperament, Merrington didn't have to be like other people if he didn't want to be.

By contrast, Alan Corker spent his life matching himself to others' needs up to a finely judged pitch of acceptance. Who was more impartial than the auctioneer tenor-throating animals and merchandise to their inherent market worth?

Gazing swiftly around before closing the door, Corker gained the impression of an Aladdin's cave of color, canvases propped on easels, small thumbed-over sculptures, and colored bottles of various sorts. Objects lined the shelves: pinecones, rocks, lumps of gnarled wood, a stuffed platypus, a Greek vase—selections from the outside carried inside and waiting for the brush. Set off were an old saddle, a pair of cracked boots on a stool, and the cape Merrington had worn in the rain, now hooked on a kind of crutch. The arrangement gave the group a life of its own. The result, on canvas, was a cartoon dance of clothes props and washing in the wind. "Life's a scream," it seemed to say. But also, "Beauty is transient, yet a very present thing."

Corker imagined putting the painting under the gavel, getting the room excited, peeling words from his imagination like hundred-dollar notes, and giving to the painting the feeling of an outsider coming home at long odds.

Merrington was more than he seemed; Corker already knew that. But this picture was more than Merrington—pointing to a truth Corker had always known in the blustery world around him, but hadn't quite focused on to see so brilliantly.

For Alan Corker was at a point in life when he wanted to have that effect on people too. Not just to have passed through the world, but also to have whatever was true in the world passed through him. But sometimes your gap closed so tight that nothing got through. Of course there was always a seeking part of him, wanting a little bit more. It had given him pluck in the amateur ring and was there in his singing when he was a bit older: a longing uncorrupted by second thoughts. It was why, between marriages, he'd cut back on his drinking and returned as a worshiper to St. Aidan's. It hadn't worked, except in the choir he'd met Lizzie, echoing a love of his youth, when he'd passed the minister's house and yodeled for the daughter. That was quite a time; then it was over too.

But what, Corker asked himself, was truly, widely, and generously amazing about him at all? He was in the groove as successor to Careful Bob down the years. That defined him locally. That Liz found him remarkable, cause for praise, was the definition of her loving him. What about the rest?

Something was left over for Corker as a man, and he had to face dealing with it as a man. It rose into his understanding as a drive to line up with sex and the providing instinct. But it seemed more elevated, and he could only express it as a question: where was the gleaming room, equivalent to Merrington's private studio, where Corker himself kept a few amazing secrets, ready for show?

Up the mountain was the best fattening country Careful Bob had ever stumbled across: those crafted, exemplary paddocks surrounded by state forest and tall timber shedding long clattering strips of bark. With ceilings open to the sky and walls wide, they were Corker's amazing room.

As a rule, Corker kept the wonders of the Bullock Run in the family. It was his workaday refuge, the place he went to on weekends and long summer evenings when the day's dealing was done—just twenty minutes' drive from the agency door to the locked gate. But he decided to invite Merrington up there.

Let him see something wild after his own heart, Corker resolved. They would make a full day of it. He would bring Liz's boys, Matt and Johnny, who followed his every move; the boys would ride the farm bikes while

Corker and Merrington took to the ridges on horseback, and Liz and Patricia Merrington spread a picnic lunch on the creek bank near the waterfall. If the arrangement fell at the right time, then the twins might join them—a bonus for Corker's feelings and a chance for Merrington to meet them and for them to decide about the sitting he'd offered.

That year was a hectic one in Corker and Liz's lives. She had a full teaching load and extra marking at night. Looking for cattle, Corker ranged wide, embarking on long drives and conducting his life via car phone out into the Riverina and north to the Upper Hunter, skirting Sydney, where on the horizon construction cranes wavered like long-legged mosquitoes, helping to make over the city for the Olympics. Several times passing, he called his daughters to arrange a coffee or a Chinese meal, but it didn't work out.

Corker's was an old problem: offering his clients the best-priced animals while securing top dollar when they moved through to the selling end, which, cattle being what they were, was in the same market moment. "Tip the Scales with a Corker" had been a slogan since Careful Bob was a boy in shorts, but it was still only as good as the most recent sale. Wool, by comparison, was in a trough, so Corker had the leisure to acquire, for the two or three concerns that cared enough to try, a line of fine wool breeders challenging his own in readiness for when the industry looked up.

Almost when the details seemed too hard to arrange, the twins phoned to set a date mid-term for their seventeenth-birthday dinner—"at home," as Corker liked to say. However, the farmhouse on the town boundary of Trout Junction where they'd started their lives had long ceased to be their center. Once, they'd ridden small bicycles with ribbons flying from the handlegrips, past the hayshed and out into the ordinary backstreet leading down to the primary school. Corker had an enduring image of them wobbling all over the road as he paced behind them to make sure they were safe.

Now when he phoned, there was the same feeling of protectiveness, but he felt wrong footed, intrusive. "Why not come Friday evening and go back Sunday night?"

Objecting, they said they would rather travel on the train arriving early Saturday afternoon and returning late the next morning.

"I don't see the point of a short stay," Corker insisted. "Less than twenty-four hours!"

He couldn't keep the edge of complaint from his voice, making him seem all obstinate fatherhood to his daughters, whereas to others, including Liz, "Nothing impossible" was his motto and geniality-plus his reputation.

"Dad, can we do it our way for once?"

Corker handed the phone to Liz, feeling as if they always did it their way.

Corker's definition of being a man in a family of women was containment of feeling, while the women expressed theirs every way they could. They seemed to have extra lines open to each other while the men's exchange barely connected. Maybe Corker wanted it that way, liked it better; except sometimes it bothered him, and when it did, it seemed more important than anything else.

Liz learned that the twins were sacrificing a Saturday-night party with their Sydney friends, for which a Friday-night party was to be substituted. So a Saturday arrival it would have to be.

"You sympathized with them," said Corker as she put the phone down.

"I was young once."

"So was I, but I paid my dues."

"Alan, your mother told me you were abominable: never at home, driving hundreds of miles to parties and dances and leaving her dangling when she longed to know who you were interested in."

"Not at seventeen. I was a lot older. Besides, it's their birthday, I'm their father," said Corker flatly.

"Darling, they love you to bits, you're the anchor in their lives."

Except when he up-anchored that once, he thought, creating uncertainty that they thought might never end.

Corker stood on the platform, his heart full. His daughters stepped down from the train: freckle-faced Abbey with a head of flossy red hair wound up in a bandana; Tina with short, blonde spiky ends. Last time, Abbey was blonde and Tina red.

After kissing him, they turned to Liz, hugging her to the count of ten. "No other luggage?" he asked as they shouldered their backpacks. They had large paper bags but wouldn't let him carry even those. He knew, of course, how skilled they were at packing minimal luggage after a childhood of shuttle domesticity. They skipped ahead, arms linked in Liz's, leaving Corker with the familiar emotion of wanting more than they could give. In the car, he drove with a tolerant half-smile, just holding the wheel and being of service.

At the house, Matt and Johnny came running out and dragged the girls to the dog kennels to muss the border collie's coat, and then to the basketball hoop clamped to the hayshed. The boys threw baskets to the girls' applause until called in for afternoon tea. On the veranda, Corker asked them about school marks, and they said they'd already told him, but he couldn't remember being told, so they patiently spelled it out.

"Tell them how they look," whispered Liz.

"Oh, by the way," he said as he fidgeted with his teaspoon, "you girls look sensational." He smiled the easy, loafing smile his clients liked.

"Do you think so, Dad? Really?"

"Yes, smashin'," he confirmed, appropriating one of Liz's North Londonisms.

They were pleased.

Then they were back with Liz, the three of them flinging dresses on beds and pooling jewelry. Corker went to swab the concrete floor of the ram shed and waited for them to come over. As the sun sank lower, he calculated that if they rushed, they had time to reach the Bullock Run for a dose of country feel before they scrubbed up for the restaurant. When he went back to the house and put the idea to Liz, she said she'd never heard anything so absurd. The girls were in the bathroom, steam coming out from under the door in volcanic folds.

At dinner at the Pizza Haven they announced, "No speeches!"

And this left Corker with a lump in his throat because he wanted to say something tipsily profound over the remains of the garlic bread and demolished Mexican Special. What was it again?

"I've always been glad I had daughters because sons might get big and clock me."

Matt and Johnny, in their wet, slicked-back hair and spotted bow ties, gave him a grin.

"Definitely a speech," groaned Abbey.

"So we're less of a threat," asked Tina with a martial-arts scowl, "because we're weak?"

"You don't understand. I always had the fantasy of a togetherness thing.

That we'd sample vineyards in France. You'd link arms with me like you do with Liz, and heads would turn and people would say, '*Sacre bleu!* They're incredible *jeune filles*, they're his daughters.' "

"Name the day," said Tina with a downward lilt to her voice. Everyone knew that Corker was hard to uproot from his working life and that his typical holiday arrangement was an expenses-paid trip to New Zealand mud springs—his reward for selling farm products.

"Look," said Corker, producing two felt-covered jewelry cases from his jacket pocket and shuffling them like a conjurer. "Whose is which?"

It was an old birthday routine. Whichever the girls received—gold wrist bracelet or silver ankle bracelet—they would swap perpetually, everything interchangeable in their lives. Their friendship with each other was, Corker felt, a safety net they had when he wasn't around. Once he'd tried to say this to them and hadn't been understood—or perhaps only too well understood. If you offered perceptions and got a prickly response, did that mean the message went through?

They came around the table, hugged him and kissed him, then smiled conspiratorially at Liz because they knew she'd had a hand in pushing him to get what they wanted and steering him to the jewelry store.

Corker had them now. But there was still a gap: their twinship, their life in the city with their mother—an intimacy sealed from Corker—their girls' web of secrets, their casting of him as cranky and contradictory when he often was not. All this left him feeling excluded as a matter of course, even unloved at bedrock when he considered how much he gave and how little flowed back of what he wanted and what would be only too simple for them to give. But what difference did it make really? He loved them. He underwrote their lives without question and always would. If there was ever a mortal threat to them, he would stand with sword and shield, warding off danger. Frankly, he would die for them, though with a lament on his lips: *Farewell, dear Lizzie my love, I must leave thee now.*

"Dad, you're tipsy!"

"What did I say?"

"You were humming some old 'choral' item or other."

Liz squeezed his hand under the table.

Corker ordered another bottle of red and watched it go straight into three out-thrust tumblers and so went for another. At the bar it was one friendly drunk after another wanting a part of him. He returned to the table to find the next round of pizzas arrived and everyone tucking in.

"What a strange, jokey little man," said Abbey, looking back over her shoulder.

Corker looked up and glimpsed Ted Merrington disappearing through the flywire door and into the dark street with Patricia Merrington a few paces behind him.

"As if it was our fault there weren't any tables," said Tina. "That was amazing."

"What do you mean?"

"Your friend did a routine for us," said Liz. "The disgruntled, pop-eyed blimp who doesn't get what he wants."

"But look what he did," said Abbey, flourishing a paper napkin with a lightning sketch in black Biro of a nest of hair and two bright eyes over a strong, small chin. "He made me prettier than I am. But I like that."

"You are pretty," said Corker.

"Oh, he perked up when he saw these two," said Liz.

"He invited us for dinner," said Tina.

"When?"

"Tomorrow night if we want to come. He said he'd talk to us about our major projects."

They stared Corker down and watched his discomfited surprise at having his daughters rushed.

"You'd cancel your train for him?"

"Would we?" The girls consulted, then looked up at Corker, holding the moment teasingly.

"Your father's been wrangling that invite for months," said Liz.

"Hardly," Corker said with an awkward laugh.

It amused her, Liz said, that Corker went on advancing his sought-after friendship while the friendship itself, as far as she could tell, existed mostly in Corker's imagination.

Corker told them about his plans for a full day out on the Bullock Run.

"Oh, that Bullock Run again," said Abbey, raising her eyes to heaven.

Liz turned to the girls. "When your dad and I first met, he took me there, paddock by paddock. Then we came at last to the old mustering hut. That was where I loved my new country and your Alan Corker in the same breath." She leaned her head on his shoulder. "The Bullock Run is the life we made from our broken halves. The hut showed what we could do together. Once it was all bits and pieces. We nailed up board and batten, refloored it in native pine, and installed the iron stove and unrolled the Egyptian-pattern rug."

"That Bullock Run," groaned Abbey to her sister, "was where I lost my thongs, remember? The iridescent ones with the electric daisies?"

"Have you got proper toilet facilities yet, Dad?" asked Tina. "Or is it still the mattock and the Sorbent roll?"

"I'm not saying we'd camp out."

"I can't see Mr. Merrington squatting on his haunches," said Abbey, "being jabbed by a prickle."

"Do I cancel the idea?"

"Well, darling, I'm for it," said Liz. "The only thing is," she added, "you should wait until they have us down there as promised. Then we can ask them back."

"All right," said Corker.

"Because I'm longing to see their stuff," said Liz, with a sly felonious giggle, having heard the Merringtons had a Fairweather, a Margaret Preston, an early Arthur Boyd, a wartime Tucker, a Grace Cossington Smith, and a superb Veronica Baxter, bought for a song. So there was a learning experience awaiting her in that house as she made herself over as an Australian teacher in the cultural field.

"There's certainly a lot of it," nodded Corker, who'd given Liz several confused accounts of what he'd seen. The night of the drinks, it had been very little. As for more recently, he didn't say he'd gone wandering through the house after leaving the package on the kitchen table, only that he'd peered through the window. This gave him the chance to describe the stick man blowing in the wind.

"That might be a Nolan," said Abbey.

"Or a Boyd," said Tina knowingly. "He painted *The Trout River Near the Sea*. It's his most famous."

"It could be one of those," said Corker. He knew it wasn't, but it confirmed an instinct he had that Merrington was on the money with his paint box.

Corker relished the one day of the week when he slept past five and the phone didn't start ringing at daylight. But the next morning, early, there was a clattering in the kitchen and a lot of hushed whispering, so he pulled a pillow over his ears and went back to dreaming. When he reached across for Lizzie, she wasn't there, and a while later she came back to bed. "Where have you been?" he asked. No answer, or if there was one, he missed it as he drifted off again with her fingers stroking his back, a motion interrupted as she turned a fresh page of her book, and he waited, his body craving the resumption of her touch like a fish getting closer to the surface of water and blazing light.

There was a knock at the door. Abbey and Tina entered with breakfast trays.

"What's this?" Corker sat up.

"Nothing much," said Tina.

"Only all those outrageous luxuries they wouldn't let you carry at the station," said Liz.

Humbled, Corker glanced out the window into the bright early day, fighting back sudden tears while breakfast was attentively laid out on the bedspread. The window framed granite boulders and pale, bare soil. A straggle of wrinkle-backed ewes filed across the corner of the view. Merinos were always such sad sacks. The black shadow of poplars elongated on the ground. When Corker looked back into the room and bit a square of toast dripping with butter and Vegemite, he felt that if he died at that moment and that was all he ever had, it would be enough.

"Careful, Dad," said Tina, as Corker shifted his knees and made a tray tilt.

Abbey buttered a croissant and spread it with strawberry jam, then put it on a small china plate and handed it to him. What antennae these girls had, smiling into his eyes, their hearts unerringly picking up what was right. Even when the faintest signal came in, they felt its force.

One day soon afterward, the agency door rattled the way Corker had expected: a bit demandingly, a bit overdone. He didn't need to raise his head to know the source of the touch.

"Look what the cat dragged in," said Henry.

"Mind the phone," Corker told Henry, seeing Merrington's barging outline ripple through the double glass doors.

Corker strode to the front of the shop and made a heartfelt greeting: "Good morning to you!"

Merrington looked pink cheeked and fresh. "Off the grog," thought Corker as he took a punch to the shoulder from Merrington. A token of friendship perhaps, it was delivered with a short man's pugilistic reach and would leave a bruise.

"I'll have that legendary cuppa I've heard about."

"Name your poison, Ted."

Merrington looked along the shelf. "Could I have a Milo?" he play-actingly whimpered.

"Good choice."

"Strong, two sugars."

"Coming up."

"Ouch!" Merrington said as they sat down in the swivel wing chairs under the stairs.

"Sciatica still troubling you?"

"I had a fall. Galloped the paddock crosswise and connected a chukka, but then my pony—not mine, lent by Frizell—chose its moment to belly-flop. Flattened out like the bejeezus. Actually, Corker, I found myself forking up and stepping off. But I was jolted, and the old trouble's back. Limped around using my polo mallet as a walking stick. Not much sympathy from Frizell."

"You mean Lionel Frizell?" asked Corker.

"Kit, the son. He's a bit of a lad."

As if Corker didn't know it. These Frizells lived at Pullingsvale, a hundred kilometers away, where the high tumbled country of the Trout district flattened to a wide grassy plateau. Horse breeding was favored there, and the polo calendar dictated the year. The grandparent Frizells, now pushing up capeweed in the family plot, had been valued clients of Careful Bob in the distant past, whereas Lionel and Kit rarely paid without a summons, and Corker had long since closed their account. But sometimes they met at cattle sales, and when eye contact was made, a check would be scribbled and passed over with an air of largesse, putting Corker on the drip-feed till next time.

Merrington took a deep breath through flaring nostrils. "Polo is my game," he declared with calculated immodesty. "I'm less than useful, though Kit says he'll try me as a 'B' reserve player one day, so I must be doing something right."

"You certainly must be."

"If it doesn't work out, there's always the Galloping Wombats—if they'll take me on." He flashed an inquiring grin.

Corker ignored it and busied himself with the electric jug. Obviously, Merrington knew that he played polocrosse sometimes; knew it, too, as a game for tradesmen and pony clubbers, in polo parlance.

Corker said dryly, "The Wombats have their standards. But you wield a mean length of polypipe, Ted, I've noticed, with a classy wrist action."

"Touché," said Merrington, giving his Milo a slurp. "By the way, Kit and Annabelle are coming for dinner on Saturday night. Why don't you and your good wife join us?"

So there it was after all this time: the invitation, rather offhand and at short notice.

Over the rim of his mug, Merrington peered at Corker with a twinkly expectation. It occurred to Corker to beg off, make an excuse, let the whole thing drop.

Merrington grabbed a copy of *The Land* and read out the long-range forecast.

"El bloody Niño strikes again. This has happened to me before, Alan. Every time I take up a new piece of country—rain to the north, rain to the south, but wherever I happen to throw down my swag, there's bugger-all."

"It's dry," agreed Corker, amused at the way Merrington talked himself up.

"Your bumph said 'safe district.' I should have allowed for the bullshit factor."

That Merrington blamed his agent for weather patterns was a pretty good joke. It raised a stock agent to the level of god and made every humorous bite a supplication. For this reason, whatever Merrington wanted, Corker was ready to give to him at that moment. He still had to know what it was, though.

"This is Australia," said Corker. "Safe means divide by two and take away the number you first thought of. Anyone with half a brain knows that."

Merrington pulled a small, defeated face. "I'll remember it next time you build my hopes."

The point was obvious, and Corker came to it. "Short of feed, Ted?"

Merrington squirmed. "It's not only that, it's the feeding out. I can't even hoist a bale without feeling as if my arms have been torn from their sockets."

"Where did you get your hay?" Corker suddenly asked.

Merrington blinked in puzzlement. "You mean because I didn't buy it from you?"

"Yes."

"I had a shedful back on the old place after I de-stocked, so I trucked it over when they settled, and I had my other cows there too. Now I've got too many—bad timing."

Corker leaned back in his chair, his smile changing from a jagged slit in galvanized iron to something cozier, more forgiving. Better men than Merrington had made mistakes on a larger scale.

"Ted, you're an artist. I hate to think of you doing farm work when you could be doing those wonderful canvases."

"Needs, must," said Merrington, with a kind of shining baffled look, expressively honest, unprotected, pleading.

Corker made a decision. "Look, Ted, have you got an hour or two?"

"Right now? I'm stuck while Tinker Brothers do a driveshaft for me."

"OK, let's go." Corker grabbed his hat. "I want to take you somewhere."

Nothing much was said when they came to the locked gate where the yards were. Nothing much needed to be said as they got under way and started climbing the high, sparkling ridges of the Bullock Run.

Merrington merely asked, "This paddock yours?" And then at the next vista, "This one, too?"

Each time Corker nodded, and Merrington took it in.

The late-afternoon light played its part compounding impressions, speaking for abundance, coming in thick golden slabs from around steep corners and through old forest trees, parted in bars of shadow on the track. Surely, thought Corker, this was a picture.

Merrington sat with his shoulder jolting against the passenger door. He seldom spoke, but Corker could almost hear the cogs in that gnarly brain. Light shone across into the heart of the mountain, purple against the tightly massed trees, the eucalypts giving out their oils and mists of oils, blue-growth tips among the red-growth tips creating mixtures of color. An artist would know that without being told.

The Toyota climbed the winding gravel track, its tires spitting stones into gullies of fern. Up higher were exposed ridges of silver-topped ash and conical anthills that looked like mud-built houses. Native reeds sprouted among the dry stones. Corker said that he often imagined all of Australia in these four thousand acres: the walloping variety of the country, from the Southeast forests to the outcrops of the Kimberley; the distillation of abundant space in a wagtail balanced on a blade of grass, nipping at ripe seed heads. He'd seen them in both places: cousins across a line wider than imagination.

While the agent waxed artistic, Merrington's mind was on the property aspect.

"Four thousand, you say?"

"More or less."

"All this your timber?" he asked with a grunt. The ash was sieberi, prized as hardwood for house frames.

"Yep."

"Why don't you chop them?"

"I wouldn't want to. Would you?"

"I might," said the artist, "if it came to the crunch."

"That's honest," said Corker.

Merrington started talking about the geology up there. It emerged he knew a lot. Each gully of the main creek had a story to tell that Corker had never heard better told, dramatized with a commentary that might have been lifted from the Nature Channel. As Merrington spoke, Corker saw changes to the landscape speeded up, the patterns of erosion at work. Where the creek had cut terraces over the years, now thick with tussock and reed and mazed by cattle pads, Merrington dated the trees. Corker realized that on the lower terraces were no trees older than when Careful Bob first brought him there. It showed that since then there had been limited ravages and no landslips or mini Grand Canyons, as in the Beetlejuices' dismal, overcleared subdivision lower down. There, entire creek banks floated into neighbors' paddocks when it rained, and grass, rocks, and cowpats looked like wedges of cake flipped from the main plate.

Corker interpreted all of this as Merrington praising him, giving him points.

But then Merrington snapped. "Why are you doing this, Al? Do you think I'm loaded?"

Corker laughed. "I'm not selling it."

"No?"

"Never. It's for my kids and their kids. I think of myself as holding it in trust."

"That noble sentiment," muttered Merrington.

"If they don't want it, I'd rather give it back to the blacks."

"If you mean that," Merrington said with a sideways look, "I could introduce you to someone."

"Let's wait and see."

"So what's the deal?"

"I'm offering you a respite, Ted, a place to spell your cows and build them up, saving you grass at home."

"Really? Truly?"

It was odd and rather touching that Merrington hadn't understood this. He spent so much time working around or behind people that he missed the obvious open palm.

"I can't pay you." Merrington jutted out his jaw.

"A painting would do."

"I'll think about it." Merrington looked off vaguely.

Corker said, "All right," then waited.

Nothing more was said. It was preferable anyway, thought Corker, to wait until Liz made the pick.

She didn't take long.

On Saturday night, while she clutched her welcoming G & T, her eyes settled on a brown, contorted face: an elderly woman staring with drab authenticity from a paint-peeling frame.

"That's strong," she said.

"Everyone says so." Merrington gestured at other pictures with his whisky tumbler. "Can't you be less predictable?"

She thought it probably wasn't one of his then. It was wonderfully good.

But then: "I painted her when I was seventeen."

It was said so quietly and simply that Liz replied, "I'm sorry," realizing she had learned something sad. Early promise and its downhill slide.

"I've done a lot since," insisted Merrington.

"Well, I like it as much as anything in the house," dared Liz. She had ticked off the famous names with a newcomer's excited pedantry as Merrington led her around—Nolan, Boyd, Tucker, Preston, Veronica Baxter—until they reached the one that affected her most.

"You want it?" Merrington looked sullen.

"You mean as Alan's quid pro quo? Could I?"

"That's the slippery question. She was my mother's great-aunt—face like boilerplate, don't you think?"

"One of those two-hundred-year-old tortoises," Liz said, nodding. "I love the character shining through. It's an unusual soft palette, all those browns and pinks."

"Like mud, my family said." Now Merrington flicked a sharklike smile. "The sitter declined the portrait, you know. They weren't comfortable with a boy genius in their midst. So I jammed it up their arses with my first show. A huge success, and I was hailed as the enfant terrible of my day. Made quids."

"Luvverly."

"I'm talking of almost forty years ago."

"Heavens."

Liz was right about the disappointment then. Such old resentment couldn't explain, though—could it?—Merrington's simmering fury, which she caught now as the main part of him but had missed when she saw him dancing across the playground that first time, when he lectured the Year Twelves with rib-splitting wit on the shortcomings of every living Australian painter with money in the bank.

Then she'd thought him a Peter Pan, and his comic turn in the Pizza Haven gave the same impression; a not particularly grown-up version of a man but certainly not a boring one. And he'd been so understanding with the twins. For that alone, much else was forgivable.

There was some kind of secret burning him, though, and Liz wondered what it was. Why didn't he like it when people liked him—and, in the case of Alan, when they liked him a lot? What did he hate in himself like poison?

Merrington drifted back to the drinks table, stunning himself with spirits before the wine started flowing.

"You're such a living embodiment of art history then," said Liz rather gauchely, trying to push things along.

Merrington had no reaction, but brightened when Liz added, "The twins asked me to tell you they appreciated your offer of conversation."

"And the sitting," Merrington reminded her, "don't forget the sitting at going rates, times twa."

They heard a car outside.

Kit Frizell and the young Annabelle were an hour late but were welcomed effusively by Merrington even though he had fumed about their unpunctuality several times.

Annabelle was hardly older than the twins—early twenties at most. During introductions she held Liz's eye and smiled in a friendly, inquisitive way, as if to say, Won't this be fun, but watch out. In the studio was a painting of her almost finished, which Merrington was giving as a late wedding present. It had a washed-out look, swirling blues and greens. Liz's summation to herself was that it lacked both character and accuracy, and that was its main difference from the painter himself, who was overdosed on definition.

The male hug was new to country manners, but Kit Frizell gave Corker a clumsy version of one and, when the others weren't watching, took a crumpled check from his pocket.

"How does a grand affect you?" He confidently grinned.

"It'll do for now."

Over dinner—plenty of bargain red and a beef stew with mashed potatoes and string beans, Ardmona pears and hot custard to follow—Merrington raised topics from the head of the table.

"Anyone heard of Ion Whitten?"

Nobody had except Liz and Annabelle. Whitten was a radio broadcaster at the serious end of the dial, and apparently Merrington hated him, though they had never met. He said Whitten took his holidays in Romania or some such blighted country and bought underage girls from their starving mothers for a few cheap dollars. Had this on good authority.

Jumping up and knocking his chair back with a vigorous clatter, Merrington descried a fantasy he had of coming up behind the broadcaster on a dark night, giving him a thumping and teaching him a lesson he would never forget. For the sake of those poor, ruined children, he would cripple the man's larynx with a rabbit chop, disabling him for the microphone, and break his legs with an iron picket, putting him in a wheelchair for life.

"For life!" agreed Corker, tossing back his wine.

"'Struth," said Kit Frizell, grinning.

"What sort of evidence do you have?" asked Annabelle. "I mean, this is serious stuff."

Patricia Merrington gave a chiding sniff in the direction of the young woman as if to say, My husband, right or wrong, is a terrific card.

Merrington scuttled around the table, topping up wineglasses.

Liz changed the subject. "Who can define the word *jackaroo*? Alan gives me a different answer every time."

Annabelle shot straight back, "Young man of good family paid peanuts to slave in hope of advancement."

"Oh, I like that!"

"It's certainly not a holiday job," said Corker, remembering Merrington's claim to have jackarooed on school vacation many years ago. The judgment was out before he realized.

"Beg yours?"

"Well, remember you told me—"

Merrington snorted. "Of course I remember what I told you! Want to see my X-rays, or do you want to step outside?"

Kit Frizell touched Corker's elbow and winked. "Don't stay past midnight. Fun till then."

Merrington tapped his fork on the edge of the bruised-blue willow-pattern dinner service. When Corker looked up, a pair of hooded, hawkish eyes met his. Maybe it was time to go now.

"Do you want to put a price on that mountain grazing, Al, or just leave it to your wife to bargain me in?"

"I'd rather leave it to Lizzie," said Corker. "What do I know about art? Anyway, it's a private arrangement, price not being the most important factor, and I'd rather not discuss it in front of these people anyway."

Merrington laughed. "That's ripe. I'm being asked to let go a prized item of juvenilia in exchange for agistment. Am I to do it for a mere song? Let's have a vote."

"You've lost me," said Kit Frizell, raising his hands in goofy surrender.

At this moment, Patricia Merrington left for the kitchen with an armload of plates, sending her husband a glance fearful with appeasement.

Corker felt cold and humorless. To have given, and to have hoped—well, that was past attempting.

Merrington turned to Annabelle. "What should I do, young one? Let go the picture?"

"You're asking me?" She pointed a finger at herself, leaned forward and laughed, then tossed her long blonde hair back over her slim shoulders. "It depends what you want to do," she said with quick clarity.

"I'm being squeezed, I believe."

Corker interrupted, his voice blowing through the silenced room like a dry wind clearing a way for itself as it went.

"I made a gesture of friendship, Ted. That's all it was. But if you want me to tell you, I will. The grazing's worth lots. Take it or leave it. Otherwise, believe me, you're out of the game and the RSPCA, will slap a writ on you for starving your herd. That picture's cheap at the price."

"I'll choose another picture," said Liz.

"Can't have that," said Corker. "It's the one, or the offer is zilch."

There was a long, uncertain silence, and then Merrington loudly mocked a yelp of pain. "Done!"

He brought the painting around, a few days later, insisting on finding the best place in the house to hang it—"Where she'll feel at home," he quipped. Liz was wary of him at first, then enjoyed the visit. She was moved when Merrington stood in front of the picture and said his good-byes, folding his hands in front of himself in a ceremonially meek posture, like a small, chastened boy, addressing a few words to the old aunt. "Wherever you are in outer space, look down on us kindly for our sins."

"Amen," said Liz.

They took tea on the veranda corner that overlooked the ram paddock. It was where Corker sat with his shotgun on wild nights, waiting for town dogs to try their worst.

Merrington said he was booking models because there was an exhibition coming up, and were Abbey and Tina interested?

"I believe they are," said Liz, "because they're on a savings junket for the overseas experience."

Liz had, besides, on the absolute Q.T., made a phone call to Annabelle Frizell to ask if there'd been anything out of order when she sat for

Merrington—artists being what they were in the moustache-twirling department.

"Not a jot," Annabelle confirmed, "not a whisper. Though I think I scared him, and aren't your girls strong? Anyway, Patricia's there in the next room, doing her weaving."

So Abbey came down three weeks later. Tina had found work at Just Jeans. Abbey stayed the weekend at the Merrington house, starting early, finishing late.

"What was it like?" Corker asked as he drove her back to the station.

"It was all right. Plenty of hours, but a bit boring. You try and sit without moving for days on end. He asked me to come again the weekend after next."

"Will you?"

"I have to, don't I, if I want the trip?"

"I'm matching your earnings dollar for dollar," said Corker.

"I know that, Dad. He asked lots of questions about you: how you got your land cheap, how Grandpa did. He thinks you're smarter than most."

"Does he indeed. Then that's all right, then."

But Corker was over Merrington pretty much.

It was Liz who collected Abbey after the next weekend of sittings: Abbey collapsed in tears, hunched in the passenger seat, almost as soon as they drove from the Merrington front yard. What she told Liz shocked her, but Abbey, shrieking, made her promise not to tell anyone.

Liz said she would have to tell Alan.

"No, not Dad. I handled it all right, didn't I? I told him to stop, and he stopped it."

"You were brilliant in the circumstances."

"Dad'll only do something about it. He'll say something. He'll tell people. He'll go to the police. Oh, my God. He'll make a mess."

She sat huddled against the car window.

"That's what really has to happen," said Liz.

"He said it was our secret and 'Don't tell Al.'"

Liz felt sick.

She waited until Abbey had left on the train, and then she went home and told Corker. "Abbey wants to handle this herself," she said at the end. She doubted if Corker heard her.

Later that night Corker sat on the veranda, waiting for dogs to come slinking around his sheep. Full moon: it was when they came, the shadows of poplars shortening and the hare in the moon sitting up, ears twitching amid the craters and seas of white.

Corker's anger poured through his thoughts unstoppably. It didn't feel like his own emotion, but like something drawn from a poisonous sac Merrington knew better than he did. How could he have been such a fool as to miss what was going on? All those occasions when Merrington needled him, and it was hateful, parasitic, harmful.

He didn't think of himself then, but of Abbey and Tina. He remembered all those times he followed their bikes through the sparkling mornings, keeping them safe until school. The feeling had never left him.

It was mostly newcomers' dogs he caught, their owners never believing their animals had it in them—claiming their dogs weren't sheep killers, believing they never hurt anyone. They kept those arguments to the end.

Dogs loved sheep with a madman's fetish. They bailed them frightened in corners and savaged them helpless. Only the ram stood ground with a line of grand courage when Corker strode to the rescue, nights when he came upon Hollywood Boy hurling dogs from his shoulders and meeting their return rush like a hardwood plank tufted with fiber.

Intoxicated with discovery, the dogs returned to their owners' knees and bestowed aroused gazes. Corker could guess the welcome. "What have you been up to, rascal?"

Pretty soon Corker would make a phone call. "I'm sorry, but it can't happen again."

"Can't? Who are you to say that?"

"I'm Corker, the stock agent."

If he saw the owners in town, he eyed them over. No longer did he seem the genial and pleasant bloke they'd heard about. They went around to see where the damage was done, down near the farm boundary fence where a laneway ran between poor weatherboard houses with roofs of rusting tin. Across the end was well-strained ringlock with strands of barb on top and below. There was a sign painted on a steel drum filled with concrete: LOOSE DOGS WILL BE SHOT. They hadn't seen it before, or if they had, had thought it was graffiti.

On nights when wind sucked and rain blew, they listened as sounds were carried. Was that a distant wild yelping, was it their imaginations, was it the pop of a shotgun muted by storm? It made the hairs on the back of the neck stand up.

It was a misty dawn a few days later when stock trucks arrived at a side fence of Merrington's place, well away from the house. Bolt cutters were used. The fence was roughly cut and wire rolled back. Merrington woke late, hearing confused bellows, and went up the hill to find his herd returned to him from the Bullock Run. Placed under the veranda eaves, away from the drizzle, was the painting he'd done at seventeen, so full of the pain of life and the wisdom of age precociously captured.

One afternoon as shadows deepened, Corker drove to the Bullock Run. Time had passed, but there wasn't a moment when his anger had abated. Just the appeal of Abbey stayed his hand. She wanted to follow it through and couldn't say what she would do or how she would do it—and so they let the matter stay between them, suspended. It had been like this for a while now, as Corker bent to the rule of women but assessed suitable planks that would do for a man. He stashed them in various places, ready for a change of policy, and always carried an iron pipe in the car in case he met Merrington on a lonely road somewhere and couldn't help himself.

Cresting the last ridge, Corker made the overlook in time to see his sleek beasts like ghosts standing in the rye and sharing the pasture with kangaroos. Big grays too, major eaters, but he didn't shoot them. If he had a painter's skill, he thought, he would take a lifetime to get them down: the way they spread alarmed across the far slope, hopping like fleas, or else the one standing fast, the big buck with his chest growling and head cocked sideways, protecting his females with troubled integrity.

What else could Corker do up there except sculpt the gullies with a hoe and spray against burr and thistle, keeping them clean for abundance? Sometimes he waited on a high ridge, cradling a 30.30 for when a file of marauding pigs would appear, and when they came, busy tuskers rambling, snouting on short legs, turning the pasture over with the wastefulness of fools, he sent them spinning with well-placed rounds of snap and rapid. Apart from fencing and drenching, there was nothing much else to do, and then it was time to get back to his sheep.

Cattle were easier than sheep by far. But cattle were more the measure of a man in the world Corker occupied. This was a wisdom Corker puzzled over as he drove back to town, listening to the sound of his tires spitting gravel.

Yiyun Li

Prison

YILAN'S DAUGHTER died at sixteen and a half on a rainy Saturday in May, six months after she had gotten her driver's license. She had been driving to a nearby town for a debate when she lost control. The car traveled over the median and ran into a semi. The local newspapers put her school picture side by side with the pictures from the site of the accident, the totaled black Nissan and the badly dented semi, the driver standing nearby and examining the damage to his truck, his back to the camera. The article talked about Jade's success as an immigrant's daughter—the same old story of hard work and triumph—how she had come to America four years earlier knowing no English and had since then excelled in school and become the captain of the debate team. It also quoted Jade's best friend, saying that Jade dreamed of going to Harvard, which was a dream shared by Yilan and her husband, Luo, and that she loved Emily Dickinson, which was news to Yilan. She wished she had known everything about Jade so she could fill the remaining years of her life with memories of her only daughter. At forty-seven, Yilan could not help but think that the important and meaningful part of her life was over; she was now closer to the end than the start, and within a blink of the eyes, death would ferry her to the other side of the world.

The year following Jade's accident, however, stretched itself into a long tunnel, thin aired and never-ending. Yilan watched Luo age in grief and knew she was doing the same in his eyes. He had been a doctor in China for twenty years; they had hoped he would pass the board exam to become an American doctor, but too old to learn to speak good English, he now worked in a cardiology lab as a research assistant and conducted open-heart surgery on dogs twice a week. Still, they had thought that the sacrifice of both their careers—Yilan had been an editor of an herbal medicine journal—was worthwhile if Jade could get a better education.

The decision to immigrate turned out to be the most fatal mistake they had made. At night Yilan and Luo held hands in bed and wept. The fact that they were in love still despite twenty years of marriage, the death of their only child, and a future with little to look forward to was almost unbearable in itself; sometimes Yilan wondered how it would feel if they could mourn in incommunicable solitude.

It was during the daytime, when Luo was at work, that Yilan had such thoughts, which she felt ashamed of when he came home. She felt she should do something before she was torn in half into a nighttime self and a crazier, daytime self, and before the latter one took over. After a few weeks of consideration, she brought up, at dinner, the idea of adopting a baby girl from China. They would get a daughter for sure, for nobody would be willing to give up a son.

Luo was silent for a long moment before he said, "Why?"

"All these stories about American parents wanting their adopted girls to learn Chinese and understand Chinese culture—we could do at least as much." Yilan's voice was falsely positive.

Luo did not reply and his chopsticks remained still over his rice bowl. Perhaps they were only strangers living in the illusion of love; perhaps this crazy idea would be the grave digger of their marriage. "Another person's unwanted child won't replace her," Luo said finally.

Even though his voice was gentle, Yilan could not help but feel a slap that made her blush. How could she expect that a girl not of their blood—a small bandage on a deep, bleeding wound—would make a difference? "Such nonsense I was talking," she said.

But a few days later, when they retreated to bed early, as they had done since Jade's death, Luo asked her in the darkness if she still wanted a child.

"Adopt a baby?" Yilan asked.

"No, our own child," Luo said.

They had not made love since Jade's death. Even if pregnancy were possible at her age, Yilan did not believe that her body was capable of nurturing another life. A man could make a child as long as he wanted perhaps, but the best years of a woman passed quickly. Yilan imagined what would become of her if her husband left her for a younger, more fertile woman. It almost seemed alluring to Yilan: she could go back to China and find some solace in her solitude; Luo, as loving a father as he was, would have a child of his blood.

"I'm too old," Yilan said. "Why don't I make room for a younger wife so you can have another child?" Yilan tried hard to remain still and not to turn her back to him. She would not mind getting letters and pictures from him from time to time; she would send presents—jade bracelets and gold pendants—to the child so she would grow up with an extra share of love. The more Yilan thought about it, the more it seemed a solution to their sad marriage.

Luo grabbed her hand, his fingernails hurting her palm. "Are you crazy to talk like this?" he said. "How can you be so irresponsible?"

It was a proposal of love, and Yilan was disappointed that he did not understand it. Still, his fury moved her. She withdrew her hand from his grasp to pat his arm. "Ignore my nonsense," she said.

"Silly woman," Luo said. He explained his plan. They could find a young woman to be a surrogate mother for their fertilized egg. Considering potential legal problems that might arise in America, the best way was to go back to China for the procedure. Not that the practice was legal in China, he explained—in fact, it had been banned since 2001—but they knew the country well enough to know that its laws were breakable, with money and connections. His classmates in medical school would come in handy. His income, forty thousand dollars a year, would be insufficient for carrying out the plan in America, but they were rich for the standard in China. Besides, if they brought the baby back to America, there would be less worry about the surrogate mother later wanting to be part of the baby's life, as had happened to an American couple.

Yilan listened. Luo had been a surgeon in an emergency medical center in China, and it did not surprise her that he could find the best solution for any problem in a short time, but the fact that he had done his research and then presented it in such a quiet yet hopeful way made her pulse quicken. Could a new baby rejuvenate their hearts? What if they became old before the child grew up, and who would look after her when they were too frail to do so? An adopted child would be a mere passerby in their life—Yilan could easily imagine caring for such a child for as long as they were allowed, and sending her back to the world when they were no longer capable—but a child of their own was different. "It must be difficult," Yilan said hesitantly, "to find someone if it's illegal."

Luo replied that it was not a worry as long as they had enough money to pay for such a service. They had little savings, and Yilan knew that he was thinking of the small amount of money they had got from Jade's life insurance. He suggested that they try Yilan's aunt, who lived in a remote mountain area in a southern province, and he talked about a medical school classmate who lived in the provincial capital and would have the connections to help them. He said that they did not have much time to waste; he did not say "menopause" but Yilan knew that he was thinking about it, as she was. Indeed it was their last chance.

Yilan found it hard to argue against the plan, because she had never really disagreed with Luo in their marriage. Besides, what was wrong with a man wanting a child of his own? She should consider herself lucky that Luo, with a practical mind and a methodical approach to every problem in life, was willing to take such a risk out of his love and respect for her as a wife.

Yilan was surprised, when she arrived at her aunt's house in a small mountain town, by the number of women her aunt had arranged for her to consider. She had asked her aunt to find two or three healthy and trustworthy young women from nearby villages for her to choose from, but twenty thousand yuan was too big a sum for her aunt to make any decision, so what she had done, instead, was to go to a few matchmakers and collect a pile of pictures of women, with their names, ages, heights, and weights written on the back. Some pictures were even marked with big, unmistakable characters about their virginity, which made Yilan wonder how much these women, or her aunt and the matchmakers, understood the situation. Even she herself doubted now that she saw all these faces, staring at her, from which she had to pick a hostess for her child. What was she to look for in these women?

"No virgins, of course, or first-time mothers," Luo said when she called collect and told him of the complications that they had not expected. He was waiting for his flight, two months later than Yilan's, to the provincial capital where, with the help of Luo's classmate, Yilan would have already finished her hormone therapy for the ovulation. It would have been great if he could have accompanied her to pick out the surrogate mother, and to the treatment before the in vitro fertilization, but he had only a few weeks of vacation to spare, and he had decided that he would wait till the last minute to travel to China in case the procedure failed and he needed to spend extra time for another trial.

"You mean we want to pick someone who has already had a child?" Yilan said.

"If we have options, yes. A second-time pregnancy will be better for the child," he said.

Luo had arranged to rent an apartment for a year in the provincial capital where Yilan and the surrogate would spend the whole pregnancy together. It was his idea, as they had to be certain that the baby they got in the end was theirs—he could easily imagine them being cheated: an unreported miscarriage and then a scheme to substitute another baby, for instance, or a swapping of a baby girl for a baby boy. It surprised Yilan that Luo had so little trust in other people, but she did not say anything. After all, it was hard for her to imagine leaving her child to a stranger for the pregnancy and coming back only for the harvest; she wanted to be with her child, to see her grow and feel her kick and welcome her to the world.

Yilan had expected a young widow perhaps, or a childless divorcée, someone who had little to her name but a body ready for rent. A mother would make the situation more complicated. "We can't separate a mother from her child for a year," she said finally.

"Perhaps it's not up to us to worry about it if someone is willing," Luo said. "We're buying a service."

Yilan shuddered at the cold truth. She looked out of the telephone booth—the four bright orange telephone booths in the main street, in the shape of fat mushrooms, were the only objects of modern technology and art in this mountain town, and to protect them from vandalism as well as probing curiosities, the booths were circled by a metal fence and one had to pay the watchperson a fee to enter one of the booths. The watchperson on duty, a middle-aged man, was dozing off in his chair, his chin buried deeply in his chest. A cigarette peddler across the street sat by his cart with his eyes turned to the sky, daydreaming. A teenager strolled by and kicked a napping dog, and it stirred and disappeared among a row of low houses behind which, in the far background, was the blue-and-green mountain.

"Are you still there?"

"I'm wondering," Yilan said, and took a deep breath, "why don't we move back to China?" Perhaps that was what they needed, the unhurried life of a dormant town, where big tragedies and small losses could all be part of a timeless dream.

Luo was silent for a moment and said, "It's like a game of chess. You can't undo a move. Besides, we want our child to have the best life possible."

Our child, she thought. Was it reason enough to make another child motherless for a year?

"Yilan, please," Luo said in a pleading tone. "I can't afford losing you."

Shocked by the weakness in his tone, Yilan apologized and promised that she would follow his instructions and choose the best possible woman. It saddened her that Luo insisted on holding on to her as if they had started to share some vital organs during their twenty years of marriage. She wondered if this was a sign of old age, of losing hope and courage for changes. She herself could easily picture vanishing from their shared life, but then perhaps it was a sign of aging on her part, a desire for a loneliness that would eventually make death a relief.

The next day, when Yilan brought up her worries about depriving a child of her mother, her aunt laughed at her absurdity. "Twenty thousand yuan for only one year!" her aunt said. "Believe me, the family that gets picked must have done a thousand good deeds in their last life to deserve such good fortune."

Yilan had no choice but to adopt her aunt's belief that she and Luo were not only renting a woman's womb, but what was more, they were granting her and her family opportunities that they otherwise would not have dreamed of. Yilan picked five women from the pile, "the first pot of dumplings," as her aunt called it, to interview, all of them mothers of young children, according to the matchmakers. Yilan and her aunt rented a room at the only teahouse in town, and the five women arrived in their best clothes, their hands scrubbed clean, free of the odor of the pigsty or the chicken coop, their faces overpowdered to cover the skin chapped from laboring in the field.

Despite her sympathy for these women, Yilan could not help but compare them to one another and find imperfections in each one. The first one brought the household register card that said she was twenty-five, but she already had sagging breasts under the thin layers of her shirt and undershirt. It did not surprise Yilan that the village women did not wear bras, luxuries they did not believe in and could not afford, but she had to avert her eyes when she saw the long and heavy breasts pulled downward by their own weight. She imagined the woman's son—two and a half, old enough to be away from his mama for a year, the woman guaranteed Yilan—dangling from his mother's breasts in a sling and uncovering her breasts whenever he felt like it. It made Yilan uncomfortable to imagine her own child sharing something with the greedy boy.

The next woman was robust, almost mannish. The following woman looked slow and unresponsive when Yilan's aunt asked her questions about her family. The fourth woman was tidy and rather good-looking, but when she talked, Yilan noticed a slyness in the woman's eyes. The fifth woman was on the verge of tears when she begged Yilan to choose her. She listed reasons for her urgent need of money—husband paralyzed from an accident in a nearby mine, aging parents and in-laws, two children growing fast and needing more food than she could put in their mouths, a mud-and-straw house ready to collapse in the rainy season. Yilan thought about all the worries that would distract the woman from nourishing the baby. She was ashamed of her selfishness, but then she did not want her child to be exposed so early to the unhappiness of the world. Not yet.

At the end of the morning, Yilan decided to look at more women instead of choosing one from the first batch. Even though Luo had explained to her that the baby would be entirely their own—they were the providers of her genes and the surrogate mother would function only as a biological incubator—Yilan worried that the baby would take up some unwanted traits from a less-than-perfect pregnancy.

When Yilan and her aunt exited the teahouse, a woman sitting on the curb by the road stood up and came to them. "Auntie, are you the one looking for someone to bear your child?" she said to Yilan.

Yilan blushed. Indeed the young woman looked not much older than Jade. Her slim body in a light green blouse reminded Yilan of watercress; her face was not beautiful in any striking way but there was not the slightest mistake in how the eyes and nose and mouth were positioned in the face—the woman was beautiful in a way not to provoke but to soothe.

"We're looking for someone who has had a child before," Yilan said apologetically.

"I have a child," the woman said. From a small cloth bag she wore around her neck with an elastic band, she brought out a birth certificate and a household register card. The birth certificate was her son's, four years old now, and she pointed out her name on the register card that matched the mother's name on the birth certificate.

Yilan studied the papers. Fusang was the woman's name, and she was twenty-two according to the register card, married to a man twenty years older. Yilan looked up at Fusang. Unlike the hair of the other married women, which was short or in a bun, Fusang's hair was plaited into one long braid, still in the style of a maiden.

"Young girl, nobody's recommended you to us," Yilan's aunt said.

"That's because I didn't have the money to pay the matchmakers," Fusang said. "I had to follow them here."

"Why do you want to do it?" Yilan said, and then realized that the answer was obvious. "Where's your son?" she asked.

"Gone," Fusang said.

Yilan shuddered at the answer, but Fusang seemed only to have stated a fact. Her eyes did not leave Yilan's face while the two women were talking.

"What do you mean 'gone'?" Yilan's aunt asked.

"It means he's no longer living with me."

"Where is he? Is he dead?" Yilan's aunt said.

For a moment Fusang looked lost, as if confused by the relevance of the question. "I don't know," she said finally. "I hope he's not dead."

Yilan felt her aunt pull her sleeve, a warning about the young woman's credibility or her mental state. "Does your husband know you're coming to see us?" Yilan said.

Fusang smiled as if she were waiting for the question to come and the fact that Yilan had asked only proved her judgment right. "My husband—he doesn't know his own age."

Yilan and her aunt exchanged a look. Despite the disapproval in her aunt's eyes, Yilan asked Fusang to come and see them again the next day. By then she would have an answer, Yilan explained. Fusang seemed unconvinced. "Why can't you tell me now? I don't want to walk all the way here tomorrow again."

"Which village are you from?" Yilan's aunt asked.

Fusang said the village name and said it had taken her two and a half hours to walk to town. Yilan took out a ten-yuan bill and said, "You can take the bus tomorrow."

"But why do you need to think about it?"

Unable to look at Fusang's eyes, Yilan turned to her aunt for help. "Because we need to find out if you're lying," Yilan's aunt said.

"But I'm not. Go ask people," Fusang said, and put the money carefully in the bag dangling from her neck.

Fusang had been sold to her in-laws at the price of two thousand yuan. Their only son was a dimwit whom nobody would want to marry, and they had to buy a young girl from a passing trader, one of those moving from province to province and making money by selling stolen children and abducted young women. Luckily for the old couple, Fusang was docile and did not resist at all when they made her the dimwit's wife. When asked where she had come from or about her life before, however, her only answer was that she had forgotten. The in-laws, for fear she would run away and they would lose their investment, kept her a prisoner for a year, but the girl never showed any sign of restlessness. The second year of the marriage, she gave birth to a son who, to the ecstasy of the grandparents, was not a dimwit. They started to treat her more like a daughter-in-law, granting her some freedom. One day, when the boy was two, Fusang took him to play outside the village. She came home reporting he was missing, and the villagers' search turned up nothing. How could a mother lose a son? her enraged in-laws asked her. If not for her dimwit husband, who had enough sense to protect Fusang from his parents' stick and fists, she would have been beaten to death. In the two years following the boy's disappearance, both in-laws died, and now Fusang lived with her husband on the small patch of rice field his parents had left them.

This was the story of Fusang that Yilan's aunt had found out for her. "Not a reliable person, if you ask me," her aunt said.

"Why? I don't see anything wrong."

"She lost her own son and did not shed a drop of a tear," Yilan's aunt said. After a pause, she sighed. "Of course, you may need someone like that," she said. "It's your money, so I shouldn't be putting my finger in your business."

Yilan found it hard to explain to her aunt why she liked Fusang. She was different from the other village women, their eyes dull compared to Fusang's. Young and mindlessly strong, Fusang seemed untouched by her tragic life, which would make it easier for her to part with the baby—after all, it was not only a service Yilan was purchasing but also a part of Fusang's life

The next day, when Fusang came again, Yilan asked her to sign the paper, a simple one-paragraph contract about an illegal act. Fusang looked at the contract and asked Yilan to read it to her. Yilan explained to Fusang that she would stay with Yilan through the pregnancy, and all living and medical expenses would be covered by Yilan; there was not any form of advance, only the final payment that Fusang would get right before Yilan and the baby left for America. "Do you understand the contract?" Yilan asked when she had finished reading it.

Fusang nodded. Yilan showed Fusang her name, and Fusang put her index finger in the red ink paste and then pressed it down below her name.

"Have you had any schooling?" Yilan asked.

"I went to elementary school for three years," Fusang said.

"What happened after the third grade?"

Fusang thought about the question. "I wasn't in the third grade," she said with a smile, as if she were happy to surprise Yilan. "I repeated the first grade three times."

Luo arrived two days before the appointment for the in vitro fertilization. When he saw Yilan waiting at the railway station, he came close and hugged her, a gesture too Western that made a lot of people stop and snicker. Yilan pushed him gently away. He looked jet-lagged but excited, and suddenly she worried that Fusang might not arrive for the implantation of the embryo. It had been two months since they had talked, and Yilan wondered if the young woman would change her mind, or simply forget the contract. The nagging worry kept Yilan awake at night, but she found it hard to talk to Luo about it. He did not know Fusang's story; he approved of her only because she was young and healthy and her body had been primed for pregnancy and childbirth.

Fusang showed up with a small battered suitcase and a ready smile, as if she were coming for a long-awaited vacation. When Yilan introduced her to Luo, she joked with him and asked if it would be hard for him to be away from his wife for a year, and what he would do. It was an awkward joke, to which Luo could respond only with a tolerating smile. He acted deferential but aloof toward Fusang, the right way for a good husband to be, and soon Fusang was frightened into a quieter, more alert person by his unsmiling presence.

The procedure went well, and after two weeks of anxious waiting, the pregnancy was confirmed. Fusang seemed as happy as Yilan and Luo.

"Keep an eye on her," Luo said in English to Yilan when they walked to the railway station for his departing train.

Yilan turned to look at Fusang, who was trailing two steps behind like a small child. Luo had insisted that Fusang come with them. "Of course," Yilan replied in English. "I won't let our child be starved. I'll make sure Fusang gets enough nutrition and sleep."

"Beyond that, don't let her out of your sight," Luo said.

"Why?"

"She has our child in her," Luo said.

Yilan looked at Fusang again, who waved back with a smile. "It's not like she'll run away," Yilan said. "She needs the money."

"You trust people so easily," Luo said. "Don't you understand that we can't make even a tiny mistake?"

Shocked by Luo's stern tone, Yilan thought of pointing out that she could not possibly imprison Fusang for the whole pregnancy, but they did not need an argument as a farewell. She agreed to be careful.

"Be very vigilant, all right?" Luo said.

Yilan looked at him strangely.

"It's our child I'm worrying about," Luo said as if explaining himself. And after a moment, he added with a bitter smile, "Of course, for a loser like me, there's nothing else to live for but a child."

Yilan thought about the patients he had once saved, most of them victims of traffic accidents, as he had served for the emergency center that belonged to the traffic department—they used to make him happy, but since when had he lost faith in saving other people's lives? "We can still think of coming back to China," Yilan said tentatively. "You were a good surgeon."

"It doesn't mean anything to me now," Luo said, and waved his hand as if to drive away the gloom that was falling between them. "All I want now is a child and that we give her a good life."

. . .

The first few days after Luo left, Yilan and Fusang seemed at a loss for what to do with each other's company, Yilan made small talk but not too often—they were still at the stage where she had to measure every word coming out of her mouth. And the only meaningful thing, besides waiting, was to make the apartment more comfortable for the waiting. A shabbily furnished two-bedroom apartment in a gray, undistinguishable building among many similar buildings in a residential area, it reminded Yilan of their first home in America, with furniture bought at the local Goodwill store and a few pieces hauled in from the apartment Dumpster. Jade, twelve and a half then, had been the one to make the home their own, decorating the walls with her paintings framed in cheap frames bought at the dollar store; she had always been good at drawing and painting, which baffled Yilan, as neither she nor Luo had an artistic cell in their bodies.

Yilan had brought with her a few books of paintings that Jade had loved, and now, when the stay in the apartment was confirmed, she took them out from her luggage and put them on the rickety bookcase in the living room. "I brought these for you," Yilan said to Fusang, who was standing by the living room door, watching Yilan work. Clueless like a newborn duckling, Fusang had taken on the habit of following Yilan around until Yilan told her that she could go back to her own bedroom and rest. "In your spare time," Yilan said, and then paused at her poor choice of words. "When you feel okay, spend some time looking at these paintings."

Fusang came closer and wiped her hands on the back of her pants. She then picked up the book on top, paintings by Jade's favorite artist, Modigliani. Fusang flipped the pages and placed a hand over her mouth to hide a giggle. "These people, they look funny," she said when she realized Yilan was watching her.

Yilan looked at the paintings that she had tried hard to like because of Jade's love for them. "They are paintings by a famous artist," Yilan said. "You don't have to understand them, but you should look at them so the baby will get a good fetal education."

"Fetal education?"

"A baby needs more than just nutrients for her body. She needs stimuli for her brain too."

Fusang seemed more confused. Yilan thought about Fusang's illiterate mind. Would it be an obstacle between the baby and the intelligence of the outside world? Yilan did not know the answer, but it did not prevent her from playing classical music and reading poems from the Tang Dynasty to Fusang and the baby. Sometimes Yilan looked at the paintings with Fusang, who was always compliant, but Yilan could see that Fusang's mind was elsewhere. What did a young woman like Fusang think about? Jade used to write journals that she did not think of hiding from Yilan, so Yilan at least got to know the things Jade had written down. Fusang, however, seemed to have no way of expressing herself. She talked less and less when the increasing hormones made her sicker. She spent several hours a day lying in bed and then rushing to the bathroom with horrible gagging sounds. Yilan tried to remember her own pregnancy; Jade had been a good baby from the beginning, and Yilan had not experienced much sickness at all. She wondered how much it had to do with a mother's reception, or rejection, of the growing existence within her body. She knew it was unfair of her to think so, but Fusang's reaction seemed unusually intense. Yilan could not help but think that Fusang chose to suffer from the pregnancy. Would the baby feel the alienation too?

Such thoughts nagged Yilan. No matter how carefully she prepared the meals, with little salt or oil or spice, Fusang would rush to the bathroom. Yilan tasted the dishes—tofu and fish and mushrooms and green-leafed vegetables. They were perfectly bland; she did not see why Fusang would not eat.

"You have to force her," Luo said over the phone. "You're too soft handed."

"How do you force a grown-up to eat when she doesn't want to?" Yilan said in a low, frustrated voice. She had told Fusang to take a nap in her bedroom when she picked up Luo's phone call, but now she hoped that Fusang would hear the conversation and understand their displeasure.

"There should be a clause somewhere in the contract. You could tell her that we will not pay her the full sum if she doesn't cooperate."

"You know the contract doesn't protect anyone on either side at all," Yilan said.

"She doesn't know. You can frighten her a little," Luo said.

"Wouldn't a frightened mother send some toxic signals to our baby?" Yilan said, and then regretted her sarcastic tone. "Sorry," she said. "I don't mean to be so cross with you."

Luo was quiet for a moment. "Think of a way to improve," he said. "I know it's hard for you, but it's harder for me to stay here, doing nothing."

Yilan imagined her husband spending his days at the lab and nights thinking about their baby. She should be more patient with him. It was not like she herself was pregnant and had a right to throw a tantrum at a helpless husband.

That evening, when Fusang returned to the table with a hand on her mouth, Yilan said, "You need to try harder, Fusang."

Fusang nodded, her eyes swollen and teary.

"You're a grown-up so you have to know the baby needs you to eat."

Fusang glanced at Yilan timidly. "Do you think I can eat some really spicy food?" Fusang said.

Yilan sighed. Spice would give the baby too much internal fire, and the baby would be prone to rashes, a bad temper, and other problems. Yilan wondered how she could make Fusang understand her responsibility to have a good and balanced diet. "Did you also crave spicy food last time you were pregnant?" Yilan asked.

"Last time? For three months I only ate fried soybeans. People in the village all said I would give birth to a little farting machine," Fusang said, and giggled despite herself.

Yilan watched Fusang's eyes come alive with that quick laugh. It was what had made Yilan choose Fusang the first time they met. Yilan realized she had not seen the same liveliness in the young woman since they had moved to the provincial capital. "So," Yilan said, and softened her voice, "did you end up having a baby like that?"

"No. Funny thing was that his dad really worried. Isn't he a real dimwit, with a brain full of lard?" Fusang said, her voice filled with tenderness.

It was the first time Fusang had talked about her previous life, full of mysteries and tragedies that Yilan had once wanted to know but were now made unimportant by the baby's existence. Yilan had thought that Fusang would just remain a bearer of her child, a biological incubator, but now that Fusang mentioned her husband with such ease, as if they were only continuing an earlier conversation, Yilan could not hide her curiosity. "How is your husband? Who's taking care of him?"

"Nobody, but don't worry. I asked the neighbors to keep an eye on him. They won't let him starve."

"That's very nice of them," Yilan said.

"Of course," Fusang said. "They're all thinking about my twenty thousand yuan."

Yilan thought of telling Fusang not to underestimate people's kindness, that money was only a small part of a bigger world. She would have said so, had Fusang been her own daughter, but Fusang had lived in a world darker than Yilan could imagine, where a girl could be stolen from her family and sold, and a son could disappear into other people's worlds. "Are you going back to your husband?" Yilan asked.

Fusang studied Yilan for a moment and said, "I'll be honest with you, Auntie, if you don't tell this to others. Of course I'm not going back to him."

"Where will you go then?"

"There is always some place to go," Fusang said.

"It would be hard for a young girl like you," Yilan said.

"But I'll have the twenty thousand yuan you pay me, right?" Fusang said. "Besides, what do I fear? The worst would be to be sold again to another man as a wife, but who could be worse than a dimwit?"

Yilan thought about the husband who had enough feeling and intelligence to save Fusang's life from his parents. She could easily end up with someone much more to be feared, and twenty thousand yuan, barely enough to cover two years of rent for an apartment such as the one they lived in, was far from granting her anything. Yet Fusang seemed so sure of herself, and so happy in knowing that she had some control of her future, that Yilan had no heart to point out the illusion. She thought about her Chinese friends in America, a few divorced ones who even though much older than Fusang could still be a good choice for her. But would it be a wise thing to make that happen when in reality the best thing, as Luo had said, was to conclude the deal after the baby's birth and never have anything to do with Fusang again?

They became closer after the conversation. Fusang seemed more settled in the apartment and in her own body, and she no longer followed Yilan around like a frightened child. Despite her husband's phone calls reminding her about nourishing both the baby's body and her brain, Yilan stopped filling every moment of Fusang's life with tasks. They found more comfort in each other's absence. In fact, Yilan enjoyed reading and listening to music and daydreaming alone now, and a few times, in the middle of a long meditation, Yilan heard a small voice from Fusang's bedroom, singing folk songs in a dialect that Yilan did not understand. Fusang's singing voice, low and husky, was much older than her age, and the slow and almost tuneless songs she sang reminded Yilan of an ancient poem that had kept coming to her since Jade's death: a lone horse of the Huns running astray at the edge of the desert, its hooves disturbing the old snow and its eyes reflecting the last hopeful light of the sun setting between tall, yellow grasses.

Twice a day, Yilan accompanied Fusang to a nearby park for an hour-long walk. Yilan told strangers who talked to them that Fusang was her niece. Nobody doubted them, Fusang's hand grasping Yilan's arm in a childlike way. Yilan did not let Fusang go with her to the marketplace for groceries—there were many things that Yilan wanted to protect Fusang and the baby from: air and noise pollution from the street always crowded with cars and tractors, unfriendly elbows in front of the vendors' stands, the foul language of vendors arguing with customers when the bargaining did not work out.

Fusang's body seemed to have changed rapidly within a short time. By the tenth week of the pregnancy, the doctor prescribed an ultrasound, and half an hour later, Yilan and Fusang were both crying and laughing at the news of a pair of twins snuggling in Fusang's womb, their small hearts big on the screen, pumping with powerful beats.

Yilan and Fusang left the hospital arm in arm, and on the taxi ride home, Yilan changed her mind and asked the driver to send them to the restaurant that had the best spicy dishes in town. She ordered more than they could consume, but Fusang had only a few bites of the spicy dishes. "We don't want the twins to get too hot," she said.

"It may not hurt to let them experience every taste before they are born," Yilan said.

Fusang smiled. Still, she would touch only the blander dishes. "I've always wondered what it'd be like to have twins," she said. "To think we'll have two babies that will look just the same."

Yilan hesitated at Fusang's use of "we" and then explained that the twins came from the implantation of multiple embryos and that they would not be identical. They might not be the same gender either.

"Let's hope for a boy and a girl then," Fusang said.

Yilan gazed at Fusang. "At my age, I wouldn't want to bargain."

"Auntie, maybe you hate people asking, but why do you want a baby now?"

Yilan looked at Fusang's face that glowed a soft peach color. The news of the twins seemed to have transformed Fusang into an even more beautiful woman. This was what Yilan was going to miss, a pregnant daughter sitting across the table from her, sharing with her the joy of a new life.

"Are you angry, Auntie? I shouldn't have asked."

"I had a daughter and she died," Yilan said. "She was five years younger than you."

Fusang looked down at her own hands on the table and said after a moment, "It's better now. You'll have more children."

Yilan felt the stinging of the tears that she tried to hold back. "It's not the same," she said. Luo had been right—nobody would be able to replace Jade. For a moment, she wondered why they would want to take the pains to get more children, whose presence could be taken away as easily as Jade's; they themselves could disappear from the twins' lives and leave them among orphans of the world. Weren't they the people in the folktales who drank poisonous fluid to stop a moment of thirst? But it was already too late to regret.

"You should stop thinking about your daughter," Fusang said. "It's not hard at all if you try."

Yilan shook her head and tried hard not to cry in front of the young girl.

"Really, Auntie," Fusang said. "You'll be surprised how easy it is to forget someone. I never think about my son."

"But how can you forget him? He came from your own body," Yilan said.

"It was hard at first," Fusang said, "but I just thought of it this way: whoever took him will give him a better life than his own parents. Then it didn't hurt to think of him, and once it didn't hurt, I forgot to think about him from time to time, and then I just forgot."

Yilan looked at the young woman, her eyes in the shape of new moons, filled with innocent smiles as if she were not talking about the cruelest truth in life. Fragile and illiterate as she was, Fusang seemed to have gained more wisdom about life than Yilan and Luo. Yilan studied Fusang: young, beautiful, and pregnant with Luo's children—who could be a better choice to replace herself as wife than Fusang? Such a thought, once formed, became strong. "Have you ever thought of going to America?" Yilan said.

"No."

"Do you want to?"

"No," Fusang said. "My tongue is straight and I can't speak English."

"English is not hard to learn," Yilan said. "Take me as an example." Take Jade, she thought.

"Are you matchmaking for me, Auntie? If possible, I want someone younger this time," Fusang said, laughing at her own joke.

Yilan could not help but feel disappointed. Indeed Luo was too old for Fusang—her father's age already. It did not feel right, to marry someone your daughter's age to your husband. "Where are your parents?" Yilan asked Fusang. "Do you want to go back to them after this?"

"My mother died when I was two. I've never known her."

"What about your father? Do you remember him?"

"He leased me to a beggar couple for ten years so I could support myself by begging with them. They were like my own parents and had raised me since I was eight. They promised to return me to my father when I was eighteen, with the money I made as my dowry, so he could marry me off, but then they died and I was brought to my husband's village and before I knew it, aha, I was sold."

"Who sold you? Why didn't you report it to the police?"

"The man said he could find me a job, so I went with him. The next thing I knew, I was locked in a bedroom with a dimwit. And when they finally let me free, my son was already born," Fusang said, shaking her head as if intrigued by a story that did not belong to her. "What's the good of reporting then? They would never find the man."

Yilan looked at Fusang's calm face, amazed at how the young woman was strong enough to live through such pain and was still able to laugh at it, and meanwhile was compliant and never questioned the justice of the world.

Yilan and Fusang left the restaurant and decided to take a long stroll home. They were the reason for each other's existence in this city, and they had no place to rush to. Fusang's hand was on Yilan's arm, but it was no longer a hand clinging for guidance, their connection something between friendship and kinship. When they walked past a department store, they went in and Yilan bought a few maternity outfits for Fusang, cotton dresses in soft colors of pink and yellow and blue, with huge butterfly knots on the back. Fusang blushed when the saleswoman complimented her on her cuteness in the dresses. Yilan found it hard not to broadcast the news of the twins. An older woman passing by congratulated Yilan for her good fortune as a grandmother, and neither Yilan nor Fusang corrected her.

When they exited the store, Yilan pointed out a fruit vendor to Fusang. It was the season for new bayberries, and they walked across the street to buy a basket. As they were leaving, a small hand grasped Yilan's pants. "Spare a penny, Granny," a boy dressed in rags said, his upturned face smeared with dirt.

Yilan put the change into the boy's straw basket, which held a few scattered coins and paper notes. The boy let go of Yilan's pants and then grabbed Fusang's sleeve. "Spare a penny, Auntie."

Fusang looked at the boy for a moment and squatted down. "Be careful," Yilan said, but Fusang paid no attention. She put a hand on the boy's forehead and he jerked back, but Fusang dragged him closer and said in a harsh tone, "Let me see your head."

The boy, frightened, did not move. Fusang stroked his hair back and gazed at his forehead for a moment. "What's your name?" she said, shaking the boy by his shoulder. "How old are you? Where are your parents? Where is your home?"

Before the boy could answer, a middle-aged man ran toward them from the street corner. "Hey," he said in a dialect not of the province. "What are you doing to my son?"

"But he's not your son," Fusang said. "He's mine."

The boy recoiled from Fusang, his eyes filled with trepidation. The man pulled the boy away from Fusang and said to Yilan, "Is she your daughter? Can't you see she's scaring my child? Don't think we beggars do not deserve respect and that you can shit on our faces."

Yilan looked at the man, his yellow crooked teeth and big sinewy hands bearing the threat of a lawless wanderer. He could easily hurt the twins with a mean punch to Fusang's belly. Yilan held Fusang back and said in a placating tone, "My niece lost a son, so please understand that she might make a mistake."

"But I'm not mistaken," Fusang said. "My son has a scar here on his forehead, like a new moon, and he has that too."

Already a group of people had gathered for the free street show. Someone laughed at Fusang's words and said, "Five out of ten boys have a scar somewhere on their heads, haven't they?"

"Hear that?" the man said to Fusang. "How can you prove he's your son?"

"Can you prove he's your son?" Fusang said. "Do you have his birth papers?"

"Beggars don't bother to bring useless things with us," the man said. He picked up the boy and put him on his shoulders. "Brothers and sisters, if you have a penny to spare for me and my boy, please do so. Or we'll leave now so this crazy woman won't bother us."

Fusang grabbed the man's arm, but with a small push he sent Fusang stumbling back a few steps before she sat down on the ground. Yilan's heart quickened.

"If you dare leave now, you will not have a good death," Fusang said, and started to cry. Neither her curse nor her tears stopped the man. The circle scattered to let him and the boy pass, and besides a few idlers who stayed to watch Fusang cry, the others left for their own business.

Yilan imagined the twins in Fusang's womb, shaken by anger and sadness that they did not understand. Yilan did not know how to comfort Fusang nor could she believe in Fusang's claim of the boy's identity. After a moment, Yilan said, "Are you all right?"

Fusang put a hand on her belly and supported herself with another hand to stand up. "Don't worry, Auntie," she said. "The babies are okay."

"You could've hurt them," Yilan said. Her words sounded cold, and right away she regretted it.

Fusang quieted down and said nothing. Yilan called a taxi, and on the ride home, they let silence grow and distance them into strangers. When they got back to the apartment, Yilan told Fusang to take a rest and not to dwell on the incident; Fusang did not reply but followed Yilan to her bedroom.

"You don't believe me, Auntie," Fusang said, standing at the door. "But he's my son. How can a mother make a mistake?"

Yilan shook her head and sat down on her bed. A moon-shaped scar could happen to many boys and it proved nothing. "You told me that wherever your son was, he was having his own life," Yilan said finally. "So don't think about him now."

"I thought he would have a much better life," Fusang said. "I thought people who wanted to buy a boy from a trader would treat him as their own son. I didn't know he would be sold to a beggar."

Yilan had heard of stories of people buying or renting children from poor villages and taking them into the cities to beg. The owners made big money from the small children, whom they starved and sometimes hurt intentionally so the children, with their hungry eyes and wounded bodies on display, would look sadder and more worthy of charity. She tried to recall the boy's eyes, whether they bore unfathomable pain and sadness unfit for a child his age, but all she could remember was the man's big hand on the child's small arm when he was taken away from Fusang.

"Had I known this," Fusang said, "I wouldn't have let the trader take him away. I thought any parents would be better than his dimwit father and me."

"Did you give your son away to a trader?" Yilan asked.

"We couldn't give the boy a good life," Fusang said. "Besides, his grandparents deserved it because of what they had done to me."

Yilan was shocked by the venom in Fusang's words, the first time Yilan detected the young woman's emotion about her past. "How could you make such a mistake?" Yilan said finally. "You're the birth mother of your son and no one could replace you."

"But if someone could give him a better life—," Fusang said. "Just like you'll take away the twins and I won't say a thing, because you'll give them more than I can."

"The twins are our children," Yilan said, and stood up abruptly. She was stunned by Fusang's illogic. "You can't keep them. We have a contract."

"If they're in my belly, won't they be my children too?" Fusang said. "But don't worry, Auntie. I won't keep them. All I'm saying is sometimes mothers do give away their children."

"Then stop thinking of getting him back," Yilan said, and then regretted her frustration. "And perhaps he's not your son at all," she added in a softened voice. "Your son may be living a happy life elsewhere."

Fusang shook her head in confusion. "Why is it that no one wants to believe me?" she said. "He is my son."

"But you have no way to prove it," Yilan said.

Fusang thought for a long moment. "Yes, there is a way," she said, and suddenly became happy. "Auntie, can you give me half of my money now? I'll go find the man and offer ten thousand yuan to buy the boy back from him. He won't sell the boy if he's his son, but if he only bought the boy from a trader, he'll surely sell the boy to me, and that will prove that he is my son."

Yilan did not know how to reply. Ten thousand yuan was a big sum and Fusang might be able to buy the boy from the beggar, if indeed he was only the owner of the boy instead of the father, but that did not make the boy Fusang's son. Or did it matter whether he came from her blood or not? She believed him to be her son, and he might as well become her son, but what did Fusang have, except for the rest of the money she would earn from the pregnancy, to bring the child up? Fusang was still a child herself, acting out of wrong reasoning; she too needed a mother to pass on generations of wisdom to her.

"Auntie, please?" Fusang said, her pleading eyes looking into Yilan's. "I can send him to his father for now if you don't like having him around."

"But you're planning to leave your husband," Yilan said. "Plus, he can't possibly take care of a small child."

"I'll find someone to take care of him in the village," Fusang said. "I'll stay with my husband if you think I shouldn't leave him. Please, Auntie, if we don't hurry, the man may run away with my son."

What would Fusang do with a small child? Yilan thought. She found it hard to imagine Fusang's life without her own presence, but what would Luo say if she told him about the situation and suggested they find a way to help Fusang and her son to America? Luo would probably say there was no clause about an advance or any other form of payment beyond the twenty thousand yuan. How could she persuade him to see that sometimes people without any blood connection could also make a family—and Fusang, wasn't she their kin now, nurturing their twins with her blood?

"Auntie?" Fusang said tentatively, and Yilan realized that she had been gazing at the young woman for a long time.

"Fusang," Yilan said. "Why don't we sit down for a moment? We need to talk."

But Fusang, mistaking Yilan's words as a rejection, stepped back with disappointment. "You can say no, but remember, your children are here with me. I'll run away and sell your children if I like. I can starve them even if you find a way to keep me here," Fusang said, and before Yilan could stop her, she ran into the kitchen and climbed onto the dinner table. Yilan followed Fusang into the kitchen and looked at Fusang, her small figure all of a sudden a looming danger.

"I can jump and jump and jump and make them fall out of my body now," Fusang said. "I don't care if I don't earn your money. I have a husband to go back to. I will have more children if I like, but you won't ever see the twins if you say no to me now."

Yilan looked at Fusang, whose face was no longer glowing with a gentle beauty but with anger and hatred. This was the price they paid for being mothers, Yilan thought, that the love of one's own child made anyone else in the world a potential enemy. Even as she was trying to find reconciling words to convince Fusang that she would do whatever she requested, Yilan knew that the world of trust and love they had built together was crushed, and they would remain the prisoners of each other for as long as they stayed under the same roof.

Michel Faber

Bye-bye Natalia

Trapped in the dingy, airless Internet café, Natalia picks at the frayed black lace of her dress while the photograph of her American pen pal loads into the computer. He's sent it at an unwieldy file size, and it's taking ages to come through. A horizontal sliver is slowly, slowly, slowly expanding downward, giving her a glimpse of the top of Bob's head and nothing more. He's bald, it seems. Or almost bald. She's not usually attracted to bald men. Although Alexander Melnik, the lead singer of her favorite Ukrainian group, Inward Path (now defunct, like just about everything else in her life), used to wear a woolly hat onstage, suggesting that he probably didn't have much hair on top, either. She should be more tolerant. There is a lot at stake.

The hem of her dress is unraveling. The lace is old: she likes to tell her friends that it was originally part of the shawl of a nineteenth-century countess who was executed by the Russians. In truth she found it in a basket of assorted remnants at a street market in Kiev and has no idea how old it is. Old enough to be coming to bits, anyway. If only she had a needle and thread, she could mend some of it while waiting for more of Bob's face to manifest on the PC screen. His brow is mostly there by now. It is slightly wrinkled but tanned. He lives in Montana.

Natalia looks at the clock on the café wall. She has been sitting here too long already: soon her allotted time will run out and she'll have to pay for another session. Squinting in the gloom—the Internet den is kept dark so that the male customers can enjoy their fight games better—she checks how many hryvnias she has in her purse. Not many.

She considers e-mailing Bob and asking him to resend his picture, this time at a more manageable size of 50 KB or less. She lifts her hands, preparing to type. Then she lowers them again. She doesn't want to get on the wrong side of Bob. Not that he's nasty—he seems uncommonly well meaning—but he's a little touchy, a little suspicious. They've exchanged half a dozen e-mails so far; in the third, she made the mistake of signing off as Natasha instead of Natalia, and he seized upon this as evidence of something fishy. Who exactly was she, he demanded, "Natalia" or "Natasha"? She explained to him that in Ukraine, each person has many versions of their Christian name. *Natalia*, *Natasha*, *Nata*, *Natashinka*: it's all the same, she told him. Which wasn't quite true, of course. Some versions were more affectionate than others; you would only use them with someone you were fond of. After Bob's "who exactly *are* you?" message, she reverted to Natalia in more ways than one.

But this is not the way she wants it. She wants to become intimate with him, to win his trust. She wants, in the end, to be his Natashinka. And that won't happen if she finds fault with his e-mail technique, will it? She must ration the number of times she challenges him. She mustn't waste his valuable American time. She must wait patiently for his unwieldy picture to load. His eyes are there now. They are blue as the Montana sky behind his head.

If she'd remembered to bring her Walkman, she could have been playing her Inward Path tapes while she waited. Natalia's Walkman is her most precious possession: all it needs is a couple of cheap batteries and it functions happily. Such a simple mechanism: society can crumble, governments and wars can come and go, but put a couple of AAs into the Walkman and its tiny spindles revolve at the same speed as ever. Miraculous. Grigory, her old school friend who now works in the faux-Soviet nightclub on Primorsky Boulevard, is the proud owner of a portable CD player that looks like a miniature flying saucer; he makes fun of her ugly gray plastic cassette player with its tarnished stickers. But Inward Path's first three albums never made it onto CD; they were cassette-only releases, for the local fanbase. *Golodomar*, *Antiar*, and *Labyrinth*—she owns them all, and a cassette version of their one and only CD, *Citadel*. She has played them hundreds of times on her trusty little machine.

Bob's face has pretty much finished downloading. His chin isn't there yet. His mouth is stretched in a toothy smile. The teeth are white and regular. What is it with Americans and straight white teeth? God, they must clamp braces on babies in the womb.

Natalia self-consciously licks her teeth with her tongue. They are not perfect. Two of them are crossed over each other. One of them is chipped. She has lots of fillings, even though she's only twenty-five. Even so, Bob picked her out of hundreds of others on the BlackSeaBrides.com website, so she must have impressed him as an acceptable-looking girl. She didn't show her teeth in the photo, but then she isn't much of a smiler. She likes to look serious. One of her old schoolfriends, Anya, frustrated that her job as a radiologist wasn't paying enough to cover rent and groceries, offered herself to the BlackSeaBrides.com website on the same day as Natalia. Anya posed in a low-cut evening dress that was little more than a nightie, displaying lots of cleavage, a naked leg balanced on a footstool, high heels. She simpered at the camera, as if to say to the unknown men sizing her up: Fancy the merchandise? Well, just say the word and it's yours. Natalia posed in the same gear she always wore: her black Goth dress, lace-up boots, the woolen cardigan knitted by her grandmother. She looked slightly downward, as if deep in thought. She probably was. She was probably thinking, What . . . the fuck . . . am I doing?

Bob's chin has appeared. It's not much of a chin, to be honest. Not the square jaw of the American cowboy hero. But Bob is as close to a cowboy hero as they come in the modern world. He owns a cattle ranch, run by employees chosen by his father. He owns a few horses, a big house and a small apartment in the city. His marriage broke up eight years ago and his kids live with his ex-wife in some other part of the United States. He is lonely. Loneliness radiates from his e-mails like a nuclear aura, like a giant spill of industrial waste. "I've done all right," he told her at the very beginning of their correspondence. "I got no complaints. But if I could have a person to share all this stuff with, that would be the icing on the cake."

What was it about her that made this Montana cattle rancher think she might be the icing on his cake? Why didn't he pick one of the hundreds of other Natalias and Anyas and Olgas, all displaying themselves on Black

SeaBrides.com, all listing their vital statistics, their university education, their lack of bad habits, and their desire to give themselves to the right person? "There was something sinsere about your face in the photo's," he told her in one of his early e-mails. "Theres a lot of women just out to take a man for a ride. I could tell you werent like that. And the part where you wrote about your brother in hospital. It shows that you are a caring person."

Natalia does indeed care about her brother. It's Montana Bob she's not sure if she could care about, even if she were elevated to the status of Mrs. Bob, riding her own horse in the American summer. Maybe she could. Surely she could. He seems quite a decent sort of guy, considering the circumstances of their romance, which, let's face it, aren't so romantic. But he's not a sex tourist and he's not a creep. At least, not as far as she can tell. Didn't he tell her about the divorced wife and the teenage children in his second e-mail? By the standards of Internet matchmaking, that's pretty impressive. Also, he says he likes alternative music! She'll have to ask him what groups he means; it might be a good way of minimizing the age difference between them. Which isn't that huge, actually. Anya is swapping e-mails with an Iowa computer salesman who's fifty-two. Bob is in his late thirties. Plenty young enough to be into alternative music. Bob writes:

> Here is a picture of me taken by one of my employees. It's not a very good picture but at least it's in focus! The picture of you on the website was really something special. I've looked at it a lot. You have such a soulfull expression in it. And I love your dress, the same dress you are wearing in the photos you sent in the letter. Those photos have been looked at a lot too, I can promise you, but not as much as the website one, because I can blow that up FULL SCREEN and I almost feel you are in the house with me. I hope one day you will be. As my guest. Anyway, I was talking about your dress. The photos were taken at different times in different places but you are wearing the same dress in every shot. Is it your only dress or do you just like it a lot? I like it a lot too. It's excotic and really different. I feel I am ready for something different in my life, something out of the ordinary. I am ready to learn about foreign cultures and things I never thought about

before. I don't want to become an old fart before my time. That's a noughty word—fart. I don't usually use noughty words but in the States, fart also means an old boring person. Not that I have anything against old people. Natalia, I am rambling here. It's late and I'm tired. I will write to you again tomorrow when I am fresh. Please try to write back more often as I get such an enormous buzz when I get an email. It puts a smile on my face all day.

Natalia sits staring at the big tanned face on the computer screen. Marek, the guy who works behind the counter of the Internet café, looks at it, too, pretending not to. He knows damn well what's going on here. He's seen it before.

After a couple of minutes, Natalia wonders why she even bothered to wait for the picture to download. It's really not relevant what Bob looks like. He is a rope being dangled down to her from a helicopter as she stands on the roof of a burning building. She has to grab that rope as soon as possible.

Dear Bob,

Thank you for sending your picture. It was very good and clear, and I can see in it that you are a kind man. Big sky of Montana is behind you, and it makes me very much wish that I could be with you under that sky together. Forgive me for writing a not so long email. I am working most of day and have not so much time for going to Internet café. I will try to go more times, but job conditions here in Ukraine are not so friendly. Also my brother is still in the hospital and I go to see him as many times as possible. I am very glad you like alternative music. What groups are your favored ones? I like very much The Cure and Sisters of Mercy and Metallica and Ministry. Some of this music is not easy to buy in Ukraine but some of our record-shop owners travel now to Poland to get supplies. But my most favored group of all time is Ukrainian group called Inward Path. Their words are in English, but full of poetry of Ukraine spirit. They made many cassettes but I fear they are not nowadays working any more. This music was important part of my life.

Natalia sits for another minute, trying to think of something to add, something that will steer the e-mail toward a natural conclusion.

Bye-bye, Natalia, she types at last.

Outside, it's a brilliant sunshiny day. Odessa is living up to its tourist-brochure image. All the trees are in leaf. The billboards are glossy and international. The shop fronts are exactly the same as what would be on offer in the main streets of London or Paris, except for the alleyways in between the Prada and Armani stores, where mangy dogs still scratch themselves and ugly old men still play cards at rickety, rain-damaged tables. There are sleek new cars weaving through the traffic, in among the rusted junk heaps driven by the gypsies. Western pop music is on the breeze. The girls wear fluffy zip-up tops, pastel nail polish, cute boots, low-slung jeans that expose their belly buttons and bum clefts. Their jeans are artfully ragged. Poverty chic. It's been months since she saw the old guy with no feet, pedaling his makeshift buggy in the middle of the road. She kind of misses him. At least the bent-backed old women are still sweeping the leaves with their ancient brooms.

Nostalgia for the bad old days: there's plenty of it around, if you look beyond the nightclub wonderland inhabited by Grigory and his pals. The twenty-first century has no use for the idealistic, dowdy drones who kept the gears of communism oiled. Anyone who's too crippled, unattractive, or elderly for the new millennium is advised to stay in the shadows and wait to be cleaned away.

At least Natalia has a good job—what passes for a good job in Ukraine. She works in a record shop. Her idiosyncratic, soulful, somewhat gothic appearance is considered a plus for customer relations, despite the fact that most of the music the shop sells is vacuous pop and easy-listening rock, the sort of stuff that should be tossed hastily into a plastic bag by a supermarket cashier. But capitalism wraps its products in more mystery than they deserve, and so Natalia has been installed behind the counter of New Sounds, to suggest to passersby that she is in some way intimately connected with the arcane, mysterious regions where Art is made, that she has passion and knowledge far deeper than the shop's crassly commercial facade might suggest.

And indeed she does. She could tell you about philology, the subject of her university degree. And she would love to evangelize on behalf of her favorite music; she would love to win new converts to Inward Path, if only New Sounds sold Inward Path albums, which it doesn't. The boss hasn't even heard of them. The boss spends his days in a swivel chair talking to Germany on the phone, nodding at the mention of the latest American sensation, and saying, "I'll have ten. No, fifteen."

Natalia's lunch break is over. She hurries back to New Sounds on Sadovaya Street and takes up her position behind the shop counter. Her first customer is an Austrian woman who wants the latest album by Robbie Williams. The woman is disappointed with the price. "This isn't much cheaper than I could get it at home," she complains, as though she has caught Natalia in the act of some barefaced scam. "I'm sorry," Natalia replies.

It's a balmy Tuesday. The shop closes at six and the summer sun is still high in the sky. Natalia walks straight to the Internet café. The gawky young men are pretending to kill enemies with their pale, big-knuckled fingers. Natalia finds her place among them and checks her e-mails. There's a new one from Montana Bob. No photographs this time, thank God. Not that she isn't curious to see more pictures of the man she may, if all goes well, spend the rest of her life with. It's just that she's in a hurry to go and see her brother, and she hasn't time to sit in the Internet café waiting for a gigantic image to load in.

> I am mega busy right now. I have acessed your email away from home (I'm in town) but I want to reply anyway. When I'm working I do this a lot—check if there is any message from you. I know I should wait until I have quality time but I can't wait, that's how much it means to me to get one of your emails. Keep them coming! The Cure—what can I say. The Cure are excellent, thier song Fridays I'm In Love was a big hit here in the States. They had some wierd videos didn't they—wierd in an interesting way. Some of my friends have a real thing against The Cures' front man because he is a guy wearing make up. I say you've got to be tolerant in this world. And besides, the guy is using it (make up) to make a living. I would definately rate The Cure one of my top 20 bands from England in the 80-ies. Ministry and the sisters of Mercy I don't know unless you are talking about

Christian Rock which is pretty big in these parts. Some of it is good but the messages can get quite heavy, if you're not a heavy church goer, which I am not. I think you can be spiritual without all that stuff. (Don't tell my parents though!)

Anyway, back to music. Metalicca are the best. They have been going for years but they are still at the top of the tree. Seriously rocking dudes. Do you like Black Sabbath? It's not a good idea to even mention thier name around here because people think it has something to do with satanic rights. But in my opinion they are just a great rock band. I like Ozzy Osbourne's solo stuff but Black Sabbath was something special, there was a mystery about it, like they were flying through the sky on a dark stormy night. I know that sounds cheesy but that's the only way I can express it. I must have listened to Sabbath Bloody Sabbath a hundred times when I was at school—the one with the naked women on the front cover! Natalia, please tell me about Inward Path. If they are special to you they must be pretty damn special. And don't worry about the cassettes not working anymore. I am a genius when it comes to fixing cassettes that got tangled up in the machine or snapped or whatever. I take them apart, splice them, put them back together, restore the tension. Good as new. If I wasn't running a ranch I could have had a business fixing cassettes! Except it's all cds these days. And downloads. I don't download music myself, do you? I don't feel something is mine unless I can hold it in my hands. Natalia I am rambling again—and I should be getting on with my job. Must shoot!

Natalia disconnects from the Net and checks the clock. As she rummages in her purse for change to pay for her session, she imagines herself getting into bed with Bob. Imagines herself naked, lifting the sheets of a king-sized American bed and exposing the hairy torso and erect penis of a bald, well-meaning guy from Montana. The thought doesn't disgust her. Genuinely well-meaning guys are hard to find. And there is more to the picture than just two people and a bed. Outside Bob's bedroom lies a whole country. A country with properly functioning hospitals and reliably available medicines.

. . .

On her way to see Sasha she stops off at a convenience store and buys two bars of chocolate and a packet of apple strudel thingies from Holland. Then she walks toward the Odessa Steps, mingling with the Japanese tourists and European holidaymakers ambling along the boulevards. Her Slavic looks and the bohemian tattiness of her clothing render her immune to the advances of the hawkers; they refrain from pushing kitsch statuettes of Lenin in her face or handing her leaflets about cut-rate plastic surgery. A young man she vaguely remembers from university stands right near the Steps, holding a live iguana and a Polaroid camera. He tenses up for a moment as he considers pressing the iguana onto her so that he can sell her a snap of her embracing it, then he decides against the idea. He doesn't appear to recognize her. But then, their university days are so long ago. A previous century. Nothing they studied is of any use now. Hot dogs, cappuccinos, Hugo Boss, blow jobs: that's what matters now.

A young Asian couple are smooching picturesquely under the statue of Richelieu, photographed by an accomplice. Natalia doesn't want to spoil their picture by walking through it, but their kiss goes on forever and she has to get moving.

"Excuse me," she says, in English. It's the universal language, after all.

She starts to descend the Odessa Steps, but instead of continuing down to the quay, she detours through the trees at the side. A few tourists squint after her in the sunlight, clearly wondering if she's savvy to a tourist attraction not mentioned in the guidebooks. But they won't follow. Their guidebooks are unanimous in advising visitors not to venture outside the designated safe areas.

Behind the trees, the landscape gets messy. There is a well-trodden path through the garbage-littered scrub, an alternative nature trail for dogs. Within a couple of minutes Natalia has reached the encampment.

There are two dwellings: a small concrete hut that was once used by caretakers for storing cleaning equipment and a vacant space under an electricity generator that's been walled shut with sheets of cardboard. A pair of jeans hangs on an improvised washing line spanned between a metal pole and a tree. Yana, a sixteen-year-old prostitute, greets Natalia with a broad smile. Her tangled hair is full of dandelion. A small child Natalia can't recall seeing here before is toddling about, wiping her tiny white hands on her knitted tunic. Dmitry is playing with the dog as usual, enjoying the sunshine. His shirt is open, revealing his lean, wiry body. The dotted scars where surgical stitches have been removed show up white against the tanned flesh. He dances off-balance, waving a cigarette in one hand and teasing the dog with the other. The dog is chewing one of the many ruined shoes scattered around the camp.

"Sasha's asleep," says Dmitry to Natalia as she approaches the hut.

"Good," she says.

There are three mattresses crammed into the floor space, so that she must step onto them to enter, careful not to fall. A middle-aged woman she doesn't recognize is sleeping under a mound of grubby windcheaters: probably the mother of the kid outside. The middle mattress is empty except for some pages torn from a coloring book and a scatter of cheap coloring pens. These are the only new elements in the shelter. The walls are still decorated with mildewed posters advertising Monolit Turkelt furniture, a decorative tea towel featuring scenes from Ukrainian folklore, and an ad for a Russian boy band who performed in Kiev in 2002. The broken cassette player still has a tape called *Acid Euro Trance 5* gathering dust on top of it, untouched for all the time that her brother has lived here.

Natalia squats down on the edge of the third mattress, which has Sasha stretched out on it, nestled next to his junkie friend Andrej. The golden evening sunlight beams in on them. They look handsome and innocent together, both lightly dressed in T-shirts and military trousers. The brilliancy of the light makes them appear freshly washed and unmarked.

"Hi, Sasha," says Natalia. "I brought you some things."

Her brother wakes calmly and sits up, rubbing his eyes. Andrej doesn't stir. Veterans of the streets, they've both trained themselves to recognize which noises they need to worry about and which noises they can afford to ignore.

Sasha takes a cursory glance at his sister's semi-transparent bag of food. "I don't need it," he says, serene and surly at the same time. He is two years older than her. He has been a removal man, a house painter; he has been to Germany, Poland, Pridnestrovye. He knows how to take care of himself.

"Maybe you can have some later," says Natalia, putting the bag down on the spare mattress next to the coloring pens.

"I have everything I need here."

"Even apple strudel?"

"The people from Way Home brought us a bag of buns earlier on."

Natalia nods. Way Home is a local charity that tries to lure kids off the streets. Their volunteers distribute cheap food and basic medical supplies, and invite homeless youngsters to relocate to their shelter. Her brother is too old to qualify. "Did they bring you some condoms?"

"Don't say such words," says Sasha with a sly half-smile. "Filthy-tongue Nata. Daddy would wash your mouth out with soap."

Natalia sighs irritably. "Daddy's not around anymore."

"Is that the fairy tale you tell your American sugar daddy?" Sasha retorts. He's fully awake now and sharp as always. "Will there be room in his mansion for me, do you think? Maybe a small cot in the corner of the bedroom?"

"You've got it all wrong. He's just a guy I correspond with."

"Correspond my arse. Does he like boys, too? Maybe if they're young and pretty? You could send him a photo of the way I used to look when I was ten. Who knows, he might go for it. You could sneak me in, wrapped in a blanket. What do you say, Nata?"

"Let's not argue. It's a beautiful day."

They sit together on the edge of the mattress, looking out. Dmitry is still playing with the dog. He seizes the animal by the snout, wrenching the whole head violently back and forth. He knows exactly how far he can go before the dog gets dangerous. Whenever he releases his hold, the dog falls back and looks disappointed, then lunges forward for another wrestle. Natalia and Sasha settle into the entertainment. The small child stands half hidden behind the jeans on the washing line and watches, too. Yana has disappeared, presumably gone off to beg. No one speaks. The air is punctuated from time to time with whistles, toots, and Tannoy announcements from the Odessa docks below.

"But seriously," says Natalia, "have you got condoms? Clean needles?"

"Stop nagging. You're in no position to lecture me."

"I'm in the best position of all."

"Yeah, on your back, with your legs spread."

Natalia blinks, stares unwaveringly at Dmitry and the dog.

"You know I don't do that anymore," she says.

"What about for your American?"

"He just writes me e-mails about Metallica and the Cure. I'm trying to get him into Inward Path."

"Oh, God," groans Sasha, falling back onto the mattress, his head bouncing off Andrej's thigh. "Don't you ever give up about Inward Path? They're ancient history, Natasha. You might as well be mooning over Ivan Rebroff or Billy Joel. Do you really think this American guy is going to get excited about your crappy old cassettes by a bunch of Ukrainian heavy metal losers?"

"Inward Path weren't heavy metal. They were dark metal."

"Heavy . . . dark . . . what's the difference . . . ," he mumbles scornfully, laying his punctured arms across his face.

"What about your precious dance music?" she points out. "You divide it up into about fifty different categories."

"Let's not argue," he says. "It's a beautiful day."

"I have to go," says Natalia, wiping her cheeks with her sleeve.

It takes Natalia half an hour to get home on the bus. She lives on the outskirts of Odessa, in a *communalka*, one of the old communist-era apartment buildings. She has a room of her own (with a sink, thank God), and shares kitchen, laundry, and bathroom facilities with four other people, none of whom she particularly gets along with. The middle-aged couple and the old pervert are all right, but there's a girl quite close to Natalia in age who really gets on her nerves, watching loud TV that penetrates through the thin walls. This girl, Irina, clogs the toilet with sanitary pads and switches on the worst Russian pop music as soon as she wakes up. She filches Natalia's shampoo, topping up the bottle with water. The communal bathtub always has a pink tidemark around it when Irina's finished with it: the scum of thick cosmetics. "The cool thing about this cardigan," she once told Natalia, showing off a fake cashmere number bought for her by her latest boyfriend, "is that it doesn't look like some senile old bag knitted it." There are mornings when Natalia can't stomach breakfast because of the stench of Irina's perfume in the kitchen. They've been living together for eleven months and it feels like a lifetime.

Natalia warms up some leftover *golubtsy* in a frying pan, or tries to. The fear of being collared by one of her neighbors makes her too hasty at the stove and the meat inside the cabbage leaves is only lukewarm. She wolfs it down, then guiltily wipes her greasy hands on a tea towel that nominally belongs to Mrs. Kotova.

Locked inside her room, she lies briefly on the bed, staring up at the Cypress Hill poster on the ceiling. (She doesn't actually like Cypress

Hill—hip-hop rubbish about smoking dope—but the poster is a giant enlargement of their *Black Sunday* album cover and its dark sepia vista of a storm-wreathed graveyard speaks to her.) Every available inch of space on her walls (not that many inches altogether, to be frank) is covered with similarly gloomy imagery: hollow-eyed maidens in chains, demons, snakes, medieval castles shrouded in moonlit vapor. They make her happy, these things. Or, to be more precise, they don't make her unhappiness any worse. The mindless cheerfulness of dance music, the sentimentality of singer-songwriters, the childish naivete of pop: they all grate on her like propaganda. Better to face up to the truth.

Does Bob, way over there in Montana, have any hope of understanding the way she feels? It's hard to gauge how much he really has inside him. When he writes, he likes to keep things breezy. Maybe it's the language barrier? Then she remembers there is no language barrier for him. So maybe he just isn't very smart. Is it important that a man should be smart if all you want from him is that he should save your life? She struggles to recall everything he has ever said. Their correspondence, although only a few weeks old, is already substantial; some of his messages must have taken him hours to write. But what can she remember? At this moment, just that he doesn't care for rap.

If only she had her own computer, she could communicate with him more often; they could exchange messages through the night, when all the world was quiet, their responses flying backward and forward at intervals of only a few minutes, almost like a conversation.

Trying harder, she mentally retrieves one of his earliest e-mails to her—the second, or maybe the third. He showed his profounder side in that. Talked about the emptiness of normal life, the search for something untainted by compromise and commerce, the sense of needing to take a bold step into the unknown, to be prepared to be bewildered and reborn. The e-mail had run for pages and had used words she'd never heard a man use before.

Now she stands on her bed and fetches, from the stack of books and papers on top of the wardrobe, her folder of Inward Path lyrics. She'll pick out her favorite ones and type them into an e-mail for him. He asked her, didn't he? Explaining what makes great music great is impossible, especially in a foreign tongue, but she can at least give him a flavor of Inward Path's poetry.

"Bleeding," from *Citadel*—that's a must. Especially the part that always goes straight through her, where Melnik sings:

As on the day gone by
I talk to you, my faithful blade
You run with crackling flame
So careless so easy
Opening blood stream
Through flesh without pain
In spite of the sand in my eyes
And dust in my mouth
I try to talk through the pressure
Of silence
Trying to touch—like screaming
Come, talk to me, 'cause I'm bleeding
Desperate heart
Tries to break out
Through the bones and flesh.

Then there's "Desolation," from *Antiar*—although the words of that one are actually by Valery Bryusov, a Russian Symbolist poet of the late nineteenth century, which might be too much trouble to explain to Bob. The same goes for "Into the Night" (words by Eduard Bagritsky) and "Antiar" itself (words by Pushkin). Although Bob would know Pushkin, surely? Everybody in the world knows Pushkin, even Americans.

Next day, she works at New Sounds till lunchtime and then has the rest of the afternoon off. It's her regular arrangement with the boss, to make up for the weekends she gives to the shop. He waves to her from his position at the telephone, a pen clamped between his teeth. She waves back and heads straight for the Internet café.

It's busy today. She has to wait for a computer. Three foreign tourists are seated at the machines that are usually free for her—the less popular machines near the window, exposed to distracting sunlight. She waits patiently, in silence, while the foreigners—Germans, it seems—do what they came for. There are two guys and one woman. One guy checks e-mails and spends ages lost in thought, staring at the screen through thick glasses.

The woman browses through real-estate websites, loading in image after image of flats for sale in Minsk, Odessa, Kharkov, Nikolaev, Kherson, Lvov . . . She compares the decorative order of various bathrooms and sitting rooms, jots down phone numbers and measurements. The other guy is visiting an Internet chat room, swapping one-liners with his virtual pals. Natalia's German isn't so hot, but she gets the gist from words like *gefickt*, *Hure*, and *Arsch*. His chair, when he's finally finished with it, is hot—so hot that it makes her uncomfortable through the thin fabric of her skirt. Her Montana Bob is a teddy bear among such hyenas.

She has to make this quick. She has an appointment in Krivaya Balka at 3 P.M. and it takes forever to get out there. Copying out screeds of Inward Path lyrics is unfortunately not feasible. She types the crucial verse of "Bleeding" and the part in "Life Grows Weak" about standing before mighty nature like a drop in the sea and a leaf on the wind. She considers typing the whole of "After Beginning" but settles for the final stanza only:

Was it the stars that sped toward me
Or I into abysmal night
A mighty hand seemed to uphold me
Over the abyss my flight.

Her heart is beating loud in her rib cage. No doubt partly because she's under pressure of time and she dislikes being under pressure of time. But also because she finds it stressful to commit the poetry of Inward Path to an uncertain journey through cyberspace. What if Montana Bob isn't having a particularly profound day?

"They made a very strong rendition of the song 'Paranoid' by your old love Black Sabbath on their album of 1994, *Golodomor*," she adds.

She glances up at the clock. She has five more minutes here before she has to run for the bus. Her heart beats louder than ever. She knows there's something more that Bob wants from her, and that it's been too long since she's slipped him any of it. The tone of their correspondence has grown too cordial; it needs an injection of sex. Not pure, unadulterated sex: he would have trouble dealing with that. But a cocktail of romance, reassurance, and a dash of the erotic: that's what he's hanging out for, she can tell. And why not? It's what she wants too.

> Bob, I must go now but I have something significant to tell you, I know you are a good man. There are many bad men in the world and I have been hurt by some of them in my life. I have a lot of love and tender actions that I can give to the correct person, a man who will hold me and take care of me, and I will give him in return a wife to make him proud among his friends and family, as well as in our private place, where the utmost happiness can occur. I have intuition that you are that man.

The Outpatients Department is in one of the shabbiest, most desolate parts of Odessa, an area characterized by defunct factories and dusty roads half-pulverized by heavy vehicles. The clinic is behind a Jewish cemetery. It looks like a mammoth toilet block. It has the words INFECTIOUS DISEASES bolted to the concrete facade, in large totalitarian letters.

Natalia walks into the building side by side with a young man in smart-casual clothing. They have nothing to do with each other, except that they both got off the bus at this stop and evidently they both have an appointment in this clinic. Natalia wonders how this young man got infected; he's no doubt wondering the same about her. At the entrance of the clinic, he steps back deferentially, motioning for her to enter first. A gentleman.

The clinic isn't busy today. The two Ministry of Health doctors aren't in; one is pursuing his private practice, the other is on vacation. The only doctor on duty is René from Médecins Sans Frontières. René has been treating Natalia for a year now, ever since she got anemia and almost died. Together they've seen Natalia's blood count creep back toward sustainable human levels. Together they've discussed what Natalia's options will be if the Ministry of Health gets bogged in another corruption scandal and there's a break in the supply of antiretroviral drugs. Natalia's options are, to be honest, not plentiful. They consist of hoping that the government of Ukraine will grow ever more efficient, compassionate, and accountable.

"When are you leaving?" Natalia asks Dr. René as he fills a small syringe with her blood.

"Not yet, not yet," he says, in his soft Belgian accent.

"But soon?"

"Head office says six months."

"That's soon."

"I'd like to stay," says René.

"Then why don't you?" She feels as though she's making a pass at him. Sasha would probably accuse her of trying her luck with every foreigner who comes into range.

"We've discussed this before," says the doctor. "Médecins Sans Frontières is supposed to be an emergency aid organization. We go in when there's a crisis and the local authorities aren't coping. We're not designed to be an alternative national health service."

"If I'd trusted our own doctors, I'd be dead now."

"But you're alive. And a lot of local doctors are much more knowledgeable about HIV than they were a couple of years ago. There's no reason why the Ministry of Health can't carry on your ARV therapy."

"Except that Ukraine is fucked."

"I'm sorry you feel that way, Natasha." The doctor is embarrassed, uneasy, and he retreats into gentle banter. "You were so wonderfully patriotic when I first saw you. Just a few blood cells away from the grave, and you were telling me all about Pushkin."

"Pushkin can't help me now."

"You're doing fine, Natasha. Just take it one day at a time."

He turns away from her, ostensibly to write her name on the plastic capsule containing her blood. She's made him feel bad. She wishes she could make up for it. He is an idealistic young man who'd no doubt be much happier sewing up wounded refugees in Africa than sitting here in a dismal office with a dusty plastic model of the AIDS virus on his desk. He has been bashing his head against ex-Soviet bureaucracy for months on end, even sometimes buying medicines with his own money in sheer frustration at the slow grinding of the official gears. Although he and Natalia converse in English, she hears him speak on the phone and to the receptionists, and his Russian is better each time. He must be working his butt off.

"Thank you. Bye-bye," she says.

"Till next week," he says, closing his Filofax. There's a photograph of his wife and children sellotaped to the front.

On the bus, Natalia feels so exhausted she keeps falling asleep. Her ear and cheek collide with the window, over and over. The bus becomes crowded as it shudders closer to the center of town, and she clutches her handbag with the ARV drugs in it. Thieves are bolder nowadays. Odessa is full of tourists and refugees from the collapsed communist empire. Junkies are everywhere.

She dozes and visits Montana in her mind. It won't be like New York or Los Angeles, those vast teeming cities Grigory is so desperate to relocate to. It will be like Crimea, perhaps. But with modern hospitals. No doubt there will be some corruption in the American health care system, too, but at least in America, people are used to demanding, and getting, what they want. They don't queue meekly in gray corridors waiting for permission to die.

There are some days when Natalia feels that every decision she makes is wrong. One trivial misjudgment triggers the next, and then another, and another. Today she jumps off a bus that would have taken her all the way home, because she catches a passing glimpse of the Internet café and has a sudden urge to check for news. But the Internet café is shut. A sign on the door says, in English, BACK IN 5 MINUTES. She waits fifteen. Then she decides to fill time by visiting Sasha. She goes to a delicatessen and buys chocolate and a bag of *vareniki* dumplings that are going cheap but still look perfectly good. Only when she's halfway to the Odessa Steps does she remember that Sasha doesn't like cold *vareniki*, only hot. Maybe he's less choosy nowadays?

At the encampment, she finds that Sasha isn't there. Gone to Ekaterinskaya Street, says Dmitry. Natalia knows that's Sasha's favorite place for begging. It's a hot spot for foreigners, the sort of faux-traditional avenue where British and American tourists sit at open-air bistros squinting bemusedly at misspelled menus, reassuring each other not to worry about making a mistake because everything is dirt cheap. Natalia sets off, still carrying her little plastic bag of groceries.

By now, she actually dreads meeting Sasha: his begging is excruciating for her to witness. He has a rubbish-skip guitar with four or five strings, brutally out of tune, and he busks with it, performing the worst kind of American soft-rock songs, Bryan Adams, the Eagles, Meat Loaf, Bon Jovi, "A Horse with No Name," "Hungry Heart," "We Built This City on Rock and Roll," you name it. He sings them in a weird kind of subdued yammer, like a loud radio overheard at a distance. His sheer awfulness seems to charm the clientele. Some days, he earns more than a schoolteacher or a nurse.

Natalia walks up and down Ekaterinskaya Street. Sasha is nowhere to be seen. Growing hungry, but not wanting to eat the food she's bought for her brother, she buys a Greek salad she can't afford in a convivial-looking café. It's lousy. She walks up and down Ekaterinskaya some more. At one point she almost breaks her neck, feeling as though someone has lassoed her around the shins. It's the lace hem of her dress; it's come loose altogether. She lifts it in her fist, unsure what to do with it. If she had something as simple as a pin, she could pin it up. She hasn't got a pin, and there's nowhere around here where she could buy one, even though Odessa prides itself on selling everything nowadays, from turquoise chrome cell phone slipcases to anal sex.

Natalia considers tearing the hem off, but she feels she's made so many wrong decisions already today that she would probably regret it. So she walks to the bus stop, carrying the dangling black lace in front of her like a dog's leash, and goes home.

Four hours later, Natalia takes her seat in front of a computer at the Internet café. It's an hour before closing. She has never been here so late before. The place is almost empty; only two game-playing lads remain, injecting their lonesome beeps, buzzes, and bombs into the glowing stillness. Outside, there's been a sudden change in the weather: a drop in temperature, stiff winds. An improperly secured billboard flaps loudly right outside the building as Natalia taps out the code to gain entry to her e-mail program. Her wrists are bulky with the sleeves of an ugly nylon windcheater, hardly a fashion item, but she just can't get warm enough. The hem of her dress is temporarily attached with masking tape. She looks ridiculous, she knows.

The game-playing boys laugh. Their laughter has nothing to do with her. Nothing in the world has anything to do with her. The boys have simply had enough of killing and being killed. They're getting up to spend the rest of the night with Mum and Dad.

> Dear Natalia,
>
> I can't tell you how happy I was to recieve your email. It was the email of my dreams. Without wanting to put down my first wife, my first marriage would have been a lot better if she had your attitude. I sometimes think that here in America, we take everything

for granted and don't treat relationships with the respect and honor they deserve. I am not saying that I deserve that much respect and honor, I am a guy with faults like anybody, what I mean is love. Love is a miracle and a precious thing. There are so many billions of people in the world, passing each other by in the street, bumping into each other in the grocery store, working together at the office and so on. What do they feel for each other—zero. But just sometimes, out of all those billions of strangers, two people connect. They break through somehow. They show trust and they get trust back.

Natalia, I don't want to scare you off, talking about marriage. I know that sounds wierd, seeing as I found you on a marriage website, but now that we have got to know each other I can see that you are a very special person and I want you to have the special husband you deserve. I am sure you must have felt exposed and unconfortable posing on that website, knowing that thousands of guys were looking at you, undressing you with thier eyes. I admit I was undressing you too, but at the same time I was looking for something else, something deeper. In fact I refused to take the other girls seriously, the ones that had bikini shots and thier jugs hanging out. When I saw you in that dress, it was like being transported back to an older time, a time when love and honor really meant something. A time when a man would bow for a lady and kiss her on the hand and stuff like that. God, I hope you are not laughing. I am serious, my dear Natalia. You are not the only one that has been hurt before, and I don't want to count my chickens.

What I propose is that you come to Montana for a holiday. No heavy expectations, no nothing. I will pay for everything, your fare, all expenses. You can stay in my daughters old room, if you prefer. We won't put a time frame on it. You can take as long as you need to get to know me (and Montana!). Montana is not the most exciting place in America and I'm sure I am not the most exciting guy but I have a good hopeful feeling about this. Intuition, like you said! Well now, Natalia, I have been talking about my feelings and my heart is going boom boom boom, and I think it's time I tried to calm down a little! So back to music.

I'm sure Inward Path are a seriously rocking outfit as I don't believe you would be so crazy about them if they weren't. And I look forward to hearing some of thier stuff soon. To be straight with you though, some of thier lyrics are too gloomy for me. Don't you think? I mean, you quoted one, Life Grows Weak, and there's all this stuff about no future, no peace of mind, eyes are bleeding, going insane, I'm lost and destroyed, we'll stay all alone. I don't go for that. Natalia, I am a glass half full instead of a glass half empty kind of guy, if you know what I am saying. There's a lot of sadness and aweful stuff happening in this world and the way I figure it is, you got to be positive or it brings you right down. There's plenty things in my own life I could lose sleep over but I just start each new day thinking OK, this is the first day of the rest of my life. And I think we should put careful thought into choosing the music we listen to, to make sure it's putting something good into our lives instead of something negative. My all-time favorite artist is actually Bruce Springsteen. He is the Boss. I'm on fire, Dancing in the dark, Born in the USA, Born to run, She's the one, Promised land, Jungle land, Hungry heart, Cover me—they are all totally classic in my book. He even has a song called "I wanna marry you!"

Natalia sits in silence. Her arms are trembling with cold. The flesh of her legs is goose-pimpled. She wishes she were at home in bed, curled up in a ball, blankets wrapped tight around her, warm as an opiate. This Bruce Springsteen thing is bad news, very bad news. Worse news than if Bob had confessed to her that he is a pervert and is very much looking forward to masturbating onto her shoes or into her eyes. Sexual disgust she can handle. But Bruce Springsteen . . .

She blinks in amazement at her own ridiculous fastidiousness, her snobbery, when her life is at stake. What does it matter if the man who is offering to be her husband likes the dullest music in the world? What does it matter that her brother sings "Hungry Heart" as one of his busking scams on Ekaterinskaya Street, filling gaps in the lyrics with sarcastic Ukrainian and vamping the "Huh-huh-hungry" chorus for all he's worth? What does it matter that Bob was probably lying about knowing the Cure? What does it matter what music anyone likes? Viruses and medicines fight to the death inside one's body, a claustrophobic dark-red package of blood and meat where music never penetrates, unless you count the rhythm of the heartbeat. No sound, surely, can ever matter more than that rhythm.

Natalia raises her hands to begin typing her response. Bob will be waiting. What with delays and different time zones, she's probably kept him waiting too long already. She must say yes at once, in case he gets spooked and changes his mind. How much easier it would be if she could just shout "Yes!" right here in the Internet café on Zhukovskovo Street and have him magically hear her in Montana. Then she wouldn't need to think of a preamble, a way of phrasing her agreement so it doesn't come across as overeager or too casual or stilted. It's not the important words that are treacherous, it's the little ones that lead there.

Dear Bob,

How to tell him what his proposal means to her? How to make her assent sound natural and gracious? Is it too soon to discuss the practicalities of airfare, visa, departure date? Should she use the word "love" in the opening line?

She decides to tackle the Bruce Springsteen thing first. To stop it hanging in the air between them. Then she can write the beginning.

Bruce Springsteen is

That's as far as she gets for several minutes. Then:

> a very important song writer in American music and it is natural that you admire him extremely. I

Several more minutes pass. Maybe five. Then:

> also admire how he writes always from point of view of very ordinary person even though he has now a big fortune. He is poet of the proletariat. Is that a word in American? It comes from Russian but I think it exists also in English for a long period.

Maybe in American there exists different word? Anyway, whenever I hear music of Bruce Springsteen, I

Five, ten more minutes pass while she considers what she can share with Montana Bob about how she feels when she hears Bruce Springsteen. All sorts of statements float into her mind, some honest, some not so honest, some equivocal. At one point, she almost types, "Some days, when I am faced with Ukrainian situation, I wish I could sing truly in chorus with Bruce Springsteen that I was Born in the USA!" A sentence like that would strike a chord with Bob, she's sure. Exactly the combination of warmth, humility, good humor, and exotic cuteness he would get off on most. But of course, it's out of the question. Everything is out of the question. She racks her brains for an alternative. The word "I" hangs suspended on the screen so long that a screen saver comes on. Natalia touches the mouse and the galaxy of ricocheting spheres disappears, replaced by her half-written e-mail and its dangling pronoun at the end. She stares at it until her eyes sting. Finally she makes her decision and clicks a single key with one pale finger.

A box pops up containing a stylized think balloon and an automated question. *Are you sure you want to discard Message 1—Dear Bob?*

Natalia makes the box disappear and disconnects from the Net. She rises from her chair. The young guy at the counter almost jumps out of his skin.

"Jesus," he says. "I didn't notice you were still here. You were so quiet. Invisible."

Natalia opens her purse, rummages around in coins of almost no value, pulls out a ten-hryvnia banknote.

"No change," says the young guy. "The boss has taken all the cash. It's OK, just pay us next time. You'll be back tomorrow, yeah?"

He stands slightly in the way, as if angling to chat to her for a few minutes longer, in exchange for giving her credit. Natalia blushes, weaves elegantly around him, and makes her escape.

"Thanks," she says. "I'd better get home."

Natalia walks the streets. She is in no hurry to get home. Earlier this evening, Mrs. Kotova caught her using the Kotovas' electric kettle to make herself a cup of coffee and they had a tense discussion about morality. "Wear and tear," Mrs. Kotova kept repeating. "Wear and tear. Every time the electricity passes through the coil, the coil gets pushed a bit closer to packing it in. Every time a towel is touched, every time a mat is trodden on, every time a tap is turned . . . it all adds up."

Natalia knows it all adds up. She knows it very well.

A car slows down as it passes her; a gypsy hoping she'll ask him to be her taxi driver. She keeps her eyes straight ahead. The buses don't quit till after midnight. She isn't cold anymore. Is it the disease or the medication that makes her body temperature rise and fall so steeply? Right now, she feels as though she could discard her windcheater and her cardigan, just toss them into the breeze and walk in her lacy dress, the raggedy bits fluttering like feathers, her flesh pale under the moon. Night obscures some of the city's modern trimmings; the clean, undiscriminating darkness simplifies the view to long, lonely avenues lined with sycamores. With eyes half closed, she could be a nineteenth-century countess, taking a stroll. A masked ball is still in full swing, but she has grown bored and wants a breath of fresh air. She may visit the house of a poet she has taken pity on, a poor sweet boy always on the brink of madness, a doomed idealist who raves about revolution while she dabs his fevered brow with the sleeve of her dress.

Another vehicle slows while it passes. It's the Faith-Hope-Love van, on the lookout for prostitutes to assist. A middle-aged woman Natalia doesn't recognize is at the wheel, no doubt with a hamper of free condoms at her side. Natalia doesn't need any free condoms. She keeps walking, eyes fixed straight ahead.

Eventually, she reaches the faux-traditional restaurant that has the revolving billboard outside. It was here that she had her epiphany, a couple of months ago. It was here that she decided to teleport herself right out of Ukraine, to rematerialize in a new world where Irina's face-powder scum around the bathtub would rapidly fade into the forgotten long-ago.

The restaurant is closed now; its peasant-garbed staff have gone home to their own sordid flats to watch subtitled TV. But the sign is still here, still rotating. BLACKSEABRIDES.COM. "Unique and beautiful women for correspondence and marriage. Translation, accommodation, flower deliveries available. Visit our website for beach pics, glamour pics, testimonials from satisfied customers. All major credit cards accepted. Sincere females 18 and up always wanted."

Natalia waits for the sign to turn, curious to see what's on the other side. Nothing, at the moment. Advertising is expensive. Maybe the price needs to drop a little. Not every business in Odessa is booming.

She walks on. Ahead, she can see the luminous marble steps of the museum where her grandmother used to work as a guide. What would her grandmother advise her to do now? Probably give her an earful for being rude. You can't just stop writing to a man who has proposed to you. You owe him a reply, even if it's just to say good-bye.

There's too far to go, she can't walk it. But she'll walk a little farther, to give everyone plenty of time to get tired and go to bed. She reaches into her handbag and fetches out the earphones for her Walkman, fits them snugly into her ears. With a well-practiced motion, not even looking inside her bag as she does it, she inserts *Antiar* into the player, presses the middle button. The instant the music starts, she visualizes the cassette cover, vivid as an icon in church, as mysterious and disturbing and thrilling now as it was when she was sixteen: a giant insect poised to prey on a tied-up woman.

The mighty Alexander Melnik could be anywhere now—serving French fries in a Kiev roadside diner, frowning over a laptop in a Moscow-bound plane, teaching Gogol to rich Germans in Cologne, injecting homebrew opiates into his festering thigh in a filthy cellar just around the corner from here—but in Natalia's ears he is reunited with his younger self, without the slightest hesitation, majestic-voiced once more, singing directly into the cells of her body.

We go into the night!
We go into the night!
Like fully ripe stars, at random we fly . . .

Natasha finds a rhythm of walking that's compatible with the furious tempo of Velchev's drums, and smiles, defiant in her intention of playing the same fucking song a million times over, until the rest of the world finally sees the glory of it, or her batteries run out, whichever comes first.

William Trevor

Folie à Deux

Aware of a presence close to him, Wilby glances up from the book he has just begun to read. The man standing there says nothing. He doesn't smile. A dishcloth hangs from where it's tucked into grubby apron strings knotted at the front, and Wilby assumes that the man is an envoy sent from the kitchen to apologize for the delay in the cooking of the fish he has ordered.

The place is modest, in the Rue Piques, off the Rue de Sèvres; Wilby didn't notice what it is called. A café as much as a brasserie, it is poorly illuminated except for the bar, at which a couple are hunched over their glasses, conversing softly. One of the café's tables is occupied by four elderly women playing cards, and there are a few people at tables in the brasserie.

Still without communicating, the man who has come from the kitchen turns and goes away, leaving Wilby with the impression that he has been mistaken for someone else. He pours himself more wine and reads again. Wilby reads a lot, and drinks a lot.

He is a spare, sharp-faced man in his forties, clean shaven, in a gray suit, with a striped blue-and-red tie striking a stylish note. He visits Paris once in a while to make the rounds of salerooms specializing in rare postage stamps, usually spinning out his time when he is there, since he can afford to. Three years ago he inherited his family's wine business in

Ireland, which he sold eighteen months later, planning to live on the proceeds while he indulged his interest in philately. He occupies, alone now, the house he also inherited at that time, creeper clad, just outside the County Westmeath town where he was born. Marriage failed him there, or he it, and he doubts that he will make another attempt in that direction.

His food is brought to him by a small, old waiter, a more presentable figure than the man who came and went. He is attentive, addressing Wilby in conventional waiter's terms and supplying, when they are asked for, salt and pepper from another table. "*Voilà, monsieur*," he murmurs, his tone apologetic.

Wilby eats his fish, wondering what fish it is. He knew when he ordered it but has since forgotten, and the taste doesn't tell him much. The bread is the best part of his meal and he catches the waiter's attention to ask for more. His book is a paperback he has read before, *The Hand of Ethelberta*.

He reads another page, orders more wine, finishes the *pommes frites* but not the fish. He likes quiet places and doesn't hurry. He orders coffee and—though not intending to—a Calvados. He drinks too much, he tells himself, and restrains the inclination to have another when the coffee comes. He reads again, indulging the pleasure of being in Paris, in a brasserie where Muzak isn't playing, at a small corner table, engrossed in a story that's familiar yet has receded sufficiently to be blurred in places, like something good remembered. He never minds it when the food isn't up to much; wine matters more, and peace. He'll walk back to the Hôtel Merneuil; with luck he'll be successful in the salerooms tomorrow.

He gestures for his bill, and pays. The old waiter has his overcoat ready for him at the door, and Wilby tips him a little for that. Outside, it being late November, the night is chilly.

The man who came to look at him is there on the street, still dressed as he was then. He stands still, not speaking. He might have come outside to have a cigarette, as waiters sometimes do. But there is no cigarette.

"*Bonsoir*," Wilby says.

"*Bonsoir*."

Saying that, quite suddenly the man is someone else. A resemblance flickers: the smooth black hair, the head like the rounded end of a bullet, the fringe that is not as once it was but still a fringe, the dark eyes. There is a way of standing, without unease or agitation and yet awkward, hands lank, open.

"What is all this?" Even as he puts the question, Wilby's choice of words sounds absurd to him. "Anthony?" he says.

There is a movement, a hand's half gesture, meaningless, hardly a response. Then the man turns away, entering the brasserie by another door. "Anthony," Wilby mutters again, but only to himself. People have said that Anthony is dead.

The streets are emptier than they were, the bustle of the pavements gone. Obedient to pedestrian lights at the Rue de Babylone, where there is fast-moving traffic again, Wilby waits with a woman in a pale waterproof coat, her legs slim beneath it, blond hair brushed up. Not wanting to think about Anthony, he wonders if she's a tart, since she has that look, and for a moment sees her pale coat thrown down in some small room, the glow of an electric fire, money placed on a dressing table: now and again when he travels he has a woman. But this one doesn't glance at him, and the red light changes to green.

It couldn't possibly have been Anthony; of course it couldn't. Even assuming that Anthony is alive, why would he be employed as a kitchen worker in Paris? "Yes, I'm afraid we fear the worst," his father said on the telephone, years ago now. "He sent a few belongings here, but that's a good while back. A note to you, unfinished, was caught up in the pages of a book. Nothing in it, really. Your name, no more."

In the Rue du Bac there is a window Wilby likes, with prints of the Revolution. The display has hardly changed since he was here last: the death of Marie Antoinette, the Girondists on their way to the guillotine, the storming of the Bastille, Danton's death, Robespierre triumphant, Robespierre fallen from grace. Details aren't easy to make out in the dim streetlight. Prints he hasn't seen before are indistinguishable at the back.

At a bar he has another Calvados. He said himself when people asked him—a few had once—that he, too, imagined Anthony was dead. A disappearance so prolonged, with no reports of even a glimpse as the years advanced, did appear to confirm a conclusion that became less tentative and, in the end, wasn't tentative at all.

In the Rue Montalembert a couple ask for directions to the Métro. Wilby points it out, walking back a little way with them to do so, as grateful for this interruption as he was when the woman at the traffic crossing caught his interest.

"Bonne nuit, monsieur." In the hall of the Hôtel Merneuil the night porter holds open the lift doors. He closes them, and the lift begins its smooth ascent. "The will to go on can fall away, you know," Anthony's father said on the telephone again, in touch to find out if there was anything to report.

M. Jothy shakes his head over the pay packet that hasn't been picked up. It's on the windowsill above the sinks, where others have been ignored, too. He writes a message on it and props it against an empty bottle.

At this late hour M. Jothy has the kitchen to himself, a time for assessing what needs to be ordered, for satisfying himself that, in general, the kitchen is managing. He picks up Jean-André's note of what he particularly requires for tomorrow and checks the shelves where the cleaning materials are kept. He has recently become suspicious of Jean-André, suspecting shortcuts. His risotto, once an attraction on the menu, is scarcely ever ordered now; and with reason, in M. Jothy's opinion, since it has lost the intensity of flavor that made it popular, and is often dry. But the kitchen at least is clean, and M. Jothy, examining cutlery and plates, fails to find food clinging anywhere or a rim left on a cup. Once he employed two dishwashers at the sinks, but now one does it on his own, and half the time forgets his wages. Anxious to keep him, M. Jothy has wondered about finding somewhere for him to sleep on the premises instead of having the long journey to and from his room. But there isn't even a corner of a pantry, and when he asked in the neighborhood about accommodation he was also unsuccessful.

The dishcloths, washed and rinsed, are draped on the radiators and will be dry by the morning, the soup bowls are stacked; the glasses, in their rows, gleam on the side table. "*Très bon, très bon,*" M. Jothy murmurs before he turns the lights out and locks up.

Wilby does not sleep and cannot read, although he tries to.

A marvel, isn't it? Miss Davally said, the memory vivid, as if she'd said it yesterday. You wouldn't think apricots would so easily ripen in such a climate, she said. Even on a wall lined with brick you wouldn't think it. She pointed at the branches sprawled out along their wires, and you could see the fruit in little clusters. "Delphiniums," she said, pointing again, and one after another named the flowers they passed on their way through the garden. "And this is Anthony," she said in the house.

The boy looked up from the playing cards he had spread out on the floor. "What's his name?" he asked, and Miss Davally said he knew because she had told him already. But even so she told him again. "Why's he called that?" Anthony asked. "Why're you called that?"

"It's my name."

"Shall we play in the garden?"

That first day, and every day afterward, there were gingersnap biscuits in the middle of the morning. "Am I older than you?" Anthony asked. "Is six older?" He had a house, he said, in the bushes at the end of the garden, and they pretended there was a house. "Jericho he's called," Anthony said of the dog that followed them about, a black Labrador with an injured leg that hung limply, thirteen years old. "Miss Davally was an orphan," Anthony said. "That's why she lives with us. Do you know what an orphan is?"

In the yard the horses looked out over the half doors of their stables; the hounds were in a smaller yard. Anthony's mother was never at lunch because her horse and the hounds were exercised then. But his father always was, each time wearing a different tweed jacket, his gray mustache clipped short, the olives he liked to see on the lunch table always there, the whiskey he took for his health. "Well, young chap, how are you?" he always asked.

On wet days they played marbles in the kitchen passages, with the dog stretched out beside them on the stone floor. "You come to the sea in summer," Anthony said. "They told me." It was Miss Davally who had told him, knowing about the family who came every July to the same holiday cottage on the cliff above the bay that didn't have a name. Miss Davally knew about everyone in the neighborhood, even people who didn't quite belong to it. The July visitors made the long journey south from County Westmeath—a provincial wine merchant and his wife, a child who might be lonely, not having brothers or sisters, as Anthony hadn't, either. "It's not an intrusion I hope?" she apologized when she called on them, and was friendlily reassured. Afterward, when the boys themselves became friends, she often drove Anthony to the cottage on the cliff, so that hospitality might be returned. An outing for her, too, she used to say, and sometimes she brought a cake she'd made, being in the way of bringing a present when she went to people's houses. She liked it at the sea as much as Anthony did; she liked to turn the wheel of the bellows in the kitchen of the cottage and watch the sparks flying up while she heard about life in a sleepy Westmeath town. And Anthony liked the hard sand of the shore, and collecting flint stones, and netting shrimps. The dog prowled about the rocks, sniffing the seaweed, clawing at the sea anemones. "Our house," Anthony called the cave they found when they crawled through an opening in the rocks, a cave no one knew was there.

Air from the window Wilby slightly opens at the top is refreshing and brings with it, for a moment, the chiming of two o'clock. His book is open, face downward to keep his place, his bedside light still on. But the dark is better, and he extinguishes it.

There was a blue vase in the recess of the staircase wall, nothing else there; and paperweights crowded the shallow landing shelves, all touching one another—forty-six of them, Anthony said. His mother played the piano in the drawing room. "Hullo," she said, holding out her hand and smiling. She wasn't much like someone who exercised foxhounds; slim and small and wearing scent, she was also beautiful. "Look!" Anthony said, pointing at the lady in the painting above the mantelpiece in the hall.

Miss Davally was a distant relative as well as being an orphan, and when she sat on the sand after her swim she often talked about her own childhood in the house where she'd been given a home: how a particularly unpleasant boy used to creep up on her and pull a cracker in her ear, how she hated her ribboned pigtails and persuaded a simpleminded maid to cut them off, how she taught the kitchen cat to dance and how people said they'd never seen the like.

Every lunchtime Anthony's father kept going a conversation about a world that was not yet known to his listeners. He spoke affectionately of the playboy pugilist Jack Doyle, demonstrating the subtlety of his right punch and recalling the wonders of his hell-raising before poverty claimed him. He told of the exploits of an ingenious escapologist, Major Pat Reid. He condemned the first Earl of Inchiquin as the most disgraceful man ever to step out of Ireland.

Much other information was passed on at the lunch table: why airplanes flew, how clocks kept time, why spiders spun their webs and how they did it. Information was everything, Anthony's father maintained, and its lunchtime dissemination, with Miss Davally's reminiscences, nurtured curiosity; the unknown became a fascination. "What would happen if you didn't eat?" Anthony wondered; and there were attempts to see if it was possible to create a rainbow with a water hose when the sun was bright, the discovery made that, in fact, it was. A jellyfish was scooped into a shrimp net to see if it would perish or survive when it was tipped out onto the sand. Miss Davally said to put it back, and warned that jellyfish could sting as terribly as wasps.

A friendship developed between Miss Davally and Wilby's mother—a formal association, first names not called upon, neither in conversation nor in the letters that came to be exchanged from one summer to the next. *Anthony is said to be clever*, Miss Davally's spidery handwriting told. And then, as if that perhaps required watering down, *Well, so they say*. It was reported also that when each July drew near Anthony began to count the days. *He values the friendship so!* Miss Davally commented. *How fortunate for two only children such a friendship is!*

Fortunate indeed it seemed to be. There was no quarreling, no vying for authority, no competing. When, one summer, a yellow Li-Lo raft washed up, still inflated, it was taken to the cave that no one else knew about, neither claiming that it was his because he'd seen it first. "Someone lost that thing," Anthony said, but no one came looking for it. They didn't know what it was, only that it floated. They floated it themselves, the old dog limping behind them when they carried it to the sea, his tail wagging madly, head cocked to one side. In the cave it became a bed for him, to clamber onto when he was tired.

The Li-Lo was another of the friendship's precious secrets, as the cave itself was. No other purpose was found for it, but its possession was enough to make it the highlight of that particular summer and on the last day of July it was again carried to the edge of the sea. "Now, now," the dog was calmed when he became excited. The waves that morning were hardly waves at all.

In the dark there is a pinprick glow of red somewhere on the television set. The air that comes into the room is colder now and Wilby closes the window he has opened a crack, suppressing the murmur of a distant plane. Memory won't let him go now; he knows it won't and makes no effort to resist it.

Nothing was said when they watched the drowning of the dog. Old Jericho was clever, never at a loss when there was play. Not moving, he was obedient, as he always was. He played his part, going with the Li-Lo when it floated out, a deep black shadow, sharp against the garish yellow. They watched as they had watched the hose-pipe rainbow gathering color, as Miss Davally said she'd watched the shaky steps of the dancing cat. Far away already, the yellow of the Li-Lo became a blur on the water, was lost, was there again, and lost again, and the barking began, and became a wail. Nothing was said then, either. Nor when they clambered over the shingle and the rocks, and climbed up to the shortcut and passed through the gorse field. From the cliff they looked again, for the last time, far out to the horizon. The sea was undisturbed, glittering in the sunlight. "So what have you two been up to this morning?" Miss Davally asked. The next day, somewhere else, the dog washed in.

Miss Davally blamed herself, for that was in her nature. But she could not be blamed. It was agreed that she could not be. Unaware of his limitations—more than a little blind, with only three active legs— old Jericho had had a way of going into the sea when he sensed a piece of driftwood bobbing about. Once too often he had done that. His grave was in the garden, a small slate plaque let into the turf, his name and dates.

They did not ever speak to one another about the drowning of the dog. They did not ever say they had not meant it to happen. There was no blame, no accusing. They had not called it a game, only said they wondered what would happen, what the dog would do. The silence had begun before they pushed the Li-Lo out.

Other summers brought other incidents, other experiences, but there was no such occurrence again. There were adjustments in the friendship, since passing time demanded that, and different games were played, and there were different conversations, and new discoveries.

Then, one winter, a letter from Miss Davally was less cheerful than her letters usually were. *Withdrawn*, she wrote, *and they are concerned*. What she declared, in detail after that, was confirmed when summer came. Anthony was different and more different still in later summers—quieter, timid, seeming sometimes to be lost. It was a mystery when the dog's gravestone disappeared from the garden.

. . .

In the dark, the bright-red dot of the television light still piercingly there, Wilby wonders, as so often he has, what influence there was when, without incitement or persuasion, without words, they did what had been done. They were nine years old then, when secrets became deception.

It was snowing the evening he and Anthony met again, five years later, both of them waiting in the Chapel Cloisters for their names, as new boys, to be called out. It was not a surprise that Anthony was there, passing on from the school that years earlier had declared him clever; nor was it by chance that they were to be together for what remained of their education. "Nice for Anthony to have someone he knows," his father said on the telephone, and confirmed that Anthony was still as he had become.

In the dim evening light the snow blew softly into the Cloisters, and when the roll call ended and a noisy dispersal began, the solitary figure remained, the same smooth black hair, a way of standing that hadn't changed. "How are you?" Wilby asked. His friend's smile, once so readily there, came as a shadow and then was lost in awkwardness.

Peculiar, Anthony was called at school, but wasn't bullied, as though it had been realized that bullying would yield no satisfaction. He lacked skill at games, avoided all pursuits that were not compulsory, displayed immediate evidence of his cleverness, science and mathematical subjects his forte. Religious boys attempted to befriend him, believing that to be a duty; kindly masters sought to draw him out. "Well, yes, I knew him," Wilby admitted, lamely explaining his association with someone who was so very much not like the friends he made now. "A long time ago," he nearly always added.

Sometimes guilt pricked. Passing the windows of empty classrooms, he several times noticed Anthony, the only figure among the unoccupied desks. And often—on the drive that ended at the school gates, or often anywhere—there was the same lone figure in the distance. On the golf course where senior boys were allowed to play, Anthony sometimes sat on a seat against a wall, watching the golfers as they approached, watching them as they walked on. He shied away when conversation threatened, creeping back into his shadowlands.

One day he wasn't there. His books had been left tidily in his desk, his clothes hanging in his dormitory locker, his pajamas under his pillow. He would be on his way home, since boys who kept themselves to themselves were often homesick. But he had not attempted to go home and was found still within the school grounds, having broken no rules except that he had ignored for a day the summoning of bells.

Dawn comes darkly, and Wilby sleeps. But his sleep is brief, his dreams forgotten when he wakes. The burden of guilt that came when in silence they clambered over the shingle and the rocks, when they passed through the gorse field, was muddled by bewilderment, a child's tormenting panic not yet constrained by suppression as later it would be. Long afterward, when first he heard that Anthony was dead—and when he said it himself—the remnants of the shame guilt had become fell away.

He shaves and washes, dresses slowly. In the hall the reception clerks have just come on duty. They nod at him, wish him good day. No call this morning for an umbrella, one says.

Outside it is not entirely day, or even day at all. The cleaning lorries are on the streets, water pouring in the gutters, but there's no one about in the Rue du Bac, garbage bags still waiting to be collected. A bar is open farther on, men standing at the counter, disinclined for conversation. A sleeping figure in a doorway has not been roused. What hovel, Wilby wonders as he passes, does a kitchen worker occupy?

In the Rue Piques the brasserie is shuttered. They might have liked to have him there, conveniently on the premises at night, but no lights are showing anywhere. Cardboard boxes are stacked close to the glass of three upstairs windows, others are uncurtained; none suggests the domesticity of a dwelling. Le Père Jothy the place is called.

Wilby roams the nearby streets. A few more cafés are opening and in one coffee is brought to him. He sips it, breaking a croissant. There's no one else, except the barman.

He knows he should go away. He should take the train to Passy, to the salerooms he has planned to visit there; he should not ever return to the Rue Piques. He has lived easily with an aberration, then shaken it off: what happened was almost nothing.

Other men come in, a woman on her own, her face bruised on one side, no effort made to conceal the darkening weals. Her voice is low when she explains this injury to the barman, her fingers now and again touching it. Soundlessly, she weeps when she has taken her Cognac to a table.

Oh, this is silly! his unspoken comment was when Miss Davally's letter came, its implications apparent only to him. For heaven's sake! he crossly murmured, the words kept to himself when he greeted Anthony in the Cloisters, and again every time he caught sight of him on the golf course. The old dog's life had been all but over. And Wilby remembers now, as harshly as he has in the night, the bitterness of his resentment when a friendship he delighted in was destroyed, when Anthony's world—the garden, the house, his mother, his father, Miss Davally—was no longer there.

"He has no use for us," his father said. "No use for anyone, we think."

Turning into the Rue Piques, Anthony notices at once the figure waiting outside the ribbon shop. It is November the twenty-fourth, the last Thursday of the month. This day won't come again.

"Bonjour," he says.

"How are you, Anthony?"

And Anthony says that Monday is the closed day. Not that Sunday isn't, too. If someone waited outside the ribbon shop on a Monday or a Sunday it wouldn't be much good. Not that many people wait there.

Wind blows a scrap of paper about, close to where they stand. In the window of the ribbon shop coils of ribbon are in all widths and colors, and there are swatches of trimming for other purposes, lace and velvet, and plain white edging, and a display of button cards. Anthony often looks to see if there has been a change, but there never has been.

"How are you, Anthony?"

It is a fragment of a white paper bag that is blown about, and Anthony identifies it from the remains of the red script that advertises the *boulangerie* in the Rue Dupin. When it is blown closer to him he catches it under his shoe.

"People have wondered where you are, Anthony."

"I went away from Ireland."

Anthony bends and picks up the litter he has trapped. He says he has the ovens to do today. A Thursday, and he works in the morning.

"Miss Davally still writes, Anthony, wondering if there is news of you."

Half past eight is his time on Thursdays. Anthony says that, and adds that there's never a complaint in the kitchen. One speck on the prong of a fork could lead to a complaint, a shred of fish skin could, a cabbage leaf. But there's never a complaint.

"People thought you were dead, Anthony."

. . .

Wilby says he sold the wine shop. He'd described it once, when they were children: the shelves of bottles, the different shapes, their contents red or white, pink if people wanted that. He tasted wine a few times, he remembers saying.

"Your father has died himself, Anthony. Your mother has. Miss Davally was left the house because there was no one else. She lives there now."

No response comes; Wilby has not expected one. He has become a philatelist, he says.

Anthony nods, waiting to cross the street. He knows his father died, his mother, too. He has guessed Miss Davally inherited the house. The deaths were in *The Irish Times*, which he always read, cover to cover, all the years he was the night porter at the Cliff Castle Hotel in Dalkey.

He doesn't mention the Cliff Castle Hotel. He doesn't say he misses *The Irish Times*, the familiar names, the political news, the photographs of places, the change there is in Ireland now. *Le Monde* is more staid, more circumspect, more serious. Anthony doesn't say that, either, because he doubts that it's of interest to a visitor in Paris.

A gap comes in the stream of cars that has begun to go by; but not trusting this opportunity, Anthony still waits. He is careful on the streets, even though he knows them well.

"I haven't died," he says.

Perfectly together, they shared an act that was too shameful to commit alone, taking a chance on a sunny morning to discover if an old dog's cleverness would see to his survival.

For a moment, while Anthony loses another opportunity to cross the street, Wilby gathers into sentences how he might attempt a denial that this was how it was, how best to put it differently. An accident, a misfortune beyond anticipation, the unexpected: with gentleness, for gentleness is due, he is about to plead. But Anthony crosses the street then, and opens with a key the side door of the brasserie. He makes no gesture of farewell, does not look back.

Walking by the river on his way to the salerooms at Passy, Wilby wishes he'd said he was glad his friend was not dead. It is his only thought. The pleasure boats slip by on the water beside him, hardly anyone on them. A child waves. Raised too late in response, Wilby's own hand drops to his side. The wind that blew the litter about in the Rue Piques has freshened. It snatches at the remaining leaves on the black-trunked trees that are an orderly line, following the river's course.

The salerooms are on the other bank, near the radio building and the apartment block that change the river's character. Several times he has visited this vast display in which the world's stamps are exhibited, behind glass if they are notably valuable, or on the tables, country by country, when they are not. That busy image has always excited Wilby's imagination and as he climbs the steps to the bridge he is near he attempts to anticipate it now, but does not entirely succeed.

It is not in punishment that the ovens are cleaned on another Thursday morning. It is not in expiation that soon the first leavings of the day will be scraped from the lunchtime plates. There is no bothering with redemption. Looking down from the bridge at the sluggish flow of water, Wilby confidently asserts that. A morning murkiness, like dusk, has brought some lights on in the apartment block. Traffic crawls on distant streets.

For Anthony, the betrayal matters, the folly, the carelessness that would have been forgiven, the cruelty. It mattered in the silence—while they watched, while they clambered over the shingle and the rocks, while they passed through the gorse field. It matters now. The haunted sea is all the truth there is for Anthony, what he honors because it matters still.

The buyers move among the tables, and Wilby knows that for him, in this safe, secondhand world of postage stamps, tranquillity will return. He knows where he is with all this; he knows what he's about, as he does in other aspects of his tidy life. And yet this morning he likes himself less than he likes his friend.

Mary Gaitskill

The Little Boy

MRS. BEA DAVIS walked through an enormous light-fluxing corridor of the Detroit airport whispering to no one visible: "I love you. I love you so much." The walls of the corridor were made of glowing, translucent oblongs electronically lit with color that, oblong by oblong, ignited in a forward-rolling pattern: red, purple, blue, green, and pale green. "I love you, dear," whispered Mrs. Davis. "I love you so." *You didn't love him*, said the voice of her daughter Megan. *You had nothing but contempt. Even when he was dying you*—Canned ocean waves rolled through the corridor, swelling the colors with sound. "You don't understand," whispered Bea. The ocean retreated, taking the colors solemnly and slowly back the other way: pale green, green, blue, purple, red. Red, thought Bea. The color of anger and accident. Green: serenity and life. She stepped onto a moving rubber walkway behind a man slumping in his rumpled suit. "I love you like I loved him," she whispered. Very slightly, the rumpled man turned his head. "Unconditionally." The man sighed and turned back. A woman with a small boy passing on the left peered at Bea curiously. Does she know me? thought Bea. "What a wonderful idea," she said out loud. "These lights, the ocean—like walking through eternity."

The woman smiled uncertainly and continued past; her little boy turned his entire torso to stare at Bea as his mother pulled him on. Maybe she did know me, thought Bea. We lived here long enough. She smiled and waved at the little boy until he turned away, a calf tethered behind his mother's busy hips.

They had not lived in Detroit but in the suburb of Livonia, in a neat brick house with a crab apple tree in front of it. The tree had spreading branches that grew in luxuriant twists; in the spring it exploded with pink blossoms, and in the summer the lawn was covered with the silken flesh of its flowers. Megan and Susan ran through the yard with Kyle, the neighbor boy. Megan, seven, climbed the crab apple tree, wrapping her legs around a branch and crowing for her mother to take a picture. Green, blue, purple. Red. It had not been a happy time for the family, and yet her memories of it were loaded with small pleasures. Dancing to the Mexican Hat Dance in the living room, the girls prancing around, and Mac swinging her in his arms yelling: "A hundred pounds! A hundred pounds!" The willow trees on 8 Mile Road, the library with the model of Neverland, the papier-mâché volcano at the Mai Kai Theater, glowing with rich colors. Kyle and Megan putting on Gilbert and Sullivan's *Mikado* in a neighbor's garage with the little girls down the block—she had a picture of it in one of the photo albums: Kyle was very dashing in slippers and his mother's silk robe with black dragons on it. The little neighbor girls wore gowns with silk scarves tied round their waists. Megan, the director, wore a top hat and a mustache. Susan sat in the driveway with the other siblings and parents, her thin arms wrapped round her body, staring off into the sky.

At the end of the corridor was an escalator with people pouring onto it from all directions. Bea mounted it and stood still while on her left people rushed facelessly past her. Going up, she felt as if she were falling, but falling where?

She had just come from a visit to Megan in upstate New York. Megan was a forty-two-year-old lawyer married to a travel writer—no children yet, but Bea hadn't given up hope entirely. They had driven to Manhattan to see a play, the windows down and country music on the CD player. She was at first disappointed to see that they were seated in the mezzanine, but it was all right—the actors' limbs were as subtly expressive as eyebrows or lips or the muscles of the neck. Afterward they had dinner in a big open-faced restaurant on a cobbled street with tables spilling out, women sitting with their legs comfortably open under the tables, their bra straps showing a little and their chests shining slightly in the heat. There was a huge bar with the artful names of drinks written on a board above it, and a mirror behind it, and a great, languidly stirring fan on the ceiling. Young men courted girls at the bar; a small girl with one knee on a tall stool leaned across the bar to order a round of drinks, and her silvery voice carried all the way to their table. They started with French fries served in a tin cone with mayonnaise on the side. Bea wondered aloud what it would be like to have a glass of sherry, and Jonathan called the waiter, a grave-faced young man with an entire arm tattooed. "I like the casual air of this place," she'd said. "I like the rough napkins instead of linen."

"It's a nice place," said Megan. "Though I've been noticing, there's an awful lot of really ugly people here right now."

"You think?" asked Jonathan. "You think it's changed over already?"

"Just look," said Megan. Her voice was strangely hot the way it would get as a little girl when she was overtired and about to get hissy. "That guy is like an anteater in leisurewear. That girl, she can't wear that dress, look at her stomach."

"You sound like Tomasina and Livia, at Woolworth's and the Greyhound bus terminal. Look at her, look at her."

"What?" said Jonathan.

"Mom's talking about her sisters," said Megan. "They would go on purpose to places where ugly poor people would be and comment on them. We didn't come here to do that, it's not the same thing."

Not far off, thought Bea. Megan hated her aunt Livia, but here she was, "Look at her." Except without Livia's lightness. It was dead serious to Megan. At some other point during dinner, she'd said to her daughter, "You've always been so beautiful," and Megan had said, "I certainly never thought that was your opinion,"

"How could you say that?" said Bea. And Megan was silent. A woman at the table next to them turned to look at Megan, then at her. Was this woman ugly, badly dressed? Bea had no idea. The waiter came back and informed them that they were out of sherry.

She looked up and saw the woman with the little boy halfway up the escalator; the boy was gazing intently down into the corridor of light. He was six or seven years old, heavyset, with dark, glowing skin, possibly Hispanic or part black. His mouth was full and gentle, and his eyes were long-lashed and deep, with a complicated expression that was murky and fiery at the same time. The child disappeared with the movement of the escalator; a moment later, Bea stepped off the clanking stair unknowingly buoyed by his bright face. She looked at her watch; she had a layover of an hour and a half before her flight to Chicago. In front of her was a snack shop, a bookstore, and a store that sold knickknacks, decorative scarves, hats, and perfume. Decorative scarves and hats, thought Bea. The most gallant members of the accessory family.

Inside, the shop gleamed with glass and halogen light and dozens of little bottles. Shallow cardboard boxes of scarves were displayed under a glass countertop with neat shelving, whimsical hats sat atop Styrofoam dummy heads. She tried on hats before a mirror in a plastic frame, and "The Finale" from Act Two of *The Mikado* played in her head—she knew it from the recording Mac used to have, which had somehow disappeared after the funeral.

"That looks good," said the woman behind the counter.

"Thank you," said Bea, and excitement rose through her. Characters were threatened with boiling in oil and beheading and forced marriage—and in between, the full cast was onstage singing with urgent joy. "As I drew my snicker-snee!" sang Livia. "My snicker-snee!" Ten-year-old Beatrice pretended to cower on her knees before her sister's snicker-snee. Pitty Sing the cat tore through the room. Tomasina whooped and forgot about the play; their mother was coming up the walk, stripping off her clothes because it was hot and she was too imperious and impatient to wait till she got through the door. Her daughters ran to the window, bursting with admiration for the long, slender limbs that were as strong and beautiful as the flowering dogwood she walked past. Thirty years later, Megan, chin up and arms outstretched, presented the little neighbor girls bowing and tittering in their gowns and silk scarves. And she was strong and beautiful, too.

"Here," said the saleswoman. "This scarf has a Brazilian flavor that works really well with that." "Brazilian" was a ridiculous word for the scarf, but it *was* arresting, with bold wavy stripes of gold and brown, and the saleswoman's brown eyes were warm and golden when Bea met them with her "Thank you."

That weird snapshot of Susan—what had she been looking at anyway? You couldn't tell from the picture. Her big glasses had caught the glare of the sun so that in the camera's eye she was intently blind; her small body, hard and flexible as wire, expressed buzzing inner focus. She certainly didn't seem to be looking at the play.

"You're right," said Bea to the lady behind the counter, "this scarf does do something for this hat."

"On you it does." The woman's hair was an ostentatious bronze, her skin was damaged and over-tanned. But her jewelry was tasteful and her makeup perfect.

An old-school sales type, thought Bea approvingly. You don't expect to find that at an airport. "I'll take them both," she said.

Pleased with her purchase, she continued down the corridor toward her gate, past more gleaming eateries and shops. Her thoughts now were suffused not by *The Mikado* but by the look Susan had on her face when her sister presented that childish spectacle in the garage. It occurred to her that although Susan had become many things since then, that particular look of blindness and glaring, sunlit vision still described her. She was a sort of therapist, and it was part of her therapy to read people's "auras" and, by moving her hands some inches above their bodies, to massage these auras. She read tarot cards, believed in past lives, and occasionally phrases like "astral plane" or "physical plane" appeared in her conversation. It was nonsense, but harmless and—

Should she stop and get something to eat? Here were people at an Internet café, humped over keyboards and dishes of fried food, typing with one hand while they gobbled with the other, writing e-mails and surfing chat rooms while televisions blared from three corners of the room. How interesting it was to be a person who, while considering eating at the airport Internet café, could remember riding a mule on a mud road to catch the bus to school. You used to sit in the Greyhound terminal waiting for the bus, and except for the roar and wheeze of the buses, it was quiet and you had to really look at the people across from you. You had to feel them, and if it was hot you had to smell them. There might be children chasing each other up and down, or men playing chess on a cardboard table set up on the sidewalk outside, or a woman holding a beautiful baby. Now people waiting to travel crouched over screens, hopping from one outrageous place to the next, and typing opinionated angry messages—about the war in Iraq or a murder in Minneapolis or parents who were keeping their daughter alive even though she'd been in a coma for ten years—to strangers they would never see let alone smell. Above their heads, actors silently sang and danced and fought; scenes of war and murder flashed like lightning, and heads of state moved their lips as chunks of words streamed under them. You could sit there on the physical plane, absently loading piles of fried food into your mouth while your mind disappeared through a rented computer screen and went somewhere positively astral.

No, Bea thought as she walked on. She just wanted to go to the gate. She wanted to think about riding to the school bus on her grandfather's mule named Magic. That had happened the winter they had stayed at their grandparents' farm while their parents looked for a place to live in Chicago, and the farm was way off the main road, on a dirt path that had treacherous ice patches in the winter. Their grandfather put all three of them up on Magic the mule and led them down the path to where the school bus was. It was fun to sway on the hairy, humpy back, knowing that Magic's feet were sure. Bea remembered the way the mule's heavy hooves would make blue cracks in the ice; she remembered boughs of pine, thick with snow that fell off in clumps as she passed, brushing against her body.

Megan had no patience for Susan's past lives and tarot cards. She thought it was precious and self-indulgent, and Bea could see why. When Megan was fifteen and Susan thirteen, Aunt Flower, their step-grandmother, who hated cats, told them that Granddaddy had killed Pitty Sing's litter by putting them in a bag and swinging them against the side of the house. In fact, more than one litter had been killed, but none so brutally, nor so late in life, and Bea saw no reason for the children to hear about any of it. Susan was already crying when she came to Bea, with Megan trailing sulkily behind, upset about the kittens, too, but provoked by Susan's wild, high-pitched sobs.

"She said . . . she said that Pitty Sing was crying," said Susan, weeping. "She said Pitty Sing was crying, and grabbing his pant leg, begging him to stop."

"She told us as an example of a time she had sympathy for cats," explained Megan. "Even *she* was sad when Granddaddy told her about it. Because of Pitty Sing grabbing the pant leg."

"That is cruel, it's sadistic!" cried Susan. "Granddaddy is mean!"

"Honey." Bea put her arm around Susan's hot little back. "It's not the same as it would be now. There was no birth control for cats back then, and you couldn't keep all the kittens. You had to kill them, otherwise they'd starve."

"That's what I told her!" said Megan. "I think it's awful, too, but—"

"But like that? Bashing them against the side of the house?" Susan pulled away from her mother and searched her face with wet, hysterical eyes. What was she looking for? "Something was wrong there. Something was wrong!" She turned away, her voice rising into a scream. "I hate Granddaddy, I hate him!"

"Oh shut *up*!" said Megan.

Bea stopped thinking for a moment and looked at the stream of faces pouring past her: young, old, middle aged. Their expressions were tense and lax at the same time, and they moved mechanically, without awareness, focused only on getting somewhere else.

In fact, Susan had been right. Something was wrong. There were only three kittens in that litter and their mother had told them they could each have one; she had already given each of them her particular kitten. Then they came home from school, and she told them that Daddy had decided that four cats was too much and that the kittens had been taken away. It was the same summer she had come up the walk, smiling and triumphant as she stripped off her clothes, the dogwood flowering radiantly as she came.

Here was her gate, A6. It seemed that she always departed from gates that were low alphabetically and numerically—an example of something to which Susan might attach mystical significance. She sat down with a proprietary "oof." Well, Susan had made her beliefs work for her. She had made a life. She had a "partner," a woman named Julie, who managed a bookstore. Susan had worked on Bea's "aura" several times, and if the "therapy" didn't help, it was still pleasant to have her daughter's hands working above her, close enough to feel the heat of her palms, working to give her mother healing and happiness. She took out her book-club novel—something literary from another century, the name of which she had a hard time remembering—and a newsmagazine. She looked through her purse, found her glasses, looked up, and—there he was again, the little dark-skinned boy she had seen earlier. He was singing as he danced across a row of plastic chairs, hopping neatly over each armrest, his face glowing with pleasure. Bea smiled to see him.

She put her glasses on, smiling to remember Susan at his age, when she and Mac found her in their bedroom, leaping up and down on their big bed like it was a trampoline, ecstatically whipping her hair about and crying, "Eeee! Eeee! Eeeeee!" Bea was about to make her get down, but before she could, Mac kicked off his shoes and climbed up onto the bed with his daughter. "Eeeee!" he yelled, and he grabbed her hands and jumped with her. Bea said, "Careful, Mac, careful!" but she was smiling. Dinner was about ready to come out of the oven; she could still remember the meaty smell of it, and the big green leaves of the bush outside pressing against the windowpane. "Daddy!" shouted Susan. "Daddy!" His shirt had come out of his pants, and his face was pink and joyous.

Nothing but contempt—

Bea put her book down and felt her face flush. It was Megan who had contempt. Contempt for her father's sadness and his failure at medical school and his job at a pharmacy. Contempt for his rage, especially for his rage; when he lost his temper and slapped her, her blue eyes were hot with nearly sensual scorn. It wasn't that his violence didn't hurt her—it did. His sarcasm and ignoring hurt her, too. But in adolescence, scorn rose up from her hurt like something winged and flaming. At fourteen, she lectured Bea on sexism as if her mother were a perfect idiot. When Bea drove her to a sleepover, or to buy new shoes, or any other time they were alone together: "It's unfair. He acts like a big baby and then he bosses you! You should stand up to him or leave!"

It was true that Bea in some small way liked to hear her daughter say these things. It was unfair, his constant complaining, his throwing the fork across the dining table and expecting her to just pick it up, get him a new one, and act as though nothing had happened. Somebody had littered the edge of the yard. He yelled, "I'll show you littering!" and then went out and dumped a bag of potatoes in the neighbor's drive. When Bea came home from the hospital with newborn Megan, she'd come early on Monday evening instead of Tuesday morning, because she'd been eager and Tomasina had been there to give her a ride. They had no phone at home, so she couldn't call ahead and thought she might surprise him—but when she and her newborn child arrived, young Daddy wasn't at home. He was out having drinks and dinner with Jean, a woman he worked with. Bea had waited until after he was dead to tell it: how she was there all alone with her baby and how, when he finally got back after midnight and found her there he *ran* into the laundry room, taking his shirt off as he went, stammering nonsense about wanting to help the lady they'd hired to do the laundry. The next day Bea had looked in the hamper and she saw it: his shirt covered with sticky lipstick kisses.

The air filled with floating announcements directing everyone every which way: *Flight 775—Flight 83—Ready for Boarding—Gate A4—Gate A5—Memphis—Delayed Until Further Notice—Cincinnati—Flight—*

Her mother came up the walk, stripping down to her slip in the heat, flowering all around. She announced her adultery in public, in glorious secret. They didn't know until they found the love letters after she died. But looking back, it was there in her proud walk, for anyone who had eyes to see. Mac scuttled and hid when he hadn't even succeeded at cheating!

"Jean was a smart cookie," said Bea, "and she never would've kissed him all over the shirt like that if she'd done anything untoward. I think she meant that as a message to me."

"*That's* what you think?" said Megan.

"Yes. I think he tried and she said no."

"And you're telling me you don't have contempt for him?"

"Stop it, you little idiot! You little—"

Aware that people were staring, the mother of the dark-skinned boy lowered her voice to a furious mutter as she dragged her child back to his seat by the crook of his elbow. Was she even his mother? She was pale with thinning blonde hair and a small mouth—on the other hand, her body was heavy like his, tall and voluptuous. Bea tried to catch the child's eye, but he was looking down, all the life gone out of his face.

"Honey," said Bea. "You don't understand. I felt sorry for him. It's different."

Megan stared, and her face grew remote.

Flight 775—Final call. Bea picked up her book and remembered Prue Johannsen, the oldest member of the book club, who had twice when she meant to say "the cemetery" said "the airport" instead. The memory gave Bea a sensation that she could not define. Prue was a beautiful ninety-year-old woman with bright eyes and a long, still-elegant neck, sloping and gentle as a giraffe's. She was a widow and she visited her husband's grave often. "I went to the airport this afternoon," she'd say. "I think I'll have them plant some purple flowers instead of the red."

What a strange world, thought Bea. A strange, sad, glowing world. In this world she had married a boy who courted her with a vision of them traveling together, in the jungle, in the desert, in the mountains of Tibet, bringing healing to the sick and learning from life. In this world, her boy-husband became a man who got up in the morning and said, "I think I'll just kill myself," and at night threw a fork across the dining room table. It was the same world, but now he was dead and yet she was not a widow. At night her darkness came while she lay alone watching light and shadow on the wall. Streetlamp, telephone wire, moths, bits of leafy branch; sometimes a pale rectangle of light suddenly opened its eye, revealing a ghost of movement inside it as someone in the apartment across the street used the toilet or the sink.

"I feel so old and so worthless." Beautiful Prue Johannsen had said that one night after *Mrs. Dalloway*. Everyone said, "No!" But they all knew what she meant.

Bea got to her feet, full of sudden energy. She went to a nearby kiosk attended by a long-fingered East Indian bent like a pipe-cleaner man. She bought a bottle of water and a candy bar filled with caramel and nuts. Instead of going directly back to her seat, she walked around the gate area and approached the little dark boy and his blonde mother. The mother looked up, not unpleasantly. Her eyes were deep and long-lashed. She doesn't remember me, thought Bea.

"Excuse me," she said, smiling. "You look familiar to me. Did you ever live in this area?"

"No. But my sister does."

The little boy, still looking down, bumped his feet together and hummed.

"Hmmm—" Bea nervously half-laughed. "Do I look at all familiar to you?"

"I don't think so." The woman's eyes were civil, but her voice was vaguely tinged with common sarcasm.

Coarse, thought Bea, and unobservant. "Well, I guess when you've lived as long as I have, a lot of people look familiar to you."

"I know you," said the child, still looking down. "You were in the magic cave. Downstairs."

His mother looked irritated. "The *what*?"

"He means the walkway connecting the terminals," said Bea. "It *is* like a magic cave, with the lights and the ocean!"

At this the boy looked up; his gaze was alive and tactile, like a baby touching your face with its hands.

"What a beautiful little boy," said Bea. "And imaginative too!"

"A beautiful little pain in the butt, you mean." But the mother's face was grudgingly pleased. Her name was Lee Anne; her son was Michael. They had been visiting her sister, who lived in a suburb called Canton, and were waiting for their return flight to Memphis, which had been delayed. Bea and Lee Anne talked about Canton and Livonia, where Bea's family lived; Bea described the crab apple tree, with its hard, dark fruit and fleshy, open flowers. While they talked, Michael walked around and around them, as if he were dying to run or dance. Could you eat the crab apples? he wanted to know. Could you throw them at people? Could you put them on the floor at night, so crooks would slip and break their butt?

"Michael, sit down," said Lee Anne.

He sat, and immediately began to rock and nod his head.

"Well," said Bea, "I—"

"You talk to yourself," said Michael, rocking. "In the magic tunnel, you talk to yourself."

"Don't be rude!" snapped Lee Anne. She whacked her son on the head with the flat of her hand. "And quit rocking like a retard."

"It's all right," said Bea. "I probably was."

"That doesn't matter, I still don't want him being rude." She stood, looming over Bea with an air of physical dominance that was startling before Bea realized it was habitual, not personal. "Listen, could you just watch him for a minute? I want to see if I can talk to these bozos here." She gestured at the check-in counter, where a man and a woman in short-sleeved uniforms made automaton motions.

"Certainly," said Bea. Lee Anne held her eye for a second as if to make sure of her, then went on toward the check-in counter, her hips expressing steady, rolling force.

"She's the one who said you talk to yourself," said Michael sullenly. He was still now, and very sober.

"It's okay, honey. I do talk to myself sometimes."

He raised his head and touched her again with his tactile gaze. Except this look did not have the feel of a baby's touch. It was as warm and strong as the arms of the man he would become. "Who do you talk to?"

"Somebody who's gone. Somebody I used to love."

Used to. He turned away, but still she felt it coming from him, warmth as strong as the arm of a man laid across her shoulders. Feeling welled up in her.

Attention: Those passengers waiting for Flight #83 to Memphis—

"I talk to my father sometimes," he said. "Even though he's gone."

She started to ask where his father was and stopped herself. Feeling welled up.

—will be boarding in approximately five minutes.

"My father is fighting in Iraq," said Michael. He looked at her, but his eyes did not reach out to touch her. They looked like they had when he rode above her on the escalator—deep and fiery, but with something murky obscuring the fire.

"You must be proud," she said.

"I am proud!" His eyes were bright, too bright. He was beginning to rock. "My father is our secret weapon! He's fighting on the shoulders of giant apes! He's throwing mountains and planets!"

Impulsively, Bea knelt and took the boy's shoulders to stop him rocking. She looked into his too-bright eyes. "And he is proud of you," she said. "He knows he has a very good boy. He is very proud."

When she thought back on it, it seemed that with her words all the murkiness had vanished, leaving his eyes clear, as if each were lit by a single fiery star.

"Okay, Mikey, it's time to go." Lee Anne was back and full of business. "We're outta here." She hoisted a backpack up on a chair and slipped one arm through a strap. She glanced at Bea. "Nice talking to you." She shouldered the pack with a graceful swooping squat, then picked up a bulging canvas bag.

"Yes, you too. And best to your husband in Iraq."

Michael shot Bea a look. Lee Anne's face darkened unreadably. "He's been telling you stories," she said. "I don't have a husband. I don't have anybody in Iraq."

And they were gone. Bea saw Lee Anne slap her son on the head once more before they disappeared. Oh don't, thought Bea. Please don't. But of course she would. The woman was alone and overworked, probably never married, probably hadn't wanted the child. At least I talked to him, thought Bea, I talked to him and he responded—he responded almost like an adult speaking a child's language.

And she got on the plane. The stewardess smiled at her, and she slowly made her way down the neutral space of the aisle. She found her seat, stowed her bag, took out her book and opened it. Children had always responded to her. When Megan and Susan were little and they fought, she rarely had to punish them; she just talked to them in her love voice, and usually they would forget their fight and look at her, waiting to see what she would say next. She could say, "Let's go out into the yard and see if we can find a little field mouse or a special clover!" And quietly, they would take her hands and go.

The stewardess came down the aisle, closing the overhead compartments, making sure the passengers were tucked into their seat belts. What luck; she had the seat to herself.

Before they went to sleep, too, her children would talk to her about anything, artlessly opening their most private doors so that she could make sure all was in order there. When Megan wet the bed, she would come half-asleep to her parents' room, pull off her wet gown, and get between them in her mother's chemise, a little white sardine still fragrant with briny pee. Even at thirteen, Susan would run to her crying, "Mama, Mama!" Once she even sank down on the floor and butted Bea's stomach like she wanted to get back inside it.

The plane pushed back. Now no private door was open to her; not even Megan's face was open to her. Susan didn't come to her even when she was raped in a parking structure, didn't even tell her about it until ten years later, when she could say, clipped and insistent, that it wasn't "such a big deal."

The plane turned on the runway like a live thing slowly turning in heavy water. Sunlight glinted on its rattling battered wing. Still, Megan had flown her out to visit and taken her to a play. Susan and her girlfriend were coming for Easter. Both girls came to visit every Christmas, and had since they moved away from home. When she left Mac and was living from apartment to wretched apartment, the girls divided their Christmas time with scrupulous fairness; Megan spent two nights in Bea's apartment while Susan spent two nights with Mac, then—switch. The two of them spent Christmas Eve with her and Christmas Day with him, then the other way next year.

But she knew they'd rather see her than Mac. Sometimes Susan even sneaked in extra time with her mother, pretending to Mac that she'd left on Tuesday when she had really stayed through Wednesday with her mother. It was cruel but so was Mac. When the girls stayed with him, he walked through the house yelling about how terrible Bea was or declaring that he wanted to die, and that if it weren't Christmas Eve he'd kill himself that night. When he did calm down and talk to one of his daughters, it was about grocery-store prices or TV shows—"And I tell him over and over again that I don't watch TV!" said Susan, laughing. Susan laughed, but Megan got mad and fought with him.

"Oh, give it a break!" she yelled. "You've been talking about how you're going to kill yourself for the last ten years and you know you aren't going to!" And then she told her mother and Susan about it.

"When I was there I did a meditation with him," said Susan.

"With him?" asked Megan, "or at him?"

"I told him I was going to pray," said Susan. "And we sat together in the dark."

They were in the living room, she said, at night with the shades open so they could see the heavy snow fall. Susan went into "a light trance." In this light trance, she "connected" with Mac as he lay on the couch, seemingly in a light trance of his own. She connected with his heart. In his heart she saw a small boy, maybe five or six years old, alone in a garden. The garden was pleasant, even beautiful, but it was surrounded by a dense thicket of thorns so that the boy could not get out and no one else could get in.

"I asked him if he wanted to come out," said Susan. "And he just shook his head no. He was afraid. I told him I loved him and that other people out here love him, too. He looked like he was thinking about it. Then Dad got up and went to the bathroom."

Megan sniggered. The plane picked up speed. Bea thought, Mac was six when his parents died. But she didn't say it.

Stop it, you little idiot! You little—

That child, dancing on the chairs, full of hope and life. Making up a hero father whom he could be proud of, longing for him, longing to be worthy of him. Didn't the mother see? *How dare you?* said Megan. *How dare you disrespect his service?*

The plane steadily rose, but she felt as if she were falling.

Mac died in his apartment, with the girls taking care of him, or trying to. She did not spend the night there; she did not sit at his side. But during the day she came to be with Megan and Susan. They had a hospice nurse who monitored him, washed him, and told them how much and how often to give him morphine. The nurse's name was Henry, and they all liked him—Susan said that Mac seemed to like him, too. When he was finished upstairs, they made coffee for him, and he would sit in the living room talking and looking at pictures of Mac when he was young. Megan showed him the picture of Mac in his army uniform, just before he shipped out. "He volunteered," she said. "Before he was even eighteen, he signed up."

"That's not true," said Bea. "He was eighteen. And he only signed up because he knew he'd be drafted anyway."

Televisions came down from the ceiling in whirring rows. White-faced, Megan left the room. Henry looked at Bea, looked away. Colors flowed across the rows of dark screens, making hot rectangles, oblongs, and swirls. In the kitchen Megan faced her, eyes glittering with rage. *How dare you? How*—Bea said no to a beverage but accepted the packet of peanuts. She looked out the window, holding the nuts. The sky was bright, terribly bright, but still she felt the darkness coming. *Do you remember the first time, Beatrice, how passionate we were? How we sweated so it was like we got joined together by our own spilled juice? You were so beautiful, so innocent, and so wild you scared me a little, did you know that?* Mac had written these things on brown grocery bags, cut to the size of notepaper to recycle and to save money. He never sent them; she found them, stacks of them, when she and the girls were going through his things. *We could have that again, I know it. Remember, Beatrice, and come back. Please, Beatrice, remember what we had.*

Faces bloomed on the overhead screens, clever, warm, and ardent.

Once, he had held her in his arms, and the emotion in his flesh softened the outgoing force of his body; his emotion bled into her and filled her so that she could barely speak except to say his name.

And still she couldn't cry. A stewardess came down the aisle, headphones draped gracefully over her arm. It had been two years and she had not cried for him once. The stewardess smiled and offered her draped arm. Bea shook her head and turned away, into the darkness. *I am old and* *worthless, and I am going home to shadows on the wall. Susan—Megan—*She raised her fists and weakly beat upon her forehead. *Why are they so far away? Why don't they have children? Why does Megan stare at me so coldly when I tell her she is beautiful?*

Shadows on the wall: streetlamp, telephone wire, moths, bits of leafy branch. A pale rectangle of light. When the darkness came, these things lost their earthly meaning and became bacteria swimming in a dish or cryptic signaling hands or nodding heads with mouths that ceaselessly opened and closed, while down in the corner, a little claw pitifully scratched and scratched. Loving, conceiving, giving birth; if human love failed, it was bacteria swimming in a dish, mysterious and unseeable to itself. From a distance, it was beautiful but also terrible, and it was hard to be alone with it night after night, without even an indifferent husband lying with his warm back to you.

Hard to bear, yes. But she could bear it. She had been a child herself and so knew the cruelty of children. She knew the strength of giving even if you did not get what you wanted back. She had thrown her body across a deep, narrow chasm; her daughters had walked to safety across her back. They had reached the other side, and she had stood again, safe and sound herself; all was as it should be. The darkness passed. She picked up her book. And he came to her: Michael, the little boy.

He came first as a thought, a memory of his face that interrupted her reading in the middle of the second page. He had so much in his eyes, and so few words to express it. How could his mother give him the words? Or the music or pictures? She thought of him again, the murkiness clearing from his eyes. And then she felt him. She felt him in a way she would later find impossible to describe.

"He was looking for me," she would say to Susan sometime after. "He needed me."

But it felt like more than that. She felt what was in his eyes, hot and seedlike and ready to unfurl. Waiting for the right stimulus, like a plant would wait for the sun. Vulnerable but vast too, like a child in her arms. *Yes, you are,* she thought. *Yes, yes, you are.*

When she told Megan, Megan surprised her by saying she'd had experiences like that, too. "But you never know," she said, "if it's really the other person communicating with you or if it's just your mind."

"No," said Bea. "It wasn't my mind. It was him. It felt just like him."

Love me. See me. Love me. He had no words, but what he said was unmistakable.

"What did you do?" asked Susan.

"I answered him," said Bea. "I tried, anyway. I tried so hard I wore myself out."

I see you, she answered. *You are a wonderful boy and you will grow into a wonderful man. I love you; I love to look at you.* She put her arms around him, gently, not too tight. She held him and talked to him until finally she felt him ebb away, as if he were going to sleep. She reclined her seat and closed her eyes. *Just don't get lost in the thorn garden. We need you right here. Don't go behind the thorns.* Tears poured down her cheeks, and she turned her head to hide them. *We need you right here.*

She waited a long time to tell Megan because she was afraid of being sneered at. She waited a long time to tell Susan because she was afraid Susan would talk about the astral plane. But she didn't. She just said, "I've heard people who had abusive childhoods say they survived because they had a good experience with an adult outside the family. Even one, even if it was tiny."

Bea opened her eyes. Before her were clouds, vast and white, their soft clefts bruised with lilac and pale gray. She wiped her eyes with her little peanut napkin. She leaned back in her seat. *Good night, Mama.* Closing her eyes, she remembered the sudden warmth and heaviness as Megan sat on the edge of the guest bed in the dark. She remembered her singing "The Sun, Whose Rays Are All Ablaze" from *The Mikado*, her voice off-key but still piercing in the dark. She sang and then bent down, and her nightgown fell open slightly as she kissed her mother good night. Beatrice crumpled the peanut napkin with an unconscious hand as she began to dream a dream that began with that kiss.

William H. Gass

A Little History of Modern Music

THE SPRING semester is almost over, Professor Skizzen said as he slowly paced, almost drifted, from one side of the classroom to another, a manner he had just recently adopted; only a week, a week and a half remains, and most of you will leave the campus, leave this community, for your summer vacation and your menial job in a fast food restaurant. Then after a few months—to play the alternatives—those of you who haven't failed this class or some lesser subject; those of you who haven't transferred to one of the cheaper Ivies, graduated to the job market, or run away to Europe or the circus; those who remain will return. That means most of you will be back, for who fails at Wittlebauer? we are so built upon success. Of course, in order to come to college you had to fly from your nest, bid bye-bye to your yard, your toaster, your elm tree with its tired swing—too many loved things for me in this shaved hour to touch on or to name—and from that vantage point . . . hold on . . . you may have brought your toaster with you to school—true—bags of clothes, toaster—yes, certainly—indispensable—anyway, from that perspective what you shall do next is fly back to your old neighborhood. Take your toaster if that pleases. Note this—you shall go home even if the elm is dying. Even if an aunt is. Even if you don't want to. This cycle—of departure and return—evaporation and rain—yo and yoyo—will be repeated in one form or another your entire lives.

I beg your pardons, all. . . . I used a misleading migratory metaphor—branch, nest, yard, garden—not wise, because the migratory bird has two homes, its cool summer cottage and its warm winter cabana. Hands if you see the difference. When you achieve physicianhood you may be able to afford it. But let me turn this inadequate image to account. Twin homesteads are not unknown to sociological research. Our earth has two poles. Such divided loyalties are regularly demonstrated by those in the dough, though one habitation is usually the castle while the other is a cabin. If you have too many homes, however, as the jet-setter presumably does, we are compelled to say you are homeless as only the very rich can be. Such people are on permanent vacation—not to and fro, but fro and fro. A woeful situation.

Miss Rudolph, if you have a cough that bad you should go to the infirmary.

The dorm room, here, is your local habitation from which every morning, if you can manage it, you rise from your bed and wobble off to crunch some sugar-laden processed wheat or corn before it sogs in the bowl. You proceed through a habitual schedule throughout the day and return at the end to that same rubble of a room to study, perhaps to play, to chat with a friend, before sleep once again takes you into its chamber of dreams and its crude simulation of death. Perhaps you will drive a tin lizzie back to your home, or your family car will come for you—father and Aunt Louise—or you will ride a bus with a bunch of strangers from another world. . . .

What?

Ah, I see. . . . We don't say that anymore. . . . Too bad. Lizzie makes an appropriate sound. Anyway, while you are traveling, you will leave the car to fuel, leave it for relief, leave it to snack, to stretch your legs—candy, restroom, gasoline, coffee—get out, lock, and return. The vehicle will seem in such moments to be your special place, your familiar surroundings where your guard can roll down like one of its windows, where your can of pop, wad of highway maps, or sweet roll waits. Small cycles turn inside of wider ones. Wheels within wheel. Like Ezekiel's wheels, wheels with eyes, eh? Show of hands . . . Ah, yes, no surprise, ignorance is epidemic.

In my home my desk is yet another haven—for my pencils and the seat of my pants—and when my mother calls from her garden her sound will be one I go to as if it were a beacon. Meanwhile, noises on the street I shall ignore. They are not a part of the composition. They revolve about other suns, have other eyes and other axles. Yet you know that when you arrive home, leave and arrive, yin to yang, come to go, this familiar cycle and its center won't roll on forever, because you expect to have a job one day, a car and dog and garage of your own, an office to go to, a kitchen to cook in, main and subsidiary bases like a diamond to traverse—ball diamond don't you play on? bases to stand safely at, stages on any journey, on life's way don't you say?—and so you expect the future will be full of places to return to. You expect homes to be here and there all over the place all the time. To spring up like spring does every year, and fresh blooms crack open, birds sing, new leaves hatch. Imagine. Homes to come home to, homes to leave. Everywhere. Imagine.

Who is imagining as you were instructed? Hands. Hands up.

Home is not just the last square on the Parcheesi board—oh I beg your pardon once again—occult reference—shame makes my cheeks show red—it is not just the tape you break at the end of the race or the plate you run to put your foot on—score—that's clearer for you?—but it is a set of things, habits of using them, patterns of behavior, met expectations, repeated experiences.

Now, then, take notice, pay a quarter, will you? for my voice and your attention: these homey spaces—so many—familiar voices, scents, satisfactions—comfort food, don't you say?—will be more important to you than other things, they can even dominate your thinking, monopoly your feeling, they will be in the major keys, but there will be minor keys, too, lesser variations, hierarchies will appear like old royalty arriving at a Viennese café where there will be requests from the customers, preferences in tables, order in the kitchen, ranks throughout the staff, competition in the silver, even among the pots and pans, bowls fit for barons shall sit on peasant plates, an ordinance will promulgate, a subordinance will sound like a summoning to church.

How many of you knew I was speaking of music all along? its inherent hierarchies? Show of hands, please. Hah . . . You are such good students. Why do I complain?

Because many of you have not turned in to me your analysis of that little tune I gave you. Such a simpleton task. A simpleton could do.

Where there is alter there is subalter. Where there is genus please expect species. Order among the tones. Order among the instruments. There is no note born that doesn't have a lineage, a rank, a position in the system. The force of past performances. Imitations of the masters. Traditions of teaching. Centers of learning. Habits of listening. Among them who will rule? for someone must rule. The horns? surely not the winds. This theory, not that, shall be abided. Therefore the French style will be enforced, the German manner obeyed, the Russian soul (it is always the Russian soul) obliged.

Where music is, Vienna is. The maestro is. You think music takes place in isolation, in some hermetic solitude? Cakes, coffee, gossip, and the Gypsy violin—loopy swoons and much mealy schmaltz surround the violinist's form and dismal dress. Huge, too, the opera *haus*. High the hats. Gaiety. Flirtations. The hunt. The waltz. Vienna tuned out the terrifying world to listen to Strauss. To *Fledermaus*. A social round of balls. Yet there must be a leader or there will be chaos, all those instruments braying at once. There must be a home to come home to, didn't the Austrians at one time suppose, while longing for the Reich to envelop them like a mother's milky white warm arms? There is a home for you. The bosom of the family. The leader raises his baton, Stukas scream from the skies.

Did not Odysseus strive to reach his wife kid dog and palace—you remember him? ah many of your hands need washing I can see—too few pink palms . . . through countless trials and tribulations, too, remember the delays, the teases—one two three ten twelve thirty troubles, trials, tribulations, did I say?—lures of ladies, comforts of creatures—in wait like rocks—to bring the wayfarer down, to sink his soul to his sandals. So, too, we depart from the tonic, we journey farther and farther afield until it seems we've broken all ties with the known world, we are farther away than anyone has ever been, we are at the edge of the earth, we can forebear the Wagnerian downfall, the brink, that splashes into silence . . . when . . . lo, behold, magically, the captain, the composer sees a way, steers us through the storm, and we modulate do we not? sail ride walk to the warm and welcoming hearth again, the hiking path winds but takes us to our hotel in safety just as the signs said they would: what relief at what a climax . . . the sight of a spire, familiar stones at one's feet, the smell of a pot on the stove. Nice walk, good hike, healthy return.

Poor Miss Rudolph. Glad you're back. Nice of you to cough in the hall. No music there.

Or shall we let a cough be music? With our new instruments of bedevilment might we not record all sorts of sounds out there in the world that calls itself—that call themselves—real; where squeaks and squeals and screams are on the menu, where dins assail us by the dozens—the crinkle of cellophane, whishiss of small talk, the fanning of five hundred programs—where we fill our ears with one noise in order not to hear another . . . yes record, preserve not only the roil of the sea but the oink of pigs and moos of cattle, the wind rattling the cornstalks like the hand of an enemy on the knob, and put them in . . . in the realm of majesty, of beauty, of purity, in . . . in music, let them in—poor Miss Rudolph's cough included—why?—why would we come to such a detrimental thought? or why should we learn to sigh at silence as if it were a sweet in the mouth, as if it were a pillow soft as a sofa, why should we order our instruments off! as if silence were an end? Only to invite ruck to rumpus us, to ruin our holy space?

Just then we had a silence, did you hear? a rest. Broken like a pane of glass by . . . explanations.

Because music has its holies, has its saints, has sounds all its own that no one else, no else like thing, no motion that the muck of matter makes, nowhere is one like them. These tones. Pure tones, resolute tones, resonant tones, redolent, refulgent, confident tones. We have artisans whose ancient art is to fashion instruments so different from the heartless machines that now chop idle raucouses into eekie parts and blast them at our ears like earclaps, earboxes, boomdoomers, save us save us save us from those ruffians, yes . . . give us smooth wooded bodies instead that glow in anticipation of being played, shining trumpets proud of their purpose, soothing tubes from which much love emerges, and virtuosos who have devoted their lives to learning how, from these wily and noble objects, to elicit the speech of the spirit. Consider: a quartet of them: four men or women. Centuries of preparation will go into their simplest tuning—a single scrape of a bow—nor will they be togged like Topsy or some ugly ragamuffin, but garbed and gowned for these rites, these magical motions that make truly unearthly sensations. This is where we should worship if we had the wit. Today Köchel Five Fifteen will pray for us. Play on our behalf. Be our best belief. Besides, this C major quintet is assigned. You will note how the apparently harmless theme sinks into C minor only to startle us with a chromatic passage meant to be stunning and achieving a vibrant numbness. That's the way to talk to God.

Now, children of our century, inheritors of what is left of the earth, calculate the consequences. Of a cough.

The musicians begin. After sufficient silence is imposed on the audience—for the slate is being wiped, a space cleared of all competition (note that, but return all notes before you leave, we dare not lose any)—then, and only then, they play. There are vibrating strings. Vibrating air in vibrating spaces. Vibrating ears. Vibrating brains. Do the notes fall out of them like spilled beans? out of these instruments as if they were funnels?

By the way, did you know that "spill the beans" means to throw up? Hands please. You others may sit upon yours and be uncomfortable.

No, the notes do not confess. They emerge like children into an ordered universe; they immediately know their place; they immediately find it, for the order you hear was born with them. Did I not just say so? Hands? Every one of them, as each arrives in its reality, immediately flings out a sea of stars, glowing constellating places. As a dot does upon a map or grid. As a developer on an empty field sees himself standing on a corner in a city that's yet to be. For these notes are not born orphans, not maroons surrounded by worse than ocean, but they have relatives, they have an assignment in a system. Did I not just say so? do you suppose that this will be on an exam?

Relations . . . As you have in your family. Aunts, uncles, haven't you? oh I dare say, and addresses, underclothes, honor codes, cribs. The whole equipment of the gang. Yes, for even gangs have their organization, their nasty-nosed bullyboy boss and the boss's chamberlain—first violin.

But now . . . now remember the honest reality of that home—so sweet—a home . . . there's no place like it just as the song says. Let us have a second thought about that collection of clichés. . . . Those relatives—remember them?—arrived like ruinous news: they broke the peace; they ate the candy; they spoiled naps; they brought their own rules. Their kids cried. And you were punished for it. Sweet home? Dad is seeing his secretary on the sly, Mom is drinking long lunches with her female friends or shopping as if a new slip or a knickknack would make her happy. Sweet home is where heartfelts go to die. Sweet home is where the shards of broken promises lie, where the furniture sits around on a pumpkin-colored rug like dead flies on a pie. Home is haunted by all the old arguments, disappointments, miseries, injustices, and misunderstandings that one has suffered there: the spankings, the groundings, the arguments, the fights, the bullying, the dressings-down, the shames. Yes, it is a harbor for humiliations. A storehouse for grudges. A slaughterhouse for self-esteem.

Families are founts of ignorance, the source of feuds, the fuel for fanatical ideas. Families take over your soul and sell it to their dreams.

Somewhere during the slow course of the nineteenth century, the children of the middle class woke up to the fact that they were children of the middle class—well, some of them did. They woke one morning from an uneasy sleep and found they were bourgeois from toe to nose; that is to say, they cherished the attitudes that were the chief symptoms of that spiritually deadly disease: the comforts of home and hearth, of careers in the colonies, of money in the bank where God's name was on the cash, of parlor tea and cake, of servants of so many sorts the servants needed servants, of heavy drapes and heavy furniture and dark woodwalled rooms, of majestic paintings of historic moments, costly amusements, private clubs, a prized share in imperialist Europe's determined perfection of the steam engine and the sanitary drain. Daughters who could demand dowries were in finishing school where they were taught to tat, paint, play, and oversee kitchens; sons were sent to military academies, or colleges that mimicked them, where they would learn to love floggings, reach something called manhood, stand steady in the buff, and be no further bother to their parents. And in these blessed ancient institutions both sexes would learn to worship God and sovereign, obey their husbands, serve and love their noble nation, and dream of being rich.

It was inevitable. It was foregone—the drift of the young to Paris. Where the precocious began to paint prostitutes; they began to write about coal miners; and they began to push the diatonic scale, and all its pleasant promises, like the vacuum-cleaner salesman, out the door. They took liberties as if they had been offered second helpings; they painted pears or dead fish instead of crowned heads; they invented the saxophone. They shook Reality in its boots. Fictional characters could no longer be trusted but grew equivocal. First there was Julian Sorel, then Madame Bovary. Novels that undermined the story and poems that had no rhymes appeared. Painters tested the acceptability of previously tabooed subjects, the range of the palette, the limits of the frame. With respect to the proscenium, dramatists did the same, invading, shocking, insulting their audiences. Musicians started to pay attention to the color of tones. They pitched pitch, if you can believe it, from its first-base position on the mound. They fashioned long Berliozian spews of notes, composed for marching bands as well as cabarets, rejected traditional instrumentation, the very composition of the orchestra, and finally the grammar of music itself. . . . Notes had traditional relations? they untied them. Words had ordinary uses? they abused them. Colors had customary companions? they denied them. Arts that had been about this or that *became* this and that. The more penetrating thinkers were convinced that to change society you had to do more than oust its bureaucrats, you had to alter its basic structure, since every bureaucrat's replacement would soon resemble the former boss in everything including name. Such is the power of position when the position is called "the podium."

Who shall build from these ruins a new obedience?

They . . . who are they, you ask? they are the chosen few, chosen by God, by *Geist*, by the muse of music: they are Arnold Schoenberg, Alban Berg, and Anton von Webern. They chose, in their turn, the twelve tones of the chromatic scale, and thought of them as Christ's disciples. Then they sat them in a row the way da Vinci painted the loyals. I don't want to convey the impression that this disposition was easy, no more than for da Vinci. Suppose out of all the rows available, the following was the order of the group—ding dong bang bong cling clang ring rang chit chat toot hoot—and that we found the finest instruments to produce each one, the finest musicians to bring them forth, and sent them—the musicians, I mean, but why not the notes?—to Oxford to Harvard to Yale to Whittlebauer, to Augsburg even—thank you for the titters—to receive the spit of polish.

Yes, it is true, this music will be keyless, but there will be no lock that might miss it. Atonal music (as it got named despite Arnold Schoenberg's objection) is not made of chaos like John Cage pretended his was; no art is more opposed to the laws of chance. That is why some seek to introduce accidents of happenstance into *its* rituals like schoolboys playing pranks. Such as hiccups. Miss Rudolph's cough. No, this music is more orderly than anybody's. It is more military than a militia. It is music that must pass through the mind before it reaches the ear. But you cannot be a true-blue American and value the mind that much. Americans have no traditions to steep themselves in like tea. They are born in the Los Angeles of Southern California, or in Cody, Wyoming, not Berlin or Vienna. They learn piano from burned-out old men or women who compose birdsongs. Americans love drums. The drum is an intentionally stupid instrument. Americans play everything percussively on intentionally stupid instruments and strum their guitars like they were shooting guns. But I have allowed myself to be carried away into digression. Digressions are as pleasant as vacations but one must return from them before tan turns to burn.

Imagine, then, that we have our row: ding dong bang bong cling clang ring rang chit chat toot hoot. Now we turn it round: hoot toot chat chit rang ring clang cling bong bang dong ding. Next we invert it so that the line looks like the other side of the spoon. Hills sag to form valleys, rills become as bumpy as bad roads: hat tat chot chut rong rung clong clyng bang bing dang dyng. We are in position, now, to turn this row around as we did our original. Or we can commence the whole business, as Schoenberg himself does at the beginning of *Die Jakobsleiter* by dividing the twelve tones into a pair of sixes. Thus the twelve tones are freed from one regimen to enter another. What has been disrupted is an entire tradition of sonic suitability, century-old habits of the ear.

Then come the refinements, for all new things need refinements, raw into the world as they are, wrinkled and wet and cranky. The rule, for instance, that no member of the twelve gets a second helping until all are fed. They have a union, these sounds, and may not work overtime. Compositions, too, will tend to be short. Audiences will admire that. For instance, Webern begins his Goethe song, "Gleich und Gleich," with a G-sharp. Then follows it (please hear it with your heads): A, D-sharp, G, in a nice line before slipping in a chord E C B-flat D, and concluding F-sharp, B, F, C-sharp. You see, or rather, you intuit: 4 in a line, 4 in a chord, 4 in a line. Neat as whiskey.

What a change of life, though, is implied by the new music.

I hear a distant bell. It might have come from any bracelet in this room, from a bell flower that my mother's grown, a garden row, or from some prankster in the audience. Shall we include it in our composition, or tell it to shush?

Because this rustic buzz is as regular, dare we say, as clockwork, it is only half an accident, like a typewriter's clacking, the tiptaps of Morse code, a few wails from police sirens, and the hoot of a railroad train that Cocteau wanted to include in his conception of *Parade*—you know this ballet, hands?—suggestions that Diaghilev killed—hands for him? who you say? so, no applause. Sweet sweet deity, why have you put such ignorance in this world?

With this question I conclude my little history of modern music.

Reading *The O. Henry Prize Stories 2008*

The Jurors on Their Favorites

Chimamanda Ngozi Adichie on "Touch" by Alexi Zentner

I admired a number of stories in this collection and spent some time thinking about which to pick. For a moment I thought that I should perhaps be clever and select the story that took the most risks and was ambitious and original, etc. But I didn't. The more short stories I read, the more I realize that while I respect many different types, my ability to love a story remains stubbornly fixed on the same criteria: I like a story to tell a story and to teach me something about what it means to be human and to not be terribly self-conscious or ironic for irony's sake, and most of all, to have emotion. "Touch" does all of these. Its themes of love and loss may be familiar, but it has such memorable characters, such a strong sense of atmosphere, such grace, and all of these done with a wonderfully light touch, that it easily transcends its themes. The language—axes cutting smiles into pines, sawdust flying down men's shirts like mosquitoes, the river like a mouth in a brief yawn—transported me to this small self-enclosed world of people who live through winters of cold-shattered thermometers, a Nature-shaped world that is ordinary and yet filled with wonder. I was moved by the elegiac telling, the unapologetic tenderness that never became maudlin, and the characters—the men hacking out a livelihood with a sort of disinterested dignity, the romantic but tough father, the mother who is determined not to lose any more, the daughter who looks wide eyed at life, the narrator for whom my heart broke at the end. I will remember this story for a long time. After I read it, as I lay in bed waiting for sleep, this image haunted me: a father and a daughter frozen in a river, both reaching out to touch, but not quite touching, the other.

Chimamanda Ngozi Adichie was born in Nigeria in 1977. She is from Abba in Anambra State, but grew up in the university town of Nsukka. Adichie's first novel, *Purple Hibiscus*, won the Hurston/Wright Legacy Award for debut fiction. Her second novel, *Half of a Yellow Sun*, won the Orange Broadband Prize for Fiction. She lives in Nigeria.

David Leavitt on "What Do You Want to Know For?" by Alice Munro

In the early 1980s, when I first started writing, the short story enjoyed a brief renaissance. Long regarded as merely a sidebar to the far more significant spectacle of the novel, the story—thanks in great part to the efforts of a small group of writers and editors—suddenly asserted itself as a form worthy of attention in its own right. Reading stories by writers such as Raymond Carver, Deborah Eisenberg, Amy Hempel, Lorrie Moore, and Grace Paley, young writers like me suddenly saw provocative possibilities where before there had only been the pallid "minor" offerings of authors for whom glory resided exclusively in the novel. That some of these emerging writers *only* wrote stories added to the form's new appeal and heralded a brief golden age in which (wonder of wonders) story collections actually *sold*; one or two even hit *The New York Times* bestseller list.

Alas, that golden age did not last long, and, starting in the early nineties, the novel once again usurped what little of a spotlight remained for prose fiction. This does not mean, however, that the story is dead. On the contrary, as the exemplary selection that Laura Furman has culled this year attests, the story is as vibrant as ever.

More than anything, it is the vitality, variety, and audacity of these stories that impresses. Who would guess, for instance, that a fragile alliance formed between a lonely musician and the parakeet whom his girlfriend has left in his care could evolve into a love story of truly operatic intensity? Yet in Ha Jin's fabulistic, funny, and very moving "A Composer and His Parakeets," this is exactly what happens. Michel Faber's "Bye-bye Natalia" is an exercise in linguistic ventriloquism, as the e-mail relationship between an HIV-positive Ukrainian would-be mail-order bride and her Montanan suitor proceeds apace—until a fatal misstep in musical taste derails it. (That the author is Dutch, and lives in Scotland, only adds to my amazement at the story's pitch-perfect renditions of its protagonists' voices.) William H. Gass's "A Little History of Modern Music" is exactly that: a lecture, rich in divagations, given by a fatigued professor to a group of bored students; it is also a summing up, about nine pages in length, of the sorrowful trajectory of twentieth-century history. As for Lore Segal's "Other People's Deaths," this story provides further evidence that its estimable and witty author, whose work appears so rarely in print, deserves a wider audience. Who else but Segal, after all, would think of turning an account of a young widow's grief into a comedy of manners focused on the bungled, often selfish reactions of her friends to the unwelcome fact of death?

One story in this collection bowled me over. Not surprisingly, it comes from a writer whom many consider the greatest short story writer of her age: Alice Munro. As is the case with most of Munro's work, the apparent modesty, even artlessness, of "What Do You Want to Know For?" belies the story's intricacy, not to mention the breadth of its concerns. "I saw the crypt before my husband did," the narrator begins—and launches into an account of her own mysterious preoccupation with this crypt, which sits in the middle of an almost abandoned cemetery in rural Ontario. As the story progresses, the narrator adds, with very little fuss, that a lump has just been found in her left breast. The weeks following this discovery—weeks marked by long waits between medical appointments—she and her husband devote to an investigation of the history and origins of the abandoned crypt.

"What Do You Want to Know For?" is frank, brave, and strangely helpful. I recall Grace Paley once saying that, for her, a great story has to be "about everything." This is the sensation with which I came away from "What Do You Want to Know For?"; that, in the course of reading the story, I had learned a great deal not only about the cemeteries of western Ontario, but about—there is no other way to say this—how to live. "It seems as if you must always take care of what's on the surface," Munro writes late in the story, "and what is behind, so immense and disturbing, will take care of itself." Such interpolations, deadly in the hands of a less experienced and (I daresay) less wise writer, become, when Munro takes them up, part of a story's delicate architecture. Hers is an art of layering in which the other ingredients are perfectly rendered dialogue, unforgettable details of place and history, and the scrupulous analysis of human interaction. As seemingly meandering as the rural roads down which its narrator and her husband drive, "What Do You Want to Know For?" carries us to a conclusion that is at once startling and inevitable, and leaves us in awe of this writer who can trick us into believing that a carefully planned journey was really just a wander through the countryside. I can think of no writer who exerts such control over her material—control as absolute, and as invisible, as God's.

David Leavitt is the author of the story collections *The Marble Quilt* and *Collected Stories* and several novels, including *The Lost Language of Cranes* and *The Body of Jonah Boyd*, as well as two nonfiction books, *Florence, A Delicate Case* and *The Man Who Knew Too Much: Alan Turing and the Invention of the Computer*. He is the recipient of grants from the Guggenheim Foundation and the National Endowment for the Arts, and a New York Public Library Literary Lion. Leavitt codirects the creative writing program at the University of Florida and edits the journal *Subtropics*. He lives in Gainesville, Florida.

David Means on "Folie à Deux" by William Trevor

A Few Thoughts about Short Fiction in General and William Trevor's "Folie à Deux" in Particular

A great short story peels back and exposes some singular mystery about the human condition while, at the same time, it refuses to give the reader any semblance of an easy answer. It might hint at one, but it never offers it up.

It roils into itself, turning inward in a strange motion—maybe an arabesque, or a backflip—so that, in the end, the entire piece seems to attain a kind of purity that justifies its stylistic quirks, the unique aesthetic tics of the author, and in the process betrays the idea of a set aesthetic standard while, at the same time, paradoxically, seems to close in on traditions as tight as ancient Sufi dervish tales.

It radiates outward, never finished, sending an essential question about human existence, honed and sharp, vivid and pure, forward into the infinite narrative space beyond the mind's eye while, at the same time, it seems to collapse itself into a tight nugget of narrative space.

It offers only a glimpse. But a glimpse can often give much more than a long stare. (And a novel is like a long stare.) The reader, always subconsciously aware that the culmination is just a few pages ahead, just over the horizon, starts reading with an awareness that he or she will be left holding the bag, drawing upon the imagination to extrapolate from the glimpse.

It seems open to infinite varieties of modes and shapes, forcing the reader to accept a pure form of literary art, one that poetically exploits its own limitations.

A great story—and there are several in this collection—bears up nobly under the close scrutiny of a reader while, at the same time, it resists being tweezed apart. It resists giving up its technical secrets and sometimes defies the scalpel and tweezers of critical discourse, perhaps because its success depends on deep poetic impulses, and it is impossible—for me at least—to explain to the reader how poetic impulses operate. One thing is for sure: a great story, even a good one, thickens our sense of the perplexing essence of being human.

Thoughts on William Trevor's "Folie à Deux"

Hovering, moving in and out of viewpoints, is a kind of omniscient eye, and it is this eye that concludes: "For Anthony, the betrayal matters, the folly, the carelessness that would have been forgiven, the cruelty. . . . The haunted sea is all the truth there is for Anthony, what he honors because it matters still." This is a revelatory moment in the story, but it is also a deeply poetic moment. What does it mean to say that "the haunted sea" is all the truth there is for a man? Clearly, we're not meant to think—and I certainly didn't—that Anthony pushed away from his world simply because of a childhood incident. A good reader, able to feel the wider connotations of the words "haunted sea," will bring to bear upon the story his or her own reflection. Perhaps the sea is meant to represent the seat of the soul and the deep, unfathomable pains that linger in the heart and, for some of us, push us into a state of depression in which the will to go on falls away.

The paradox of the story—at least the way I read it—was that, clearly, Anthony did go on with his life after he "lost his will to go on." He moved to Paris and found pleasure in his work. He is content—I wouldn't dare say happy—to clean the ovens, tend to his duties at the café, and to live far away from Ireland. Trevor refuses to give us more of Anthony's life, forcing us, as all good stories do, to deduce from the glimpse, to use our sympathetic capacities, to extrapolate outward.

Near the end, Trevor's eye allows us a fleeting, tight glance into Anthony's point of view, and we see that at one time he read *The Irish Times* and got the news that his parents were dead. We get the feeling that, from his vantage, his life makes sense. To Wilby, he says, simply, "I haven't died." This statement resonates deeply. It is a statement both of fact and of existential rebellion. It is clean and pure. It is all Anthony can say to Wilby, a man who has speculated and pondered and tried, drawing from fleeting memories of the past, to make sense of seeing his friend again, alive. (Anthony's statement echoes Herman Melville's character Bartleby. The simple, short utterance of an imponderable soul.)

Two men meet, the I/thou of their souls bumping for a quick moment on a street in Paris, and in that meeting there is—as there always is when two people come upon each other—a potential for deep revelation, for some complex exchange, for a long conversation, for a mending of wounds, for a bond to form or a bond to break. As readers, we know this is a key moment, and we lean in close to the story and—if we're reading the way we should—let the poetics of the moment resonate. (The reader should go back and look carefully at the way Trevor composes this pivotal moment, using his panning eye to move us from Wilby's point of view into Anthony's, splintering the narrative, giving us a tactile sensation of divided lives, causing us to feel the intricacy of the meeting while, at the same time, making us aware of the magnitude of the fact that no matter how hard Wilby tries, he'll never locate the secret narrative behind Anthony's life.)

Trevor is a master at evoking a certain kind of loneliness—often mistaken for a form of darkness. His work is sometimes criticized as being too dark, lingering too much on the tragic. But really his stories are not so much about darkness as about loneliness, not so much about loneliness as a particular kind of solitude and isolation.

With all the neuroscience in the world, the nature of character proves a mystery. All behavior is, at the narrative level, enigmatic. One event—even the trauma of sending a dog to its death, chasing a blow-up raft into the waves—cannot explain the vagaries of Anthony's strange behavior. In the end, each thing we do, each decision we make, each love we feel, each memory we have, when tweezed apart and held for close observation, stands as part of a mystery. Because the world is just too vast and too complex and has too many factors—like a wild, chaotic storm wending itself into various graspable but fleeting symmetries—to be nailed down precisely.

But the miracle is that Trevor does nail the truth down with his art and with the poetic musicality of his form and with the way the story ends, moving alongside Wilby in the salerooms, passing the orderly display tables where the stamps, held fast in their frames, behind glass, are arranged in an orderly fashion. This is the miracle of a great short story, the paradox of what a writer like Trevor can do at his best, giving us just a glimpse, a few fragments of one thing, and then another, that can be held in the mind as a multifaceted whole, rotated, reread from one angle and then another, giving you a sense of having the entire picture, and yet, at the same time, one that is truthfully incomplete. Like the lives we live.

David Means is the author of three story collections, including *Assorted Fire Events*, which won the 2001 Los Angeles Times Book Prize and was a finalist for a National Book Critics Circle Award. His latest collection, *The Secret Goldfish*, was short-listed for the Frank O'Connor International Short Story Award and has been translated into eight languages. His recent work has appeared in *The New Yorker*, *Zoetrope*, *Harper's Magazine*, *The Best American Short Stories*, *Best American Mystery Stories*, and *The O. Henry Prize Stories 2006*. He teaches at Vassar College and lives in Nyack, New York.

Writing *The O. Henry Prize Stories 2008*

The Writers on Their Work

Shannon Cain, "The Necessity of Certain Behaviors"

My story began when I asked myself a couple of questions: What would happen if a modern-day city dweller were confronted with a whole new set of social rules for intimate relationships? What if she turns out to really dig those new rules?

I am drawn to stories in which characters grapple with intimate situations that make them feel odd or foreign. Part of what satisfies me about "The Necessity of Certain Behaviors" is that it takes for granted that the villagers' society works just fine and puts up for question the functionality of the "normal" world Lisa comes from. There are more paths to love and morality than many of us are ready to accept.

Earlier drafts of this story ignored the question of why there weren't any children and old people in the village. When I dealt with that aspect of their anthropology, the piece opened up and became (for me, at least) a story about community. It's probably the most spiritual thing I've written. I think these villagers, with their focus on joy and their devotion to meaningful ritual, have a few things to teach us about how to be happy.

Twenty-four literary magazines turned this story away before it found a loving home at the *New England Review*.

. . .

As a child, Shannon Cain lived in Colorado, New York, Maryland, Connecticut, California, and Arizona. Cain is a graduate of the MFA Program for Writers at Warren Wilson College and 2005 recipient of a fellowship from the National Endowment for the Arts, and her stories have appeared in *Tin House* and *The Massachusetts Review*. Cain is the executive director of Kore Press, and she lives in Tucson, Arizona.

Anthony Doerr, "Village 113"

I first saw Rome, Italy, from a railing high on the Janiculum Hill: thousands of rooftops, domes, gardens, bell towers, apartments, the buildings extending back across the plain, strings of distant towns climbing the hills at the horizon. Air pollution had pooled over the city in a sort of bluish haze, and it seemed to me, for a blink, that the city had been submerged beneath a lake.

A few months later, while I was still living in Italy, I read an article by Peter Hessler about the Three Gorges Dam. The dam, I learned, is about 2,300 meters (1.4 miles) long. Superimpose it over Rome, and it would reach from the edge of the Colosseum to the edge of the Piazza del Popolo, dwarfing the entire historic center. I realized I was buying diapers and drinking Chianti and reading Pliny the Elder while five thousand miles away the world was changing in huge, irrevocable ways.

At some point I decided to try to merge the two experiences: the ways in which history is continually being submerged, and my own continuing failures to understand adequately the larger world.

I guess "Village 113" was an attempt to rectify (partially) my own embarrassing ignorance about lives more difficult than my own. Maybe most of my work comes out of that.

Anthony Doerr is the author of a story collection, *The Shell Collector*; a novel, *About Grace*; and a memoir, *Four Seasons in Rome*. His work has won the Rome Prize, Barnes & Noble's Discover Prize, the New York Public Library's Young Lions Award, and inclusion in two previous *O. Henry Prize Stories*. In 2007, *Granta* put Doerr on its list of best young American novelists. He lives in Boise, Idaho.

Michel Faber, "Bye-bye Natalia"

"Bye-bye Natalia" owes its existence to Médecins Sans Frontières. I participated in their "Writers in the Frontline" project, which sent authors to emergency zones all over the world. Ukraine qualified as an emergency zone because of the AIDS epidemic raging through a frighteningly large percentage of the population, incubated by hordes of prostitutes and homeless people in cities like Odessa. I spent a week in MSF clinics and on the streets, and recorded about ten hours of interviews. On my return to the UK, I wrote a newspaper article as agreed, with all proceeds going to the charity.

However, MSF also planned to issue an anthology of fiction inspired more freely by their projects. "Bye-bye Natalia" was written for this book, which fell through for dispiriting reasons I won't go into. However, the story turned out to be one of my very best and bears no sign of being a commission. It feels unforced and instinctive. I think the fact that I'd already written a newspaper article about the AIDS calamity in Odessa meant that I got all the journalistic stuff out of my system. What was left was Natalia. I never met her, or even anyone like her, but her world was very real to me, waiting only for her to appear in it.

Anyone who's read my Victorian novel *The Crimson Petal and the White* will know that I'm interested in the dynamics of mutually exploitative sexual relationships—the delicate balances of deception and self-deception. "Bye-bye Natalia" explores similar territory, but with a soundtrack of Ukrainian death metal and, I hope, a greater degree of compassion.

Michel Faber was born in 1960 in Den Haag, Netherlands, and grew up in Australia. Faber worked as a nurse and did not submit his novels and short stories for publication until he had been writing seriously for twenty years. His novels are *Under the Skin*, *The Courage Consort*, *The Hundred and Ninety-Nine Steps*, and *The Crimson Petal and the White*. His short story collections are *Some Rain Must Fall*, *The Fahrenheit Twins*, and *The Apple*. Faber lives in the Scottish Highlands.

Mary Gaitskill, "The Little Boy"

"The Little Boy" started with a story told to me by a woman in an airport. We were sitting in a boarding area, having for some reason a conversation about book clubs, which turned into a conversation about an experience she'd had with a little boy in an airport. It was an experience that clearly touched and troubled her; she felt the child needed help and she could offer him very little but her wishes of love and hope—wishes so intense that they seemed like love and hope she actually gave, not only to him but to herself. (She didn't say it, but I felt she was in need of love and hope too.)

Mary Gaitskill was born in 1954 in Lexington, Kentucky. She has published two story collections, *Bad Behavior* and *Because They Wanted To*, and two novels, *Two Girls, Fat and Thin* and *Veronica*. Her work has been nominated for the PEN/Faulkner Award, the National Book Award, and the National Book Critics Circle Award. Her story "Secretary" was the basis for a movie of the same name, and Gaitskill was the recipient of a Guggenheim Fellowship. She lives in New York State.

William H. Gass, "A Little History of Modern Music"

I wanted to write something based upon the most primal fictional form: somebody telling a story. But what story? I have often given lectures on various topics that were, in a sense, short surveys of a particular section of cultural history, and history is ultimately a kind of storytelling too. I decided to combine the fictional narrative with the lecture exposition and the historical record. I am working on some musical material right now, so a musical period as revolutionary as the one we have just passed through seemed a good choice—lots of conflict and drama. I also wanted to play with several rhetorical techniques that have to do with finding metaphorical models in ordinary life for otherwise distant phenomena. Hence the comparison of keyishness to one's home and the sonata form to daily affairs. Finally, I was interested in using all these things to reveal not so much some truth in the narrative proper, but a few revelations about the narrator (teacher) himself, and his relation to his material, for if there is anything that students are likely to take away from a course in the humanities, when the subject matter has disappeared into their past, it is the tone the professor takes toward his or her material—what sort of grasp, what kind of passion, what degree of irony, defensiveness, scorn, or love is present.

. . .

William H. Gass was born in Fargo, North Dakota. He is the emeritus David May University Professor in the Humanities at Washington University in St. Louis. He has published two volumes of short stories, *In the Heart of the Heart of the Country* and *Cartesian Sonata*; three novels; and numerous volumes of critical essays, including *Reading Rilke* and *On Being Blue*. His most recent collection, *A Temple of Texts*, won the Truman Capote Award for Literary Criticism. William H. Gass lives in St. Louis, Missouri.

Ha Jin, "A Composer and His Parakeets"

Two years ago I came across an interview given by a painter. In it the artist mentions he lost his parakeet in an automobile accident and afterward he couldn't get over the loss and kept painting the bird. He called the parakeet his son. I was fascinated by his brief account and wanted to create a full story out of it. At the time I had been working on the libretto of *The First Emperor* for the Metropolitan Opera, which gave me some firsthand knowledge of how an opera is made. So I decided on a composer as the protagonist. I had in mind a collection of short stories, all about the immigrant experience; naturally, this story was meant to be part of the collection and was set in a New York immigrant community. Also, I was interested in exploring the chance nature of artistic creation and the role that personal emotion plays in the process and outcome. At the beginning of the story, the composer believes only in the theory and vision in composition, but at the end those become less relevant to him. It is the personal loss that gives some unique human quality to his art.

In the immigrant experience, loneliness and fear are most common emotions. That is why the composer is described as a lonesome man, who suddenly finds friendship and love in a homely parakeet. As a matter of fact, the bird belongs to his girlfriend, so the man's emotion is a kind of sublimation of what he desires but cannot find in his relationship with the woman. Furthermore, this emotion branches out into his art and makes his music different from what he envisioned. These ideas were clear to me, but the writing process was slow and arduous, mainly because I had been writing novels over the years and had almost lost the feel for short fiction, which I am getting back gradually.

. . .

Ha Jin was born in China in 1956. He has published five novels, three collections of short stories, and three volumes of poetry. His most recent book is *A Free Life*. He has received the National Book Award, the PEN/Faulkner Award, the Hemingway Foundation/PEN Award, and other prizes. His short fiction has been included in *The Best American Short Stories* and many other anthologies and was chosen for the Pushcart Prize four times. Ha Jin teaches writing and literature at Boston University. He lives outside Boston.

Edward P. Jones, "Bad Neighbors"

Class conflict among black people is an important part of the story. It's not often a part of fiction—many have died due to racism, but not as many because one's wealthier neighbor rules a larger part of your world. But the oppression of class has been there, I suppose, since the first days of this country.

One might also say the story is about the inability to see beyond the surface, an old, old topic.

Edward P. Jones was born in Washington, D.C., in 1950. He attended the local public schools and won a scholarship to Holy Cross College. Seven years after he graduated from college, he earned his MFA at the University of Virginia.

Jones's first collection of short stories, *Lost in the City*, won the Hemingway Foundation/PEN Award, was short-listed for the National Book Award, and received a Lannan Foundation award. His novel, *The Known World*, won the Pulitzer Prize for Fiction and the National Book Critics Circle Award, was a finalist for the National Book Award, and won the international IMPAC Dublin Literary award and a Lannan Literary Award. In 2004, Edward P. Jones was named a MacArthur Fellow.

His most recent story collection is *All Aunt Hagar's Children*. He has taught creative writing at the University of Virginia, George Mason University, the University of Maryland, and Princeton University.

Edward P. Jones lives in Washington, D.C.

Sheila Kohler, "The Transitional Object"

There are, of course, some real details in the story: I do come from South Africa and I did study psychology at the Institut Catholique in Paris, though I was married by then with three children. I did know a man, a psychiatrist, who looked something like the professor in the story. Like most women, I have experienced something similar to the molestation in this character's story. Though none of my professors behaved as this man does, there were several men who did.

However, here, fiction enabled me to allow this very young woman to turn the tables on her molester. In other words, I was able here to render a passive situation active by the young woman's actions, to reverse the reality of the situation. I find this reversal of a traumatic experience is often one that lies at the heart of my fiction.

Sheila Kohler was born in South Africa. She is the author of six novels: *Bluebird, or the Invention of Happiness*; *Crossways*; *Children of Pithiviers*; *Cracks*; *The House on R Street*; *The Perfect Place*; and three story collections, *Stories from Another World*, *One Girl*, and *Miracles in America*. Kohler's work was included in *The O. Henry Prize Stories 1988* and also received the Open Voice award, the Smart Family Foundation Prize, and the Willa Cather Prize. She was awarded the Dorothy and Lewis B. Cullman Center for Scholars and Writers Fellowship of the New York Public Library. She has taught at Sarah Lawrence College, City College of New York, Brooklyn College, the New School, Bennington College, the West Side YMCA, and Princeton University. Kohler lives in New York City.

Yiyun Li, "Prison"

Two years ago I was invited to write a story about pregnancy and motherhood, which seemed just the right assignment as I was pregnant with my second child. I started the story with a woman, very pregnant and exhausted, lying on an old sofa her husband had found in a Dumpster, but the story was going nowhere, as the character refused to nourish my story. So I asked myself a question, as many writers do, when a story gets stuck, what if the character wants a child but she is mentally and physically unfit to get pregnant? The question then led to another question: how do I know that she wants the child—perhaps she doesn't want the child, or she wants a baby for a reason more complex than just becoming a mother? I love to ask the "what if" questions when I write stories. With the two questions I started to rewrite the story, and this time it was a character lying in bed thinking of death more than birth as she felt closer to the end than the beginning, and that was the first draft of "Prison."

Yiyun Li grew up in Beijing, China, and came to the United States in 1996. Her stories and essays have appeared in *The New Yorker*, *Zoetrope*, *Tin House*, *The Best American Short Stories*, and elsewhere. Her debut collection, *A Thousand Years of Good Prayers*, won the Frank O'Connor International Short Story Award, the Hemingway Foundation/PEN Award, the Guardian First Book Award, and other awards and prizes. *Granta* recently named her one of the best young American novelists and she has received awards and grants from the Whiting Foundation and the Lannan Foundation. Li teaches at Mills College and lives in the Bay Area.

David Malouf, "Every Move You Make"

Like Jo, when I first came to Sydney, in my case in 1968, I encountered several houses of the kind described in my story, all the work of the same builder, though he did not have the same name as my character or the same physical attributes or past. I am very interested in place—a singular house or landscape is often what sets a story going. I find it easier to "see" characters if I can see the world they are moving in. For the characters themselves I take hints from real people, generally ones I have had a chance of observing but do not really know; it is easier then to imagine a life for them. Jo in "Every Move You Make" is based on such a person but she is not Hungarian, does not belong to the context of the story I created for her, and did not have this affair.

At a certain point in the writing I got stuck, as I often do, and had to set the story aside to see how it might go on. This was resolved only after a couple of years in fact, when I read a magazine article about the mentally disabled brother (or maybe twin, I can't remember) of a famous and famously attractive actor, who all his life has been haunted by this maimed and till then hidden reflection of himself.

David Malouf was born in Brisbane, Australia, in 1934. He has published novels, stories, essays, poems, and opera libretti. His novel *The Great World* won the Commonwealth Writers' Prize in 1991 and the Prix Femina Étranger. *Remembering Babylon* won the inaugural IMPAC Dublin Award and the Los Angeles Times Book Prize in 1995. Malouf was the sixteenth laureate of the Neustadt International Prize for Literature. His most recent book is *The Complete Stories*. David Malouf lives in Australia.

Roger McDonald, "The Bullock Run"

There is something in men that longs for transcendence but ends in destructiveness. "The Bullock Run" began with a sentence: "It was miserable weather but satisfying work for men." The story unfolded from there. The stock agent Alan Corker, restored to himself after the disjunctions of midlife, is a lucky man, loving his wife and daughters, loved by them, and secure in his place in the world. But he wants something more, and in a pang of seeking friendship finds what he wishes for, but not in the way he expects—something left over for him as a man that he must deal with as a man.

"The Bullock Run" is one of a series of interconnected stories about men's lives in commotion. Until I started these stories I had rarely tried writing short stories, and never to my own satisfaction. I admired the generosity of writers able to create the breadth of an entire novel's-length of incident and place within a few short pages.

Roger McDonald was born at Young, New South Wales, in 1941. He is the author of seven novels, including *1915*, *Water Man*, *The Slap*, and *Mr. Darwin's Shooter*, and two books of nonfiction, *The Tree in Changing Light* and *Shearers' Motel*, an account of traveling through the Australian outback with a team of New Zealand sheep shearers. In 2006, his novel *The Ballad of Desmond Kale* won Australia's foremost fiction prize, the Miles Franklin Award. He lives near Braidwood, on the Southern Tablelands of New South Wales.

Steven Millhauser, "A Change in Fashion"

I'm deeply attracted to the theme-and-variations form. It invites you to begin simply and then to elaborate more and more boldly. Such attractions can't really be accounted for, but I'd argue that in this case it's more than just a quirk of temperament. The world is full of examples. You start by building a log cabin in the woods, and before you know it you're constructing a skyscraper. One day you throw a log across a stream, the next day you find yourself working on the Brooklyn Bridge. A path in the woods becomes a superhighway. A flip book leads to the history of the cinema. I find these movements seductive and exhilarating, and also disturbing. They seem to contain a secret that's about to be revealed.

Steven Millhauser was born in Brooklyn and grew up in Connecticut. His books include *The Knife Thrower*, *Martin Dressler*, and *Edwin Mullhouse: The Life and Death of an American Writer 1943–1954 by Jeffrey Cartwright*. His work has appeared in *Harper's Magazine*, *Tin House*, *The New Yorker*, and *McSweeney's Quarterly*. His most recent book is *Dangerous Laughter*, a collection of stories. He lives in Saratoga Springs, New York.

Alice Munro, "What Do You Want to Know For?"

What to say about "What Do You Want to Know For?"

It's the only story I've ever written that is hardly a story. From beginning to end, it *happened*.

Of course, I saw things in it I couldn't resist writing about. The cairn, my breast. If I made that up you'd consider it utterly something-or-other. Also the lamp, the conversation, even, I think, "Onward Christian Soldiers." I've never done anything like this before. But I am happy about it.

Alice Munro was born in 1931 in Wingham, Ontario. Her most recent short story collection is *The View from Castle Rock*. She is a three-time winner of the Governor General's Literary Award and has won the Lannan Literary Award, the W. H. Smith Award, and the Rea Award. Her stories have appeared in *The New Yorker*, *The Atlantic Monthly*, *The Paris Review*, and other publications, and her collections have been translated into thirteen languages. In 2006, Munro received the Edward MacDowell Medal. She divides her time between Clinton, Ontario, and Comox, British Columbia.

Olaf Olafsson, "On the Lake"

When I was a boy I spent parts of my summers by Lake Thingvellir in Iceland, where my parents had a little cabin. The lake is very cold, its waters coming from springs beneath the lava floor. When I was ten, two young men, my neighbors, drowned in the lake on a summer night after their boat capsized.

Visiting Lake Thingvellir a couple of years ago I happened to see a man and his young son fishing in a boat not far from where I used to spend my summers. When they returned to land, a young woman—the boy's mother, I assume—ran down from a small cottage to meet them. She took the boy in her arms and the three of them walked up a small hill to the cabin the woman had come from. There was no indication of discord.

A couple of days later I started "On the Lake." I wrote it in about a week and didn't change much when I was done, not more than a sentence here and there. I guess the story must have been dormant someplace in my mind, waiting to be told. The simple image of this young couple and their son was enough to unleash it.

Olaf Olafsson was born in Reykjavik, Iceland, in 1962. He studied physics as a Wien Scholar at Brandeis University. The author of a collection of short stories, *Valentines*, and three novels, *The Journey Home*, *Absolution*, and *Walking into the Night*, Olafsson lives in New York City.

Lore Segal, "Other People's Deaths"

"Other People's Deaths" talks about our human inadequacy in the face of a friend's calamity. There are readers who misunderstood me to be exposing the shabby humanity of my bunch of (fictitious) intellectuals, but we're all in this together. I was remembering the neighbor who crossed to the other sidewalk after my husband's death, and I was thinking of my failing to write to an old student whose son had died. Calamity, says my story, is a foreign country whose language and usage we will never learn and, yes, what we say might be unwelcome, silly, and give pain. Also there are the friends who call night after night.

I have heard about a nurse sitting by the side of a child in an oxygen tent. The child asks, "Am I dying?" and the nurse lays her head on the pillow beside the child's head. That might be an answer.

Lore Segal was born in Vienna, Austria. At the age of ten she left Hitler's Austria and went to England with a transport of Jewish children. From 1948 to 1951, she lived in the Dominican Republic and immigrated to the United States in May 1951. Segal is a novelist, translator, and writer for children, and her novels include *Other People's Houses* and *Her First American*. Among her children's books are *Tell Me a Mitzi* and *Why Mole Shouted*. Her translation of *The Juniper Tree and Other Tales from Grimm* was illustrated by Maurice Sendak. Lore Segal's recently published *Shake-*

speare's Kitchen is a book of related stories. Retired from teaching creative writing, Lore Segal lives in New York.

Brittani Sonnenberg, "Taiping"
The summer after my freshman year of college I spent five weeks backpacking through Thailand and Malaysia, writing for a travel guide. It wasn't the glamorous job I'd imagined; the work schedule was grueling and I was often alone in off-season resort towns. Bukit Larut was such a place. I arrived at the faded British hill station late in the afternoon, as the shadows were lengthening. Six soldiers played cards in the lobby, pausing when I entered to ogle me and laugh. The guesthouse owner, a strange man who spoke alternately in a high falsetto and in a gravelly bass, took my bags. My room was full of decaying colonial furniture. Wasps crawled over the bathroom tile. During dinner I noticed a small young girl who seemed to work at the guesthouse. Her eyes looked years older than her tiny frame. I watched her cast scornful glances at the guesthouse owner as he puttered around with plates for the guests, swishing to and from the kitchen in his sarong. He was both a man and a woman, and his guesthouse was both British and Malay, and everything felt haunted. I wrote "Taiping" to try to understand Bukit Larut and that man. Having spent much of my life overseas as an expatriate in China, Singapore, and Cambodia, I am accustomed to being the foreign observer. Exploring the narrator's character in "Taiping" reminded me that feelings of foreignness occur within cultures, too. This thought, along with the belief that grief is borderless, gave me the courage to attempt a character so different from myself.

Brittani Sonnenberg grew up in Europe, America, and Asia. She has worked as a journalist in Phnom Penh and Hong Kong, and as a writing instructor at the University of Michigan. Her stories have appeared in *Ploughshares* and *Minnesota Monthly*. Sonnenberg lives in Ann Arbor, Michigan.

Rose Tremain, "A Game of Cards"
I think the short story is a difficult and petulant form. It's almost as demanding as poetry in its aspiration to say something important while continuing to insist on its own shortness.

The core idea examined in this story is simple. It's the notion that at a certain moment in a human life, which may arrive somewhere between the ages of fifty-five and sixty-five, we begin to glimpse the shape *of the whole damn thing*. Certain roads are no longer passable. And when this last realization strikes home, people often entrap themselves in a corrosive form of mathematics. They start measuring their own achievements and levels of happiness or anxiety and so forth against those of their friends.

And it follows that, if this addition reveals a dismaying chasm of difference, friendships may alter, or even be lost.

The image I selected to illuminate this was the card game—a companionable pastime, which is nevertheless both competitive and lethally finite. In the story, the close friends, Gustav and Anton, have been playing gin rummy together for years. Sometimes Gustav wins; sometimes Anton wins. But the expectation of Gustav, who narrates this story, is that neither will get so far ahead on a winning streak that the other one suddenly feels demoralized and depressed. His hopes for their lives, as they enter the dangerous zone of their sixth decade, are identical.

He wants everything to remain more or less as it is, with no outside intervention arriving to disrupt a friendship that has always been at the center of his life and without which he knows he might give in to existential despair.

Gustav's terror of outside intervention is underlined by the setting of the story in "neutral" Switzerland, a country that never suffered the horror and destruction of the two great twentieth-century wars. Readers will soon understand that the slightly old-maidish voice with which Gustav tells the story is intended to *echo* the voice of Switzerland—careful, precise, and, to some extent, disassociated from the wider world.

They will also see that at the heart of the story there is a conundrum: the characters of Gustav and Anton are wildly opposed. Gustav is a materialist and a pedant; Anton is a musician and a dreamer. Gustav believes the friendship to be safe, because his own desire for ordinariness has kept the dreamer in Anton locked down. But, just as cards withheld for a long time in the hand can suddenly be revealed as winners, so dreams buried for a long time in the psyche can suddenly reappear and alter the shape of a life.

Rose Tremain was born in London and educated in London and France. Her novels and short stories are published in twenty-five countries and have won numerous prizes, including the Whitbread Novel Award and the Prix Femina Étranger. In 2007, Tremain was made a CBE in the Queen's Birthday Honours List. She lives in London and Norfolk.

William Trevor, "Folie à Deux"

William Trevor was born in 1928 at Mitchelstown, County Cork, and spent his childhood in provincial Ireland. His novels include *Fools of Fortune*, *Felicia's Journey*, and *The Story of Lucy Gault*. He is a renowned short story writer and has published thirteen story collections, from *The Day We Got Drunk on Cake* to his most recent, *Cheating at Canasta*. Trevor lives in Devon, England.

Tony Tulathimutte, "Scenes from the Life of the Only Girl in Water Shield, Alaska"

In college I had a roommate from Whale Pass, Alaska, a remote hamlet where he spent a childhood and adolescence without telephone, plumbing, or neighbors. Watching television required an ad hoc satellite rig and electricity cranked out of a generator. I once asked him—in what I hope was a not-condescending, sincerely curious way—how he had turned out so normal. (He answered: "MTV?")

My story is a collection of the many and disparate impressions that emerged as I developed the fictional setting. I wrote the scenes all at once, using the modular structure simply to arrange my ideas; later I realized that it allowed me to emphasize only the interesting moments in what otherwise seems (to Shelley, at least) like a tedious and unremarkable life. Reintroducing and combining the section titles likewise allowed me to connect parts of the story to one another without necessarily having to put them in any set order. Only as I approached later drafts did I order the scenes so that they would converge, providing the reader with the distance and perspective on the events in Shelley's life that she herself lacks.

In final drafts I noticed that many scenes dealt with the conflict between independence and intimacy, and eventually I decided to include only those scenes. This, however, obliged several begrudging omissions: the VHF radio correspondence with a methamphetamine-addicted religious fanatic, the boat tour of the surrounding islands, several guitar interludes (really), and Shelley's beloved pet deer.

. . .

Tony Tulathimutte was born in 1983 in western Massachusetts. He graduated from Stanford University with bachelor's and master's degrees in symbolic systems with a minor in creative writing. "Scenes from the Life of the Only Girl in Water Shield, Alaska" is his first publication. Tulathimutte lives in San Francisco, California.

Alexi Zentner, "Touch"

I realized "Touch" might be a decent story when I heard my wife crying. I wrote the first draft of "Touch" about three years ago. At the time, both of our daughters were under the age of three. I was a full-time stay-at-home dad and had been writing sporadically during my daughters' naps. We finally broke down and decided to hire a babysitter to come to the house two mornings a week for two hours. I learned very quickly that I had to make the most of those two hours.

"Touch" started with an image of a girl's body under a frozen lake. I'm always drawn to stories of love and duty, stories about family and the pull of desire, and I was haunted by the translucent nature of ice and the question of what it would mean to have somebody I love trapped like that, so close and yet untouchable. I was also driven by the landscape of the story. I was raised in southern Ontario, and, though I have dual citizenship and have lived in the United States since I was eighteen, the Canadian national mythology has stuck with me. When I look at my notes—a few quick sentences I scratched down after the image of Marie trapped under the ice came to me while I was trying to fall asleep—I notice how much, even then, weather and the cold played a part in the conception of the story. I wrote that I wanted the story to be "a lyrical description of the weather and the ice, a small, Canadian village." In retrospect, the idea that weather and place were enough to carry a story on their own seems naïve to me. But there's something to be said for the hopeful energy that naïveté can bring to a project. Despite the changes in my life since I wrote "Touch," I try to bring that same naïveté with me to the first draft of every story I write.

When I wrote "Touch," I'd never met another writer, never been to a workshop, and really didn't have any idea if what I was writing was good or not. Much of that has changed, but I still can't tell if what I'm writing on any given day is good or not. Which leads me back to my wife. I had left her with an early draft of "Touch," and when I came back into the room she was holding the story and crying. She said we could keep the babysitter.

Alexi Zentner was born in Kitchener, Ontario. His short stories have appeared in *Tin House* and *Southwest Review*. He lives in Ithaca, New York.

Recommended Stories 2008

The work of picking the twenty O. Henry Prize Stories each year is at its most difficult when it comes to the end and there are more than twenty stories in the pile of admirable, interesting stories. Once the final choice is made, the stories remaining are our Recommended Stories, listed, along with the place of publication, in the hope that O. Henry readers will seek them out and enjoy them. For the first time this year, we're honoring the Recommended Stories online. Please go to our Web site, www.ohenryprizestories.com, for excerpts from the stories and information about the writers.

Kimberly Chisholm, "Generation," *The Threepenny Review*
Lauren Groff, "L. DeBard and Aliette," *The Atlantic Monthly*
Miranda July, "The Swim Team," *Harper's Magazine*
Samuel Ligon, "Drift and Swerve," *Alaska Quarterly Review*
Irina Reyn, "The Wolf Story," *One Story*
Karen Russell, "The Barn at the End of Our Term," *Granta*
Andao Tian, "The Death of My Mad Uncle," *Natural Bridge*

Publications Submitted

Because of production deadlines for the 2009 collection, it is essential that stories reach the series editor by May 1, 2008. If a finished magazine is unavailable before the deadline, magazine editors are welcome to submit scheduled stories in proof or in manuscript. Work received after May 1, 2008, will be considered for the 2010 collection. Stories may not be submitted by agents or writers. Please see our Web site, www.ohenryprizestories.com, for more information about submission to *The O. Henry Prize Stories.*

The address for submission is:

Professor Laura Furman
The O. Henry Prize Stories
The University of Texas at Austin
English Department
1 University Station, B5000
Austin, TX 78712

The information listed below was up-to-date as *The O. Henry Prize Stories 2008* went to press. Inclusion in the listings does not constitute endorsement or recommendation.

AGNI Magazine
Boston University
236 Bay State Road
Boston, MA 02215
Sven Birkerts, Editor
agni@bu.edu
www.bu.edu/agni/
Semiannual

Alaska Quarterly Review
University of Alaska Anchorage
3211 Providence Drive
Anchorage, AK 99508
Ronald Spatz, Editor
aqr@uaa.alaska.edu
www.aqr.uaa.alaska.edu/
Semiannual

Alimentum
PO Box 776
New York, NY 10163
Paulette Licitra
editor@alimentumjournal.com
www.alimentumjournal.com
Semiannual

American Letters & Commentary
PO Box 830365
San Antonio, TX 78283
David Ray Vance and Catherine Kasper, Editors
AmerLetters@satx.rr.com
www.amletters.org
Annual

American Literary Review
PO Box 311307
University of North Texas
Denton, TX 76203-1307
John Tate, Editor
americanliteraryreview@gmail.com
www.engl.unt.edu/alr
Semiannual

The American Scholar
Phi Beta Kappa Society
1606 New Hampshire Avenue NW
Washington, DC 20009
Robert Wilson, Editor
scholar@pbk.org
www.theamericanscholar.org
Quarterly

American Short Fiction
PO Box 301209
Austin, TX 78703
Stacey Swann, Editor
editors@americanshortfiction.org
www.americanshortfiction.org
Quarterly

The Antioch Review
PO Box 148
Yellow Springs, OH 45387-0148
Robert S. Fogarty, Editor
review@antioch.edu
www.review.antioch.edu
Quarterly

Apalachee Review
PO Box 10469
Tallahassee, FL 32302
Laura Newton, Mary Jane Ryals, and Michael Trammel, Editors
www.apalacheereview.org
Semiannual

Arkansas Review
Department of English and Philosophy
Box 1890
Arkansas State University
State University, AR 72467
Tom Williams, Editor
delta@astate.edu
www.clt.astate.edu/arkreview
Triannual

Ascent
English Department
Concordia College
901 S. Eighth Street
Moorhead, MN 56562
W. Scott Olsen, Editor
ascent@cord.edu
www.cord.edu/dept/english/ascent
Triannual

The Atlantic Monthly
The Watergate
600 New Hampshire Avenue NW
Washington, DC 20037
C. Michael Curtis, Senior Fiction Editor
letters@theatlantic.com
www.theatlantic.com
Monthly

Avery
Avery House Press, Inc.
7601 Carrington Drive
Apartment G
Madison, WI 53719
Stephanie Fiorelli, Adam Koehler, Andrew Palmer, Editors
submissions@averyanthology.org
www.averyanthology.org
Biannual

Backwards City Review
PO Box 41317
Greensboro, NC 27404-1317
editors@backwardscity.net
www.backwardscity.net
Semiannual

The Baltimore Review
PO Box 36418
Towson, MD 21286
Susan Muaddi Darraj, Managing Editor
www.baltimorereview.org
Semiannual

Bat City Review
Department of English
The University of Texas at Austin
1 University Station, B5000
Austin, TX 78712
batcity@batcityreview.com
www.batcityreview.com
Annual

Bellevue Literary Review
Department of Medicine
Room OBV-612
NYU School of Medicine
550 First Avenue
New York, NY 10016
Ronna Wineberg, J.D., Fiction Editor
info@BLReview.org
www.BLReview.org
Semiannual

Black Warrior Review
Box 862936
Tuscaloosa, AL 35486-0027
Molly Dowd, Editor
bwr@ua.edu
webdelsol.com/bwr
Semiannual

BOMB Magazine
80 Hanson Place
Suite 703
Brooklyn, NY 11217
Betsy Sussler, Editor in Chief
info@bombsite.com
www.bombsite.com
Quarterly

Boston Review, A Political and Literary Forum
35 Medford Street, Suite 302
Somerville, MA 02143
Deborah Chasman and Joshua Cohen, Editors
review@bostonreview.net
www.bostonreview.net
Published six times per year

Boulevard Magazine
6614 Clayton Road, Box 325
Richmond Heights, MO 63117
Richard Burgin, Editor
www.richardburgin.net/boulevard.htm
Triannual

Briar Cliff Review
3303 Rebecca Street
PO Box 2100
Sioux City, IA 51104-2100
Tricia Currans-Sheehen, Editor
currans@briarcliff.edu
www.briarcliff.edu/campus_info/bcu_review/home_bcu_review.asp
Annual

Cairn
St. Andrews College
1700 Dogwood Mile
Laurinburg, NC 28352
Lindsay Hess, Editor
press@sapc.edu
www.sapc.edu/sapress

Callaloo
English Department
Texas A&M University
4227 TAMU
College Station, TX 77843-4227
Charles Henry Rowell, Editor
callaloo@tamu.edu
xroads.virginia.edu/~public/calla
loo/home/callaloohome.htm
Quarterly

Calyx, A Journal of Art and Literature by Women
PO Box B
Corvallis, OR 97339-0539
Beverly McFarland, Senior Editor
calyx@proaxis.com
www.proaxis.com/~calyx/journal
.html
Semiannual

The Carolina Quarterly
Greenlaw Hall, CB 3520
University of North Carolina
Chapel Hill, NC 27599-3520
Elena Oxman, Editor
cquarter@unc.edu
www.unc.edu/depts/cqonline
Triannual

The CEA Critic
Humanites Division
Widener University
One University Place
Chester, PA 19013
Daniel Robinson, Editor
dxr003@mail.widener.edu
www.as.ysu.edu/~english/cea/
Critic.htm
Semiannual

The Chattahoochee Review
2101 Womack Road
Dunwoody, GA 30338-4497
Marc Fitten
www.chattahoochee-review.org
Quarterly

Chelsea
PO Box 773
Cooper Station
New York, NY 10276-0773
Alfredo de Palchi, Editor
www.chelseamag.org
Semiannual

Chicago Review
5801 S. Kenwood Avenue
Chicago, IL 60637
Joshua Kotin, Editor
chicago-review@uchicago.edu
humanities.uchicago.edu/review
Quarterly

Cimarron Review
205 Morrill Hall
English Department
Oklahoma State University
Stillwater, OK 74078
E. P. Walkiewicz, Editor
cimarronreview@yahoo.com
cimarronreview.okstate.edu
Quarterly

The Cincinnati Review
University of Cincinnati
McMicken Hall, Room 369
PO Box 210069
Cincinnati, OH 45221-0069
Brock Clarke, Editor
editors@cincinnatireview.com
www.cincinnatireview.com
Semiannual

Colorado Review
Department of English
Colorado State University
Fort Collins, CO 80523
Stephanie G'Schwind, Editor
creview@colostate.edu
coloradoreview.colostate.edu
Triannual

Commentary
165 E. 56th Street
New York, NY 10022
Neal Kozodoy
editorial@commentarymagazine
.com
www.commentarymagazine.com
Published six times annually

Concho River Review
English Department
Angelo State University
10894 ASU Station
San Angelo, TX 76909-0894
Mary Ellen Hartje
me.hartje@angelo.edu
www.angelo.edu/dept/english
Semiannual

Conjunctions
21 E. 10th Street
New York, NY 10003
Bradford Morrow, Editor
webmaster@conjunctions.com
www.conjunctions.com
Semiannual

Crab Orchard Review
Southern Illinois University
Carbondale
1000 Faner Drive
Faner Hall 2380, Mail Code 4503
Carbondale, IL 62901
Allison Joseph, Editor
www.siu.edu/~crborchd
Semiannual

Crazyhorse
Department of English
College of Charleston
66 George Street
Charleston, SC 29424
Carol Ann Davis and Garrett
Doherty, Editors
crazyhorse@cofc.edu
crazyhorse.cofc.edu/
Semiannual

Cream City Review
Department of English
Box 413
University of Wisconsin–
Milwaukee
Milwaukee, WI 53201
Phong Nguyen, Editor
www.creamcityreview.org
Semiannual

Daedalus, Journal of the American Academy of Arts & Sciences
Norton's Woods
136 Irving Street
Cambridge, MA 02138
James Miller, Editor
daedalus@amacad.org
www.mitpressjournals.org/page/
editorial/daed
Quarterly

Denver Quarterly
Department of English
University of Denver
2000 E. Asbury
Denver, CO 80208
Bin Ramke, Editor
www.denverquarterly.com
Quarterly

Epoch
251 Goldwin Smith Hall
Cornell University
Ithaca, NY 14853-3201
Michael Koch, Editor
www.arts.cornell.edu/english/
epoch.html
Triannual

Event
Douglas College
PO Box 2503
New Westminster, BC V3L 5B2
Canada
Billeh Nickerson, Editor
event.douglas.bc.ca
Triannual

Fence
303 E. Eighth Street, #B1
New York, NY 10009
Lynne Tillman, Fiction Editor
fence@angel.net
www.fencemag.com
Semiannual

The Fiddlehead
University of New Brunswick
PO Box 4400
Campus House
11 Garland Court
Fredericton, E3B 5A3
Canada
Ross Leckie, Editor
fiddlehd@unb.ca
www.lib.unb.ca/Texts/Fiddlehead
Quarterly

The First Line
PO Box 250382
Plano, TX 75025-0382
David LaBounty, Editor
info@thefirstline.com
www.thefirstline.com
Quarterly

580 Split
Mills College
PO Box 9982
Oakland, CA 94613-0982
Michelle Simotas, Managing Editor
editor@580split.com
www.580split.com
Annual

Five Points
PO Box 3999
Atlanta, GA 30302-3999
David Bottoms and Megan Sexton, Editors
info@langate.gsu.edu
webdelsol.com/Five_Points/
Triannual

The Florida Review
Department of English
PO Box 161346
University of Central Florida
Orlando, FL 32816
Jeanne M. Leiby, Editor
flreview@mail.ucf.edu
www.flreview.com
Semiannual

Fugue
University of Idaho
200 Brink Hall
PO Box 441102
Moscow, Idaho 83844-1102
Justin Jainchill and Sara Kaplan, Editors
fugue@uidaho.edu
www.uidaho.edu/fugue/
Semiannual

Gargoyle
3819 N. 13th Street
Arlington, VA 22291-4922
Lucinda Ebersole and Richard Peabody, Editors
gargoyle@gargoylemagazine.com
www.gargoylemagazine.com
Annual

The Georgia Review
University of Georgia
012 Gilbert Hall
Athens, GA 30606-9009
Stephen Corey, Editor
scorey@uga.edu, garev@uga.edu
www.uga.edu/garev
Quarterly

The Gettysburg Review
Gettysburg College
Gettysburg, PA 17325-1491
Peter Stitt, Editor
pstitt@gettysburg.edu
www.gettysburgreview.com
Quarterly

Glimmer Train
1211 NW Glisan Street
Suite 207
Portland, OR 97209-3054
Susan Burmeister-Brown and
Linda B. Swanson-Davies,
Editors
eds@glimmertrain.org
www.glimmertrain.org
Quarterly

Good Housekeeping
Hearst Corp.
W. 57th Street
New York, NY 10019
Laura Matthews, Literary Editor
www.goodhousekeeping.com
Monthly

Grain Magazine
PO Box 67
Saskatoon, SK S7K 3KI
Canada
Kent Bruyneel, Editor
grainmag@sasktel.net
www.grainmagazine.ca
Quarterly

Granta
12 Addison Avenue
London W11 4QR
United Kingdom
editorial@granta.com
www.granta.com
Quarterly

The Greensboro Review
MFA Writing Program, English
Department
3302 Hall for Humanities and
Research Administration
UNCG
Greensboro, NC 27402-6170
Jim Clark, Editor
jclark@uncg.edu
www.greensbororeview.org
Semiannual

Gulf Coast
Department of English
University of Houston
Houston, TX 77204-3013
Claudia Rankine, Executive
Editor
editors@gulfcoastmag.org
www.gulfcoastmag.org
Semiannual

Hadassah Magazine
50 W. 58th Street
New York, NY 10019
Tom Blunt, Editor
tblunt@hadassah.org
www.hadassah.org
Monthly

Happy
46 St. Pauls Avenue
Jersey City, NJ 07306-1623
Bayard, Editor
bayardx@gmail.com
Quarterly

Harper's Magazine
666 Broadway
11th Floor
New York, NY 10012
Ben Metcalf, Literary Editor
letters@harpers.org
www.harpers.org
Monthly

Harpur Palate
English Department
Binghamton University
PO Box 6000
Binghamton, NY 13902-6000
Katherine Henion and J. D. Schraffenberger, Editors
hpalate@binghamton.edu
harpurpalate.binghamton.edu
Semiannual

Harvard Review
Lamont Library
Harvard University
Cambridge, MA 02138
Christina Thompson, Editor
harvard_review@harvard.edu
www.hcl.harvard.edu/harvardreview
Semiannual

Hawai'i Pacific Review
Hawai'i Pacific University
1060 Bishop Street
Honolulu, HI 96813
Patrice M. Wilson and Catherine Sustana, Editors
www.hpu.edu/index.cfm?section=uniquelyhpu1110
Annual

Hayden's Ferry Review
Box 875002
Arizona State University
Tempe, AZ 85287-5002
Salima Keegan, Managing Editor
hfr@asu.edu
www.haydensferryreview.org
Semiannual

Hemispheres
Pace Communications
1301 Carolina Street
Greensboro, NC 27401
Randy Johnson, Editor
hemiedit@aol.com
www.hemispheresmagazine.com
Monthly

HGMLQ: Harrington Gay Men's Literary Quarterly
Thomas Nelson Community College
99 Thomas Nelson Drive
Hampton, VA 23666
Thomas Lawerence Long, Editor
community.tncc.edu/faculty/longt/HGMFQ/index.htm
Quarterly

Hotel Amerika
Department of English
360 Ellis Hall
Ohio University
Athens, OH 45701
David Lazar, Editor
editors@HotelAmerika.net
www.hotelamerika.net
Semiannual

The Hudson Review
684 Park Avenue
New York, NY 10021
Paula Deitz, Editor
www.hudsonreview.com
Quarterly

Hyphen: Asian America Unabridged
PO Box 192002
San Francisco, CA 94119
Melissa Hung, Editor
editorial@hyphenmagazine.com
www.hyphenmagazine.com
Triannual

The Idaho Review
Boise State University
Department of English
1910 University Drive
Boise, ID 83725
Mitch Wieland, Editor in Chief
english.boisestate.edu/idahoreview/
Annual

Illuminations
Department of English
College of Charleston
66 George Street
Charleston, SC 29424-001
Simon Lewis, Editor
www.cofc.edu/illuminations
Annual

Image, A Journal of the Arts & Religion
3307 Third Avenue West
Seattle, WA 98119
Gregory Wolfe, Editor
image@imagejournal.org
www.imagejournal.org
Quarterly

Indiana Review
Indiana University
Ballantine Hall 465
Bloomington, IN 47405-7103
Abdel Sakur, Editor
inreview@indiana.edu
indianareview.org
Semiannual

The Iowa Review
308 EPB
University of Iowa
Iowa City, IA 52242-1492
David Hamilton, Editor
www.iowareview.org
Triannual

Jabberwock Review
Department of English
Mississippi State University
Drawer E
Mississippi State, MS 39862
jabberwock@org.msstate.edu
www.msstate.edu/org/jabberwock
Semiannual

The Journal
Department of English
Ohio State University
164 W. 17th Avenue
Columbus, OH 43210
Michelle Herman, Fiction Editor
thejoural@osu.edu
english.OSU.edu/journals/the_journal/
Semiannual

Kalliope, A Journal of Women's Literature & Art
Florida Community College at Jacksonville
South Campus
11901 Beach Boulevard
Jacksonville, FL 32246
Dr. Margaret Clark, Editor in Chief
maclark@fccj.edu
www.opencampus.fccj.org/kalliope/index.html
Semiannual

Karamu
English Department
Eastern Illinois University
Charleston, IL 61920
Olga Abella, Editor
www.eiu.edu/~karamu
Annual

The Kenyon Review
Kenyon College
Walton House
Gambier, OH 43022
David H. Lynn, Editor
kenyonreview@kenyon.edu
www.kenyonreview.org
Quarterly

The Laurel Review
Green Tower Press
Department of English
Northwest Missouri State University
Maryville, MO 64468-6001
Rebecca Aronson and John Gallaher, Editors
catpages.nwmissouri.edu/m/tlr
Semiannual

Lilies and Cannonballs Review
PO Box 702
Bowling Green Station
New York, NY 10274-0702
Daniel Connor, Editor
info@liliesandcannonballs.com
www.liliesandcannonballs.com
Annual

The Literary Review
285 Madison Avenue
Mail Code: M-GH2-01
Madison, NJ 07940
René Steinke, Editor in Chief
tlr@fdu.edu
www.theliteraryreview.org
Quarterly

The Long Story
18 Eaton Street
Lawrence, MA 01843
R. P. Burnham, Editor
rpburnham@mac.com
homepage.mac.com/rpburnham/longstory.html
Semiannual

The Malahat Review
University of Victoria
PO Box 1700
STN CSC
Victoria, BC V8W 2Y2
Canada
John Barton, Editor
malahat@uvic.ca
malahatreview.ca
Quarterly

Mandorla
Department of English
Campus Box 4240
Illinois State University
Normal, IL 61790-4240
Roberto Tejada, Editor
www.litline.org
Annual

Mānoa
English Department
University of Hawai'i
1733 Donaghho Road
Honolulu, HI 96822
Frank Stewart, Editor
mjournal-l@hawaii.edu
www.hawaii.edu/mjournal
Semiannual

The Massachusetts Review
South College
University of Massachusetts
Amherst, MA 01003-7140
David Lenson, Editor
massrev@external.umass.edu
www.massreview.org
Quarterly

McSweeney's
849 Valencia Street
San Francisco, CA 94110
Dave Eggers, Editor
printsubmissions@mcsweeneys.net
www.mcsweeneys.net
Quarterly

The Means
Self-Evident Press, LLC
PO Box 183246
Shelby Township, MI 48318
Tanner Higgin, Editor
tanner@the-means.com
www.the-means.com

Meridian
University of Virginia
PO Box 400145
Charlottesville, VA 22904-4145
Fiction Editor
meridian@virginia.edu
www.readmeridian.org
Semiannual

Michigan Quarterly Review
University of Michigan
3574 Rackham Building
915 E. Washington Street
Ann Arbor, MI 48109-1070
Laurence Goldstein, Editor
MQR@umich.edu
www.umich.edu/~mqr
Quarterly

Midstream: Bi-monthly Jewish Review
633 Third Avenue
21st Floor
New York, NY 10017-6706
Leo Heber, Editor
midstreamthf@aol.com
www.midstreamthf.com
Bimonthly

The Minnesota Review
Department of English
Carnegie Mellon University
Pittsburgh, PA 15213
Jeffrey J. Williams, Editor
editors@theminnesotareview.org
www.theminnesotareview.org
Semiannual

Mississippi Review
The University of Southern Mississippi
118 College Drive
Box 5144
Hattiesburg, MS 39406-5144
Frederick Barthelme, Editor
fbx@mississippireview.com
www.mississippireview.com
Semiannual

The Missouri Review
357 McReynolds Hall
University of Missouri–Columbia
Columbia, MO 65211
Speer Morgan, Editor
tmr@missourireview.com
www.missourireview.com
Quarterly

Natural Bridge, A Journal of Contemporary Literature
Department of English
University of Missouri–St. Louis
One University Boulevard
St. Louis, MO 63121
Steven Schreiner, Editor
natural@umsl.edu
www.umsl.edu/~natural
Semiannual

New England Review
Middlebury College
Middlebury, VT 05753
Stephen Donadio, Editor
NEReview@middlebury.edu
go.middlebury.edu/nereview
Quarterly

New Letters
University of Missouri–Kansas City
5101 Rockhill Road
Kansas City, MO 64110
Robert Stewart, Editor in Chief
newletters@umkc.edu
www.newletters.org
Quarterly

New Millennium Writings
PO Box 2463
Room M2
Knoxville, TN 37901
Don Williams, Editor
www.newmillenniumwritings.com/
Annual

New Orleans Review
Box 195
Loyola University
New Orleans, LA 70118
Christopher Chambers, Editor
chambers@loyno.edu
www.loyno.edu/~noreview
Semiannual

The New Renaissance
26 Heath Road
#11
Arlington, MA 02474-3645
Louise T. Reynolds
tnrlitmag@aol.com
www.tnrlitmag.net
Semiannual

News from the Republic of Letters
c/o Zachary Bos, Deputy Editor
PO Box 247
Boston University Station
Boston, MA 02125
Keith Botsford, Editor
nickmatchwell@gmail.com
www.bu.edu/trl

The New Yorker
4 Times Square
New York, NY 10036
Deborah Treisman, Fiction Editor
fiction@newyorker.com
www.newyorker.com
Weekly

Night Train Magazine
212 Bellingham Avenue, #2
Revere, MA 02151-4106
Rusty Barnes, Editor
rustybarnes@nighttrainmagazine.com
www.nighttrainmagazine.com
Semiannual

Nimrod
800 S. Tucker Drive
University of Tulsa
Tulsa, OK 74104
Francine Ringold, Editor in Chief
nimrod@utulsa.edu
www.utulsa.edu/nimrod
Semiannual

Ninth Letter
Department of English
University of Illinois, Urbana-Champaign
608 S. Wright Street
Urbana, IL 61801
Jodee Stanley, Editor
ninthletter@uiuc.edu
www.ninthletter.com
Semiannual

Noon
1324 Lexington Avenue
P.M.B. 298
New York, NY 10128
Diane Williams, Editor
www.noonannual.com/
Annual

The North American Review
University of Northern Iowa
1222 W. 27th Street
Cedar Falls, IA 50614-0516
Grant Tracey, Editor
nar@uni.edu
www.webdelsol.com/NorthAmReview/NAR/
Published five times per year

North Carolina Literary Review
Department of English
2201 Bate Building
East Carolina University
Greenville, NC 27858-4353
Margaret Bauer, Editor
bauerm@ecu.edu
www.ecu.edu/nclr
Annual

North Dakota Quarterly
Merrifield Hall, Room 110
276 Centennial Drive, Stop 7209
Grand Forks, ND 58202-7209
Robert W. Lewis, Editor
ndq@und.nodak.edu
www.und.nodak.edu/org/ndq
Quarterly

Northwest Review
1286 University of Oregon
Eugene, OR 97403
John Witte, Editor
jwitte@uoregon.edu
darkwing.uoregon.edu/~nwreview/
Triannual

Notre Dame Review
840 Flanner Hall
University of Notre Dame
Notre Dame, IN 46556
William O'Rourke, Editor
www.nd.edu/~ndr/review.htm
Semiannual

One Story
PO Box 150618
Brooklyn, NY 11215
Hannah Tinti, Editor
questions@one-story.com
www.one-story.com
Published about every three weeks

Ontario Review
9 Honey Brook Drive
Princeton, NJ 08540
Raymond J. Smith, Editor
www.ontarioreviewpress.com
Semiannual

Open City
270 Lafayette Street
Suite 1412
New York, NY 10012
Thomas Beller and Joanna Yas, Editors
editors@opencity.org
www.opencity.org
Triannual

Opium Magazine.print
161 W. 15 Street
Suite 6E
New York, NY 10011
Todd Zuniga, Founding Editor
todd@opiummagazine.com
www.opiummagazine.com
Semiannual

Orchid
PO Box 131457
Ann Arbor, MI 48113-1457
Keith Hood, Editor
editors@orchidlit.org
www.orchidlit.org
Semiannual

The Oxford American
201 Donaghey Avenue
Conway, AR 72035
Marc Smirnoff, Editor
smirnoff@oxfordamericanmag.com
www.oxfordamericanmag.com/
Quarterly

Oyster Boy Review
PO Box 299
Pacifica, CA 94044
Damon Sauve, Editor
email@oysterboyreview.com
www.oysterboyreview.com
Quarterly

Painted Bride Quarterly
Drexel University
Department of English and Philosophy
3141 Chestnut Street
Philadelphia, PA 19104
Kathleen Volk Miller and Marion Wrenn, Editors
pbq.drexel.edu
Annual

Pakn Treger
National Yiddish Book Center
Harry & Jeanette Weinburg Building
1021 West Street
Amherst, MA 01002-3375
Nancy Sherman
pt2006@bikher.org
www.yiddishbookcenter.org
Semiannual

Paper Street
PO Box 14786
Pittsburgh, PA 15234-0786
Dory Adams, Editor
editor@paperstreetpress.org
www.paperstreetpress.org
Semiannual

Paradox
Paradox Publications
PO Box 22897
Brooklyn, NY 11202-2897
Christopher Cevasco
www.paradoxmag.com
Semiannual

The Paris Review
62 White Street
New York, NY 10013
Philip Gourevitch, Editor
queries@theparisreview.com
www.parisreview.org
Quarterly

Parting Gifts
3413 Wilshire Drive
Greensboro, NC 27408
Robert Bixby, Editor
rbixby@earthlink.net
www.marchstreetpress.com
Semiannual

Phantasmagoria
English Department
Century Community and Technical College
3300 Century Avenue North
White Bear Lake, MN 55110
Abigail Allen, Editor
Semiannual

Phoebe, A Journal of Literature and Art
MSN 2D6
George Mason University
4400 University Drive
Fairfax, VA 22030-4444
Ryan Effgen, Editor
phoebe@gmu.edu
www.gmu.edu/pubs/phoebe
Semiannual

Pilot Pocket Book
PO Box 161
Station B
119 Spadina Avenue
Toronto, ON M5T 2T3
Canada
Reuben McLaughlin, Lee Sheppard, and Bryan Belanger, Editors
editor@thepilotproject.ca
www.thepilotproject.ca
Annual

The Pinch
Department of English
University of Memphis
Memphis, TN 38152-6176
Kristen Iverson
www.thepinchjournal.com
Semiannual

Pindeldyboz
23–55 38th Street
Astoria, NY 11105
Whitney Pastorek, Executive Editor
editor@pindeldyboz.com
www.pindeldyboz.com
Annual

Playboy Magazine
730 Fifth Avenue
New York, NY 10019
Amy Loyd, Literary Editor
sirc@ny.playboy.com
www.playboy.com
Monthly

Pleiades, A Journal of New Writing
Department of English
Central Missouri State University
Warrensburg, MO 64093
Kevin Prufer and Wayne Miller, Editors
pleiades@cmsul.cmsu.edu
www.cmsu.edu/englphil/pleiades/
Semiannual

Ploughshares
Emerson College
120 Boylston Street
Boston, MA 02116-4624
Robert Arnold, Managing Director
pshares@emerson.edu
www.pshares.org
Triannual

Polyphony HS
The Latin School of Chicago
59 W. North Boulevard
Chicago, IL 60610
Paige Holtzman, Editor in Chief
polyphonyhs@latinschool.org
www.polyphonyhs.com
Annual

Post Road
PO Box 400951
Cambridge, MA 02140
Mary Cotton, Managing Editor
fiction@postroadmag.com
www.postroadmag.com
Semiannual, e-mail submissions only

Prairie Fire
Artspace
423-100 Arthur Street
Winnipeg, MB R3B 1H3
Canada
Andris Taskans, Editor
prfire@mts.net
www.prairiefire.ca/
Quarterly

Prairie Schooner
201 Andrews Hall
University of Nebraska
Lincoln, NE 68588-0334
Hilda Raz, Editor in Chief
kgrey2@unlnotes.unl.edu
www.prairieschooner.unl.edu
Quarterly

Prism International
University of British Columbia
Buchanan E-462
1866 Main Mall
Vancouver, BC V6T1Z1
Canada
Ben Hart, Fiction Editor
prism@interchange.ubc.ca
www.prism.arts.ubc.ca
Quarterly

Provincetown Arts
PO Box 35
650 Commercial Street
Provincetown, MA 02657
Christopher Busa, Editor
cbusa@comcast.net
www.provincetownarts.org
Annual

A Public Space
323 Dean Street
Brooklyn, NY 11217
Brigid Hughes, Editor
info@apublicspace.org
www.apublicspace.org
Quarterly

Quarterly West
University of Utah
255 South Central Campus Drive
Department of English
LNCO 3500
Salt Lake City, UT 84112-0494
Paul Ketzle and Mike White,
Editors
utah.edu/quarterlywest
Semiannual

The Rake
800 Washington Avenue North
#504
Minneapolis, MN 55401
Tom Bartell, Editor and Publisher
submissions@rakemag.com
www.rakemag.com
Monthly

Raritan
Rutgers University
31 Mine Street
New Brunswick, NJ 08903
Jackson Lears, Editor in Chief
raritanquarterly.rutgers.edu/
Quarterly

Redivider
Writing, Literature, and Publishing Department
Emerson College
120 Boylston Street
Boston, MA 02116
Laura van den Berg, Editor in Chief
pages.emerson.edu/publications/redivider/
Semiannual

Red Rock Review
English Department, J2A
Community College of Southern Nevada
3200 E. Cheyenne Avenue
North Las Vegas, NV 89030
Richard Logsdon, Editor in Chief
richard_logsdon@ccsn.nevada.edu
sites.csn.edu/english/redrockreview
Semiannual

River Styx
3547 Olive Street
Suite 107
St. Louis, MO 63103-1014
Richard Newman, Editor
bigriver@riverstyx.org
www.riverstyx.org
Triannual

Salmagundi
Skidmore College
815 N. Broadway
Saratoga Springs, NY 12866
Robert Boyers, Editor in Chief
pboyers@skidmore.edu
cms.skidmore.edu/salmagundi/
Quarterly

Santa Monica Review
Santa Monica College
1900 Pico Boulevard
Santa Monica, CA 90405
Andrew Tonkovich, Editor
antonkovi@uci.edu
www.smc.edu/sm_review
Semiannual

Seven Days
PO Box 1164
Burlington, VT 05402-1164
www.sevendaysvt.com
Weekly, fiction published annually

The Sewanee Review
University of the South
735 University Avenue
Sewanee, TN 37383-1000
George Core, Editor
www.sewanee.edu/sewanee_review
Quarterly

Shenandoah
Mattingly House
2 Lee Avenue
Washington and Lee University
Lexington, VA 24450-2116
R. T. Smith, Editor
shenandoah@wlu.edu
shenandoah.wlu.edu
Triannual

Small Spiral Notebook
172 Fifth Avenue
Suite 104
Brooklyn, NY 11217
Felicia C. Sullivan, Editor
editor@smallspiralnotebook.com
www.smallspiralnotebook.com
Semiannual

Sonora Review
English Department
University of Arizona
Tucson, AZ 85721
PR Griffis and Amy Knight
Editors
sonora@email.arizona.edu
www.coh.arizona.edu/sonora
Semiannual

The South Carolina Review
Center for Electronic and Digital
Publishing
Clemson University
Strode Tower, Box 340522
Clemson, SC 29634-0522
Wayne Chapman
www.clemson.edu/caan/cedp/
scrintro.htm
Semiannual

South Dakota Review
Department of English
The University of South Dakota
414 E. Clark Street
Vermillion, SD 47069
Brian Bedard, Editor
sdreview@usd.edu
www.usd.edu/sdreview/
Quarterly

Southern Gothic
7746 Newfound Gap Road
Memphis, TN 38125
Jeff Crook
wordartsinc@yahoo.com
www.southerngothic.org
Annual

Southern Humanities Review
9088 Haley Center
Auburn University
Auburn, AL 36849
Dan R. Latimer and Virginia M. Kouidis, Editors
shrengl@auburn.edu
www.auburn.edu/english/shr/home.htm
Quarterly

Southern Indiana Review
College of Liberal Arts
University of Southern Indiana
8600 University Boulevard
Evansville, IN 47712
Ron Mitchell, Managing Editor
sir@usi.edu
www.southernindianareview.org
Semiannual

The Southern Review
Louisiana State University
Old President's House
Baton Rouge, LA 70803-0001
Jeanne Lerby, Editor
southernreview@lsu.edu
www.lsu.edu/thesouthernreview
Quarterly

Southwest Review
Southern Methodist University
PO Box 750374
Dallas, TX 75275-0374
Willard Spiegelman, Editor in Chief
swr@mail.smu.edu
www.southwestreview.org
Quarterly

St. Anthony Messenger
28 W. Liberty Street
Cincinnati, OH 45202-6498
Pat McCloskey, O.F.M., Editor
samadmin@americancatholic.org
www.americancatholic.org
Monthly

StoryQuarterly
PO Box 29272
San Francisco, CA 94129
M.M.M. Hayes, Carol Edgarian, and Tom Jenks
manuscripts@narrativemagazine.com
www.storyquarterly.com
Triannual, online submissions only

Subtropics
PO Box 112075
4008 Turlington Hall
University of Florida
Gainesville, FL 32611
David Leavitt, Editor
www.english.ufl.edu/subtropics
Triannual

Swink
5042 Wilshire Boulevard
#628
Los Angeles, CA 90036
Leelila Strogov, Editor
www.swinkmag.com
Annual

The Sycamore Review
Purdue University
Department of English
500 Oval Drive
West Lafayette, IN 47907-2038
Rebekah Silverman, Editor
sycamore@purdue.edu
sycamorereview.com
Semiannual

Tampa Review
University of Tampa
401 W. Kennedy Boulevard
Tampa, FL 33606-1490
Richard Mathews, Editor
utpress@ut.edu
www.tampareview.ut.edu
Semiannual

The Texas Review
English Department
Sam Houston State University
Box 2146
Huntsville, TX 77341
Paul Ruffin, Editor
eng_pdr@shsu.edu
www.shsu.edu/~www_trp/
aboutr2.html
Semiannual

Third Coast
English Department
Western Michigan University
Kalamazoo, MI 49008-5092
Peter J. Geye, Editor
www.wmich.edu/thirdcoast
Semiannual

The Threepenny Review
PO Box 9131
Berkeley, CA 94709
Wendy Lesser, Editor
wlesser@threepennyreview.com
www.threepennyreview.com
Quarterly

Timber Creek Review
8969 UNCG Station
Greensboro, NC 27413
John M. Freiermuth, Editor
Quarterly

Tin House
PMB 280
320 Seventh Avenue
Brooklyn, NY 11215
Win McCormack, Editor in Chief
robspill@ix.netcom.com
www.tinhouse.com
Quarterly

Transition Magazine
104 Mount Auburn Street
3R
Cambridge, MA 02138
Kwame Anthony Appiah, Editor
transition@fas.harvard.edu
www.transitionmagazine.com
Quarterly

TriQuarterly
Northwestern University
629 Noyes Street
Evanston, IL 60208
Susan Firestone Hahn, Editor
triquarterly@northwestern.edu
www.triquarterly.org/index.cfm
Triannual

The Virginia Quarterly Review
1 West Range
PO Box 400223
Charlottesville, VA 22903-4223
Ted Genoways, Editor
vqreview@virginia.edu
www.vgronline.org
Quarterly

War, Literature, and the Arts
Dept. of English and Fine Arts
U.S. Air Force Academy
2453 Fairchild Drive
Suite 60-149
Colorado Springs, CO
80840-6242
Donald Anderson, Editor
editor@wlajournal.com
www.wlajournal.com
Annual

Washington Square Review
Creative Writing Program
New York University
Lillian Vernon Creative Writers
House
58 W. 10th Street
New York, NY 10011
Carolyn Clark, Editor in Chief
washington.square.journal@nyu
.edu
cwp.fas.nyu.edu/page/wsr
Semiannual

Weber Studies
1214 University Circle
Ogden, UT 84408-1214
Brad L. Roghaar, Editor
weberstudies@weber.edu
weberstudies.weber.edu
Triquarterly

West Branch
Bucknell Hall
Bucknell University
Lewisburg, PA 17837
Paula Closson Buck, Editor
westbranch@bucknell.edu
www.bucknell.edu/westbranch
Semiannual

Western Humanities Review
University of Utah
English Department
255 S. Central Campus Drive
Room 3500
Salt Lake City, UT 84112-0494
Barry Weller, Editor
www.hum.utah.edu/whr/
Semiannual

Witness
Oakland Community College
Orchard Ridge Campus
27055 Orchard Lake Road
Farmington Hills, MI 48334
Peter Stine, Editor
stinepj@umich.edu
www.oaklandcc.edu/witness
Semiannual

Xavier Review
110 Xavier University
New Orleans, LA 70125
Richard Collins, Executive Editor
rcollins@xula.edu
www.xula.edu/review/
Semiannual

xconnect: writers of the information age
CrossConnect, Inc.
PO Box 2317
Philadelphia, PA 19103
David E. Deifer, Editor
editors@xconnect.org
www.xconnect.org

Zoetrope: All-Story
916 Kearny Street
San Francisco, CA 94133
Michael Ray, Editor
info@all-story.com
www.all-story.com
Quarterly

ZYZZYVA
PO Box 590069
San Francisco, CA 94159-0069
Howard Junker, Editor
editor@zyzzyva.org
www.zyzzyva.org
Triannual

Permissions

"The Transitional Object" first appeared in *Boulevard*. Copyright © 2007 by Sheila Kohler. Reprinted by permission of the author.

"Prison" first appeared in *Tin House*. Copyright © 2007 by Yiyun Li. Reprinted by permission of the author.

"Every Move You Make" from *The Complete Stones* by David Malouf, copyright © 2007 by David Malouf. Reprinted by permission of Pantheon Books, a division of Random House, Inc., and Rogers, Coleridge & White Ltd., 20 Powis Mews, London W11 1JN.

"The Bullock Run" first appeared in *Mānoa*. Copyright © 2007 by Roger McDonald. Reprinted by permission of the author.

"A Change in Fashion" first appeared in *Harper's Magazine*. Copyright © 2007 by Steven Millhauser. Reprinted by permission of the author.

"What Do You Want to Know For?" from *The View from Castle Rock: Stories* by Alice Munro, copyright © 2006 by Alice Munro, published in the United States by Alfred A. Knopf, a division of Random House, Inc. and in Canada by McClelland & Stewart Ltd. Used by permission of Alfred A. Knopf, a division of Random House, Inc. and McClelland and Stewart Ltd.

"On the Lake" first appeared in *Zoetrope*. Copyright © 2007 by Olaf Olafsson. Reprinted by permission of the author.

"Other People's Deaths" first appeared in *The New Yorker*. Copyright © 2007 by Lore Segal. Reprinted by permission of the author.

"Taiping" first appeared in *xconnect*. Copyright © 2007 by Brittani Sonnenberg. Reprinted by permission of the author.

"A Game of Cards" by Rose Tremain was first published in *The Paris Review* (Issue 177, Summer 2006). Copyright © 2006 by Rose Tremain. Reprinted by permission of the author.

"Folie à Deux" first appeared in *The New Yorker*. Copyright © 2007 by William Trevor. Reprinted by permission of the author.

"Scenes from the Life of the Only Girl in Water Shield, Alaska" first appeared in *The Threepenny Review*. Copyright © 2007 by Tony Tulathimutte. Reprinted by permission of the author.

"Touch" first appeared in *Tin House*. Copyright © 2007 by Alexi Zentner. Reprinted by permission of the author.